Sue MacKay lives with her husband in New Zealand's beautiful Marlborough Sounds, with the water on her doorstep and the birds and the trees at her back door. It is the perfect setting to indulge her passions of entertaining friends by cooking them sumptuous meals, drinking fabulous wine, going for hill walks or kayaking around the bay—and, of course, writing stories.

Lifelong romance addict **JC Harroway** took a break from her career as a junior doctor to raise a family and found her calling as a Mills and Boon author instead. She now lives in New Zealand, and finds that writing feeds her very real obsession with happy endings and the endorphin rush they create. You can follow her at jcharroway.com, and on Facebook, Twitter and Instagram.

Also by Sue MacKay

The GP's Secret Baby Wish
Captivated by Her Runaway Doc
A Single Dad to Rescue Her
From Best Friend to I Do?

Forbidden Fling with Dr Right
is **JC Harroway**'s debut title
for Mills & Boon Medical Romance

Look out for more books from JC Harroway

Coming soon

Discover more at millsandboon.co.uk.

THEIR SECOND CHANCE IN ER

SUE MacKAY

FORBIDDEN FLING WITH DR RIGHT

JC HARROWAY

MILLS & BOON

First Published in Great Britain 2022
by Mills & Boon, an imprint of HarperCollins*Publishers* Ltd,
1 London Bridge Street, London, SE1 9GF

www.harpercollins.co.uk

HarperCollins*Publishers*
1st Floor, Watermarque Building,
Ringsend Road, Dublin 4, Ireland

Their Second Chance in ER © 2022 by Sue MacKay

Forbidden Fling with Dr Right © 2022 by JC Harroway

ISBN: 978-0-263-30121-2

03/22

MIX
Paper from
responsible sources
FSC
www.fsc.org   **FSC C007454**

This book is produced from independently certified FSC™ paper
to ensure responsible forest management.
For more information visit www.harpercollins.co.uk/green.

Printed and Bound in Spain using 100% Renewable Electricity
at CPI Black Print, Barcelona

THEIR
SECOND CHANCE
IN ER

SUE MacKAY

MILLS & BOON

This one is for all those special family and friends
for their wonderful support
over the past couple of weeks.

It has meant the world to me. Love, Sue.

CHAPTER ONE

'WAIT TILL YOU meet the new doc,' Jaz told Chloe as she closed her locker. 'He started last week and has already got half the hospital talking about him.'

Laughing, Chloe headed out to the emergency department workstation. 'How many times have I heard this? Every male doctor who comes to work in the emergency department starts out as the best thing since mobile phones.' Not that she often disagreed, but she did keep her distance. In her experience some of them had egos that gave them expectations of how they should be treated as perfect while quick to find flaws within her.

'Even you might look twice this time.'

Jaz had no idea how often she'd looked at the previous emergency specialist until they'd learned he had a wife and two kids back in Christchurch whom he'd forgotten to mention to the women he'd dated here. Thankfully, Chloe sighed, she'd only looked and turned down his suggestion of a night on the town together because something about him hadn't gelled.

'So who is this man? What shifts is he working this week?' Chloe was in zone three, the area for the most serious injuries and illnesses that presented, from seven to three all week. Being prepared for any changes was important to her. Especially new doctors as they nearly always had their own way of doing things—how they approached patients and what they expected from the nurses—and it was best to be prepared. Saved a load of hassle.

An orderly charged into the hub in the centre of the department, calling, 'Man down in Reception. Not breathing.'

'You're not in the army any more, Willy,' Chloe quipped as she snatched up a defibrillator from the trolley by the bench. 'Jaz, you hear that?'

'Right behind you,' her friend answered.

'Nothing like diving straight back into work,' Chloe muttered as she sped past the mostly empty patient cubicles and down the short corridor to Reception. A fortnight at her parents' home in the Marlborough Sounds using up some holidays she was owed and supposedly taking care of her mum post major abdominal surgery had been bliss. There'd been little to do since her mother was stubborn and didn't take kindly to lazing around recuperating. They'd had a couple of minor squabbles about what her mother should not be doing, all in good fun.

The time had been the perfect elixir for her own worn-out body and mind following hectic weeks working long hours with few days off because of a sudden shortage of nurses due to one giving birth ten weeks early, another suffering from a broken femur, and a third one dealing with a family crisis. Plus the doctor who'd had to quit in a hurry when her husband broke his back after falling off the roof of their house he was fixing had added to everyone's workload. As a senior nurse, Chloe was kept very busy, which mostly she liked. It had been a concern that she mightn't get her time off to go to the Sounds, but in the end it had all worked out fine. Seemed as though they were now fully up to speed on staff levels with the new doctor having started. Bring him on.

Willy thumbed the door-release button. 'I've got the door for you.'

Skidding to a stop by the sprawled body, Chloe placed the defib on the floor and dropped to her knees by the woman—not man, Willy—and immediately lifted her wrist to feel for a pulse.

Jaz appeared opposite her. 'Anything?'

'No.' Chloe tore open the woman's shirt, interlaced her fingers and began compressions on the chest. 'You take the defib.'

Jaz was already placing pads on the exposed chest. 'Anyone know the lady's name?'

'Wendy Wright,' gasped a man standing to the side, shock echoing through the room. 'My wife.'

'What happened?' Chloe asked, without looking up.

'She woke me at about five, said she'd been having sharp pains in her chest for about an hour. I wanted to call the ambulance but Wendy said no, I should bring her in. We only live five kilometres away.'

Five kilometres wasn't far, but an ambulance came fully equipped with lifesaving apparatus. Push, lift, push. Twenty-four, twenty-five. 'Jaz, you ready to administer two breaths?' Twenty-nine.

'Yes.'

Thirty. 'Go.' Chloe withdrew her hands, rolled her shoulders. 'Has your wife got any history of heart problems?' The woman looked fit and healthy, but looks could be deceiving.

'No. She goes to the gym four times a week, runs, eats healthy food, doesn't drink.'

The door heading into the department opened, then

closed. Even when the air shifted around her with an oddly familiar sensation, Chloe remained focused on Wendy, and started more compressions. Why would anyone make her feel warm at a moment like this? It was daft. Her eyes didn't leave her patient as she tried to ignore the slight lifting of the skin on the backs of her hands.

'Family history of heart problems?' Jaz asked the husband while holding the defibrillator pads ready to place on the woman's chest the moment the machine's electric current was ready.

'None.'

Push, release, push. Sweat was already breaking out on Chloe's forehead. Doing compressions was no stroll in the park.

Jaz said clearly, 'Stay back, Chloe, everyone.'

Removing her hands and making sure she wasn't touching the woman anywhere, Chloe waited, rubbing her hands up and down her arms, eyes glued to the monitor as the current struck the heart. 'Nothing.' Hands together, press, release. 'One, two, three, four.' She continued while waiting for the defib's electric current to get up to speed again. The woman's face looked deathly pale. It would be horrifying for her husband to be watching this. *Come on, Wendy. You can do this. Your heart needs to pump all by itself. Come on.*

Jaz said, 'Stay back. Second shock coming up.'

The flat green line on the screen lifted, dropped, lifted, up and down, a rough line replicating erratic heartbeats showing life. 'Thank goodness.' Relief surged through Chloe as she tipped her head back to ease the tension in her neck and shoulders from doing the compressions. Then she shrugged forward and lifted the woman's wrist and felt the pulse just to be certain.

Yes. The heart was sending blood around the body, taking oxygen to where it was most needed, keeping Wendy alive. A good result to be going on with. 'Willy, we need a bed in here. Plus a plinth to slide Wendy onto.' It made lifting a patient onto the bed easier on everyone's backs and saved further injury to the patient.

'Everything's ready and waiting on the other side of the door.' Willy was usually one step ahead of things, and rarely got it wrong about what was required.

'Good one. Bring it through.' Chloe staggered to her feet, pins and needles shooting through her calf muscles, and rubbed away the tension in her arms brought on with the compressions. It was always a worry they wouldn't get a heart restarted. She'd experienced that a few times in her career as an emergency nurse and the following despondency always took a bit of getting past, even when knowing it wasn't possible to save every person every time.

Within moments Wendy had been moved onto the plinth and Chloe was reaching for a corner to help lift it onto the bed.

'I'll take that end.'

Chloe froze, her hand inches from the plinth handle. Every muscle in her body was on high alert. Her eyes must've widened because the skin at the corners suddenly felt tight. That voice brought back so many memories she no longer had a use for. Or wanted to revisit. Not at all.

A tall, slight man reached down to take the end of the plinth, his hand missing hers by mere millimetres. Devlin Walsh. It couldn't be. But even if she hadn't recognised the voice, she knew that tiny tattoo of a star between the thumb and forefinger. No doubting who this man was. What was he doing? Ahh, got it. No wonder the air had shifted around her earlier. It had been trying to warn her of trouble. This was the new doctor. The good-looking one every female wanted to get their hands on. They were more than welcome to him.

Ladies, he knows how to break hearts without pausing for a breath. He doesn't understand the truth, even when it knocks him between the eyes. He sees life through rose-tinted, make that wealth-inspired, glasses.

'Chloe, out of the way,' Jaz said. 'We've got this.'

Blindly stepping back, she shook her head. This must not be Devlin. But it was. His all too familiar face with a firm mouth that used to tease her skin into believing it was alive with a fire of its own, the easy grace in his movements that spoke of knowledge and determination as he straightened up holding one end of the plinth, the confidence that exuded from every pore of his body. This man was none other than her ex-fiancé. Of all the people to turn up today when she was feeling relaxed and happy after a wonderful break. What had she done to upset the universe? There were plenty of doctors out there, though not necessarily available or good enough for the position here. So just because she didn't want Devlin Walsh to be the new specialist in the department, didn't mean she could have it her own way. But hell, she could still scream at the sky about this. Silently, of course.

The moisture in her mouth evaporated. After all this time she wouldn't find anything remotely exciting about Devlin. They'd been finished for almost seven years. She closed her eyes, then opened them again, but felt only annoyance. She'd lost the love of her heart and the baby she'd been carrying within a couple of weeks. Forget annoyance. It was pure anger hissing in her veins. He was real, and absolutely *not* exciting. Definitely the rat who broke her heart. Turned out when the going got tough she hadn't been good enough for his family, and therefore him. Growing up in the lowest of the low suburbs in Auckland, according to Mr and Mrs Walsh, she wasn't supposed to mix with the crème de la crème. An opinion that had never changed. Crème de la crème? More like super *rico*. So full of their own self-importance they didn't know if they were coming or going half the time. Bet they wouldn't believe she'd never missed them or their lifestyle one little bit. Not when they believed she'd got together with Devlin for his money, not because she loved him.

'Chloe, you want to grab the defib?' Jaz asked over her shoulder as the bed with their patient was pushed into the department.

The exaggerated wink Jaz gave suggested Chloe might be aware of Devlin in ways Jaz had said other women were, which reminded Chloe to get her head straight. It also made her stomach churn at the thought her friend could even imagine she'd be interested in the new doc. Not that Jaz knew much about her past, especially about Dr Walsh. He was old news. He'd never intrigue her with his wicked wit and sexy body again. Been there, fallen in love deep and fast, did the excruciating hard yards on the way out, and barely managed to survive.

But she had, and now wasn't the time to be recalling all the reasons she didn't care two hoots for him. Devlin was working in the same department as her and there was no point making the days longer than they already were. Besides, any conflict between them would just make everyone else uncomfortable around them, and hadn't she got over him? Yes, she had, so she'd act appropriately.

Putting the defibrillator back on the trolley, her hand briefly touching her churning belly lightly, she turned for the cubicle where they'd taken their patient. Reality dropped like a boulder. Devlin was here to stay. He wasn't an apparition. Unfortunately.

Welcome back, Chloe. Hope you had a great holiday because your job has just taken on a whole new dimension and it's not looking too great right now.

Deep breath. But it would improve. It had to. This time she wasn't going to be the one to leave. The experiences she'd had as part of moving on from her broken engagement had made her stronger and more resilient. Hadn't they? Guess that theory was going to be put to the test over the coming months.

Stepping up, she breathed deep, pulled on her professional face, and said, 'Hi there, Devlin. Welcome aboard.'

Devlin glanced up from their patient to Chloe Rasmussen, charging the air around him as she entered the cubicle where they'd brought Wendy. 'Hello, Chloe, and thank you. I'm slowly getting to know everyone,' he said from the other side of the bed, caution overtaking everything else as he looked at his ex-fiancée.

Unfortunately he knew her too well, so why the wave of illogical fascination crashing through him? So many years since they'd split up, and though he'd learned last week she worked in this department and would be here this morning, he'd had no qualms about that because of all those years standing between then and now. He hadn't been carrying a torch for her all that time. Not even a match. Far from it. At twenty-seven, his heart had been so invested in her that they were planning on getting married. Then he'd found out she was cheating on him just as his previous girlfriend had. Straight away he'd wrapped his love up tight, tossed it aside, and walked away. Not only from Chloe, but the dream of settling down one day and having a family. A man could only be cheated on so many times, and for him it had been twice too often. He would never again take a chance on love. Some time during the intervening years of study and training, qualifying as an emergency specialist, he had got over Chloe, as he had the first woman who'd messed with his heart. Well and truly over her.

So why the tingling heat under his ribs brought on by a simple glance?

Right now Chloe was completely focused on their patient—as he should be. Hell. He never lost focus on what was important. Which certainly was not this slight, cool, pretty woman he used to know very well. Or so he'd thought until she'd proved how wrong he could be for a second time.

She was saying, 'Wendy, I'm sorry but I have to lift your blouse to place the pads on your skin,' as she prepared to attach the ECG monitor so they'd have continuous readings and an immediate recognition of cardiac arrest should it occur again. It shouldn't, but there was no such thing as never when it came to medicine and their patients. The beeps would vary according to the heart rate so if the heart stopped they'd instantly be made aware by a sharp monotone.

Wendy blinked her eyes open, sought out her husband, and closed them again.

'Mr Wright, I'm Devlin. These nurses are Jaz and Chloe. Sorry we didn't get around to introducing ourselves earlier but it was a little tense.'

'I understand. My name's Ian.'

'Ian, which GP does Wendy go to? I need to fill in

the details that would normally have been down at Reception,' explained Jaz.

Devlin tried to listen to that nurse as she questioned the husband further, and to stop noticing Chloe as she attached the monitor leads to their patient. Getting distracted couldn't happen unless another crisis occurred in the department, and even then it was a controlled distraction. So he wasn't about to let Chloe sidetrack him any more than she already had.

Wendy's heart attack seemed to have come out of the blue. There was little info to work with, so he threw in some questions of his own. 'No history of chest pain, sore back, aches in the left arm?'

'Not that I know of.'

'Family history?' Sometimes it paid to repeat questions. Especially as at the time of Jaz's first queries the man was in shock and watching his lifeless wife lying on the floor while everyone worked to resuscitate her.

'None. Is she going to be all right?'

'We have to establish the cause of why her heart failed so there'll be tests done,' Devlin told him while dodging the question. He didn't yet have the definite answers the man was looking for. 'Did Wendy have any childhood illnesses?' Rheumatic fever would be one that'd possibly explain today's event, but she looked fit with well-honed muscles so that seemed unlikely. Besides her husband had told them she was healthy.

'Nothing.'

Jaz was tapping on the portable screen, filling in details.

Devlin sighed. He'd taken over, which showed Chloe was getting to him. Damn her. She'd lost that power years ago. Or so he'd believed. No, of course she had. 'Sorry, Jaz. Carry on. I'm going to take some bloods

and call the cardiology department.' A specialist was
needed now, not later. Except it wasn't even seven in
the morning and unless there'd already been a cardiac
emergency during the night the chances of a cardiologist being in the hospital that early were unlikely. He'd
have to get someone out of the shower or away from
breakfast. He shrugged. It was the nature of the job.
Though not his, unless there was a particularly hectic
shift and more hands were required. Which did happen
more times than he cared to acknowledge in emergency
departments, especially on a Friday or Saturday night
when downtown partying got out of control.

'Heart rate's thirty-four,' Chloe noted aloud.

Not good. 'Too low.' Did she still like to party?
Dance with abandon to loud music? Shake her shapely
backside and wriggle her hips until he'd had to have
her? 'Monitor it,' he snapped.

Perfectly shaped dark eyebrows rose. 'Yes, Doctor,
I am.'

Two mistakes in not many more seconds. He shook
his head sharply. 'Sorry, Chloe. You know what you're
doing. I get that.'

'I do.'

'You two obviously know each other,' Jaz commented, looking from one to the other of them with a
question in her eye.

'It was a long time ago,' Chloe said.

Too well. Though not well enough when it came to
the crunch. He might've once made the mistake of falling for Chloe and asking her to be his wife, but he'd
learnt a blunt lesson when she played around on him.
Don't trust women with his heart. But he could still be
professional—kind and friendly, not overbearing and
rude. Guilt ripped through him. He had been abrupt

with Chloe for no reason other than his own musings over the past. 'I haven't seen Chloe since not long after she qualified as a nurse. She was focused back then, and I'm sure that hasn't changed.'

'I try to be.' Chloe spoke sharply while her eyes remained fixed on the monitor as she prepared a cannula to insert in Wendy's arm so they could give any intravenous drugs and painkillers she required over the coming hours. They'd also be getting fluids on board through another cannula as dehydration did not help in this situation. 'Devlin was studying to become an emergency specialist back then.'

So she wasn't completely denying their past. Was that good or bad? Warmth touched his skin. Kind of odd when she'd hurt him so badly.

Suck it in, get on with being professional.

'You did well with the compressions today.' Now he sounded condescending. She really had got to him—without saying anything at all annoying. 'I mean it. I got there just behind you and Jaz, and wanted to leap in and take over, but you had it under control.' His instinct had been to push them aside to do the compressions himself. After all, he was the emergency specialist. Once he would've done exactly that, but nowadays his ego was a lot more secure and he stood back to let others perform their tasks just as competently as he could. He didn't have to prove himself any more. He was a very good emergency specialist. Yet somehow Chloe had made him feel superfluous.

Also in awe at the speed and proficiency of both women working on their patient. His palms had itched with the need to get in there and save the woman sprawled on the floor, but he'd forced himself to stay put. Everything that could have been done for Wendy was already being done efficiently and effectively. Interrupting would've only caused problems. So instead, his gaze had turned to Chloe as she'd continued her efforts. There had been no panic or stress on her face, only concentration as she'd done her job. As she was one of the permanent nurses working any of the three typical shifts, they were going to rub shoulders a lot. And he'd already snapped at her.

Great going, Dev.

Chloe might've always taken her career seriously, tried hard to overcome a lack of confidence in herself, but there'd been another, much livelier side to her when they'd been together away from work. She'd said she had years to make up for of studying and working at supermarkets stacking shelves to pay her way. She'd done a lot of that. Apparently he hadn't been enough for her; she'd needed other men as well to play catch-up with. She'd waited until they were engaged, and then let rip, apparently certain the ring on her finger meant she was safe from being dumped if the truth ever came out. Bile rose in his throat. He swallowed hard. She'd betrayed him, hurt him.

Old hat, Devlin. Get over yourself. Get over Chloe. Again.

'Want me to get the blood-test kit so I can do the tests?' Chloe asked, her face blank, her slim frame ramrod-straight and tense.

What? Damn, he was losing the plot. 'No. I'm on my way.' He forced himself to turn away and head for his desk in the centre of the department. Giving her the hug he found he inexplicably wanted to share after saving Wendy's life would be like wrapping his arms around an iceberg. She wouldn't be warm towards him after the way they'd parted. She'd been so furious when he'd left her, even though it was her own fault. Besides, to hug her at work would be bad enough. To hug her at all when she meant nothing to him any more would be just weird. No denying he wanted to though. She'd think he had lost his mind. She might have a point, he conceded as he sank onto the chair and picked up the phone to call the cardiology ward.

When indifference should be foremost in his head, that wasn't what was pricking his mind. His gaze wandered towards the cubicle where Chloe was talking to Wendy, reading the monitor, and looking more self-contained than he remembered her ever being. She'd constantly worried about not being good enough for him and his family, her lack of confidence made worse by his mother, who hadn't taken a shine to her future daughter-in-law. Then Chloe had had a brief fling with another man. Only brief because he'd quickly found out and told her they were over, though. None of it had made sense. He had adored her, had promised her the earth and had been looking forward to being married and having a family with her later on. She'd said she felt the same and he'd believed her.

Old words filtered into his head.

You and your family are all so wrapped up in your wealthy bubble that none of you see other people for who they truly are. Try standing in a different pair of shoes some time and see how the world looks from another perspective. I am as good as any of you.

He'd had no idea where that had come from, and used to shrug her doubts away, telling her she was more than good enough for him and that was all that mattered. Then she'd played around on him. If she'd felt she didn't fit in why go and do the very thing that proved his mother right about her? Did she ever have any regrets?

Or had she moved on, found someone else to settle down with, and was now happy in a way he obviously hadn't made her? Chances were she had a husband, kids, and a mortgage like most normal people. Unlike him. After twice having his heart broken, he stuck to the tried and true habit of dating amazing women and then walking away before anyone got too involved. It worked for him, kept him safe, and at the end of the day he was okay with that.

'Cardiology. Don't tell me you've got another emergency down there,' came a disgruntled male voice over the phone. 'I've been here all night.'

Devlin smiled. 'Sure have. Devlin Walsh here. A forty-three-year-old woman had an arrest in the waiting room—' he glanced at his watch '—twenty minutes ago. She's been resuscitated. No history of heart problems, appears fit and healthy.'

'This is Nick Somers. I haven't met you yet, but seems I'm about to. I'll be down shortly.' No mucking about.

Devlin liked that. 'Thanks.' Hanging up, he filled in a lab form on screen before going to get the blood kit. 'Nick's on his way down from Cardiology,' he told Chloe and Jaz when he returned to the cubicle. 'Seems they've had a busy night.'

Chloe glanced his way. 'I haven't had time to catch up with who's in here, let alone what went down during the night. I'd hardly stepped into the department and Willy was calling for help with Wendy.'

'Much the same for me,' Devlin admitted, relieved she was talking to him as she might any doctor. That stiffness in her shoulders had loosened and there was even something approaching a smile in those oval caramel eyes. It made sense she might've been a little shocked when she first saw him, since she'd been on leave and probably wouldn't have had a clue he now worked here. 'I'd better get onto finding out what other cases we have.'

'What bloods do you want done for Wendy?' She was holding her hand out for the kit.

'A troponin to see what level it's at and set the bar for further tests, plus general liver and renal tests and a CBC. Cover the bases and if Nick wants to add any more we'll have taken the correct samples.'

'Right. I'll do that.'

It was the second time she'd mentioned she'd take the bloods. Was he lagging behind that much? When he looked directly at her, his heart lurched. Those eyes used to be full of happiness whenever she was with him. Even love. Until the day he'd walked into her flat and accused her of sleeping with another man. A tsunami of pain had replaced the happiness then, pain he'd thought she deserved. Today only professionalism showed. Fair enough. That was how he wanted it to be, despite the un-expected memories of what had once been the most won-derful time of his life. He'd never trust her again so why consider if what he'd lost could be found? Even if at all possible, he wasn't running with it. She'd cheated on him.

She denied that, Dev.

Sure she did. So did his first serious girlfriend and he'd actually caught *her* in the act.

'You want me to do something else?' Chloe asked, sudden barbs in her voice at his lack of response.

'No.'

'Morning, everyone. Chloe, thank goodness you're back. The place isn't the same without your steady hand at the helm.' A short, chubby man strolled into the cu-bicle and held his hand out to Devlin. 'Nick Somers.'

'Devlin Walsh.' He shook hands, and then dipped his head in Wendy's direction. 'This is our patient, Wendy Wright, and her husband, Ian, behind you.'

'Hello, Wendy. I'm a cardiologist and will work with you to find out why your heart stopped.' He turned slightly and held out his hand again. 'Morning, Ian. Quite the stressful start to your day, I understand.'

'It certainly is. Glad to meet you.' Then he glanced at Devlin. 'Not that the doctor doesn't know what he's doing. And the nurses.'

Devlin said, 'Relax, Ian. I understand you want the best help on your side right now, and who better than a cardiologist?' Though he, Chloe and Jaz had done everything they could and needed to, and Wendy was all the better for that. Especially after the nurses had brought her back to life. Nick's job would be focused on finding the cause of the arrest and seeing that another didn't occur.

Chloe placed the blood-test kit on the bed. 'Wendy, there'll be a small prick.' She'd taken over the job he still hadn't got around to doing.

He sucked in his stomach, breathed deep to dissipate the frustration she invoked, and turned to Nick. 'I'll fill you in on the little we know.' And put all things Chloe, except her nursing skills, behind him. Again.

CHAPTER TWO

WHILE SIPPING HER TEA, Chloe stared at her running shoes. The morning had been busier than usual for a Monday so getting a break had come later and she was in need of a large caffeine fix. 'Nothing like a heart attack and a car accident to remind me that my real life is in here and not lounging on the deck overlooking the waters of the Kenepuru Sound.'

'Not to mention a hot doc that has everyone sitting up and taking notice,' Jaz added before biting into her muffin and looking smug.

'Not me.' Not in the way Jaz was suggesting. 'Don't even ask.' She'd once loved Devlin with every bone of her body and then some, and she'd thought she'd never get over him. But she had. Thank goodness or she'd be shattering into fragments right now. It had taken determination and hard work to move on, but she'd done it.

As she had her first love, Stephen, whom she'd met at nineteen. She'd moved in with him at twenty, only to find enough courage to pack her bags and leave a year later when his controlling personality had become too much to bear. She hadn't ever been up to scratch for his exacting standards; something he'd loved to taunt her about, saying how useless she was at the basic things in life, and even worse in bed. Her leaving had shocked him, and he'd swiftly returned to being the nice guy she'd first met, begging for a second chance because he wanted to show how much he cared for her. She'd been stupid enough to believe him, but it hadn't taken long for Stephen to return to his old tricks, and it was easier leaving the second time, and staying away. She'd watched her mother do the same with a man who wouldn't accept Chloe as part of the package, and treated her worse than his cat, which was downtrodden and half starved.

Her mum had adored the guy, but no one, nothing, was allowed to hurt her daughter. It was a lesson that had taught Chloe to try to be strong and not let others wield the rod, no matter how much it hurt to walk away. She hadn't done very well at that. It had been hard when she'd believed Stephen was right in that she wasn't good at most things she did. Of course, she hadn't been strong, had argued with herself about what she was doing for weeks, but she had finally managed to leave.

But breaking up with Devlin had been a whole different story. He had never treated her badly, appeared to love her as much as she did him, until that fatal day when he'd arrived at her flat, taken one look at Adam in his semi-naked state, and accused her of having a fling behind his back. *Worse*, he'd refused to believe her explanation. Plain out refused to talk to her at all. Just walked away, head high, taking her heart with him. Yeah, it had been hard to get over that, but she had.

When she met Devlin two years after leaving Stephen while on placement on a plastic surgery ward during her final year of nursing training, she fell for him hard and fast. Seemed that was how it worked for her. But Dev had been just as quick to fall for her; they'd clicked with only a look, and seemed to be on the same page over many things—except his family. But she'd loved him so much she'd tried hard to fit into his privileged lifestyle, to make his parents accept her, especially after she and Devlin became engaged. It wasn't to be. Devlin threw her love back in her face hard and fast, decimating her with his complete lack of trust in her. He didn't even ask if it was true or try to discuss it with her. She was guilty in his eyes, and that was that.

Except she wasn't guilty. That he could so easily believe such a horrible thing about her had her doubting she'd ever trust herself to fall in love again. Her mother told her not to give up, to keep an open mind, when it came to men. There were some good ones out there, the only problem being they were hard to find. Her mother was forty-four when she finally met Jack, who loved her and treated her as though she was special, and was the closest to a real father Chloe had ever known. She was his 'little' princess, even now she was thirty-two years old.

So maybe one day she'd get lucky and find a man who'd believe in her and see her for who she was. A man who didn't complain about how she washed the dishes or made the bed, like Stephen. Or a man who didn't accuse her of something she'd never do, like Devlin. He'd also come with a snobbish mother who'd said things like, 'We're going to a charity dinner, not a pub meal,' as she'd studied Chloe's outfit. Or, 'The Hugheses are coming for drinks, not one of your nursing friends,' because Chloe hadn't gone to the hairdresser that day. She was one hell of a lot stronger these days, and a match for anyone. Her hands smoothed her uniform trousers over her thighs.

Jaz's voice cut through the mixed memories. 'Devlin's got your attention like no other guy I've seen you look at. You're miles away.'

Not that far, Chloe reflected. 'Not in the way you're thinking. It was a bit of a shock seeing him again,' she admitted. 'I can't get my head around the fact that there are doctors out there wanting to work here and it's Devlin Walsh who got the position. Couldn't they have found someone else?'

'You know the board's been interviewing prospects for a while now. He's definitely got what's needed here. We've been short-staffed since Kate's husband had his accident, and, despite what you say, good doctors weren't exactly lining up to replace her. There's a level of uncertainty about what'll happen when Lloyd's back on his feet and Kate considers returning to work.' Jaz gave her a broad smile.

'Even then, she'll probably only work part time,' Chloe acknowledged.

'So you're going to have to swallow that lemon in your throat and get used to working alongside Devlin.'

'I know.' Chloe shuddered.

It wasn't a lemon, but a strange feeling that the past was coming back in spades to haunt her. Maybe even knock her down after she'd worked so hard to get up and keep moving. She had loved Devlin so much, it was scary. What if some of that love was still lurking in her heart? Ready to cause pain every time she looked at him? Going to tip her steady world upside down again? As if. She gave a mental snort. He didn't belong in her heart any more. And she was stronger nowadays. *Remember?* First though, she had to get used to working with him.

'I understand how fortunate we are. He does have a brilliant reputation as an emergency doctor.' He always did, even when training. There was something about his calm, knowledgeable demeanour that repeatedly won patients and other doctors over. Plus his dedication. He'd won *her* heart. Too easily, perhaps. Because he was wonderful. Until… Until he threw her heart back in her face. No such dedication then. He couldn't have walked away any quicker.

His disabling words rose in her head.

'You've played around behind my back.'

'No, Devlin, I haven't. I never would.'

'Then explain why that man is in your lounge dressed only in a towel.'

'He needed a shower and has no hot water. I'm just being neighbourly.'

'Do you take me for a complete fool? Well, guess what? I'm not. I will not be made to look like an idiot. We're done, Chloe. It's as simple as that.'

There'd been nothing simple about watching Devlin walk out of her flat for the last time that night. Straightforward, maybe, but simple? Hell, no. Not when her heart was in a million little pieces. Not when he wouldn't talk to her from then on, no matter how often she'd tried to make contact. Not when her world had just stopped turning.

'So how long have you been working here, Chloe?'

Tea splashed onto her thigh, soaked through her blue uniform pants. How long had Devlin been standing behind her? Surely Jaz would've noticed and said something. He'd better not have overheard them talking. She didn't need Devlin knowing Jaz had told her to get a grip, or he'd realise he could still get her in a pickle. But he probably had already, all by himself. He had a gift when it came to reading people, especially her. Except for that one, disastrous time. 'About three years. I was at one of the private surgical hospitals here in Wellington before that.'

He'd crossed to the bench and was making a mug of tea. 'You've been in Wellington all the time, then?'

Since you kicked me out of your life, you mean?

'No. I stayed on at the North Shore for nearly a year.' Wasting time hoping he'd see he'd made a huge mistake and come back to her. She'd have given him a second chance then, but that was before she'd learned to prioritise herself and her own needs. 'After that I took a break and headed offshore for a year. Next stop Wellington, and I'm settled, unlikely to leave.'

'Where did you go overseas?' He'd probably remember she never used to have any ambition to travel abroad.

She hadn't, even when boarding the flight to London on the way to Rome. It had taken coercion from her stepdad to get her packing a case with a year's clothing. 'Italy.' And only Italy. That'd surprise him even more because that length of time obviously meant it hadn't been a tour where everything was organised for her.

Sure enough, a teaspoon clattered into the sink. 'Italy? Did you work there?' He was studying her with something like amazement on his face. 'No, of course not. For one, you don't speak the language.'

'No, I couldn't work as a nurse. I boarded with a family in a small village near Milan and for my meals I taught their children English. I also took care of Nonna Rossi part time, and when I wasn't doing those things I went sightseeing, cycling everywhere. It was the most incredible experience of my life.' She'd never known such freedom, even while scraping by on very little—which hadn't been anything new for her anyway. With a roof over her head, a warm bed and food provided, and a wonderful family happy to share what they had, she hadn't needed anything more.

He winced. 'That's not something I'd thought you wanted to do.'

You didn't know me as well as you thought. Not enough to trust me anyway.

'It hadn't been.' But a lot of things had shifted in her thinking back then. The miscarriage she'd suffered not long after Devlin had left her had been a huge shock, especially as she hadn't even known she was pregnant. It had woken her up to realising she'd lost more than just a fiancé. She'd wanted to move beyond her dreams of love and children, since it obviously wasn't happening, and to find something to excite herself and give her confidence in her own ability to survive, and survive well. But she hadn't known how. It had been her stepdad, Jack, who'd got her up and running, not away from everything but heading towards something that could help her learn to be strong on her own.

'I'm impressed.'

Yeah, right. 'Don't be. I finally did something for myself.' That trip and the family who'd become such a part of her had widened her horizons so that she'd understood trying to make people love her, because her father had proved he didn't by not even waiting around for her to be born, wasn't as important as loving herself—and those like her mother and Jack, who always backed her. This was a side to her that hadn't been so obvious when Devlin was in her life.

'Sounds grand.'

There'd been nothing grand about her travels. She'd had a narrow bed in a back room in a small, dark and damp house with a family who ate lots of pasta and vegetables because they couldn't afford meat, and shared what little they had with her. And she'd loved every moment of it. Draining her tea, she stood up. 'I'd better get back.' It was barely ten minutes since she'd left the department.

Chloe put her mug in the dishwasher, reached for Jaz's and placed it in there too. 'Don't rush,' she told her friend as she headed for the door, needing Devlin-free air to breathe normally. Damn it. *Did* she still feel something for him after all this time? No, that would be too stupid. She wasn't the same woman who'd fallen for him. She no longer felt inadequate around strong, confident, privileged people. She'd learned to be herself, and accept that not everyone would see things her way. Her time in Italy had given her confidence and strength, and an inner comfort that had seen her come home and buy her little house and get a dog and live how *she* liked. Amongst that she'd learned not to look back and regret the past—except her miscarriage. Fingers crossed, one day she'd have another baby. Yet here she was, already getting in a bind over Devlin when there could never be a future between them. They'd hurt each other badly at the end. Not that she had been unfaithful to him, but he'd believed she had, so understandably he'd been hurt, too.

Jaz grinned. 'I'm coming. Wonder what we've got.'

Devlin told them, 'A three-year-old girl with a severe asthmatic episode. Mum's beside herself with fear. Clare's seeing to her.'

Chloe paused, turned back as her heart squeezed. 'The poor kid. She'll be terrified, especially if her mother's showing her fear.'

'You're right.' Dev nodded. 'They're both stressed to the max, and there's nothing anyone can do until wee Lilly's breathing properly again.'

Of course, he understood his patients' concerns. That was one of his best characteristics as a doctor. Actually, he'd been like that with her, too, about most worries she'd had. Tenderness threaded through her tight muscles, loosening the tension Devlin had brought with him. 'Where's the father?'

'He's on his way from the airport where he works. I hope he's the calm one of the family.'

'Me, too.' An easy smile started lifting her lips. Huh? Tightening her mouth, Chloe headed away.

'I'll work with Clare on this case,' Jaz said.

'Thanks, friend.' Not. She did not want to work with Devlin at all.

Swallowing the last of his tea, Devlin resisted the urge to get up and follow Chloe. Never in a million years would he have believed he'd feel anything but annoyance at spending time with her. He'd expected to be cool and calm, not sitting with his fingers gripping his mug while the blood pounded through his veins at a higher than normal rate. She looked lovelier than ever; time and experience had matured her. She'd lived in Italy for a year! Gone over on her own and stayed with a family in a village off the regular tourist track and begun to learn another language. That was not the Chloe he'd been engaged to. That Chloe hadn't been overly confident, always worried she wasn't good enough for people to stand by her. Her mother, Joy, had supported her but, from what he'd gathered, Chloe's father had never been in the picture and she felt guilty about the relationships Joy ditched when the men didn't want her daughter. Obviously she'd learnt to stand alone, since she'd moved here, where she didn't know other people. At least, she hadn't when he knew her, but any of the nurses she'd trained with might've moved south. Or maybe she now had a partner who came from here? He still had no idea if she was single or not.

Hell, when he'd dragged himself out of bed that morning after a restless night, unsure how it would go catching up with Chloe for the first time since they'd split up, he couldn't have cared less about her relationship status, yet within a few hours he'd twice wondered if there was a deep and meaningful other half in her life. Apparently Chloe still had the ability to get under his skin. So what? He'd cope. It wasn't a big deal. Some might say it was to be expected, given their fiery bust up. Not that he had anything he wanted to say to her about that. It was over, had been for years. In that time he'd moved on, qualified as a specialist, bought a house in Auckland, an apartment in Wellington, and become godfather to two of his friends' sons. His dreams of having a family with Chloe were long gone, and these days he made the most of time spent with his godsons while trying not to think about what he was missing out on.

He'd packed up and moved to a different city and a new job, and hopefully an exciting new life. All because his over-demanding parents had become even more so, lately. His brother, Patrick, had shown him by example that he could lead his own life. Patrick had disgraced the family by becoming addicted to gambling and had been told to go away until he was over his problems or he'd be cut off from the family wealth. So his brother had gone to Melbourne, got a high-end job in the financial district, quit gambling, and slowly found happiness. A new life, new friends, and a wonderful woman was all it took, he'd told Devlin. He had no intentions of returning home, which had left Devlin handling more of the family responsibilities. 'You should try it,' Patrick had added. 'You might be surprised what you find out about yourself.'

He had taken Patrick's words on board on a day when he'd put in far too many extra hours in the emergency department, where he'd lost a patient to cardiac arrest and worked hard to save a five-year-old from bleeding out after falling from a jungle-gym bar onto a glass bottle, only for their mother to start in on him about the daughter of close friends being the ideal woman to marry when he'd called in afterwards. That had been the final straw. He'd finally decided to get away and try something different. His parents were adamant he should marry that woman. She came from a similar background to his: the best schools, clothes and cars, trips to exclusive resorts around the world, high expectations over what they were to accomplish with their careers, which had to be respectable. A woman Devlin liked, but did not fancy. She was warm and funny, and devoted to her family, but that didn't add up to enough for him to think about marrying her and living with her for the rest of their lives.

Chloe. He'd been going to marry her, have children with her, be with her for ever. She'd touched him in ways he hadn't known before—or since. It was as though she could see right inside him to his vulnerabilities without using them against him. She'd given him a sense of belonging that came with no obligations.

'Devlin, we've got a stabbing victim.' Chloe, the nurse, not the woman taking up his head space, stood in the doorway, an ambulance patient form in her hand.

'Fill me in,' he demanded, following her to a cubicle where deep, teeth-gritting groans of pain were coming from.

'Tommy Drysdale, twenty-eight. Knife wounds to

the chest and upper left arm, and at least one to the abdomen. No major blood vessels damaged. Patient had to be sedated as he was angry and tried to hit the paramedics who collected him. He's also been given morphine and is on fluids.'

'Has he taken any drugs? Alcohol?' That was when fighting often occurred: even before eleven in the morning with some people, which was obviously the case here.

'None that he's admitting to, but the paramedics noted the smell of alcohol on his breath, and his speech is slurred, which could also be due to his injuries or lack of hydration,' Chloe concluded.

'True.' No doubt a mix of all of the above. 'Hello, Tommy. I'm Devlin Walsh, a doctor. This is Chloe, one of our nurses.' The twitch of concern he suddenly felt for the staff made him speak carefully. The guy mightn't be in good shape right now, but Tommy looked like trouble. 'Tell me where the worst of the pain is.'

'Everywhere. It's twelve out of ten, man. Do something about it instead of standing around talking at me.'

'How long ago was the morphine administered?' Devlin asked Chloe.

She read the form, checked her watch. 'Forty minutes. One milligram.'

'Can you please get another similar dose?'

'Sure.'

'Get me some water,' Tommy shouted. 'My mouth's dry.'

'Sorry but you can't have anything to drink or eat, at the moment.' Devlin lifted the swab applied to what appeared to be the largest wound near the right side of the horrid man's ribcage and pressed around the area. 'Any pain here?'

'Which part of everywhere don't you get?'

'I understand, but it will be worse in different places and I'm trying to find where so I know what internal damage has been done. Did you see how long the knife blade was?'

''Bout five inches.'

Dev winced, swallowed. The thought of something like that piercing his body made him shiver. He continued to check all the wounds. Whenever Tommy grunted at the pressure he applied he knew he'd found internal damage. Finally he straightened. 'I'm ordering an ultrasound of your abdomen and liver. I suspect your liver has been injured.'

Chloe held up the vial of morphine for him to check the batch number with her.

As she was pressing the drug in through the cannula, he told her, 'I'll stitch the lesser wounds. Can you call an orderly? Tell them it's urgent.'

She nodded. 'What about a moist pad for Tommy to suck since he can't swallow anything?'

'Yes, that's fine.' He walked out of the cubicle towards the cabinet containing suture needles and thread, said quietly, 'Tread carefully around him. I don't like the aggression in his eyes. I don't want anyone getting hurt.' *Especially not you.* There he went again. Thinking about Chloe more than other nurses. 'Warn anyone who might go into his cubicle to be aware.'

Her smile was grim. 'Believe me, I will. I've taken a hit before, and I don't intend letting it happen to me or anyone else again.'

His hands tightened. 'Someone hit you?'

'I took it on my shoulder. The shock of it rattled me more than the pain. It was a lesson I won't forget.'

'Good. But I don't like hearing that you were hit.

I've taken a couple of knocks, and they made my blood boil. We try to help people and some of them show no appreciation whatsoever.'

'Dev, this sounds like a hobby horse of yours.' The skin at the edges of her eyes crinkled, but her mouth was tight. 'Drop it for now. You've got some suturing to do.'

All the air went out of him. She was right. He was not proving himself to be efficient or professional—to Chloe of all people. But he liked how she pointed it out without making a fuss or raising her voice. He would follow her example and maybe they'd manage to work together without any hassles about the past. Except it sat between them like a boulder that'd have to be manoeuvred out of the way with difficulty. 'On to it.' If only he could forget the Chloe who used to make his blood sing and his heart dance. He'd forgotten that about her until now, remembered only the immense disappointment and hurt that she could betray him when she'd sworn she loved him more than anyone or anything. That had been until this morning and seeing her for the first time in nearly seven years. The better memories were fast becoming a plague, filling every space in his head, which had to be why he was overreacting. Surely it would blow over fast? He only had to remember that man in her flat for that to happen. Didn't he?

'I doubt that blade was five inches long or there'd be more serious damage, wouldn't there?' she murmured.

'Hard to say. Depends if the assailant pushed it in right up to the hilt. With aggressive stabbing, they tend to pull out fast and have another go.'

She shuddered. 'Yuck. Gives me the creeps thinking about it.'

He touched her shoulder lightly. 'Me, too.'

The stunned look crossing her face made him withdraw instantly.

Quite right, Chloe. I shouldn't have touched you. I don't have the right to touch any of the staff. I never do that.

Yet he'd just placed his hand on her. Couldn't be because he wanted to get to know her again. That'd just be setting himself up for more pain. 'I'm sorry. I briefly forgot where I was.' Not who he was with though. Their conversation had felt personal, despite talking about something that all the staff in the ED had to deal with from time to time. When she'd shivered he'd felt the same urge to hug her that had caught him out earlier in Reception.

Chloe stepped away, picked up a phone from the desk and punched a number. 'Hi, it's Chloe in ED. We need an orderly urgently to take a man for an ultrasound. If Willy's available, that'd be great. The patient's aggressive.'

Devlin picked up another phone and rang through to Radiology. 'It's Devlin Walsh in ED. Sorry to do this to you, but I've got a man needing an urgent ultrasound of the abdomen. He's got stab wounds and I need to know if any organs have been damaged.'

'No problem. The machine's in use, but should be available in ten. The next patient will have to wait, that's all.'

Nothing unusual in that. 'Thanks.' Putting the phone down, he told Chloe, 'He's next in line.'

'Willy's on his way,' she told him. 'He's ex-army and takes no nonsense.'

He wanted to high-five her. She'd been onto the problem immediately. Instead he clenched his hands and said, 'The stitching will have to wait until Tommy gets back. The bleeding from all the wounds is mostly under control anyway. I think he's got off lightly.'

'I'll leave you to tell him that.' The tension had backed out of her stance. There was even a glimmer of a smile as she sat down at the computer to update a file. Though probably not for him.

'Think I'll keep it to myself for now.' What a day this was. Not patient-wise, but when it came to behaving normally around Chloe he wasn't able to manage it. But then, she'd always been able to wind him up and have him wanting her with no effort on her part. Wanting her? He hadn't got that far. Nor was he going to any time in the future. If she could hurt him once, she could do it again. Damn it, why was he even thinking this? He'd got over her a long time ago. The anger and hurt had gone and he was a different person these days. He couldn't be sucked back into believing that when he loved someone he was actually loved back equally. Couldn't? Or wouldn't? Didn't matter, either way he wasn't getting involved with Chloe or any other woman.

His gaze fell on Chloe. That would be a shame. She was… She was still Chloe. Different, wonderful, exciting, sexy, loving. Except…

Give it a break, Dev. Go do some work.

He tossed a file into the tray on the desk and said, 'Anyone ready for a break while we still can?'

Jaz said, 'Chloe, you go first. I want to keep an eye on my patient for a bit longer.'

A scowl was directed at her as Chloe answered unenthusiastically, 'All right.'

A tea break, not a round on the wrestling mat, Devlin wanted to tease. Instead he walked beside her, quiet except for the thudding in his chest. This awkward situation could only get worse unless they dealt with it, and the sooner the better. 'Chloe. I understand you got a shock seeing me on your turf this morning.'

She didn't look his way. 'A little one but I'm over it already.'

'Then you're happy I'm here and we can get on with everything as though nothing even happened between us?' Tension was creeping into his arms and shoulders.

'Of course not.' She strode out, heading to the cafeteria at the end of the corridor. Suddenly she stopped, spun back to face him, hands tight at her sides, her eyes blazing. 'You could quit, go back to where you came from.'

If only. 'I won't do that. I'm sorry, but I'm here for the long haul.'

Her lips pressed into each other as she glared at him. She looked away, then back again. 'Okay, there are issues between us that were never resolved, and are never likely to be. In fact, they don't need to be. They're old and irrelevant now. I accept you're working here and that we have to get along for the sake of the rest of the staff and the patients. I can do this.'

'So can I. But I'd prefer that we are comfortable around each other, not uptight and wary.' Was it even possible? Probably after a month or two dodging around one another and not looking each other in the eye.

The slight flick of her tongue at the corner of her mouth told him Chloe had similar thoughts. 'You think we can manage that?'

'Only one way to find out.' He'd do his damnedest to make sure they did. 'I don't want to go on reliving what happened every time we cross paths. It's not me, nor is it like you, Chloe.' Her name skipped across his tongue and landed gently between them.

For a moment she said nothing, then finally a glimmer of a smile crossed her mouth. 'You're right. I hate carrying grudges, and this one is long dead anyway. As of now, we get along fine without becoming too friendly or talking about our previous lives in front of everyone.'

Exactly what he'd hoped for, yet the moment she said the words his gut dropped. He didn't belong in her life, nor she in his. That was going to be hard to live with. Because he couldn't write off all that they'd had together. Not now he'd come face to face with her again. Every look brought back some memory of wonderful times and why he'd fallen for her so hard in the first place.

He headed for the cafeteria. 'Coffee or tea?'

CHAPTER THREE

'Hi, Mum, how's your day been?'

Mine's been a shocker.

Chloe held her phone to her ear and watched her mutt, Genie, chase a seagull along the beach.

Make that disturbing.

Her reactions to Devlin were completely wrong. She was mad at him for coming to work in the same hospital as she did. Forget that he didn't have a clue she was there before he'd taken the job. And she was angry at the way he still affected her just looking at him. She'd thought that was long over.

'I played cards badly.' Her mother laughed. Her mum was still under don't-do-anything-strenuous orders from the surgeon.

'At least you weren't on the golf course.'

'As if Jack'd let me even look at my clubs. How was your first day back at work?'

Chloe looked out over the harbour from where she stood on the heavy, damp sand at its lapping edge. With the familiar city centre and wharves to her left and a plane taking off from the airport to her right, the first sense of calm all day crept over her. 'Nothing like I expected. You'll never guess who joined the department while I was away.'

'Not Prince Charming, if the sound of your voice is anything to go by.'

Far from it. 'Devlin Walsh.' No further explanation needed. Her mum knew how badly he'd hurt her with his accusations. She'd been upset and angry that he could even think such things about her daughter.

'Devlin's moved to Wellington?' Shock filtered through the ether. 'I didn't think he'd ever leave his family.'

'You and me both. They're a unit that no one or anything breaches.' The calm disappeared as her stomach squeezed. 'But, Mum, did you hear me? He's joined the ED so we're now working together.' She stared up and down the beach, glaring at every male figure within sight. The way her day had unfolded, there was every possibility that at any moment Devlin would come sauntering along to relax after work, rubbing in how much her life had suddenly changed from the easy, comfortable way she'd made it since moving to Wellington. Where was he living? Had he bought a house here? An apartment? It would be in one of the expensive suburbs. That was what he was used to and could afford without a blink. Since she was walking on the beach at Oriental Bay there was every likelihood he wasn't far away, this being one of the most prized areas to live in.

'This should prove interesting.' Laughter was not meant to be part of her mother's reply.

'Mum! You're supposed to be on my side. You know how much he hurt me.' Though today he'd been a gentleman most of the time.

'A lot can change in seven years, Chloe.' Her mother had become serious. Warning bells were sounding. 'Don't get too tied up in what went down back then.

You've matured and found your own strengths. Be friends at least.'

'What? After what he accused me of? I don't think so.' She shouldn't have told her mum Devlin was in town. Wasn't she supposed to support her daughter no matter what? Except she had an odd feeling she couldn't explain that it was going to be too easy to get along with Devlin, like it or not.

'I know where you're coming from, sweetheart. I still want to tear strips off him for what he did, but it's a long time ago and dragging up those feelings again will only undermine and hurt you.'

'True.' Damn it.

'What was it like working with him?'

'Fine. Just like any other emergency doctor, he was on the ball and knew how to prioritise patients. He didn't waste time when it came to getting the help they needed.' Which showed she could at least do her job without the past causing friction. He was the type of doctor she liked working alongside. It was the first time they'd been together in an ED and he was as good as his reputation in Auckland suggested. If today was anything to go by she couldn't fault him as a doctor. An image of that tall, lean body as he bent down to lift Wendy Wright's plinth filled her head. Hard to find any fault there either.

Genie dropped a stick at her feet and sat back on her haunches, staring up at her with a pleading look in her eyes.

Bending down, Chloe rubbed Genie's head and picked up the stick. As she hurled it out over the water she pulled a face. Such a normal winter's early evening, she and Genie getting their exercise and fresh air, and yet her head and heart weren't quite so relaxed as usual. 'I can't help the memories he's stirred up, Mum.'

Not only the love she'd had for him, but of their baby. Had he received her message about her miscarriage? Or had he tossed the note she'd left in his letterbox in the bin without even reading it? By that point she hadn't bothered texting him as he'd already blocked her number. She'd been about seven weeks, unaware of the pregnancy, probably because of the trauma of breaking up with Devlin, and being horrendously busy at work. She'd been nursing on a children's ward where they'd been dealing with an outbreak of influenza. Plus she'd still not given up her other job at the supermarket as she'd wanted to pay off as fast as possible the loan she'd taken out to go to nursing school. Initially Devlin had tried to insist on paying it off for her, but she'd refused. It would've taken something away from her when she'd been so proud of her accomplishments.

'Naturally the memories are still there, but, as you've never seen or heard from Devlin since that night, this could bring about final closure for you.'

Closure. She hated that word. Whenever people said it she could hear a door slamming shut. It was as though a whole part of her life would be neatly excised and she wouldn't be able to recall the twenty months she'd known Devlin, which included love and fun and excitement, and the complete certainty he believed in her, saw her strengths and weaknesses and didn't care. That had been so important after the way men had treated her all her life, as if she were an appendage to her mother, or there to fetch and carry, as Stephen had made her feel. Also, her finals and the excitement of becoming a registered nurse, the most amazing thing she'd ever accomplished, were a part of that time with Devlin. Nor did

she want to forget the embryo that had once been growing inside her, that had slipped away one cold, lonely
night with a rush of pain and despair that had woken
her in the middle of many nights since. 'Mum, I'll be
all right. We got through today, so it's only going to get
easier.' *I hope.* 'I'd better go. Genie is on a scent trail.'

Nose down, tail up, Genie was heading further along
the beach towards the Italian restaurant where people
were already sitting at tables in the window. Not a good
sign. Genie always expected treats there, and often got
them. But the big problem was the busy road between
the beach and the restaurant. At least she was still well
down the beach.

'Genie, stop, sit.'

Genie continued as if she hadn't heard.

Chloe jogged towards her dog, the lead swinging
from her hand. 'Genie, stop, girl.'

With a flick of her tail, Genie finally obeyed.

'Good girl.' Clicking the lead onto Genie's collar,
Chloe straightened up, and her breath stuck in her throat
as she came face to face with Devlin.

'Hello, Chloe. Your dog's cute. What breed is she?'
Devlin stood a couple of metres away, dressed in jeans
with a white tee shirt and navy wind jacket.

I just knew he'd be around here somewhere.

She coughed out the stalled air in her lungs. 'Genie's
a mongrel.' Not a pure breed of any kind.

A bit like me.

She didn't know who her father was, and, since he'd
walked away before she was even born, she didn't have
any longing to know him either. If she hadn't been good
enough for him to hang around to meet her, then to hell
with him. Not that she'd reached that decision early or
easily, but these days she didn't waste energy or emo-

tion on people who didn't care about her. 'I got her from the rescue centre.'

'Looks like she's got some lab in her.' He crouched down to hold out his hand for Genie to sniff. 'Hey, girl.'

Genie obliged with her nose, then sat back to allow Devlin to rub her between the shoulders.

Fickle girl.

Don't trust him. He'll hurt you.

'Most likely poodle and lab. She bounces around like one and loves to eat like the other.' And was the most affectionate creature in her life, Chloe admitted to herself. 'I got her a couple of years ago. She's the first pet I've ever had.' Why she'd waited so long to get a dog was beyond her. One of those things on her going-to-do list, along with a hundred other things she'd been slowly ticking off since she'd made it to Italy and found an inner strength she hadn't known she possessed.

Devlin stood up, watching her closely. 'I meant to get your phone number before we knocked off, but I got caught up and you were gone. Someone mentioned you usually walked your dog here and, since I live close by, I figured I'd try and catch up with you.'

That someone Jaz by any chance? 'I thought we dealt with the problem between us already.' Not that they'd actually aired their grievances.

He shrugged. 'I wasn't sure about how you felt, that's all.'

'Annoyed, if I'm honest. But there's no point raking over the past. It happened, and can't be undone. You're here, and we'll get along well enough for work.' Disappointment dragged at her. She wanted more? She flinched internally. Get out of here. Not likely. Why couldn't he have grown a pot belly and lost some of that thick dark hair?

'You seem settled. Happy.'

Where did that come from? Happy was not on her radar at this moment. She'd have to lie a little. 'I am both. It took a while but here I am, doing great.'

'Do you live around here?'

'Close. I bought a tiny two-bedroom cottage behind the theatre in Te Aro, which needs lots of maintenance I'm slowly making my way through.' Not far from here. It'd cost an arm and a leg, and she'd be paying off the mortgage till she was old and doddery, but it was hers, thanks to her stepdad backing her loan application. 'A couple of minutes' walk to Cuba Street and ten to the CBD. I mostly walk to work, too. Perfect really.'

His laugh was short and sharp. 'I'm in an apartment over the road. Near enough to Cuba Street, the CBD and the hospital, too.'

So she'd got the location right.

Their eyes met, locked. Who'd have thought it? It was funny that they'd both ended up in the same city, *and* the same hospital. Funny? Try again. More like strange. Though maybe not. New Zealand wasn't huge, and there weren't many big cities, which were the only places either of them would choose to live and work.

She looked away. Devlin's eyes were too intense to be dealing with. Once she'd loved that he could look at her like that. Not any more. He brought back memories of great times. He also made her shiver with something like longing, or was it regret? Of course, she regretted their break up, but that was long over, and there was nothing to rue now. Not even the fact that she couldn't get back with Devlin? Definitely not. If he'd been able to so easily believe she'd gone behind his back for sex then, no; she would never be ready to try again with him. 'Dev—' Damn it. 'Devlin, I'd better get going. I need to stop at the supermarket to get Genie something for dinner.'

Understanding filled his eyes. 'It isn't easy, is it?'

'You're right, it's not. But I'm not going over old territory. You wouldn't listen to me before. Why would you now?' Her pulse was deafening.

Devlin nodded. 'I don't want a rerun on the old argument, but we need to bury the hatchet so the past doesn't interfere in our daily lives. I don't think we quite got that far earlier.'

She stared at him for a long moment, and felt some of the tension back off. 'You're right on all counts. Today's brought everything back but I can deal with it. We'll get along just fine.' Because they had to. And because, 'It might be good for us.' Not sure how though.

'I'll walk to the end of the beach with you.'

Not quite what she wanted, but it was only a short distance, and maybe a step in the right direction as far as their new relationship went. 'All right. Come on, Genie.' She strode away, aware with each step she took that Devlin was right beside her. Her head spun. They might have to work together, but out here, away from their professional environment, she expected him to be heading in the opposite direction. Seemed Devlin was more comfortable around her than she was with him. Or more determined to knock out the elephant between them.

Minutes later they reached the roadside, and Chloe held her breath, waiting for Devlin's next move.

'See you tomorrow,' he said.

She nodded. 'Let's hope nothing too drastic occurs first thing. If at all.'

When she reached the other side of the busy road,

she couldn't help glancing over her shoulder, and breathed deep.

Devlin stood with his hands on his hips, watching her. Devlin Walsh was back in her life. Not in the same way, but still a bubble burst inside her and tears welled up to spill down her cheeks.

I loved you so much, Devlin, how could you believe I'd hurt you like that?

Unbelievable. She was over him, yet still hurt by the fact he'd never accepted her truth over what he'd thought had happened. Flicking her head forward, she strode out in the direction of the supermarket, her hand gripping Genie's lead like a lifeline. Genie was her reliable pal, happy as long as there was food in the bowl and a warm, dry bed to sprawl out on. How easy was that? Too easy?

Chloe owned a two-bed cottage a kilometre or two from his apartment. Did that mean she was single? Hadn't settled down with another man? Or she had and the relationship had gone belly up? She'd said she'd bought a house, not 'they' had. Devlin watched those long legs eating up the distance to the corner and remembered how she used to wind them around his waist when they made love. But it hadn't been love, had it? It had been sex, plain and simple, for Chloe. Love for him though.

Strange how today he'd had the strangest feeling something didn't ring true about their break up. By all appearances, she'd had another man on the side, just as his previous partner had. They'd both denied it, even when he'd caught them out. But there was a difference. Chloe hadn't been naked, nor in bed with the guy. She'd been quick to deny his allegations but he'd been so shocked, so hurt, that he hadn't wanted to fall for those lies again. He hadn't been able to put his finger on what, only that despite everything that had happened he was still attracted to her, could feel those too-familiar sparks of desire whenever he'd glanced at her today.

It wasn't as though there hadn't been other women since Chloe. He was a man with a healthy sexual appetite. But there hadn't been another woman he'd given his heart to. Not only because he didn't trust so readily any more—two women cheating on him was more than enough—but also because Chloe had touched him in a way he'd never entirely forgotten. She'd come into his life when they were both busy studying, and didn't have lots of free time to spend together, and they'd made the most of every opportunity to be together, and then made some more because they couldn't stay away from each other. Then he'd proposed. Chloe had burst into tears of happiness and cried yes so loud he'd have been surprised if half of Auckland hadn't heard. Her reaction had filled him with more love than he'd believed possible. It was for ever; he'd found his other half. He'd been hurt once before but with Chloe it had been like coming home, having found that special place where he'd always be safe. It just showed how badly he read women. Cath had hurt him. Chloe had sliced him in half.

Devlin took one last look at her, swallowing the longing that rose in his throat before turning around to walk the other way. How could he possibly want Chloe? Why? What was there about her that possessed him so wholly that his body ached for her, his head grew light when watching her work with a patient, his heart squeezed when she rubbed her dog's head? One day working with her, and he was in an unbelievable mess. He, who could handle death before his eyes at work without losing his sanity, could not catch up with his ex-fiancée without feeling as though the floor had disappeared beneath his feet. So much for thinking moving to Wellington would be straightforward. If only he'd known she lived here. Then what? He would still have moved here because he'd believed he was over her.

But was he? Or was his love buried so deep he couldn't feel or taste it? Had she, by repeating what Cath had done, made him feel worthless when it came to giving his heart away? Did women really only want him for his status and wealth? It had seemed as though that had been the last thing Chloe had her eye on when they got together. She'd appeared genuinely uninterested in his family's position in society, only in him. Though not enough if she could play around behind his back. If? Of course she had. He still saw that man strutting around her flat semi-naked, a smirk on his face that had Dev wanting to punch him. What if he'd been wrong though? Chloe had been quick to say he was. So had Cath in his previous relationship and she'd only proven he should accept the truth when it was right before his eyes. She'd lied. Likewise Chloe. Hadn't she? Of course she had.

Hadn't she?

His strides lengthened as frustration welled up. He'd have to take things one day at a time. Tomorrow he'd work alongside Chloe again and it would get easier. By the end of the week he'd probably be wondering what the hiccup had been about.

Except the moment Devlin walked into the ED at six-fifty the next morning his heart did a dance. Chloe was already reading patient notes on the computer while sipping tea, a furrow between her eyes, an intense expression tightening her face.

'What's up?' he asked, pulling out a seat beside her.

'Morning, Dev. I mean, Devlin,' she added hurriedly, a pretty shade of pink colouring her cheeks.

He leaned back on the chair. 'What've we got?' He'd thought he'd been early but Chloe had beaten him here.

'Forty-three-year-old man, broken ribs and punctured lung, waiting for surgery. They've got him on a regime of morphine and tramadol.' She flicked the screen, moved down through the files. 'Twenty-five-year-old woman, thirty-one weeks pregnant, eclampsia. She's going to the neonatal unit shortly.'

As Chloe continued to outline their cases, Devlin absorbed her calm attitude. She was good; no doubt about it. She talked about the patients clearly and with an understanding of the data. She didn't get wound up about the severity of the cases they saw in zone three, just told him like it was. But if he still knew anything about Chloe, she'd be hurting for her patients behind that steady face. It was in her DNA. There'd been times when he'd held her while she'd downloaded her sorrow for someone she'd been nursing. He couldn't see why that would've changed. Chloe had known hardship growing up and with that came an empathy for others not doing so well. Yet she'd hurt him.

But had she? What if he'd reacted too quickly? Hadn't listened to her pleas all because of what Cath had done? Not once did he stop and think he might be wrong. Instead he'd turned his back—and his heart— on her. Now he realised there'd never been a glimmer of guilt in her eyes any time she'd looked at him back then, or yesterday.

The pen he'd been holding dropped to the floor.

What? Of course she'd betrayed him. He'd been told she was having a fling with another trainee nurse on the ward where she was working. A guy with a reputation of enjoying all the fresh-faced nurses. His mother had been adamant Chloe had been seen with him, and she'd been backed up by one of Dev's female colleagues.

One who his mother had later tried to get him to date.

He hadn't thought of that before, had he? But he had also seen Chloe and the man together having coffee at a café along the road from the hospital. Chloe had been laughing and talking as though she didn't have a care in the world. It had been so obvious what had happened when he'd found the guy in her flat, strutting around in nothing but a towel after a shower.

What if he'd been wrong jumping to that conclusion? Maybe Chloe hadn't done anything wrong. It might've been true the man's hot water system had failed.

But his mother wouldn't lie to him. She might not have thought Chloe would be the ideal daughter-in-law, but she'd never deliberately set out to hurt him by lying about something so important, not when she knew he'd already been cheated on with the first love of his life.

'Devlin, the ambulance is here,' Chloe called out.

How the hell was he supposed to focus on a patient with these crazy thoughts tripping around his head? Suck it up and get on with what was important right now. That was how. 'Coming.'

The paramedics were rolling the bed into Resus where Chloe waited, ready to help shift their patient across to the hospital bed before replacing the ambulance monitor with the department's one.

Devlin strode up, his professional face firmly in place, and one of the paramedics handed him the notes he'd made of readings and the description of the woman's pain, which suggested heart problems. Must be something in Wellington's water bringing on heart attacks first thing in the morning. He gave a tight smile. 'Tell me what's going on.'

'Pain in the chest woke me up.' The woman, Iris, by the notes, answered tearfully. 'Like really bad pain in my left side and arm. I thought I was going to die.'

Nurse Chloe touched the back of Iris's hand. 'You're here now, and we've got everything covered. That's what matters at this point.' Nurse and caring woman all in one, he thought with a wince.

Devlin focused on the monitor, noting the arrhythmia that suggested ventricular fibrillation. Iris could've had a heart attack this morning, one that hadn't been strong enough to stop her heart but could still do a lot of damage all the same.

Jaz stepped into Resus, said quietly, 'Devlin, got a minute? We've got a patient bleeding heavily via the throat.'

'I'll be right there.' He scanned the monitors, read the notes, knew there was nothing he could actively do for the woman as long as nothing changed in her readouts. She needed a cardiologist to pay her a visit. 'Iris, I'm calling the cardiology department to get a specialist to see you. In the meantime, just do as Chloe tells you and you'll be fine.' Following Jaz, he asked, 'Is the patient coughing?'

'Some deep bellied air gasps rather than coughing.' Jaz slipped around a curtain at cubicle three. 'Judy, Hugo, this is Devlin, one of our doctors.'

Devlin acknowledged the man, presumably the husband, then dipped his head to Judy, the woman clinging to Hugo's hand. 'When did the bleeding start, Judy?'

The woman croaked, 'About three hours ago.'

Jaz wiped her mouth and chin.

Devlin continued. 'To save you talking and causing more bleeding I'll ask Hugo the details. Is that all right?'

'Yes,' Judy whispered.

At least that was what he thought she said, as she'd barely opened her mouth. 'Is Judy suffering any pain?'

'Yes, she told the paramedic it was six out of ten, but knowing Judy it's probably more than that. She's a tough old girl.'

Judy blinked rapidly.

Hugo smiled endearingly. 'Okay, not old.' He tapped his chest on the right side. 'She indicated it hurt most here. Her throat was sore last night, and still is, I think.'

Judy nodded.

'Has she suffered sore throats a lot recently? Had the flu or a cold in the last month?'

'No.'

Jaz looked at Devlin, and inclined her head towards the monitor, which just then beeped at a level that was a warning. The blood pressure was thirty-five, too low. 'Any history of low blood pressure?'

'No, the opposite. She's on tablets to lower it. I don't know what it used to be.'

'Fair enough.' A lot of people didn't really understand BP readings clearly. 'I'll look up her medical history online. I can access her medical-centre data.' Thank goodness for easy access these days. It saved lots of time on phones waiting for people to verify who he was and then going into details. 'Judy, I'm going to look at your chest and tap the area where Hugo said the pain was.'

Jaz helped lift the woman's shirt and covered her abdomen with a cotton blanket for decency.

She was good, as good as Chloe. But she *wasn't* Chloe. Already he preferred working with Chloe, even when only minutes ago he'd been in a hurry to put space between them. As it had been years ago, when he'd enjoyed being with her all the time. A tingling warmth and a lightness in his heart had always been present. Weird how it had returned now whenever they were in the same room.

No, he was over her.

Judy gasped when he pressed below her ribcage on the right. And again when he pressed further towards her abdomen. There was no reaction when he did the same on the left. 'Judy, I'd like you to roll onto your left side.'

Jaz helped the woman. 'That's it. Lie still.'

More pain was apparent when Devlin tested her back. 'Right, you can lie on your back again.' Popping the stethoscope buds into his ears, he said, 'Breathe deep, hold it. Let it out slowly.' He repeated the move three times over different regions of Judy's lungs, before tossing his gloves into the bin. 'I'm going to arrange an X-ray of your chest, specifically your lungs. I think there's fluid on your lungs.'

'That's where the blood's coming from?' Judy asked with dread in her eyes.

'Possibly, or your throat is raw and bleeding. But more likely it's the lungs. I'll also arrange some blood tests. I want to see if you've got an infection going on in there.'

Hugo reached for his wife's hand and held tight. 'We'll be all right, Jude.'

Heading to the hub, Devlin glanced over to Iris's cubicle, saw Chloe giving her a dose of medication, no doubt the painkiller he'd ordered. Calm, steady Chloe.

Hell, I've missed her.

Shock rippled through him. That was nonsense. He

hadn't even thought about her very often, deliberately burying her for ever. That had created a void within himself he hadn't understood, had put down to losing two women to other men, and feeling he wasn't quite good enough to keep a woman at his side for ever. He hadn't believed that void was about not having Chloe sharing his life, laughing, crying, loving with him. Now she was nearby, within sight and touching distance, he was remembering a lot of things about her he'd always loved. Her soft smile that unravelled the knots forming in his belly after a particularly difficult day at work. The way her right eyebrow rose slightly higher than the left when she was puzzled by something. The irritation that darkened the caramel shade of her eyes to mahogany whenever she felt she'd inadvertently let him or his family down. The soft shade of pink polish she wore on her nails—except now she wore bright orange. But there was a strong tilt to her chin, a straightness of her spine that hadn't been there before. The void was filling in a little.

'Have you phoned upstairs?' she was asking now, reminding him what he was supposed to be doing, which didn't include daydreaming about something that had run its course.

'About to. Any changes I need to know about?'

'Everything's steady.' Her focus was firmly on their patient.

Devlin felt as though he was being given the cold shoulder, but knew he was imagining it. There was no reason for her to act that way. Anyway, she wouldn't do that around here when there were colleagues and patients in all directions. She had no reason apart from their break up and him accusing her of cheating on him. Even frost dissipated after a time. Now he was being sarcastic, not his usual stance. Anyway, it was himself he was uncomfortable with today, not Chloe. That new niggling question about whether he'd been right to believe what he'd heard and supposedly thought he'd seen. 'I'll be back shortly.' He refrained from saying she was doing a good job. It would sound condescending when really he was looking for something to say that was genuine and friendly.

The tension tightened more and more over the day so that Devlin started clock-watching for the end of his shift to come round so he could get away from the stifling air that went wherever Chloe went. Air he had to share and breathe every minute.

'Chloe, you're needed in Reception.' Kirsty, the receptionist, rushed into the centre of the department. 'There's an elderly man and his wife and they can't speak English well enough to get the info we need. They're Italian.'

Was Chloe fluent enough to interpret for the couple? Wow.

'Coming. Jaz, can you keep an eye on our patients for a mo?' Chloe was heading away without waiting for an answer, obviously used to this.

'Need me out there?' Devlin followed the women.

'You speak Italian, too?' Kirsty asked.

'Not a word.'

'Then no, we've got it.'

'Fine.' He stopped outside the last cubicle before Reception. Obviously he hadn't put two and two together. Naturally Chloe would have learned at least enough Italian to get through the day-to-day tasks with the family she'd lived with.

He heard Chloe say, *'Quando e iniziato il dolore?'* then pause and say, 'Two hours.' Then, *'Su una scalada*

uno a due, dieci al massimo, quanto e forte il dolore?'
She listened, then, 'Eight.'

He was gobsmacked. Chloe wasn't hesitant over her choice of words, talking and pausing to listen to replies, giving Kirsty the answers without breaking for air. Just like an Italian. Okay, maybe not quite as rapidly, but pretty darned close. Who was this Chloe? Certainly not one he'd known, or loved, or been going to marry. The surprises just kept on coming. Impressive.

'Grazie.' Chloe was heading his way, a cheeky smile lightening her face. 'Surprised you, huh?' Her shoulder bumped his upper arm.

'You certainly have.' He nudged back. 'Go, you.'

She sucked a quick breath, muttered, 'Right. Where was I?' and disappeared around a cubicle curtain.

He headed back into the hub, shaking his head and grinning to himself. This woman was interesting. No wonder he couldn't put her aside. She was becoming a challenge. *A what?* He didn't need any challenges, and certainly not from Chloe. She was already pushing his buttons in far too many ways, and yes, he had to admit he was intrigued. He could remember how it felt being in love with her, to spend time with her in mutually enjoyable activities. He'd given her his heart within a matter of days, and she'd reciprocated. As if they were meant to be together for ever. It had felt wonderful being loved beyond anything he'd known before, to feel wanted for himself. They'd become inseparable very quickly, yet it had all turned to dust even faster.

Now he wondered who she really was, and he felt those old, familiar pricks of desire and longing all over again. With so many questions turning over in his mind, he had to find time to spend with her to ask them, to discover if he'd been wrong seven years ago. Looking around, he realised how quiet the department had become. Nothing urgent required his attention in zone three. 'Up for a coffee?' he asked Chloe. Seemed they were forever meeting over patients or going for coffee. 'I know it's not long till knock-off but we deserve one.'

Her eyebrows rose as she looked around. 'Might as well while we can. Who knows what's about to arrive?'

The speed at which they left the hub made Devlin feel like a naughty boy playing hooky, half expecting to be called back for a patient. It was fun.

With steaming mugs in hand, they sat at a table in the corner of the cafeteria and sighed simultaneously.

'What a morning,' Chloe groaned. 'Non-stop patients.'

'Then you were prattling away in another language. How cool is that? How would those people have coped without you there?'

She stared at him for a moment, then all of a sudden she beamed. 'I'm not the only person working in the hospital who speaks Italian. There's a strong Italian community in the region. But I do get a buzz whenever I get to help out.'

'I bet you do.' She looked pleased with herself. 'Guess that trip to Europe has a lot to answer for. You're more confident now, too.'

'When you're in the middle of Rome and no one understands you, and you need to find a loo in a hurry, then you learn fast.' She laughed.

Dev sipped his coffee and relaxed in the chair. What more could he want?

CHAPTER FOUR

'DO WE REALLY have to go for a walk?' Chloe stared down at Genie, sitting expectantly in front of her, the lead hanging from her teeth. There were days Chloe was so exhausted after work that the last thing she wanted was to go for a walk, but it usually turned out for the best. If Genie didn't bring the lead to her on those days and get her outside into the fresh air, then she'd mooch around getting bored and fed up with herself. Patting Genie's head, she laughed. 'Okay, you win. Again.'

Genie did a circle on the spot, understanding full well she'd won, as she always did.

'You're good for me, aren't you?' Another pat.

Another circle, Genie's tail waving all over the place.

'Watch out.' Chloe caught the water bottle that had been on the coffee table before it landed on the carpet. 'We'll go up the hill today.' If Devlin decided to go to the beach, she didn't want to bump into him.

She needed a break from those intense blue eyes that seemed to watch her every move. She wasn't sure if he was sizing her up as a nurse or his ex, or as someone he wanted to work side by side with and not worry about the past coming back to bite him on the backside. Much how she felt. Time to drop the past and move on? Again?

This time jointly, without the hurt tainting everything? Why not? Nothing to be gained holding onto the pain.

After changing into black jeans and a warm top, she let her hair down from the messy bun she wore for work and brushed out the knots, trying to shove away the unusual tiredness that sat over her. It had been a busy, but normal day in the department, if she could call working alongside the man she'd once given her heart to normal. Well, it was becoming her new normal. Of course, she wouldn't always be rostered on the same shift as him, but the doctors tended to stay on after theirs was finished, not rushing to leave particularly ill patients until the next doctors on duty were ready to take over. Spending eight hours in the same department, with the same medical staff and patients, meant they were part of a team. Something she'd once had with Devlin in her private life. Three days together, and already she wanted to get beyond the past so they were connected, if only as medical colleagues and in their thinking and approach to patients. Something they already seemed to be doing.

They'd once matched perfectly in a lot of other ways. Relaxing on the deck with a glass of wine at the end of a hard day at their respective jobs, unwinding by talking over the things that had distressed them. Similar quirky things that made them laugh until their sides ached. Sleeping in late when they had a day off, waking with their legs entwined and Dev's hand splayed across her stomach. Knowing how to touch each other while making love, bringing each other to a climax and kissing until the world spun.

But he hadn't truly understood her, hadn't been on the same page as her when she'd denied having sex with another man. It was still hard to forgive as it said he hadn't known her as well as she'd believed. To be so ready to believe the worst, not wanting to stop and listen to her, not once, suggested she'd never had a chance to prove that it was beyond her to do what Cath had inflicted on him. Almost as if he'd wanted to believe the worst. From that moment on they'd had nothing in common. Except broken hearts. They'd been deeply hurt. *Both* of them. And still, despite that, she liked what she'd seen of Devlin so far this week. Her heart did anyway, getting in a pickle at times, totally out of sync with her head, which kept reminding her she hadn't done anything wrong and, therefore, he didn't deserve her as any more than a professional colleague. But, said her heart way too often, he was still incredibly gorgeous and kind and sexy. Down, heart, down.

Genie gave her a not too gentle head-butt on her knee. *Come on, Mum.*

'Sorry, girl. Got a lot on my mind.' Shoving her wallet, keys and phone in her bum bag, she closed the door behind them and headed down the path, sunglasses and cap in place. The sun was heading towards the horizon but she never went without her glasses. 'We'll have early dinner with the boys after this.'

Wednesday nights she went to the Italian restaurant across from the beach for a meal and a catch up with brothers, Giuseppe and Lorenzo. They'd treated her like a sister ever since the day she'd been passing the restaurant and heard a man yelling for help. Inside Lorenzo had been holding a severely burned arm under the cold tap and Giuseppe had been running round in circles unsure what to do. Talking calmly in Italian, getting Giuseppe to close the restaurant and get his car ready, she'd examined the damage. Large blisters had formed over the back of Lorenzo's hand and up his arm, but it was the raw redness between his fingers that had given her concern, so she'd taken over and driven the men to the ED where Lorenzo had got the necessary care and hadn't lost too many days behind his ovens in the restaurant.

Out of the gate, Genie pulled in the direction of the beach.

'No, girl, we're going this way.' Chloe tugged gently and began striding out along the path towards the track that led to the hill, feeling a wee bit mean.

Going this way wasn't as much fun for Genie as she had to remain on the lead instead of being able to run around free on the beach, chasing gulls and leaping into the water. Instead they'd go further than planned, and get a little bit tired, before going to the waterfront for dinner. The guys always had a bowl of treats for Genie, which she lapped up with a wagging tail to show her appreciation.

'I wonder what tonight's special is on the menu.' Not that it mattered. She ate anything Lorenzo cooked.

A woman going in the opposite direction gave her a funny look, and shook her head.

Chloe didn't slow down. It didn't count as talking to herself if Genie was there, right?

All the way up the hill, and down another way through the large homes to reach Oriental Parade, Devlin was firmly on her mind. He just would not go away. Her hands tightened and loosened. How could he do this to her after so long? Hey, was she having the same effect on him? Now there was a thought. That'd make them two sad puppies, for certain. Very sad.

Her phone rang.

Devlin.

'Hi. What are you up to?' Did she sound too friendly?

'I'm heading to the beach to stretch my legs.'

Those long, muscular legs. Right. Her mouth dried.

'I was wondering if you were there already and if I could join you for a bit?'

Don't bring your legs. They'll distract me from any sane thought I might have.

'We've been up the hill, but Genie's not done yet so more exercise on the beach wouldn't go astray.'

'Great. See you in a bit.'

Great? Yes, it actually was. He was hanging out in her head all the time anyway, so why not spend time with the real deal, possibly iron out some of the kinks in their new relationship?

When she reached the water's edge, Chloe picked up a stick to hurl out over the water and promptly got soaked as Genie leapt after it. 'Thanks, my girl. Remind me not to do you any favours for a while.'

'Bet she does that to you all the time.' Devlin bloody Walsh. Why couldn't he have called out hello from further away instead of being so close?

She spun around so fast she lost her balance and would've landed on her butt if Devlin hadn't caught her arm.

'Steady. I didn't mean to scare you.'

'You didn't.' Much. More like morphed from an image in her head to a full-on, tall, sexy, *real* man still holding her arm. Pulling sharply, she freed her arm and took a step back. 'You couldn't.'

A small, lopsided smile appeared. 'I know. You never scared easily.'

She laughed, surprising herself. 'Unless there's lightning about.' Once, as a kid, she'd seen lightning strike a tree that sheep had been sheltering under. The ensuing mess had stayed with her ever since.

'I can see you've toughened up even more.' He wasn't smiling any more.

'I sure have.' This conversation was all too serious, too soon.

Genie dropped the stick on her foot.

Saved by her fur baby. Rubbing Genie's head, she threw the stick again, and got splashed once more. 'I'm a slow learner.'

Dev laughed.

And her gut went all gooey. Over a laugh? A sexy, friendly, nothing-bad-meant laugh.

He said, 'That's not how I would've described you.'

She wasn't falling for that one. She did not need to know how he'd describe her. His last, loud, harsh opinion of her was all too easy to recall despite all the time in between.

Devlin reached for the stick hanging out of Genie's jaw. 'Give me that and let's see how far I can throw it.'

As they strolled along the beach, chatting about next to nothing, Chloe snuggled into herself, letting the warmth of her jersey and this easy camaraderie take over. Just how it used to be.

'What are you doing after your walk?' Devlin asked as they retraced their steps once Genie was worn out.

She turned to look at him. 'Why?'

His chest rose on an inhale as he looked at her. 'Want to have dinner with me at that Italian restaurant over the road?'

Devlin waited, a breath stalled in the back of his throat. Where had that come from? He'd only intended a bit of time together on the beach, working slowly at chiselling away the past, finding the good things that had been part of their relationship, and then only enough to put their history away where it belonged.

'I don't know, Dev.'

Dev. Did she realise that over the last three days she'd sometimes reverted to her pet name for him? A name he'd loved, because it made him feel special, hers, and no one else's. His mother had loathed it, saying they'd named him Devlin. 'Why?' Relief should be pouring through him at her hesitancy, not this disappointment. 'I thought it might be a good way to clear the air a bit more.' Did he? At the rate he was going, he should become a storyteller.

One well-shaped eyebrow rose slowly.

He'd forgotten that move, and how it made him laugh. Except he wasn't laughing now. He wanted to sit down over a meal with Chloe and talk to her about life in general, not only work. What she had been doing throughout the years since they'd split, other than going overseas. He wanted to know more about that, too. What had changed her mind about travelling to the other side of the world where everything would be new to her? For a year at that. So much to learn and he couldn't wait to start finding out. 'What do you say?'

A red hue touched her cheeks. 'I'm already eating there tonight.'

'Oh.' His chest tightened. There was someone else in her life. Should've known. Because she was gorgeous and wouldn't be without someone special at her side. 'Fair enough.'

She slipped her sunglasses off and glared. As if he was frustrating her. 'Oh, damn it, Devlin. Okay, we'll share a table.'

He was none the wiser. Did that mean she would be alone? Or that others would be there? One other? 'I don't want to intrude.' But he did want to spend time with Chloe, make it possible to work together without the tightening in his gut, his groin, and even his heart that occurred on and off throughout their shifts.

The dog had returned with the stick and was shaking saltwater everywhere.

'Stop that, Genie,' Chloe growled through a smile, before rubbing her pet's head. 'The brothers who own the restaurant are friends and I eat there regularly. So does Genie—though she gets to sit outside the back door on her own special mat.' She drew a breath and locked formidable eyes on him. 'Yes, let's have dinner together, and, as you said, continue clearing the air. Though I don't think we've done too badly so far.' That eyebrow lifted again, then fell back into place.

'I guess being on the job, and being professional, has its place.' He tried for a smile of his own and surprised himself at how easily it came. 'When were you going to the restaurant?'

Another blush coloured her tanned cheeks red. 'When we're done here. I took Genie up the hill so she's had her walk. I was just letting her have a bit more fun.'

He didn't quite believe her but couldn't work out what was missing in that explanation. Leaving it alone, Devlin held out his hand for the stick. 'I'll throw that for her.'

Watching Genie race into the water without a care brought back a longing for a dog of his own. It was something he'd put off because he was never home enough, and now he was living in an apartment it would be totally unfair. No back yard to run around in, having to be stuck inside all day except for walks, was not how a dog should live. Especially a large dog, which was what he'd like.

'She's so good for me,' Chloe said. 'On days like today when I'm exhausted and all I want to do is sit down with a coffee and unwind she makes me go for a walk, which is what I need all along.'

'Bet you talk to her, too.'

'All the time. We have the most interesting conversations and I'm never wrong.'

'You don't say?' Picking up the stick Genie had dropped in front of him, he hurled it along the beach. 'Let's get some of that water off you, Genie.'

Chloe shoved her hands in her pockets and watched Genie dash along the beach, sending sprays of sand left and right. 'What made you decide to move to Wellington?'

Crunch went his gut. 'It was time for a change.' There was no straightforward answer. Not when it was Chloe asking. She knew how his and Patrick's parents made so many demands on their time and life choices. He wasn't ready to bring up any of that yet. *But* he had instigated this. *And* there was the possibility talking about it, however briefly, might make him even happier he'd taken back control of his life.

Her head tilted to the side, and her lips twisted. 'Interesting.'

She knew his family and how everyone had their role, which included living in Auckland, especially in the correct suburb, being available for certain dinners or cocktail parties. 'Not as interesting as you might think. I was restless, and getting more so by the day. Moving overseas seemed the perfect solution but it didn't enthuse me. Not sure why, but when a mate from training days phoned to say there was a position down here I got quite excited, which told me I should look closer.' The truth, just not all of it.

'So here you are.'

'Yep.'

'Glad you moved?'

'So far.' Had she just let him get away with such a brief explanation? 'Yes.' Of all the hospitals in the country, or the world come to that, here he was, working in the same department as Chloe. Chloe, who'd agreed to join him for dinner. No denying the flicker of excitement in his gut. He felt something for Chloe, which might be wrong, but was true all the same. Was it wrong to feel like this after all this time? Did relationships get second chances? And the big question—were they worth the risk? But, hey, he'd had his heart broken twice and wasn't exactly on top of the world when it came to the love stakes so it might be an idea to have another crack at finding true love.

Looking at her, seeing that face that used to follow him into sleep every night with a twinkle in her eyes, knowing how she liked to walk for kilometres at a time and to hang her washing using matching-coloured pegs for each item, how too much coffee made her hyper and her shoes were always lined up perfectly in the wardrobe, was touching him in ways he'd never have thought possible. This woman had been his fiancée, the love of his life, and he'd not come close to a similar feeling with another woman since their horrible break up. He'd believed he'd got over her. Now it felt as if she'd been waiting deep within him, ready to leap out and take his hand to lead him somewhere he dared not even name.

'It's kind of different being in a far smaller city than Auckland. Everything seems to be central—everything I require or like anyway,' he said a little gruffly.

'Apart from getting away from people, that is, but even then it's not a long ride to find a less populated beach or hills to hike in. Even better, you can catch the ferry to go across to Picton and suss out the Marlborough Sounds or the vineyards. For me, Mum's close yet not so close.'

'She still likes to keep an eye on you?' Devlin laughed. Joy never hovered but she always had tabs on what Chloe was up to. When he commented one day, Chloe said her mum had been like that from the day she was born and she'd had to go it alone as a parent. If only his parents had been the same with him and his brother, and not quite so demanding of them to partake in lives neither of them wanted. Sure, he understood there were obligations to being wealthy, but to have his parents think they could decide on the right woman or career position for their sons made everything awkward and often downright exasperating. And the way his mother had treated Chloe back then had made his blood boil, but he'd been wasting his breath whenever he'd tried to talk to her about it.

'Not as much as she used to. Not that I'd change anything. She's always been a great mum, even if I used to fight with her a lot as a teen. Which was normal, I guess. Jack still supports me like I'm his daughter.' There was a lot of love in her voice, making his gut squeeze.

Chloe had always worn her heart on her sleeve. He'd forgotten that. Now a picture of the distress and pain in her face when he'd accused her of cheating on him appeared in his mind. She'd been devastated. He'd supposed that was because she'd been caught out. Not once did he consider she was hurting because *he'd* broken *her* heart. It had been all about the pain he'd been suffering. *Another* woman had done the dirty on him. He'd offered Chloe his heart and future, and she'd shown little respect or care for either. Or so he'd thought. Had he been wrong? Had he? No. Another picture of a muscular man wearing nothing but a towel wrapped around his waist and a knowing smirk on his mouth, standing in Chloe's lounge, came to mind.

Stop this. Or say sorry, you can't make dinner after all.

Because if these thoughts and images continued popping up then they were going to have an awful time at the restaurant.

He couldn't do it. He wanted to spend time with her.

Devlin looked along the beach, searching for Genie. Anything to distract him, help him get back on track. The dog was sitting quietly, letting a small girl pat her. 'Genie's quite placid, isn't she?'

'Unless there's a bone, or ball, or a warm bed on a cold day involved, then yes, mostly.'

They walked along in a companionable silence, Devlin keeping his mind under control. And his hormones. Sort of, anyway. They seemed to react around Chloe all too often. More memories? No. He wasn't going there. 'Why did you choose Italy instead of France or Britain or Spain?'

A soft smile lit up her face. 'Jack convinced me to get away for a while, and when I remained hesitant he bulldozed me by setting it all up with a family he'd met when he did his OE as a twenty-year-old. I'm so glad. It was truly the best experience I've had.'

'As you know, like others I trained with, I considered going overseas for my junior doctor years, but it didn't happen. Too many other things going on, I guess. Or I wasn't as keen as I'd thought.'

Chloe glanced at him from under her fringe. 'We

were together then and planning a wedding.' There was no apology or sorrow in her voice.

Nor did he feel any. He'd finally come to accept it was what it was. These days it was the future that was disconcerting. 'It's not as if I didn't travel enough growing up.' He gave a bitter laugh. 'Mostly to resorts and cities with stunning sights to see that were on every traveller's to-visit list. Not quite the same as hunkering down in a hospital working all hours. Or doing what you did. That's truly amazing.'

'It was. You did what was right for you. That's what counts.' She stopped and called out. 'Genie, come.'

Genie trotted towards them, sniffing the air and wagging her tail.

'She's had enough.' Chloe clipped the lead onto her collar. 'Time for dinner, eh, girl?'

Genie nudged Chloe's thigh.

I did what was right for me.

Yes, Chloe was right, he had. Though now he was starting to think he might've been a bit short-sighted about missing the opportunity. At the time, because he was hurting so badly, he hadn't wanted to go to another country. To him, that would have felt like running away, and that was the last thing he'd ever do. 'A lot of junior doctors head offshore for extra experiences and they say it looks good on their CVs, but I can't say I've been held back for not going away.'

'Surely it comes down to how well you do your work? What you're like as a doctor.'

'I guess.' Not once had he missed out on a position he'd applied for, so he must've got something right, and presumably that was because he did know what he was doing and hopefully was better than good. 'I'm still as passionate about what I do as I was the day I qualified.'

Talk about spilling his guts, but then this was Chloe, who he'd always told his true feelings to about anything from work to what he'd had for dinner. She'd listened to him, never brushed him aside. Unlike his parents. Stepping up as the next Walsh generation representative in the family business, and every other organisation they had anything to do with, was their choice, not his or Patrick's. They'd both been happy to contribute but wanted to get on with their careers and other things. Their lives, basically. 'You're much the same. You were going to become a top-notch nurse no matter what hurdles came your way, and you did it.'

Beginning to walk back the way they'd come, she peered up at him with a wonky smile lighting up her face. 'Even when bed pans made me nauseous and sticking needles into someone had my stomach in a knot.'

Laughter bubbled up through him. 'Find me a medical person who hasn't had their gremlins to deal with along the way. At least mine wasn't the sight of blood.'

'That only happens in the movies.' She laughed. 'But you didn't like straightening broken bones.'

He shuddered. 'Still don't, if I'm being honest, but I've learnt to deal with it while not doing any further damage or adding to the pain of my patient.'

'What's Patrick up to?'

'Living in Melbourne, married with a child on the way, and happier than he's been in a long time.' And not likely to ever return to Auckland and the family fold. Too much to lose, he reckoned. Already there was a lightness in his own step from being in a different city, different space. Yet the phone rang constantly with his mother demanding his presence for a charity function in Auckland. Like tonight. She'd expected him to fly back for a mayoral dinner. He'd turned her down, which hadn't made him popular. Tough. He wouldn't risk fly-ing back in the morning and being late for his real job.

'Patrick's going to be a dad? Wow, that's great.' Chloe looked a little startled. 'Who'd have believed it?'

Of course, she'd remember his brother. They'd got along well, though she'd never agreed with all the gam-bling and drinking Patrick had done. 'He's calmed down a lot over the last few years.' Tell her? Why not? She shouldn't be too surprised. 'Patrick became addicted to his gambling. Dad put a hold on all his finances, told him to go away and sort himself out or he'd never get another cent.'

Chloe winced, her eyes widening. 'No support, then?'

She'd know the answer to that. Their parents be-lieved in tough love, no holds barred. Which included not showing their feelings, though sometimes he got a sense there was a lot of love being held back. 'Mum and Dad don't like showing any softness towards us in case it makes us weak.'

'Don't I know it?'

Here they were, back to the past and their broken feelings. 'Chloe—'

'Dev, stop.' Her hand wrapped around his wrist. 'That was rude, I'm sorry. But I never believed your parents were affectionate towards you or Patrick, so if Patrick was crying out for help he was in big trouble.'

The problem with having started this conversation was Chloe did know his family better than most. She'd had to put up with criticism and expectations she had no idea how to handle. 'The good side to this is Pat-rick's found his feet and is making a solid career in fi-nance, and he's happy with everything in his life. He left the country determined never to gamble again, and to stop drinking. He's done both, with a lot of support from Rachel, his wife.'

'I'm glad.'

Did she just mutter, 'One down, one to go'? He wasn't asking. He didn't need saving from anything. He was in charge of his own life and getting on with it very well, thank you very much. 'So am I. Now what are we likely to find on the menu at this restaurant?' Time to go with ordinary and easy.

'It's a small selection, only ten dishes, but each one is superb. Lorenzo keeps the prices down as his aim is to entice anyone and everyone to the restaurant to show them what Italian food is all about. He isn't interested in being a top restaurant that everyone must go to. He says it's about replicating his mother's kitchen back in Milan where all the relatives got together for a meal at least once a week.'

'I've not eaten Italian often.'

'You're not one of the it's-only-flour-and-water brigade, referring to pasta, are you?' There was that laughter again. She used to laugh a lot, but it had often been tight and full of concern that she'd got something wrong. Now it came easily and lightly, a happy sound.

'Guilty as charged.'

'So why choose there?'

'Because I saw the restaurant when I came along to the beach and when I suggested we have a meal together it seemed ideal. I also remembered how much you enjoyed pasta,' he admitted.

She blinked, glanced quickly at him and then away. 'I'd eat it all the time if only I could get off my backside and make some. The packet variety doesn't come up to scratch.'

'You still haven't taken up cooking in a big way?'

'Moved beyond the tinned soups and baked beans on toast? Not much. Though occasionally I try to put something together to share with friends. They usually suggest phoning out for something more edible.'

Friends. Not someone special, then. His step lightened. 'Cooking was never your forte. I still like to play around with flavours and proteins. Gives me a sense of accomplishment when I create a tasty morsel.'

'I prefer eating to cooking.' She laughed. 'Let's cross the road while there's a gap in traffic.' She stopped on the footpath, and Genie sat. 'Good girl.' A flick of the lead and they were off.

Dev followed, watching those firm legs striding ahead with the dog beside her. He *had* missed Chloe. There'd been a big hole in his life that he hadn't been able to fill, and now he knew what had caused it. Despite what had happened, all along he'd been lonely without Chloe at his side.

This working-together business was causing all sorts of memories and longings that he'd never believed possible to resurface. Like right now he'd love a hug. Glancing at Chloe, his arms ready to wrap around her, he hesitated. Too soon. If ever appropriate. They were barely on the same page. *Yet.* They used to get along so well he could always grab a hug, give her a kiss, without hesitation. Yes, Devlin. A hug maybe. Kisses? Never. They belonged in the past.

Chloe headed up the side of the restaurant building, Genie's tail wagging faster than ever. 'We go through the back door,' she said over her shoulder. 'At least I do. Genie has her own spot on the back veranda.'

Dev followed. 'Their most regular customers, then?'

'Possibly.' Lorenzo and Giuseppe were going to be

surprised she had someone with her. Make that a man they'd never met, nor heard of, and they'd be agog with questions.

'Hey, Chloe, how's your day been?' Giuseppe asked when she stepped into the kitchen after tying Genie up.

'Busy as usual. Guys, I want you to meet someone.' She turned to Devlin and, hand on his arm, pulled him into the hot space. 'This is Devlin Walsh. He's an emergency specialist and started in ED last week.'

Lorenzo wiped his hands on his apron and held one out to Devlin. 'Pleased to meet you. I'm Lorenzo. This is my brother, Giuseppe. Are you joining our girl for dinner?'

Our girl. As if she were the pet in this relationship. Chloe laughed. 'Yes, he is.'

'Hello, Devlin.' Giuseppe put his hand out, too, his eyes firmly fixed on Dev.

Looking for what? Chloe wondered. Deciding if he was good enough for her, as any decent brothers would?

Devlin shook hands all round. 'Nice to meet you both. This is the first time I've come into a restaurant through the back door.'

It'll be the last time if these two don't take to you, Chloe thought.

Dev must've picked on that, too, as he added, 'Hopefully I pass muster and it won't be the last.'

Giuseppe gave him a long, hard look that many would've turned away from.

Not Devlin. 'I used to know Chloe in Auckland and now we're working together, which is a first.'

Lorenzo, the more accepting of the brothers, grinned. 'Hope you know who's in charge, Devlin. No one gets away with much around our Chloe.'

'Like I said, I used to know her.'

Chloe struggled to take back control before he started telling them how well they'd known each other. 'What's the special tonight, Lorenzo?'

'Wait and see.'

'Same as last week, then.' She laughed, suddenly nervous. It had been a bad idea to agree to come here with Devlin. These guys might be keeping their questions to themselves, but past experience had taught her they wouldn't put them aside for ever. 'We'll go and sit down, get out of your hair.'

'That'd work if I had any.' Finally Giuseppe was smiling his usual broad smile. Dev had obviously passed the first step, whatever that was in Giuseppe's book. 'Come on. I'll pour you both a wine.' He gave Chloe a quick hug. 'How was your holiday? Your *mamma* is all right? And *papà*?'

'They're both good, and send their love to you two and the rest of the family.' Whenever her mother and stepdad came to Wellington they dined here, and visited with the guys' sisters and parents. 'They also said you have to go over and stay when you close for the winter break. Take the tribe with you.'

'We take three weeks and have about six weeks' worth of invitations to use,' Lorenzo called from the kitchen. 'I tell you, Joy and Jack's will be the first stop.'

Placing two glasses on the counter, Giuseppe added, 'Knowing how they will spoil us, it might be the only one. Three weeks lounging around in the Sounds, going boating, fishing, and eating fresh fish is the idyllic holiday.' He turned to the fridge for a bottle of the Chardonnay that Chloe enjoyed.

'Hang on. Devlin prefers a red.'

Giuseppe's eyebrow rose as he looked from her to Devlin. 'That's so?'

Damn, he'd worked out they might know each other better than first indicated.

Dev picked up fast. 'Old habits don't change,' he acknowledged. 'What brands of Pinot Noir do you have?' He leaned closer to the wine rack. 'Is that a South Otago one?' Lifting it out, he read the label and handed the bottle to Giuseppe. 'That one, please.'

'Good taste, I see.' Her 'brother' flicked a quick glance her way, before going back to pouring the wine and studying Dev.

She shouldn't have come here with Devlin. But what choice had she had when he'd asked? She had been tempted to say no, but not a lot in her head, or heart, could manage it. Spending time with him away from work helped cement the fact they were getting along well enough to not bite each other's heads off over any little thing. It was in their DNA to face facts, not avoid them.

But I haven't mentioned the miscarriage.

Not now. Don't even think about it. Don't spoil what was going so well.

Dev picked both wine glasses up and nodded across the room. 'Is that table with the reserved sign yours?'

'Yep. This place will be humming soon.' Half the tables were already full and people were relaxing with wine and delicious food. This was only Wednesday and early, but it was a restaurant locals used regularly. 'Wait until you see this on a Friday evening. Standing room only.'

'As if we let that happen.' Giuseppe grinned. 'Too messy when someone spills their food.'

As she sank onto her chair, Chloe told Devlin, 'The guys prefer catering for locals. More reliable, and getting to know individuals suits their personalities. Plus many folk from the Italian community are regulars. The guys often close it to the public on a Sunday so that family and friends can enjoy themselves as only the Italians know how.'

'We live and work in this area. It's home in all ways.' Lorenzo had come out with a plate of arancini al burro, which he placed on the table. 'Rice balls in batter.'

Devlin sat down. 'How long does it take to become a regular? If you're going to produce food like this I'm booking my own table.' And he hadn't even tasted one.

'You can put your name on Chloe's as long as you look out for her.'

If he didn't, he wouldn't get in the front—or back— door again. Chloe tried not to smile too widely. These guys were her brothers in all ways except genes, and likely as fierce, if not more, than real ones would be. 'Thanks, Lorenzo. Can Devlin have a menu? He doesn't know what you create yet.'

'Here.' Giuseppe flourished a folder. 'Take your time. But everything is delicious.'

Finally they were left to themselves, and Chloe felt her muscles start to relax. 'Sorry about that. They can be full on, but I wouldn't change them for anything.'

'A couple of characters, for sure.' Dev studied her as he sipped his wine. 'I like that you've got friends like them. Everyone needs someone to fall back on at times.'

'Who said I've ever done that with them?'

'There's a sense of comfort and safety that touches you whenever you talk to them. What happened?'

Great. Walked into that one without even realising. She'd forgotten how well Dev could read her. But after all these years, she'd thought he'd have lost that skill with her at least. 'It's not important.'

Devlin sat back and waited. He knew she wouldn't

be able to remain quiet for ever. She didn't used to be able to anyway. Then again, she'd toughened up lately. Hadn't she?

'There was a man.'

His face tightened.

'He was a regular here. Used to sit in the corner at the back, always on his own. He'd eat spaghetti bolognese every night, drink one glass of prosecco, and walk out after paying cash. Until…' She paused, took a mouthful of Chardonnay. It could still make her shiver when she thought of him. 'One night he seemed to take an inordinate amount of notice of me. He never spoke to me, or acknowledged me, just watched me while he ate and drank.'

'How long did that go on for?' There was a fierce, angry thread in Dev's voice.

'I only come in here once or twice a week, but he continued for a month.' More wine spilled over her dry tongue. 'Then one night he waited outside and started to follow me home. It was winter and dark but I knew he was there, so I did an about-turn and returned here. Lorenzo drove me home, I talked to the police but there was nothing they could do as he hadn't approached me, let alone anything else.'

'What happened?' Dev ground out.

'I never saw him again. He's never been in here since. All the guys will say is that Giuseppe had a word with him and he agreed to find somewhere else to eat. They also talked to the cops, and word has it the man left town shortly afterwards. I don't know anything else, and no one's saying a thing. But the Italian community have a reputation for looking out for their own.'

'He lives in another town and won't be returning to

Wellington any time soon,' Giuseppe said as he went past with a tray of drinks for a table at the front.

'But you never decided to leave the city yourself,' Devlin said. 'I'm impressed. Not that you were ever a gutless wonder, but you always did like to feel safe.'

'I still do, only on my terms now.' Hell, she'd told Devlin more about herself than anyone else in the last seven years. But then, he'd always been easy to talk with, and had a way about him that prompted confidence.

'I'm glad the guys were here for you.' The tightness in his voice told her he'd have done the same had he been around when it happened.

'So am I. Can we talk about something else? It gives me the creeps even thinking about that man. Did you sell your Auckland home before coming south?' If he had it would mean he wasn't in a rush to return to the family, and they must be freaking out that he'd gone. Number one favourite son was meant to be there for all the society events.

'No, it's rented out, but not just as a backstop in case I change my mind over living here. This is a permanent move.'

'Sticking to your guns might not be easy.'

'You have no idea.' Then he really looked at her. 'Wrong. Of course you do.'

Bam. His parents were between them again. 'I wasn't what they'd envisaged as their daughter-in-law and, if I was going to say anything in their favour, I wasn't exactly the right type for all that socialising and being glammed up. I get that. I tried so hard to be more like your mother wished, but it wasn't in me to put having my nails done before putting my hand up for an extra shift at the hospital. I own that.'

A large, warm hand covered hers. 'I'm sorry. I did talk to them about it whenever it got too bad, but I thought you'd want to fight your own battles. You were always saying how much you fought with Joy as a kid. Maybe I should have tried harder, said more.'

She didn't want to move away from that touch. Not at all. The warmth and gentle strength in his fingers and palms reminded her of too many wonderful times with Devlin, of reliance and trust and love. Which was why she slid her hand away and picked up her glass again. There hadn't been much of that in the last days of their relationship. Though he had just admitted he could have done more for her, but the blame wasn't all his. She could have talked to him about it.

'I did, and I also wanted to know you were right behind me. I was a bit of a scrapper growing up. Any kid with only one parent and living in poverty was. It was how we survived. But the day I started training to become a nurse I vowed never to be like that again.'

'Except it's in your veins. That attitude saved you time and again from put-downs and other people's venom. I saw you react when someone was rude to you in an emergency department or on a ward. You'd lift your shoulders and chin, and glare at them to say, "Don't mess with me. Ever."' He smiled.

'So Wellington's the real deal?'

He laughed. 'Persistent, aren't you? Yes, it is. I don't intend returning to Auckland, at least until I've given this opportunity a real chance.' He was looking over her shoulder to the far wall. 'Auckland's the only place I've lived, and I want to expand my horizons, find where I'd like to be.'

This from the man who'd warned her when he'd proposed that he'd never leave Auckland permanently, that his family came first over everything. 'You're serious.'

His eyes returned to her. 'Yes, Chloe, I am.'

What had happened to change him? He was different. For one, he'd never have admitted what he'd just told her. He'd liked to appear in control of himself if nothing else, even when it was obvious his parents had a hold over him—a hold called *family*. They were his family, not hers, and even if their marriage had gone ahead she'd always have come second in their eyes. 'Tell me more.' Would he? Wouldn't he?

She nibbled one of the deep-fried balls as she waited. Better than nibbling her fingernail. Did this move have anything to do with their break up, as long ago as it was? More pressure from his parents because of what she'd supposedly done? The muscles in her legs tightened. Why this fascination about what'd been going on in Devlin's life since they'd split?

'I never really settled once you'd gone.' He blinked, as though he'd gone too far.

She wasn't suggesting he stopped. This was so unlike the Devlin of old who never admitted to having any difficulties in his private life. She picked up another ball and nibbled at it, trying to ignore the tension in her body, the dryness making eating difficult.

'Something was missing. I know we were finished, yet it took some getting used to being alone again.'

'You could've talked to me.' As she'd begged so often.

'I see that now.' He stopped, sipped his wine, continued. 'Work was fine. In fact, it became my regular go-to place most of the time.'

'It always was,' she said without hesitation. Then blushed when he studied her. 'It's true. I lost count of the number of times you'd forget we had a date and I'd learn you were working extra hours.' She'd resented that at times, even knowing he'd had to put in as much time as possible to qualify. He just hadn't seemed to have an off switch.

'Is that why you went out with your friends so much?'

If that was a loaded question, then he'd get an honest answer. 'Yes. I understood you had to put in the hours but occasionally I wanted to let my hair down—with you. I understood you weren't as free as me, your study took up more time than mine, but for you not to turn up for our dates hurt, so eventually I gave up sitting around in my flat and went out with my girlfriends.' She had to put it out there one last time. 'I did not ever cheat on you.'

Pushing his plate aside, Devlin reached for her hands, holding them tight. 'I think I know that.' He shook his head. 'No, I do know that. Now. Since I saw you on Monday in ED I just knew I'd badly messed up. I keep replaying that night, trying to see it from your perspective. You were shocked, angry and hurt. It's the anger that's woken me up to the truth. You were furious because I wouldn't hear you out.'

'You never once gave me the benefit of doubt. It was your way or no way.'

'You're right. I was so convinced you'd done the same thing as Cath, I didn't want to hear your excuses. I deleted your text messages without reading them and blocked your number, then threw away all the notes you left in the letterbox. I'm so sorry.' Sadness filled his eyes.

She was stunned. Now what? Reaching for her glass, she took a big gulp. It did nothing to change the shock souring her mouth. They wouldn't have had to go through all the pain of their break up if he'd thought this through years ago. But he hadn't, and they had broken up. Nothing could change that. So… Another gulp of wine, and the glass was empty. 'I'm glad you've finally accepted the truth, albeit seven years on.' The glass spun in her fingers. 'Now we have to move on as colleagues and maybe eventually friends.'

The sadness etched his face. 'Of course.'

'Dev, I—'

'Here you go, lovely. Main course.' Giovanni placed dishes of bubbling lasagne before each of them. 'I'll get you another glass of Chardonnay.'

Lovely. That was Giuseppe being protective, telling her he and Lorenzo were watching out for her. Had he overheard their conversation? Had he deliberately interrupted her before she said too much, put her heart on the line without thinking it through? Because she did care for Dev. Far too much. Him acknowledging his mistake had her letting go of the knots of anger and hurt she hadn't realised she still carried.

Chloe shook her head. 'My hips' favourite.'

'Like there's a problem.' Devlin laughed. 'You're never going to win the award for being overweight.'

True. She had lean genes. 'I'm lucky. But sometimes I probably test the boundaries a little bit too much.' It went back to her insecurities growing up and also how Stephen had always told her she was fat when she'd been almost skinny. 'Hard to resist food like this though.' She had finally accepted herself for who she was, and to hell with what anyone else thought. Mostly, anyway.

'I mightn't be so lucky.' Devlin forked up a mouthful, chewed, smiled with more exuberance. 'It's going to be hard to stay away from here.'

There went her quiet go-to restaurant. She'd always

be on the lookout for him and, depending on how her day had gone if they were on the same shift, she'd be happy or not so pleased to see him. 'Did you know I was living in Wellington before you moved here?'

'Hardly. I heard you'd moved south, but you could've been anywhere by now.'

'I guess I could have.' But she was here in Wellington, where Devlin had recently decided to make a permanent life. 'Where's that wine, Giuseppe?'

CHAPTER FIVE

'I'LL WALK YOU HOME,' Dev said as Chloe untied Genie outside the restaurant.

'No need. We do it all the time.' It wasn't far, the streets were well lit, and Chloe doubted she could take much more of his company without saying something she'd later regret. Like how great it would be to spend more time alone with him. Because she was seeing the man she'd first fallen for, only older and more interesting. He was calmer and more at ease with himself, something he hadn't been before.

'Not on my watch, you don't.'

'Don't forget Nonna's lunch on Sunday.' Lorenzo was standing in the doorway, arms folded across his chest.

Bet he'd heard Dev saying he'd see her home. The questions would be firing at lunch come Sunday. 'As if I'd forget her birthday.' She crossed the deck and gave Lorenzo a hug, whispering, 'Don't even think about quizzing me.'

He gave her a tighter than usual hug, said quietly, 'Bring him with you to the party, if you like.'

'I don't think so.' It was too soon, if indeed there was ever going to be a time she'd introduce Devlin to her other family. 'Catch you Sunday.'

'Nice meeting you, Devlin,' Lorenzo said over the top of her head as she pulled away.

'Likewise. I'll be back for another meal soon.'

'Good.'

Chloe stepped off the porch, Genie at her knee. Time to get home and relax. Not that she hadn't been relaxed over dinner, but there'd been this feeling that any moment now Dev was going to start asking about whether she had a man in her life, or who she'd been dating since they split up and if she was on her own, why. She wasn't ready to talk about the drought that was her love life. She'd have to admit she'd been unaware until she'd seen him again that she hadn't got over him, and, as she was still getting her head around that, she didn't really have any answers she was willing to share.

'I wouldn't be surprised if one of those guys doesn't follow us just to make sure I behave like a gentleman.' Devlin laughed. 'They really have your back, don't they?'

'You'd better believe it.' She joined in the laughter, but it was true. Both men had taken her under their wing right from that day she'd helped Lorenzo with his burns. Almost as though they'd seen past her barriers to the woman inside and the hurt she'd carried, and how she didn't trust men with her heart, unless they only wanted to be friends. 'I found me a family without trying.'

'I bet you give back as much as or more than they do.'

'No comment.' She smiled, and stretched out her steps. It was colder now and a hot shower and a cup of tea in front of the fire was tempting. As was a break from this sexy man matching her strides.

They reached her front gate in what felt like record time, and Chloe bit her tongue, trying not to invite Devlin in for a hot drink. It felt natural, but if she did she wondered if she'd be able to resist hugging him, maybe even kissing him. Her body ached to do so, to feel his warmth under her palms, know the movement of his muscles again. But for once her head was winning the battle and keeping her hormones in control. Barely, but barely was enough.

'Thanks for seeing us home,' she said as she unlatched the gate.

He was looking beyond her. 'You've got yourself a tidy little cottage. Looks like you've had the outside repainted fairly recently.'

Pride inflated her chest. 'I did it myself last summer. At first it was daunting, but the further along I got the more I found I enjoyed the prep and then the painting. The result was beyond what I had hoped for.'

'You continue to surprise me, Chloe Rasmussen. Is this your for ever home? Or is it an investment?'

'At the moment, it's my for ever place. I love living here, in *my* house, making changes as I see fit.' But hopefully one day she would settle down with the man of her dreams and make the move into another property. That dream had never been completely discarded, just the bit about who it might include. 'It's small—the second bedroom can barely fit a single bed. At the moment it's my sewing room.'

'Sewing room? As in making clothes? Or curtains for the house?' He looked stunned.

But then she hadn't known how to use a sewing machine back in the days they were together. Another thing she owed her trip to Italy for. Milan and fashion were Brigitta's passion and it had rubbed off on her, though she still didn't dress up as often as she should. Had to have somewhere to go for that. 'Dresses, coats, trousers. You name it. I can make them.' A wedding dress. Air hissed over her teeth.

Wrong, Chloe. So wrong to be thinking that.

Tell that to her heart when she was standing next to Devlin, who looked so delicious she wanted to eat him. Taste him, kiss him, touch his shoulders, back, everywhere.

He was staring at her as though for the very first time and seemed to be seeing something that fascinated him. And stirred his blood because there was something akin to lust filling his eyes. 'Chloe…' The tip of his tongue appeared between his lips.

Her pulse quickened. Her upper body leaned towards him.

Don't, Chloe. It's too soon.

But those eyes were dragging her in. The face she'd once fallen in love with was so close. She could almost feel her palm touching his chin, his cheek, her lips kissing his.

No, Chloe. Not now. Not yet.

Deep breath.

'Chloe.' Dev sighed her name as though on a breeze.

Her arms lifted, lay over his shoulders, around his neck, ever so gently pulling them together. 'Dev.'

Their lips met, carefully, tenderly. Opened under each other, pressed harder, closer.

Their tongues clashed, pulled back, moved forward again.

Chloe melted into Dev's solid body, absorbing his heat and strength and gentleness as her mouth brought more deliciousness to her starved heart. 'Dev.'

He held her tight yet softly, his hands on her backside, his thighs and belly and chest against hers, his mouth devouring her. Magic swirled in the air around them, encasing them in their own world.

Thud. Something solid banged the back of her knee.

What? Oh, it was Genie.

Devlin dropped his arms, stepped back.

Chloe blinked, looking from Dev to the dog and back to Dev. She'd kissed him. And loved feeling him against her, his mouth on hers. Loved it. What had she done? 'Goodnight,' she muttered and raced up the path to her front door, denying herself the opportunity to turn around and drink in more of those good looks and that stunning body.

Chloe slid into bed and switched the light off. Even in the total blackness, she saw Devlin's face in her mind.

'Dev.' His name whispered across her lips. The tip of her tongue traced her lips where his had been. 'Devlin.'

She shuffled down the mattress to lie on her back, staring up where the ceiling was, and a rough sigh spilled out. Followed by another. Longer, rougher, sad. Squeezing her eyes shut tight, she focused on the image of that strong face, blue eyes, and sexy mouth that had delivered the sweetest of kisses. And the most demanding ones. Kisses that turned her on in a blink.

Her eyes shot open. Yes. Devlin had turned her into a molten blob of heat and longing within an instant. Nothing new there, she'd thought. But actually there was. They were different people now. So many years spent doing different things. Of course, they'd changed. Yet there was a familiarity at being in his arms, kissing that sensuous mouth, that she couldn't deny. It had just gripped her. Could they really do this? Rewrite their past?

Staring around, she picked out the shape of her dressing table, the doorframe, in the weak light from the street lights now shoving that total darkness aside. The familiarity did nothing to quieten her thudding head—and heart. Devlin had once owned her heart. But she needed to slow down right now. One kiss at a time. Not rush in without looking around this time, or they'd be back to square one all too soon.

He'd turned her world upside down just by being himself. He might have changed but he still had the power to blindside her with softness and heat and need and annoyance. By talking to her, looking at her, touching her elbow when she tripped over a rough patch on the footpath as they'd walked home.

Damn you, Devlin. Couldn't you have stayed away for ever? Chosen another city to put your feet down in? Left me to the quiet, comfortable life I've finally made for myself?

After only three days everything had changed, and nothing would be the same again. She was already back to square one. A different square, but just as confusing.

He was the man she'd given her heart to, fallen for so deeply it had been hard to find herself afterwards, and when she had, she'd vowed she'd never give her heart or soul away again. Dev had supported her when she'd struggled with training to be a nurse, he'd been beside her when she'd qualified, had talked about how many kids they might have one day, where they'd live, who'd be the best cook and worst gardener. He'd been everything to her.

Too much, maybe? Had she taken more than she'd given? Had she relied on him too much to find her feet in an adult world where she was supposed to be in charge of her own destiny while always looking for the sky to fall in on her? A habit learned as a child when her mother had kept them on the move as she'd tried to find her own place in the world. People had come and gone throughout those early years, teachers, friends, and neighbours. While her mother had always been her rock, the time had come when she'd had to make her own way, and she'd met Stephen after leaving school and doing her pre-nursing studies. She'd probably moved in with him too quickly, but it had felt right at the time. She'd needed to be loved. Got that wrong big time. She had found the courage to leave him and thought that was it for love for a while, then along had come Devlin with his solidness, reliability, and devastating kisses, and her world had finally stopped rolling and settled. He was her match in every way. Or so she'd thought.

Wrong, Chloe. Oh, so wrong.

Except he had just apologised for hurting her, had owned his error. A lone tear trickled from the corner of her eye down the side of her face into her ear. Then another. And another.

Slapping them away, she continued staring at the ceiling. Nothing there to distract the upsetting thoughts and memories.

Sitting at the restaurant, enjoying a meal, talking like they used to had sucked her right back in, made her feel comfortable with Devlin, made her feel desirable again. It had been too easy to let the past fall away—as though it had only been a glitch between them. But it hadn't been. Yet for a few hours she'd forgotten everything else and just enjoyed being with him.

Be honest, Chloe. You more than enjoyed his company. You loved it. You might even still love him.

The tears were running fast now. Filling her ears, soaking her hair.

She flipped over and buried her face in the pillow,

her hand a fist in her mouth to prevent the raw pain exploding out. Her chest was aching from the beating it was getting. The tears were a torrent as a sob tore out of her. She couldn't love Devlin. Hadn't for a while. She'd put him aside, moved on.

Put him aside only to pick up again when he'd turned up in her life?

'No.' The denial groaned across her lips.

So why the familiar pain? The old sense of wonder whenever he was near? Why did she feel more relaxed around Devlin than she'd been with anyone else in the intervening years?

This was plain crazy. She could not love Devlin.

Something solid nudged her arm.

'Genie?'

You weren't thinking Devlin had turned up, were you?

Nudge. Bump. Bang. Genie sprawled alongside her.

Chloe rolled onto her side and reached out to stroke her pet's head, sniffing at her tears. 'Hey, my girl.' More tears spilled down her face. Damn it. *This* was love. Simple, filled with warmth and food and shelter. No complications. No accusations that not any amount of denials got rid of.

Damn it. None of this was keeping Devlin out of her mind. He was back in full force. Just like old times.

Except nothing was like their relationship back then. Now they worked together. She owned a house. She was stronger, believed in herself and didn't need to be boosted into believing she was good enough for him. That one fault in particular had caused a lot of problems in the past. Now she knew better. If someone didn't like her or the way she went about things, then that was their problem, not hers.

Genie pushed closer.

'That's enough, my girl. I do have to get some sleep.'

Another day, another shift working alongside Devlin. Her new reality. One that had her in a state of uncertainty. Except working with Delvin was fine. That kiss was tipping her off track. With it came that special bond they'd shared over most aspects of their lives. It had also brought home how good they were together. *And* how she'd like to feel that again.

She would? Of course she would. She didn't want to spend the rest of her life single, or without children. But she hadn't done very well finding another man she'd even consider getting close to and possibly settling down for the long haul with. They weren't exactly lining up for her to take notice. Then along came Dev once more and suddenly her heart was beating more erratically than it had done in years, and she just plain felt more at ease and ready for an adventure than she had in for ever. Devlin. Was this all down to his reappearance in her life?

What other reason could there be? Nothing was popping up in her head. Her hands fisted on either side of her thighs. 'Damn it. Damn you, Devlin. Why, why, why did you come to Wellington? Now I have to deal with these feelings that are marching through me like an unstoppable parade.'

Genie dropped her head on Chloe's shoulder.

'Sorry, girl. I don't know what's come over me. I'm beginning to think I might still love Devlin. Not in an "old boyfriend who could now be a friend" kind of way, but in a complete, heart-rending, body-warming, mind-blowing way.' As she used to.

Thump, thump, thump. Her nails poked into her palms. The bed shook. What had she done? Nothing.

The question should be, did she want to love Devlin again? No, she didn't. He'd accused her of cheating on him, and then refused to listen to her replies. Why would she want to love him?

Because he was the only man to ever light her fires so hot, so big, so wonderfully. That she could start reacting to him so strongly as soon as she'd seen him again had to have been a warning that all was not how she'd thought it should be, that she hadn't yet reached the point where she was truly over him. Spending the evening with him at the restaurant had only enhanced all those feelings a hundred times over, ringing giant warning bells.

What was she going to do? Leap in and see what happened? Devlin would be out of town within seconds.

Then go for it. Make him aware of you in other ways than as a nurse in the same department.

They'd already started that process over dinner, so keep up the momentum. No, there'd only be one loser and she wasn't ready to go through all that heartache again. She'd have to continue being professional at work and stay away from dinner dates or walks on the beach except with Genie.

Tossing the sheet aside, she swung her legs over the side of the bed and stood up. This was not working. She needed sleep, not nightmares—or dreams that were never going to be realised. So she'd settle for a hot chocolate drink sitting on the couch with the curtains open so she could gaze up at the stars until her pulse slowed to normal and her head stopped spinning.

Dressed in jeans and a merino jersey, Devlin sat on his deck, his feet propped on the top of the glass balustrade, a glass with a shot of malt whisky in his hand.

He should be in bed sleeping the sleep of the dead. His body ached with exhaustion, but his mind was wide awake and busy.

The weeks leading to arriving in Wellington and unpacking his household belongings and everything else he'd managed to accumulate over the years had been intense. Meeting new colleagues and learning the ropes of the department had kept him on his toes, and happy, and reminding himself this was what *he* wanted. But it was Chloe who'd thrown his calm to the wind.

From that first moment when he'd seen her dealing with the patient who'd had a cardiac arrest he'd known deep down he was in trouble. Like a ticking time bomb inside him, his body tensed on and off with regular distractions, and his head kept spinning left and right. If he still believed he could work with Chloe and not get sidetracked, then he was screwed. The last thing he wanted to be was continually distracted. It made concentrating on patients difficult. No, that wasn't true. Every time he and Chloe worked together with a patient, he was completely focused on what he was meant to be doing. It was only when they paused, or moved on to another patient, that his mind started playing games with him.

They'd kissed tonight. He'd been drawn straight back to the very first time he'd kissed her and the sense of having found his love, his better half. Tonight had been no different. They belonged together. Or at least they had. Chloe in his arms as he kissed her, her slight body wrapped around him as they made love, her tinkling laughter when they shared a funny moment. Sadness and pain in her eyes when they argued. Yes, those emotions were there every day as they worked together, when they walked on the beach. Like memories overlaid with new yet similar images. Where did this take him? Take them? Since the day he'd broken off their engagement he'd refused to think about Chloe and what he'd lost. What was the point in regrets?

Now that kiss showed he hadn't got over her. She was still in his system. Still capable of making him breathe faster. Still giving him a reason to smile. Twisting his belly whenever he looked at her. Making his heart thump.

The whisky slid over his tongue and down his throat, warming him as it went.

Chloe had told him the truth. Believing his mother had proved to be the wrong decision but had she genuinely been misled, too, and believed she'd acted in his best interests? Or had she deliberately tried to cause problems for him and Chloe? No, he still couldn't believe she'd go that far and deliberately break his heart just to get her own way with him. She must have known there was only so far he could be pushed before he pushed back. He'd left Auckland to get away from his parents interfering in his life, trying to suggest he marry someone of their choice who didn't tick his boxes.

Tick his boxes? Try tighten his belly into tiny knots of desire and heat and need.

Wiping his hand over his face in a vague attempt to hold the exhaustion at bay, he laughed mirthlessly at himself. Chloe Rasmussen had waltzed right back into his head—and his body—and there was no getting away from her. Not even out here, fifteen floors up, in the cool night air where no one could see him. He was alone, and yet he wasn't. She was always with him. That was how he'd used to feel when they were a couple. Chloe was always there for him, and in his soul when they weren't together in the same room.

She should not be with him now.

They were long finished as a couple.

Weren't they? Their kiss said otherwise. Kissing Chloe had made him feel as though he'd come home. The woman he'd once accused of having an affair. Shame gnawed at him, felt ghastly. How could he have made such an awful error of judgement and wrecked what should've been a wonderful future with the woman of his dreams?

Chloe had been all of that, and more. He'd loved her so much. Had his ego got in the way? The whisky soothed his throat but not his mind. Three days working with her, and then going out for a meal followed by that sensational kiss, and he couldn't deny he still had feelings for her. Old ones that he hadn't managed to get over after all. Like how his body went soft with longing whenever she walked into the room. How his heart tripped when she touched him. The way she slept with one hand under her cheek and the other on his chest.

Could they start over? Was he falling for Chloe as fast and deep as before? No, he wasn't falling in love with her again. Because he hadn't stopped loving her in the first place. Had he? Of course, he had, he must have. Hell. This was getting completely out of hand. He didn't know what he thought or how he felt.

Devlin jumped to his feet, drained his glass and strode inside, closing the glass door behind him. If he was going to sit out there having these dim-witted ideas, then he might as well go to bed and try to get some sleep. He'd swallow some magnesium tablets to help with that.

As he slid between the sheets, one good thought crossed his mind. He would be out of town from Friday till Monday, going up to Auckland to finalise some legal paperwork surrounding his properties and attending his cousin's wedding on a vineyard west of the city. There'd be little or no time to spend thinking about Chloe. He'd have a break from her and hopefully calm down.

Just had to get through tomorrow first. And put aside the warm sensations that kiss had brought to his body and heart.

Chloe had the wipers on full speed and still had to peer through the windscreen to see clearly. It was bucketing down and the wind was driving the rain sideways. Parking and making a dash along the street to the hospital had her wondering if calling in sick might've been a good idea. At least she'd have been warm and dry. As if she'd do that, she thought with a sigh.

'Welcome to windy Wellington,' she said to Devlin a quarter of an hour later as they both entered the ED hub at the same time, her hands itching to touch him again.

'Who'd want to be on a ferry this morning?' he agreed politely.

'Not me, that's for sure.' The Interislander ferries running between Picton and Wellington often had high winds and huge swells, and it was not fun to be on board at those times. 'Far prefer it when it's perfectly flat. Which is very rare on the Cook Strait.' Pulling up a chair, she sat down and brought up the screen to go through last night's patient list and focus on anything but Dev. 'What've we got, Jaz?'

'It was a busy night. Two car crashes, a policeman shot in the arm, and one five-year-old with RSV.' Jaz stretched, hands rubbing the small of her back. 'I hope that's not the beginning of more to come.'

'It's a fast-acting virus, highly contagious, especially

amongst youngsters, so I expect to see more cases in the coming weeks,' Devlin commented.

'Throw in this being the middle of winter,' Chloe muttered.

'Agreed.' Devlin was reading a file on the computer next to her. 'Let's hope it doesn't get out of hand.'

A yawn gripped her. Beside her Dev was doing the same, and she couldn't hold back a laugh. 'You, too?'

'Yes,' he muttered.

'Morning, everyone.'

Chloe glanced up and around, surprised to find the space filled with the day-shift staff. She hadn't been aware of anyone other than Dev and Jaz. 'Hi, Clare. Busy night by the looks of it.'

'It was. Jaz, get out of here while you can. Everyone else's gone.' Clare got down to business. 'Devlin, everyone, you've got a woman in cubicle ten, admitted at four with severe abdomen pain. Suspected kidney stone. We're waiting on blood results and the urologist is due in before seven. A forty-five-year-old male, suspected mild stroke during the night, no known history. I've given him blood thinners, and we're keeping him in under observation for a few hours.'

The list went on and Chloe divvied up the patients between the other nurses. 'I'll take triage,' she told them at the end of Clare's outline. That'd keep her out of the main area and away from Devlin most of the time. All part of downplaying her reactions to him, and staying sane for the day.

She needn't have worried about getting too close to him. The day was manic with a steady stream of patients coming through the front door by foot or through the ambulance bay on a bed. At two o'clock she got a call from the head nurse, Sandy. 'Hi, Chloe. Busy day, I hear.'

Chloe sighed. She knew what was coming. 'Who's not turning up for the next shift?'

'Shayne. He's come down with a stomach bug. You up for it?'

She was hardly going to say no, even when she was shattered. 'It's why you ring me first. You know I hardly ever say no.'

Sandy sounded a little embarrassed when she said, 'Sorry. I was panicking a bit. Had another no show yesterday and I still don't know if she'll be in or not today. Take a break, have some coffee and a snack, go for a brisk walk before you start the next shift.'

'It's stopped raining?' It had still been hosing down last time she'd been in triage and had looked out of the front doors.

'Drizzling now. You shouldn't get too wet.'

'Gee, Sandy, you're a cheer.' But a walk might do wonders for her tired body. 'I'll go across the road for a decent coffee and a slice of quiche.'

'Don't let the cafeteria staff hear you say that. They think their coffee's the best.'

It was hospital grade, a standard joke amongst the staff, who drank gallons of coffee twenty-four-seven. 'They'd lynch me, I know. Okay, I'm up for it. I'm not even going to mention hoping that we have a quiet evening.' She'd done that too often with crazy consequences.

At the far side of the hub Devlin was typing up notes. 'You staying on?'

'Yep. I'm about to take an hour's break first.' It was routine when someone carried on through the next shift.

'What about Genie? Won't she need feeding and a walk?'

'I'll phone my neighbour when she gets home from school. She takes care of Genie for me when I'm on afternoon and evening shifts.' Then Chloe recalled something. 'Damn, that won't work.'

'Problem?' Devlin had swung around on his chair and was watching her.

'Just remembered Zoe is away on a school trip.'

'I'll drop by and take her to the beach for a walk. Feed her as well.'

'You don't have to do that. I can call somebody else.' Devlin was offering to help her out. He couldn't have any hang ups about last night, then.

'I know I don't, but I'd like to. It'll get me moving, instead of sitting around my apartment with little to do.' One side of his mouth lifted in a wry smile. 'Pathetic, eh?'

'Fine, thanks. Genie'll think you're wonderful, and be beholden to you. There's food in the fridge and biscuits in the pantry. There's a spare key on a nail just inside her kennel.'

Genie would probably take it off the hook and give it to Dev. She could be fickle in her affections when it came to getting walks and food.

'Consider it done.' He stood up and stretched that long body she used to know far too well.

Still did, if her memory of muscular abs and firm buttocks was anything to go by. Then there was the way her arms had wound around him last night. As if they hadn't taken a seven-year break. Quiet, girl. He was about to go off shift, and she had another eight hours to see through. There wasn't any energy to spare for even thinking about his body. Tell that to someone who'd believe her. She could always drum up the energy to think about Dev's body. 'Thanks. I'll see you next week.' Hadn't he mentioned going north for the weekend? Maybe he'd get back sooner than expected and drop by for a coffee. Or even another kiss?

CHAPTER SIX

'HOW WAS YOUR WEEKEND?' Chloe asked on Monday morning as Dev strolled in to begin the shift looking far too sexy in the drab blue scrubs. She hadn't seen him since last Thursday, but she had dreamed about him far too often. 'Oh, Genie says hi.'

'She's a right little con. I'm sure I fed her far too much.'

'One nudge and lots of wagging wins her most things she wants,' Chloe agreed, trying not to ogle him.

'I was in Auckland. Had a family wedding to go to as well as a few things to finalise. How was yours?'

'Quiet. Went to the guys' grandmother's birthday lunch at the restaurant on Sunday, and it was fantastic. Also went downtown to a couple of bars with friends on Saturday. That was it.' Nothing too exciting, no hot man in sight.

'I went to a winery in Masterton for lunch,' Jaz piped up. 'Had the best steak I've ever had. The wine was amazing, too.'

Chloe crossed over to give her a hug. 'Happy birthday, girlfriend. I hope Toby spoiled you.'

Jaz blushed and held out her hand. 'I'd say so.'

'Wow. Would you look at that?' She took Jaz's hand

in hers to gaze at the sparkling diamonds. 'That's beautiful. Congratulations. This deserves another hug.'

Jaz grinned, and sniffed. 'I'm still pinching myself.'

Chloe sniffed too. 'You two are destined to be together. Decided on a date yet?'

I am not jealous. Much.

Oh, to be planning a wedding and dreaming of a future with the man of her heart.

'February. If I can wait that long.'

'Time will fly. There's so much to do arranging a wedding.' Not that she'd had a lot of experience. Hers had been pretty much taken over by Mrs Walsh because Chloe had been told she just wouldn't have got it right.

'We're going for small and casual. I think.' Jaz was gazing at her ring with awe in her eyes. 'There again...'

'Can I add my congratulations, too?' Devlin stepped up.

'Everyone's welcome.' Jaz grinned.

Chloe returned to her computer, her heart pounding dully. A wedding. Phew. She'd wanted a cream, off-the-shoulder, tight-fitting gown that flared over her hips to fall to the floor. Daffodils for the bouquet. Her hair falling in long curls over her shoulders, the way Dev liked it.

The pen she'd picked up slid from her lifeless fingers.

'Here.' Devlin picked up the pen. 'You all right?'

'Why wouldn't I be?' Her eyes slid upward, drank in the strapping specimen standing beside her. Yeah, well, dreams were all a load of hot air. And getting back together with Devlin was completely airy. A fantasy— with no happy ending. Hadn't she told herself she wasn't following through on the feelings she appeared to still be having for him? Their kiss had a lot to answer for, she thought morosely, knocking her carefully held together ideas to bits like this when she should be guarding her heart with everything that was in her. 'I'm good to go. Bring on the shift.' Hopefully it would be busy and there'd be no spare time for watching Devlin and reminiscing about things best forgotten.

'Devlin, we've got a cyclist who was knocked off his bike by a bus,' Cass, the triage nurse, was leading the ambulance paramedic into the department. 'GCS eight, fractures in both legs, pelvis out of alignment.'

'Take him, or her, to Resus. Chloe, where are you today?' Devlin asked.

'Resus one.'

'Right, Cass, Resus one. Tell me what we know about our patient.' He nodded at a paramedic.

Chloe raced to Resus, putting all thoughts of Devlin aside.

The paramedic was telling them, 'Male, thirty-one, James Schultz, banker, and that's it. The police got scant details from his backpack. They're following up with the banks and will be in here soon.'

'According to the receptionist there's no information on a James Schultz in the hospital data,' Cass said.

'Great,' Devlin muttered so only Chloe could hear. 'Let's hope there are no illnesses that could impact on what we have to do here.'

Chloe joined everyone to transfer the man across to the bed from the ambulance trolley. 'He's probably fit if he's a cyclist.' Though that wasn't always the case, it was more often than not. She began swapping out the ambulance leads for the hospital ones to keep track of the man's heart and BP on their equipment.

'James, I'm Devlin, a doctor in the emergency department you've been brought into. Can you hear me?'

One eye opened, sliding shut almost instantly.

'Good. You've been in a serious accident. I'm going to give you some drugs for the pain now, and then we have to assess you for all your injuries.' Devlin looked over to Chloe. 'We'll go with intravenous morphine first.'

'I'll get it. Anything else?'

'Not yet.' He was running his hands over James's skull, his fingers gently searching for soft patches that would indicate a head injury. 'Tell Amy to join us, too. She can observe and learn.'

Amy was the junior doctor on their shift. Chloe nodded. 'And another nurse.' They were going to be busy with this man.

Returning with the drug Devlin had requested, she ran it past Amy to check the expiry date and name of drug, then began inserting a cannula in the back of James's hand.

'Skull indent left side,' Devlin intoned. 'No apparent spinal damage, reacting to stimulus on feet.'

Amy watched every move Devlin made. 'His heart rate's low. Internal bleeding?'

'More than likely. That head wound's not causing too much blood loss. There're no obvious external injuries. He could've taken a handlebar in the gut area, which might've damaged the spleen or liver.' Devlin's fingers were now probing James's abdominal region. 'Swelling above the intestine. Feel that, Amy.' He stepped back to allow the trainee in. 'Chloe, can you phone Theatre and let them know we've got a patient who's going to need urgent surgery? Those leg fractures are a go, and the skull needs pressure released. I'll phone the on-duty orthopaedic surgeon and Radiology. Probably going to need a general surgeon, too, if that abdominal swelling proves there's a damaged organ.'

Reading the monitor before her, Chloe said, 'No changes here. One plus in his favour at least. I'll go make that call.'

Cass poked her head around the curtain. 'James has no known medical problems and is a competitive cyclist.'

Not for a while, he wasn't. Chloe's heart squeezed for the man. Being fit would help his recovery but it wasn't going to save him from months of pain and learning to use his legs again. If he got that lucky. Picking up a phone, she pressed the number for Theatre. 'Hello, Damien. Chloe from ED. We've got a multi-trauma case that's going to need surgery after X-rays and as soon as the orthopaedic surgeon sees him.'

'We've got a full house this morning. Let me see who I'm going to put back. Okay, there we go. Let the surgeon know we've got a bed in an hour or a bit less. I'm presuming you'll be that long anyway, by the time Radiology, the surgeon and the anaesthetist have done their jobs?'

'Sounds about right. There might be a general surgeon as well as the man is still being assessed for internal injuries.'

'So I need to swap out another op as well. Okay, onto it. Keep us posted.' Damien hung up.

'Theatre's sorted,' she told Devlin, who was sitting at the next desk talking to what sounded like the surgeon.

He gave her a quick nod, mouthed, 'Can you phone Radiology and the porters?'

'Sure.' She picked up the phone again, pressed another button. 'Hi there. Chloe from ED.'

After the calls she headed back to their patient where Devlin was again trying to get a verbal response from him.

'James, this is Devlin. Squeeze my hand if you can hear me. Good. Okay, now we're going to get you X-rayed and a surgeon is also coming to see you.'

'Do we want bloods for a cross match?' Chloe asked.

'Yes.'

'Dianna, can you get the blood kit?' she asked the other nurse. 'And wipes to start cleaning his arms and torso.'

'No problem.' Dianna opened a cupboard on the far wall.

The orthopaedic surgeon arrived, and the room began to feel crowded. But no one was surplus to requirements; they all had a job and were getting on with it quietly and efficiently.

As Chloe took the blood sample she listened to Devlin explaining to the surgeon what little they knew about the patient's injuries. Then as suddenly as James had arrived he was whisked off to Radiology and from there he'd be taken to Theatre and prepared for at least one operation. 'It's going to be a long morning for him,' she commented. Not that he'd know much about it.

'Poor blighter,' Dianna said.

'It's going to be a whole lot worse afterwards,' Devlin added. 'I'd say for a bus versus cyclist he might've got off lightly, if I can call those horrific injuries light.'

'Know what you mean,' she agreed. 'He's alive and breathing, and not totally non-compos. But I wouldn't want to be waking up to learn what's happened.'

'I wonder if there's family or a partner to be there for him.'

'Imagine facing that on your own.' She shuddered. 'There wouldn't be anything worse. Actually, that's not true, but it would be right up there.' She couldn't envisage not having someone special at her side if she were going through something like that. But she'd had to go through a miscarriage alone, hadn't she? Her gaze drifted sideways to Devlin before abruptly returning to focus on the job in hand.

Devlin was looking at her with empathy and a gentle smile.

An old anger burst into her head, and she leapt to her feet. How *could* he have believed she'd cheated on him so easily? It mightn't have looked good having Adam in her flat, but Devlin had never given her a chance to explain properly.

He might have apologised now and admitted he was wrong, but the fact remained he had reacted harshly and swiftly, and refused to hear her out, or even bother to read her note about the miscarriage. How could she think she still had feelings for him when he was capable of that? He could do it to her again. Just as quickly the chill evaporated, taking her sudden surge of anger with it, leaving her feeling hollowed out and worried about what lay ahead. More pain? Or something potentially exciting and loving?

Living here seemed to indicate he might have finally told his family he was living the life he chose, not what they expected of him. The only thing wrong with that idea was Devlin was very loyal to his family, and totally understood where his wealthy lifestyle had come from. He'd never walk away from them completely. Not for her, not for anybody. And she'd be best off remembering that.

'Chloe?'

'Yes?'

Devlin took her arm, squeezed gently. 'Let's grab a coffee while we can.'

Another squeeze, then coolness where Dev's hand had been. 'Hello?'

'Not so fast.' Cass spoke across the space. 'Two-year-old girl, runny nose, harsh coughing and temperature of thirty-eight. Possibly another case of RSV. I've put her in cubicle ten, green zone.'

'Good.' Chloe was off her chair and heading to the little girl, relieved she had someone else to concentrate on.

Unfortunately, Devlin was right behind her as she walked towards her new patient. 'This RSV seems to be escalating. Other hospitals around the country are starting to report a higher than normal rate for this time of year.'

Chloe's heart sank. 'The toddlers always seem to be the hardest hit with it. Though we did have a fifty-six-year-old woman on Friday night with symptoms. I didn't hear the outcome as I signed off shortly after she was admitted.'

'If that was the woman from Petone, then, yes, she's got the virus,' Cass told them as she held the curtain back to expose a tiny tot curled up on a woman's lap, tears streaking her scared face. 'This is Kiera and her mother, Megan. Devlin's your doctor for now, Megan, and this is Chloe, the nurse who's going to look after Kiera.'

Troubled eyes locked on Devlin, who found a smile as he studied the little girl Megan was holding gently. 'She's never been sick like this, Doctor. She never gets sick at all really. She woke me up with her coughing and crying. I might be panicking but I put her in the car straight away and drove here.'

'You did the right thing, Megan.' Devlin crouched

down so he was looking directly at the child. 'Hello, Kiera. You don't feel good?'

Kiera turned her face into her mum's breast.

'Was she all right when she went to bed last night?' he asked Megan as he reached for the little arm closest to him. His finger found Kiera's pulse and he timed the beats.

'She was grizzling but I put that down to the fact she'd been at the play centre for longer than usual because I had to work extra hours as someone was away. She gets tired if she's there longer than six hours. Did I get that wrong?'

'It's not a case of being wrong,' Chloe told her, since Devlin was focusing on the pulse rate. 'You know your daughter better than anyone else. You know when something's not quite right.'

Devlin stood up. 'Chloe's got a point. Chances are Kiera didn't even have a fever last night. If her temperature was raised, it might've been only infinitesimally high. But it is high now. We are going to attach her to the monitor so we can keep reading her heart rate and BP. I want her temperature taken hourly, more if it rises any further, Chloe.'

Chloe brought the monitor across. 'Let's lie Kiera down on the bed. Megan, we need to get those thick clothes off her to help lower her temperature. While you're doing that I'll get some water. She needs to drink little and often to avoid dehydration.'

Kiera grabbed at her, crying out, 'Mummy.'

'Shh, sweetheart. Mummy's here. We're going to put you in the bed.'

'I want to go home,' coughed the wee girl.

'Nasal oxygen, please.' Devlin took the monitor leads

Chloe held out to him and began placing them on Kiera's little chest as her mother removed her upper clothes.

'Be right back.' Chloe headed for the trolley with the oxygen tank and bags of nasal tubes. That poor child was scared and gasping for air, her face scorching red, as was the rest of her upper body now that they'd got her clothes off. Chloe grabbed a jug of water and a paper cup as well. 'Here we go. Megan, can you get Kiera to take a few sips of water while I set up the oxygen?'

'Water's not her favourite drink.' Megan managed a smile as she took the cup and jug from Chloe.

'Sorry, but it's better than a sweet drink at the moment. It's absorbed quicker and that's what she needs right now,' Devlin explained.

'Devlin, got a moment?' Cass asked from the corner. 'I want you to see another patient who's just been brought in.'

'Sure. You got this, Chloe?'

'Absolutely.' She wasn't leaving Kiera for a moment. Not until they'd got fluid into her and the oxygen flowing properly anyway.

'Good. I'll be back.'

'How's Kiera doing?' Devlin asked Chloe forty minutes later.

'She's settling down well,' Chloe answered. 'I've left her with another nurse for now.'

He held up a vial. 'Check this dose with me.' He breathed deep, savouring the light floral scent wafting from Chloe. Her abrupt change of mood before had him wondering if he'd been the cause for some reason, though she appeared to have calmed down now. Thank goodness, because he enjoyed working with her.

'Sure.' Her fingers brushed his as she accepted the vial he held out.

'Hey, I missed you over the weekend.'

Her eyes widened as they locked on him. Her tongue licked the corner of her delectable mouth.

'You were angry earlier.'

Her lips pressed together, moved left then right, opened. 'I'm confused, frustrated. I don't know what I'm doing, what you're doing, where we are.'

He got where she was coming from in spades. 'You and me both.'

'Oh, Dev.'

He pulled her into the supply closet, then kicked the door shut, enclosing them in darkness. Reaching for her, he found her mouth through sheer instinct and kissed her as though she was the only thing on earth that mattered. Which, at this point in time, she was.

CHAPTER SEVEN

'GENIE, THE LAST thing I need right now is a walk.' Chloe stared down at her pet sitting wagging her tail and holding the lead in her mouth. 'I'm tired and hungry. It's been a big day.' The patients hadn't stopped coming. No sooner had they sent one to Theatre or a ward and another two would arrive. She'd stayed on for an extra two hours helping catch up.

Wag, wag, wag.

'Yeah, I know. You don't care. I'm a broken record.' A tired smile finally made its way across her mouth and she reached down to rub Genie's head. 'All right. You win. As always. Let me get my walking shoes on. And a coat.'

More wags and a head nudge. Genie always knew when she'd got her way.

'We'll go into town and along Courtenay Place.' The beach wouldn't be fun in the rain, and sand would stick to Genie to make a mess back in the house. Never a great look. 'I can grab something to eat at the supermarket.' She was too damned tired to be bothered what she got, as long as it kept the hunger gremlins at bay.

Genie's ears had pricked up. Somehow she always knew words to do with food.

Pulling the laces tight on her second shoe, Chloe

stood up and stretched her back. 'Let's do this before I change my mind.' Not that she would. Genie needed the walk, and it wouldn't hurt her. 'Wonder what Dev's doing?' He'd left the hospital before her, since the doctors had been up to speed with patients and his shift had long finished.

Her phone rang. 'Speak of the devil.' *Down, heart.* 'Hello?'

'Hey, like to share dinner somewhere?' Dev sounded breathless. Couldn't be because he'd been doing a workout in a gym. Not his style at all.

'I'd like that.' She'd love it. Did kisses come as an entrée or dessert? 'I'm just taking Genie for a walk, then I'll be free.'

'You're not going to the beach in this weather, are you?'

It was drizzling and chilly out there. 'I'm heading downtown to keep under the shop awnings. Want to meet me somewhere? There are some good eateries on Courtenay Place.'

'What about Genie? We can't leave her sitting outside while we have a leisurely meal.'

She'd forgotten her girl in all this. 'So want to pick me up after we get back from the walk?' Another idea popped into her head. 'Or we could get Thai and bring it back here.'

'I'd like that. I'll meet you in town, then walk back to your house with you.'

'Fine,' Chloe said. Then looked at her old jeans. Not up to speed if she was meeting up with Devlin. It couldn't hurt to impress him a little. Changing into the new pair she'd bought in a sale last week, she chose a soft cream blouse and navy woollen jacket.

Outside, Chloe pulled the collar of her jacket tight

around her neck and stretched out her steps. The sooner they were under the cover of shop awnings, the better.

Genie didn't seem at all worried about getting wet, just trotted alongside her, sniffing the air every time they passed a takeaway outlet. And when they joined Devlin, she began bouncing along as though she'd caught up with her best friend.

Once they'd ordered their meal they continued walking.

'How do you cope with days like today?' Chloe asked. 'I'm talking about the toddlers with RSV.' Not that stolen kiss. 'It's heartbreaking seeing little kids so unwell.'

'By going for a long walk usually with music playing in my ear and breathing in normality.'

She hadn't noticed the earplugs hanging from his shirt pocket before. 'Joe Cocker by any chance?'

'You remember?' He grinned.

Heat scorched her cheeks. Was he referring to her dancing naked to Cocker's music in Devlin's apartment, and making love with him on the rug afterwards? 'Didn't I buy you a collection of his records when you got that ultra-modern stereo?' Records had started making a comeback and Dev had been into them big time. She'd been happy knowing there was something she could buy him he'd really enjoy and it had nothing to do with spending lots of money.

Dev was still grinning. So he did remember that afternoon. 'I've still got them all.'

So he was still into the records. That was good, as he hadn't had many interests outside medicine and family duties. Still into sex on the floor? She swallowed hard.

He continued, 'There's a shop in Queen Street that specialises in records. I bet they're making a killing.

Good old vinyl is so popular these days. Not very practical when wanting to listen to music while going for walks though.'

Damn but she loved that grin. Always had. Probably the first thing she'd loved about him. And everything else had been right behind. They'd only taken days to get close and personal and start talking about moving in together. In hindsight, it had been way too soon. They should have taken their time getting to know each other better first. He might have trusted her more then. 'Half the population would think you were talking about something that covers the laundry-room floor.'

'True. Are you saying I'm old-fashioned?'

'More of a Neanderthal.' Though she had always enjoyed listening to music with Devlin, to her there wasn't a lot of difference between LPs and CDs. Except the expense. And dollars had been in short supply for her back then. Still were compared to what Devlin was used to. The difference in their incomes hadn't really bothered her when she'd loved him so much, and it had certainly not been the reason she'd agreed to get engaged to him. Something his mother had implied more than once. Mrs Walsh hadn't understood that growing up poor had never made Chloe envious of the wealthy, and certainly hadn't meant she'd ever get married just for the money. Devlin had believed her about that, something she'd always appreciated.

'No, Genie.' She twitched the lead to emphasise the order, and Genie stopped sniffing the shop doorway and moved on.

'What do you do in your spare time?'

'General household chores, and maintenance. There's always something needing to be repaired around the house. Waterproofing windows, replacing roof tiles and rotten boards, paintwork inside and out.'

'Sounds like you really enjoy doing all that.'

'I do. I've found immense satisfaction in turning my house into a home.'

'I can understand that. You've done something for yourself and it's turned out well. And you've always wanted a home of your own after your unsettled lifestyle as a child.' He looked pleased. For her? Or because he was hoping he might find something similar with his move to Wellington?

'We should turn around. Our takeaways will be ready soon.'

A warm hand took her cold one, wrapped gentle fingers around her rigid ones. As he used to take hold of her whenever she'd been upset about something. 'I know you struggled with your past and the people who never accepted you as part of your mother's life or for other reasons. I haven't forgotten any of the stories you told me about being rejected by the men who wanted Joy to live with them but not you. How could I when they made me angry for you? Hurt for you? I also recognised that they'd made you the woman I intended to marry and live with for ever.'

Thank goodness they were walking on a busy street as workers made their way from offices to bars and restaurants or bus stops. Otherwise she might've spun into Dev's arms and clung to him, hugged him until the chill that had been in her heart from the day they broke up finally dissolved. To hell with it. She threw her arms around him anyway.

'I'm glad you came to town.' What else could she say when her heart was in her throat? Devlin had loved her back then. The way he'd looked out for her, talked her through things that upset her, gave her confidence whenever it was lacking, had spoken loudly of his feelings, with open, loving affection. But he still hadn't been able to believe she hadn't been unfaithful to him. Was some of that her fault?

Had she done something to make him believe she didn't love him as much as he'd loved her? Had she been too accepting of everything he'd said, and not fought hard enough to make him see how wrong he was? Had she put on her 'I'm not good enough for you' hat and let him win the battle too quickly, too easily? 'I'm sorry.'

Devlin's hold tightened around her and he gazed down at her. 'For what, Chloe?'

Tell him. She looked up at him, locked her eyes with his.

He was waiting, quietly, expectantly.

Maybe this was just one more piece of the past she needed to let go of to be able to feel free of him.

You're never going to. He's inside you, in your head and heart.

'For not trying harder to make you believe me. I accepted too quickly that I didn't stand a chance of changing your mind so I gave up.' A gutless reaction that came from a time when getting away from people who didn't want her as a part of their lives was the norm. She should've trusted that Dev wasn't like that, but then Stephen had begged for a second chance and she'd trusted that he'd changed, and look how that had turned out.

'There were two of us in that story. Yes, you could've kept trying, but I still wouldn't have believed you. I accepted your guilt far too easily, and I'll have to live with that every day.'

'Oops, sorry, wasn't looking where I was going,'

a young woman dressed in a business suit said as she bumped into them.

'It's fine. We should've found somewhere less busy for this conversation.' Devlin wrapped his arm around Chloe's shoulders and they began walking back towards the Thai restaurant.

Would her stomach be okay with receiving food on top of the emotions tripping through her at Dev's words? She'd try, just as she'd try to understand why he hadn't fought harder to save their future. At least she'd tried.

'You're overthinking everything,' he said close to her ear. 'But then you always did.'

Devlin frowned. He knew he'd walked away from Chloe too readily. He had been forewarned and therefore prepared to see her with another man after his mother had warned him that she wasn't always the good girl he'd believed her to be. The thing was, he'd never thought of Chloe as good, nor had he wanted that in his girlfriend. Good spoke of dull and conventional, and not up to a bit of fun. It also didn't mean being unfaithful. He'd been so stupid; why had he taken his mother's word for fact and not dug deeper? That was something he would follow up on now. Mothers were supposed to support their children, not undermine all their dreams and hopes.

Devlin shuddered to think he might've made the biggest mistake of his life seven years ago. Years wasted because he'd never stopped to consider that Chloe was innocent.

'Chloe, I should've stopped and listened to you, not walked away head held too high, thinking I was right and you were wrong.'

'Yes, you should,' she said gently.

They reached the Thai restaurant. 'You stay with

Genie. I'll grab the food.' The dog was looking impatient to keep moving. Probably ready for her own dinner and to curl up somewhere warm.

'Sure.' Chloe drew a breath. 'Dev—'

There she went again. Dev. His toes tingled. He loved it. Warm fuzzies filled him as memories of wonderful times spent with Chloe rose. 'Yes?'

'Do you honestly, truly accept that I didn't play around on you?'

'Yes, I honestly, truly believe you didn't.' It was true. Completely and utterly true. He did accept it. He breathed easier than he had for days. His chest filled with oxygen and hope. His head swam with a longing he hadn't known in for ever. In seven years, really.

You're jumping in where you haven't been invited. Rushing towards Chloe and what you used to have without thinking it through.

He frowned. He didn't want logic to intrude on this moment, but it seemed his brain was insistent on applying caution this time even though his heart seemed to be stubbornly clinging to the hope.

'You want me to go in?' Chloe asked with a frown between her beautiful eyes.

'No. I've got it.' It might be taking him a few minutes to remember why they'd stopped outside a Thai restaurant but, hey, he was on to it now. His feet were bouncing as he entered the building.

They didn't stop bouncing on the way back to Chloe's small cottage, or when he followed her inside and closed the door behind them. It was like coming home, except Chloe hadn't owned a house when he first knew her. When they'd been together they'd spent many nights in his apartment in St Helier's, overlooking the Auckland Harbour. Posh, she'd called it. Normal, was his response. She'd frowned at that, but did her best to make herself comfortable, though sometimes he'd thought she preferred her cramped one-bed flat.

Chloe tapped his arm. 'I'll feed Genie, if you want to grab some plates from the cupboard. There's an open bottle of Chardonnay in the fridge if you'd like a glass. No red, I'm sorry.'

'Chardonnay's fine.' So might salt water be at the moment. 'Shall I pour you one, too?'

Her eye roll had improved with time. Sarcastic and cheeky all rolled into one. 'What do you think?'

'I'll take that to be no, then.' He looked around the neat kitchen space and figured the cupboard above the fridge might hold glasses.

Neat? Sort of. Devlin took another look. Everything was in its place. The glasses in the cupboard he opened were lined up, but not as perfectly as they once would've been. The wooden shelf gleamed but there was a hint of dust towards the back. Control freak Chloe had backed off somewhat when it came to keeping her life orderly. She'd driven him crazy with her need to have every single item in the kitchen, lounge, bathroom, bedroom, in the right place, facing the correct way. It had been her way of controlling life, of stating, 'I am Chloe Rasmussen. Don't mess with me.' Seemed she didn't need to put that out there quite as strongly any more. She'd found her strength inside herself. It had always been there, though too easily knocked aside when she was younger.

A wave of pure happiness for Chloe washed over Devlin. He was glad. She deserved to be able to stand on her own two feet and face, without flinching at, everything the world liked chucking at people. Though if he still knew anything about her, she'd be holding her breath at the same time.

'What's up? You forgotten how to pour a glass of wine?'

The bottle was in his hand, the glasses on the bench before him, and, yes, he was in la-la land. Again. 'Want to show me?' At least they could still tease each other and not wonder where it might lead. But, hell, he so wanted it to lead to her bedroom.

The bottle hit the rim of one of the glasses, shattered it into countless shards. He was mortified!

'You've definitely forgotten.' Chloe laughed. 'Give me that before you do any more damage.'

'Sorry. Where's the dustpan?' Chloe wasn't about to get glass in her fingers. What had happened? His brain had bombed out over the idea of getting closer to Chloe. Hadn't he decided to keep the lid on his emotions around her? Time to suck it up and get on with being friendly but not too friendly.

'Here.' She was holding a brush and pan out. 'Though looks to me you shouldn't be allowed near that mess. Might cut yourself.'

That'd wake him up in a hurry. 'I'm fine.'

'If you say so.' She reached for the second, still-in-one-piece glass and put it at a safe distance from where he was cleaning up. Then she got another out of the cupboard and filled them both with the wine. 'There. That's how it's done.' Her cheeky grin hit him hard.

'I learn something new every day. Got anything I can wrap the glass in?'

A roll of paper towels appeared. 'Go easy or I might have to do some stitching on your hands. Although, if I did, you'd actually be impressed at my skill.'

'That's right, you did mention you made your own

clothes now, but I'm still trying to picture you at a table operating a sewing machine.'

'Peek in the second door on the right past my bathroom and you'll believe it. There's fabric for every occasion in there.'

'Any other skills you gained over in Italy you'd like to mention?'

She locked her eyes on him and laughed. 'The only one I'll admit to is that I learnt to live without all the hang ups I used to carry around.'

He wouldn't think about what else she might've got up to. Instead, he smiled and said, 'You wouldn't have laughed about that before.'

'No, I wouldn't have.' Her laughter didn't wane at all. Those eyes he'd never quite forgotten still sparkled with happiness and amusement.

'You're pleased to be able to surprise me, aren't you?'

'You bet.' Turning away, she got out plates and cutlery, and began taking the food containers out and removing the lids. 'This smells so yummy. We'll sit at the counter.' She set two places side by side, though not so close they'd touch each other every time they moved.

Not across from one another at the table? Too intimate? But then Chloe wasn't acting as though she wanted to get close to him. Wise woman. There was nothing to be gained other than more heartbreak. Because despite how he was coming to feel for her, getting back together wouldn't be wise. Too much water had flowed under the bridge. He might have apologised for his mistakes, but would they be thrown in his face every time they had an argument? Even if she was interested in trying again, would she ever really trust him with her heart again after he'd let her down so badly? Did he deserve her to?

He handed her one of the glasses, and carefully tapped it with the second one. 'Here's to catching up, and to working together.' That was the right tone, wasn't it? She couldn't get upset about that, surely?

Chloe tapped back. 'To us.' Her lips touched the rim of the glass.

And his stomach did a backward flip. Those lips used to be manna from heaven on his hot skin. Man, could they work him up into a state in no time at all. Sinking onto a stool beside the counter, he dragged his hungry gaze away to focus on the rice and green curried pork. At least, that was what he thought he was looking at. Not that the food was making him feel any less wound up.

For all he knew, the takeout could be something Genie had dragged in. The longing for Chloe was blotting out everything else in his head. This was going to be the longest meal he'd ever eaten. And probably the most tasteless. 'Can I put some music on?'

'Help yourself to my sound system,' she replied over the rattle of dog biscuits filling Genie's metal bowl.

'You've got Joe Cocker.' His heart rate started increasing as he flicked through the options then turned up the volume. Cocker and Chloe dancing naked went together as did cheese and macaroni.

'Yeah.' She laughed, leaning one hip against the counter and raising her glass to those desirable lips.

He was incapable of stopping himself. Ignoring every single thing he'd just told himself about holding back from her, he crossed the room, taking the glass from her hand and leading her into the centre of the lounge. 'Remember this?' he whispered in her ear.

Her head nodded against his chest. 'Of course.' And

then she was swinging her hips and kicking off her shoes, all in one graceful and sexy move.

His heart landed in his throat. His body tightened. And tightened some more as her arms rose above her head, lifting that figure enhancing blouse to expose skin. Warm, soft skin his fingers remembered too well. 'Chloe,' he croaked. 'Please stop, unless—' His throat blocked the rest of his sentence.

'Unless what, Dev?' Her voice was a purr as she danced in time to the croaky voice coming through the speakers.

'Damned if I know,' he growled and reached out to her.

She shimmied up to him, rubbed her belly against him, tightening him further. 'I don't know if this is right or wrong. I only know I want you right now, Dev. I need you.'

'Likewise, Chloe.' With that, he let go of the last knot in his heart holding him back and hauled her up against his whole length, lowering his mouth to claim hers. Tomorrow was another day.

Their bodies moved in unison to the rhythm beating through the room. Their mouths held each other, touching, tasting, feeling, remembering, creating new sensations. And when they couldn't take any more Devlin lifted Chloe in his arms and laid her on the rug in the centre of the room, leaning over her, reaching for the buttons preventing access to her hot pink skin.

Chloe brushed his hand aside, slid one button free, and ran her fingers over his face. The next button and she touched his chest with feather-light softness. The third button and her hand wrapped around the bulge pushing out the front of his trousers.

Taking a lace-covered nipple between his teeth, he

nipped and licked. Held her arms above her head to give him time to bring her to a first climax while some of his control still remained. Her body shuddered and strained against him, her eyes wild with desire.

Somehow her hands were free and pulling at his belt, shoving his trousers down, reaching for him to hold and rub and squeeze, rushing him towards his own climax. Kissing a trail from her breast to her navel to the edge of her lacy knickers, he held onto the need threatening to explode out from where her hands were working their magic. Then somehow they were together in all senses of the word, their bodies joined, moving in a rhythm all of their own.

And then he knew; *this* was home.

Chloe closed her front door behind Devlin and leaned back against it, deafened by the pounding in her chest. Dev had just spent the last three hours here, in her house. They'd made love on the rug to the sound of their favourite music. They'd finally shared their take-aways at the counter, drinking wine and talking almost nonstop, and then gone to her bedroom and loved each other again with abandon.

The Devlin she remembered never lost track of what he was up to. Ahh, except when he was making love and losing control of his emotions. Oh, yeah, then he was a different man. One she could lose herself in all too easily. She had to stop going on memories and live with the updated version of the man who'd once meant everything to her.

She'd tried so hard to keep her distance from him, but now she'd given in, it wasn't enough.

A groan escaped her lips. She was done for. Back in love with the only man who'd ever made her feel special and loved and wanted. Back in love? Or had she never left? Thought she'd already worked this out. Didn't matter. She'd also decided not to do a thing about it because she needed to protect her heart, and here she was regretting letting Devlin leave the house after dinner.

The phone played its rock tune signalling a call.

'Go away. I'm not in the mood for talking.' But she headed to the kitchen where the phone lay on the bench. It might be Devlin. Hope dropped away. 'Hi, Mum. How's things? You're still taking it easy, I hope?'

'You think I'd get away with doing anything when Jack hovers around all the time, making sure I barely move off the couch from one hour to the next? I swear when I'm up and about properly he's going to regret being so caring, yet totally bossy.'

'You wouldn't change a thing.' Even to Chloe's ears, her laugh was a bit sharp.

'What's up?'

'Nothing.' Like her mother was going to believe that. 'I might be coming down with a cold.'

'That's why you sound tense and worried? Come on, spill, my girl.'

No getting away from this. 'Devlin was here. We shared a takeaway.'

'You're getting along all right, then?'

'Unbelievably well, which is hard to get my head around.' Kisses all round. Throw in making love. Yes, they were getting along just fine.

'You thought you'd both be sniping at each other because of the past. I understand that, but it has been a long time. I know how much you've grown and changed. Can the same be said for Devlin?' Her mother had always adored Devlin and had been devastated when his accusations had come to light. After that she hadn't had a good word to say about him. Actually, she hadn't said much at all. Protective mum to the fore.

'It's not so obvious, but yes, he seems less wound up and more at ease with who he is and what he's doing.' Pants on fire. If that reaction to her naked body wasn't obvious then she was on another planet. Deep breath. 'Like he's the Devlin I always thought was there, waiting to qualify and settle into the life he'd dreamed of.'

'It's possible these years apart have been good for you and your relationship.'

Chloe stared at her phone. Did her mother have some power that let her 'see' things? Putting the phone against her ear again, she asked, 'Did I hear right? You think Devlin and I could make a go of being together again? When you never had a nice thing to say about him after he kicked me out of his life?'

'What Devlin did was wrong. I told him so.'

'You what?' This was something new.

'I went and saw him, told him he had no right to insult my daughter like that, and he'd better sort his act out. Oh, and I added that he would never be welcome in our family again. I'm sorry, I shouldn't have done that, but he had to know who was right, and that you came first. Always.'

Her mother's loyalty had been unfailing throughout her life. As was Jack's. She couldn't help smiling.

'Thanks, Mum.' She'd expect nothing less. Even when it was her job to stick up for herself. Her mother was the best. 'But you just said our relationship might have gained something for the time that's gone by.'

'Yes.' Then her mother was silent.

Chloe waited.

'You met Devlin too soon. You were still finding your feet after Stephen, you were deep into your nursing training, and weren't really ready to settle down for good. Devlin was busy training to become a doctor, then an emergency specialist, and that took a lot out of him. Plus he had an extremely demanding family to deal with. Naturally you've both changed, matured, so it's possible those feelings you had for each other could always come back.'

Come back? They hadn't really gone away, as far as she was concerned. Not, not telling her mum that. 'Mum,' Chloe growled. 'You're thinking I want this to happen?'

'I have known you all your life.'

Therein lay the problem. Her mother rarely got things wrong about her daughter. Still, it didn't mean her mum was right about her and Devlin though.

Except she'd already admitted she still loved him. *And* kissed him like they belonged together, made love with him like there was no tomorrow. 'I've got to go. Genie needs to go out before settling in for the night.'

'It's barely gone eight o'clock.' Her mother laughed.

'I'm tired. We have the RSV filling the wards and our department.' Throw in nine people from a bus that rolled off the Remutaka Hill, two suspected cardiac arrests and a few other minor problems and there hadn't been time to think, let alone keep her energy levels at a peak.

'Just don't make any rash decisions.'

Too late. Maybe not a decision exactly, but her body had certainly shown her beyond doubt how she felt about Dev. 'No, Ma. Talk tomorrow.' If it was a little quieter than today, and *if* there were no distractions in uniform looking so sexy her blood didn't cool once all shift.

'I'll phone you.' Which meant there was no avoiding her mum and all the questions she'd probably come up with overnight.

Heading for the bathroom, Chloe flicked the shower on to hot and stripped off her clothes, rolling her aching shoulders and tight neck. It had been a hectic thirteen hours. Spending time with Dev out of the department had been good for her soul, helped her unwind.

Standing under the gushing water, she closed her eyes and tipped her head back, drowning herself in the welcome heat.

Dev believed her. He accepted she hadn't done the dirty on him.

Her eyes flew open. He really believed her. She still struggled to accept that after all this time. Yes, he'd changed in lots of ways. And he was prepared to stop and listen to her, had admitted he'd been wrong and apologised. But there was still one thing she hadn't mentioned to him yet. How would he react when she told him about the baby she'd lost? Would he be relieved because they hadn't been ready to be parents yet? Hurt that they'd lost a child? Upset that she still hadn't told him when she'd had plenty of opportunity to do so after his arrival here? They were supposed to be friends, if nothing else. So why hadn't she told him? Had she still not trusted him to say and do the right thing? No, it was because she'd been reeling from his reappearance in her life and she'd been trying to find solid ground before having such an emotional discussion. Hopefully, he'd understand why she'd kept it to herself.

She was supposed to be so much stronger these days, and if she didn't try to build on what they had now, she'd never know if they could make it work. One thing she was absolutely certain of: she loved him. So they needed to be able to move forward without anything holding them back. Which meant telling him about the baby.

'Chloe, you're in charge of zone green today,' Devlin informed her as she entered the department at sixty forty-five the next morning. 'And before you even begin to think you're getting off lightly, we already have three toddlers and two sixty-year-olds with RSV and two men awaiting surgery after a brawl at a pub in the early hours this morning.'

'Knew I shouldn't have got out of bed.' She laughed, then blushed and had to look away.

Dev's eyes widened and a look of need flitted across them.

She smiled. Life felt that good this morning. But there was no time to do anything about that. There was work to do, patients to help, and a handover to deal with. 'Guess I haven't got time to grab a mug of tea, then.'

'There's one on the bench with your name on it,' Devlin told her. 'I saw you coming along the footpath as I entered the hospital.'

'You're a champ. It was chilly out there this morning.' She picked up the tea and took a sip. 'Perfect.' A good guess or he'd remembered how she liked it? More likely he'd observed her making her own over the last few days.

'Why do you walk to work in the dark and cold?'

'It's not far, and parking costs aren't cheap around here. I always drive if it's raining or when I'm on nights though. Don't fancy meeting someone after they've been drinking at a pub. You've been here a while, I take it?'

He was meant to start at the same time she did. 'Yeah, couldn't sleep.' Devlin glanced at her, looked away. 'Figured I'd be more useful in here than at home trying to work out how to fix the leaking tap in my kitchen. Remind me to call the plumber at a sensible hour, will you?'

'How long's it been dripping?' There was a collection of grips and vices in her garage for that sort of problem.

'It was like it when I moved in, but I've never got around to doing anything about it. For some reason it annoyed me more than normal this morning.'

'Nothing to do with your sleepless night?' She cracked him a grin. This should be good. He'd sworn he was exhausted when he'd headed home last night. 'I'll call in after work and see what I can do for you.'

The pen in his fingers slid onto the counter. Those beautiful eyes were on stalks. 'You what?'

'I'm amazing at plumbing.'

'And changing electrical plates,' Jazz said from the other side of the hub.

'That's illegal,' Dev said.

'Only if someone finds out.' Jazz laughed. 'Our Chloe's a whizz with all sorts of minor repair jobs around the house if you're in a spot of trouble.'

'Jazz, shut it, will you?' Chloe tried not to join in her friend's laughter. 'I only do the straightforward chores. Let me know when you're going to be at home and I'll drop around with my gear.' It was time she saw his apartment anyway.

Jazz piped up. 'She doesn't come with a tool belt on her hips.'

Devlin just shrugged, continuing to look bemused.

'Right, shouldn't we be getting the show on the road?' Chloe sat before a computer and brought up the screen. By the looks of things, ED was already near to full capacity and rush hour was only beginning. It was a rare day someone didn't crash a car, fall off a bike, or trip out of a bus on the way to work.

If only that was all, Chloe thought as, many hours later, she wiped down the fevered body of three-year-old Jarvis suffering from RSV. The virus had gone rampant this winter. 'Hey, little man, let me put this under your arm, okay? That's a good boy.' She slid the thermometer in place, and held it there, keeping an eye on her watch.

'Is he worse?' Jarvis's father asked. 'He looks redder than he did half an hour ago.'

'His temperature might be peaking.' It was another degree higher than the last reading. She only hoped this was the peak, and there wasn't worse to come. Forty point five degrees was too high, almost dangerous. 'I'm going to talk to the doctor.'

'Paediatrics is overflowing,' Devlin told her when he heard Jarvis's temperature was still rising.

She already knew that. It was the reason the emergency department was chock full. So was the waiting room, where more people were waiting to be admitted and seen by a doctor. 'Are they taking more patients, or do we keep them here?' A paediatrician had been in the department most of the day, trying to keep up with the stream of sick children.

'Clare is trying to arrange for them to go upstairs, but we're waiting on orderlies to set up extra beds.' Devlin yawned. 'And I thought yesterday was busy. Looks like we'll be here later than ever.'

'There goes fixing your leaking tap today.' She tried for a smile, pushing the exhaustion aside for a brief moment.

'Always another day. I'm not there to get annoyed by it so it doesn't matter. Anyway, you don't have to do it. I'll get around to phoning a plumber some time.' He stepped around the curtain of the cubicle where Jarvis lay curled up against his dad, looking frightened. 'Hello, Jarvis. I like your shirt. That elephant looks really cool jumping over the rocks like that.'

The little boy glanced at his shirt and back at Devlin.

'Is he going to be all right?' the father asked.

Devlin spoke in a steady voice that gave out confidence even when no one knew how long it would be before they could get Jarvis's temperature down or if it might go even higher. 'We have to continue monitoring his temperature. I hope to have Jarvis moved to the paediatric ward within an hour, where the paediatric doctors and nurses can watch him continuously. He'll be more comfortable up there without other patients coming and going and creating noise and distress. The children's ward is full beyond capacity, but it is still a much more comfortable place for him to be right now.'

'You haven't really answered my question.'

Devlin sighed. 'You're right. As long as Jarvis's temperature doesn't keep rising he'll be okay. It could take a day or a few days to get it back to near normal and until then he will be kept in hospital.'

'Why so many cases? Is this something new? I've never heard of it before.'

'The virus has been around for years, but normally we don't get an outbreak like this. It's affecting the youngsters and elderly in particular. We believe the children are hardest hit because of Covid and being in lockdown so much last year. They weren't mixing with other kids and, therefore, weren't building a natural immunity to various bugs and viruses.'

The father nodded slowly. 'That makes sense, I guess. Another thing to blame on Covid.'

Chloe agreed. 'There's been a few things we've all

blamed on that virus. And still do.' The world wasn't out of trouble yet. She held a bottle of water to Jarvis's lips. 'Here, Jarvis. Drink some more water for me.'

Jarvis shook his head and pulled back from the bottle.

His father took it from her. 'Hey, Jarv, do this for Daddy, eh? You drink some and I'll drink some from my bottle. Okay?'

Big eyes focused on his father, and Jarvis slowly opened his mouth. He took a few sips and pulled away.

'That's the boy. My turn.' The father picked up another bottle from the bedside table and took some gulps. 'See? I took some big sips. I want you to try to do that too.'

Jarvis didn't move. Stared at his bottle in his dad's hand.

'Go on. Give it a go.' Chloe held her hand up, ready to high-five him.

The boy tipped his head to stare at her.

For a long moment she thought he was going to refuse. She winked.

And finally, Jarvis took the bottle in both hands and drank some water.

'Go, man.' Reaching out with her hand, she tapped his. 'You are a star.' Until next time she needed him to drink some more. To the father, she said quietly, 'Keep trying to get him to take a few sips every little while. He's burning up so the more fluids on board, the better.' There was no chance Jarvis would drink too much. He just wasn't interested. 'I'll pop back in a few minutes. I've got another patient to see now.'

Devlin followed her out of the cubicle. 'You have a knack of getting little kids to do as you ask.'

'And I didn't even have to bribe him.' She stepped

into another cubicle and up to the heart monitor attached to Daphne Harroway, very aware of Devlin right behind her. Did he want to be a dad some day? He'd be awesome. A great role model, supportive, loving and loyal; all the things kids needed and wanted. She'd been aware of him all day, even when they weren't working alongside each other. Seemed that he'd got under her skin and wasn't going anywhere. There to stay. Which didn't bode well for getting much sleep in the nights ahead. 'No changes.' Leaning close to their patient, she said, 'Daphne, can you hear me?'

No response.

Taking the woman's hand in hers, Chloe tapped her fingers one by one. 'Daphne, can you feel this? Squeeze my hand if you can.'

'Nothing?' Devlin asked. 'I'd be surprised if there was.'

The woman had been brought in from a car accident in an unconscious state and Devlin had diagnosed swelling to the brain, caused most likely by severe whiplash during the impact. There were no other injuries so they'd put her on oxygen and she was about to be moved to the neurology department.

'Have we been able to contact any relatives yet?' Dev asked as he read the monitor's printout.

'The police said they've got an address for a son, but no phone number so they've sent a constable out to Lower Hutt to make contact.' She couldn't imagine being in a situation like this and not having her mother or a close friend at her side. It would be frightening, though she was thinking as if she'd be aware, which Daphne clearly wasn't.

'I'd annoy the hell out of you by talking at you until

you came round,' Dev said quietly from the other side of the bed.

'Did I speak out loud?'

'You have the most readable eyes I've ever come across.' He grinned. Then he quickly looked serious again. 'I hope they find someone to be with her soon. A familiar voice can sometimes get through to even the most damaged brain.'

A nurse appeared in the cubicle. 'Devlin, you're needed in Resus. Forty-one-year-old male, severe stroke.'

'Coming. Join me when you can, Chloe.' He was gone.

Almost as though he hadn't been there, except he had. Her skin told her so with the tightening it did, and how the hairs lifted whenever he spoke. 'Sure,' she answered to his back. Straight and strong. That was Devlin.

Reading the monitor quietened the sensations. The oxygen pump's steady in-out movements lifting and dropping Daphne's chest kept Chloe focused and soon thinking only of her patient and not one hot, distracting doctor.

Until her shift ended, and she was able to take a break, grab a coffee and something to eat before starting on the next shift to help out until the department became less like a warzone and more of a calm, quiet place for sick people to see a doctor and be monitored, discharged or admitted to another department.

'I thought Wellington ED would be a little less hectic than the last one I worked in,' Devlin said as he joined her and the other staff who'd agreed to stay on for a few hours. 'I couldn't have been more wrong if I tried.' He had a plate of food in front of him that was going to take an hour to get through.

'Why would it be any different?' someone asked.

'Wishful thinking on my part, I suppose.' His smile was tired, and those engaging eyes were less twinkly than usual.

Chloe guessed he felt as shattered as she did as she bit into a bagel filled with chicken and salad. Everyone probably did, she admitted. They'd been working extra hours for a couple of days now. It wasn't the hours, or even the work, that got to them. It was the stress when a patient didn't make it out of the department alive, or when someone was so severely injured their future looked grim, or when one of those little kids with RSV was coughing enough to make their lungs scream with pain and their eyes spill buckets of tears as they clung to their parents in fear. Yeah, those were the things that exhausted Chloe, and the people she worked alongside. There was no getting away from the mental anguish. No one wanted to see a patient's pain, or their loved ones' distress. It was so damned hard.

But they all put on their smiley faces and got on with what was required.

And she still loved being a nurse. All of the job, not only the nice and fuzzy moments when she got to see a patient go home happy and out of pain or danger. Growing up and often feeling lonely, she'd still always wanted to help others, maybe because deep inside she'd felt they might return the kindness in some way. These days she wasn't hanging out for other people's acceptance. She had finally figured out that not everyone would like her and that was fine.

Chloe pushed her empty plate aside and sipped her coffee. Her stomach rumbled, still hungry. Reaching over the table, she snagged an egg sandwich off Devlin's plate.

'Hey, leave that. I'm starving,' he growled before biting into the ham sandwich in his hand.

'Me, too. I'll buy you a chocolate muffin if you finish everything on your plate.'

'Yes, Mum.'

'Ha-ha. You think?'

'What? That you could be a mum?' Devlin asked. Then his head reared back as shock struck. 'Umm, delete that. I never said it.'

'Why not?' Chloe asked around the sudden lump blocking the back of her throat. 'It's not an unreasonable question.' Most people would ask something similar if the conversation was heading in that direction. No one else was looking at them strangely. But she knew, deep inside where her heart was thumping, that he was thinking of her, and their past. They'd talked about children. Of course they had. They were going to get married and having a family was part of it. But now? Devlin had asked about her becoming a mother and then got flustered. She didn't follow where he was going with this, except to wonder if maybe he still did have feelings for her. 'I certainly hope I will have children some time.' She regarded the man before her, knowing he really was the only one she could ever contemplate settling down and having babies with.

When to tell him about the baby she'd lost? When she was surer of where they were going with this new relationship, perhaps? Or should she just do it as soon as their frantic work schedules permitted? What if she hadn't miscarried? She'd have been a mum for more than six years by now. Devlin would've been a dad. She closed her eyes. After all these years, she could still tear up thinking about that. Devlin holding his baby, cuddling and hugging, murmuring sweet nothings when baby wasn't sleeping, holding a bottle of warm milk to his or her mouth and watching as baby sucked and swallowed.

'I can see you on your hands and knees playing games with a couple of toddlers.' Devlin's shock was ebbing, being replaced with amusement. 'You'll be good at being a mum.' Not amusement, then, but something more like wistfulness.

If only he knew. 'I had a good role model.' This was getting harder and harder to continue talking about casually. 'Do you still think you'd like to be a father one day?' she asked.

'Absolutely. Whenever we used to talk about kids, I'd get quite excited. That hasn't changed.' His smile was lopsided. 'Imagine where we'd be if we'd stayed together. Ankle biters distracting us left, right and centre.'

'That many?' She had to tell him about the miscarriage as soon as possible. But not here.

'Maybe.' He picked up another sandwich and started scrolling through something on his phone.

Conversation finished. Thank goodness for that. It couldn't do anything other than stir up feelings best left alone when they had to get back to the department soon. Up at the display cabinet she chose two muffins, zapped her card, and returned to the table. 'Here you go. Get that into you, and keep your energy levels up for the next few hours.'

CHAPTER EIGHT

'GET A GOOD SLEEP,' Devlin told Chloe as she clambered out of his top-of-the-range car outside her house. 'At least we've got a straight forty-eight hours off work.'

She leaned against the door, wobbly with exhaustion. 'Think I'll be comatose for all of that.' Shadows darkened her face and her eyes had lost all their sparkle.

It had been a long week, working so many extra hours he'd lost count. 'What about Genie?' He could see her standing on her back legs at the fence, waiting for Chloe with a lead in her mouth.

'The girl next door has been taking her for walks after school every day.' Chloe looked around. 'Hey, girl. Not now, eh?' She turned back to him. 'Thanks for the ride. Catch up later.'

'That's a date.' Driving away, he watched Chloe in the rear-view mirror as she went through her gate to be greeted by an exuberant Genie. Chloe leaned over her, rubbing her head, and no doubt murmuring soft words of endearment. 'Lucky dog.'

Within minutes he was passing the Italian restaurant where they'd had a meal nearly two weeks ago. Was it really only two weeks since he'd first seen Chloe performing compressions on that woman on ED's reception floor? Two weeks ago he'd never have believed he could get so rattled by her again. But he was, and nowhere close to getting over the feelings of need and love that filled him all the time. Yes, love. As in feel it in every bone of his body. As in want to look out for her, care for her, make sure she wanted for nothing.

He hit the brake too hard and the car lurched sideways. Belatedly turning on the indicator, he pulled to the side of the road, waited for a gap in traffic and turned around to head back to the restaurant. It was after eight in the evening. He hadn't eaten since midday, and doubted Chloe had either. Tired as they were, food was important, too. As were a long hot shower and fresh clothes. Anyway, they could sleep together in her bed. Okay, possibly after some activity but what better way to drift off to sleep than in the warm haze after sex?

Striding into the restaurant, he went straight up to Giuseppe. 'Hello. I know you don't usually do takeaways, but could you possibly do a couple of meals for Chloe and me? We've been working every hour there is and are exhausted. I want to take some food to her house and make sure she eats before falling fast asleep on her face.'

Giuseppe studied him. 'I wondered why she hadn't been in this week.'

'It's been the week from hell, and every time she was asked to put in extra hours she agreed straight away.'

'That's our Chloe. Puts everyone else first. Right, we'll put something together for you both. What were you thinking?'

'Whatever is Chloe's favourite, and— I don't know. What's the dish of the day?'

'Fettuccine Alfredo.'

'Perfect. One of those, please. Unless that's Chloe's favourite and I need to order something else?'

Giuseppe was still watching him closely. 'She's into meatballs and tomato and garlic sauce. You don't know her that well, then?'

Here we go.

The family to the fore. He understood this man and his brother were like family to Chloe. He was glad she had people there for her, but he was here now. No point in getting on the wrong side of Giuseppe though. Nothing to be gained, and possibly a lot to lose. 'When I first met Chloe she didn't know Italian from Chinese, and that was just the food. She certainly couldn't speak a word of your language and now it appears she's as near to fluent it makes no difference.' A softness slipped through him. Chloe had grown a lot in the years he hadn't been a part of her life. Grown in ways he, and he suspected she, would never have guessed.

'*Sì.* Almost fluent. She's a very tough *signorina.*' Giuseppe was still watching him. 'You care about her?'

'Very much.' Shouldn't he be telling Chloe this first? But he was being studied like a specimen in a Petri dish and wanted Giuseppe to understand he wasn't playing games with Chloe. He was for real. 'We were a couple a long time ago, then broke up. Now I'd like to think we're starting out again.'

'She never talks about her past.'

'That's Chloe. Keeps things to her chest. I hurt her back then.' Something he was still getting to grips with, but did accept. Locking his own formidable glare on the man opposite him, he said, 'But I'm hoping she'll give me a second chance. Any more than that I'll leave to her to tell you if she wants to.'

The silence between them was accentuated by one of those odd moments when the restaurant patrons all went quiet at the same moment.

Then Giuseppe nodded. 'Fair enough. Now, about the meals. They'll be about thirty minutes. Do you want a glass of wine while you wait?'

Relief expanded Devlin's chest. 'Thanks, but I'm heading home to get cleaned up. I'll leave you my phone number in case I fall asleep in the shower.'

He didn't fall asleep in the shower, as warm and relaxing as it was. But he was late picking up the meals because his mother interrupted his plans by phoning to ask him to go home next weekend to attend a dinner being put on in recognition of his father's support for the local school's new sports facility.

'That's very short notice, Mum.'

'I know, darling, but it's not as though you're busy with anything outside your work in Wellington. You haven't been there long enough to become involved in organisations, and anyway, what would be the point? You'll be moving back here before you know it.'

'You need to get that idea out of your head, Mum. As far as I'm concerned this is a permanent move.' Like Patrick's was to Melbourne.

'Now, now. You know you're just flexing some muscle, proving a point, since you didn't get the position at Auckland General you wanted so badly. You'll be back.'

He'd turned down the job after he'd been headhunted because he didn't see eye to eye with the hospital's CEO over patient numbers. The woman thought beds should be available for urgent cases only, and not those patients who had nowhere else to go. 'Right, back to the dinner. I won't be coming up. I've got other things on, including work. You have to accept I will not drop everything every time there's an event on that you're going to. I'm sorry, but that's over for me now.' Quite frankly, he didn't care any more. He'd given so much of his life to supporting his parents when it should've been the other way round.

'Devlin, I don't like your attitude. We expect you to be here.'

'I know you do, but I cannot, will not, hop on a plane every time you call. I can't do it any more. I need to live my life, not yours and Dad's. It's not what you want to hear, I know, but I am not a drone.' His stomach crunched. He did feel bad, but he'd been raised to feel bad when he didn't bend over backwards to appease his parents. He'd had it up to his throat and higher, trying to please them. He'd begun to wonder if they'd ever seen his life through his eyes.

'This is Patrick's fault. He's fooled you into thinking his way is much better. It isn't, Devlin.'

Since moving south and working with Chloe he'd already started to understand how much he'd fallen for the lies and false compliments back home.

'Devlin, darling, you mustn't think like that. I'm only asking you for what's best for the family.'

Here we go. Heard it all before. Far too often. 'Sorry, Mum, but I won't be there next weekend. Or any other in the foreseeable future. Now, I've got to go. I'm meant to be somewhere.'

'You've got a woman already? Who is she?' Was that hope or annoyance in her tone?

He couldn't tell. What was more, he didn't care. Which didn't make him feel pleased with himself, but he wasn't changing course. Chloe was getting dinner tonight, and he was delivering it. Chloe. Hell. His mother would have fifty fits if she knew Chloe was back in his life. She'd always thought Chloe wasn't good enough for her son. 'Got to go. Talk again.' He hung up before the usual tirade began in full.

He was going to take a meal around to the most amazing woman he'd ever known, and he was going to relish any time he spent with her. He'd stuffed up completely years ago and now he wanted to make up for that. Both for Chloe, and for himself. *If* she'd let him back into her life as more than a work colleague and a friend.

His phone rang again as he was heading out to the lift. 'Devlin Walsh.'

'You're not asleep, then.' Giuseppe chuckled. 'Dinner's getting cold.'

As if. That was the last thing Giuseppe and Lorenzo would allow to happen. Guess that meant he'd passed the test. He had no doubt the Italian wouldn't be laughing if he disapproved of him. 'I'll be there in five.'

When Chloe opened her front door to his knocking, his heart hit the bottom of his stomach. Wrapped in a thick, shapeless sky-blue robe, her long hair hanging in wet lengths down her back, and her pale face devoid of make-up, she was it for him. This was Chloe as close to her real self as she could get. Memories of making love in the shower, of cuddling up on the sofa in their robes, of laughing and talking and kissing without trying to be perfect, flooded him. Time to stop remembering and start making new memories. If Chloe wanted to continue what they'd started, that was.

'Dev? What's wrong?'

'N-nothing.' Everything. Here was the woman he was meant to spend his life with. And he'd gone and blown that out of the water seven years ago all because his past experience with Cath had tarred her with the same brush and let him believe she'd hurt him. What had he done to them both? Suddenly, he hated himself. Thrusting the bag containing their meals at her, he turned to go home. He couldn't do this. Sitting across from her at the table while she sat there looking so love-able and warm and real would turn his stomach into a tight ball that wouldn't accept food, make his head ping off the walls with frustration and anger at himself for being such a fool. He waved over his shoulder. 'Enjoy your dinner.'

'Devlin, wait.' It was a demand, not a 'what have I done wrong?' query. So unlike how Chloe would've once spoken to him.

But no, he couldn't wait, or face her, or explain himself. This sense of failure was too raw, and too likely to cause trouble. They wouldn't be able to continue working together if Chloe knew how he felt about her. He'd have to quit his job and try to find another in the same region or pack up and move on again. After a few weeks? Giving up too quickly? It was so unlike him, he stumbled. 'I've got to go.'

A strong hand on his arm. 'No, Devlin, you don't. Come inside and at least have a drink.' She paused. Then after a moment, 'Please.' She spoke like a child begging someone to listen to her. And too many times she'd been denied.

His heart gave in. Hell, *he* gave in completely. Turning, he wrapped an arm over her shoulders, tucked her lithe body up against him, and took a step towards her home. And another, another. As though walking towards the noose, only it didn't feel terrifying. More electrifying and intense. As if there were a wall before him that he was going to step through and keep on going, with Chloe at his side. He was probably being a naïve idiot, but when his heart thumped and squeezed as though it couldn't get enough air to be going on with, he had to revive it.

And that meant going inside with Chloe and sharing

dinner—for starters. His fingers pressed deeper into her shoulder, held her tighter and closer. As if he'd finally come home after a long and lonely journey going nowhere.

Chloe used her hip to shut the door, not wanting to move out of Devlin's embrace. She felt as though she'd crossed a line with him, and the silly thing was she had no idea what had changed. Why she felt this way when she'd already admitted to herself she still loved him was a mystery. Perhaps she should just kiss him?

One glance at his face had her wondering if she'd be making the right move if she did. Devlin looked worried and frightened and—and loving. Loving of her? There was no one else here. But… What if—?

Grow up, Chloe. Be the strong woman you've become, not the self-doubting girl you once were.

With a dry mouth and trembling hands, she placed the bag containing dinner on the sideboard and turned to face Devlin.

Those intense cobalt eyes were watching her every move.

'Chloe?' he whispered.

That got to her as nothing else could. It was Devlin from the past, holding her heart in his hands. Slipping her arms around his neck, she stretched up on her toes and placed her mouth over his. 'Devlin,' she whispered in return. 'Devlin, I've missed you so much I can't tell you how I feel,' said so quietly he probably didn't hear a word.

Hands spread across her lower back, strong, firm and large. Familiar hands that knew her well, hands that she knew very well. 'Chloe, sweetheart, I've missed you, too.'

Her head spun. 'Really?'

'Yes, really.'

She'd said that louder than she'd thought. Maybe not such a bad thing after all. It was fine. Nothing was happening, except they were holding each other and admitting they'd missed one another, that was all. Her mouth opened, her lips moulded to his, and she pressed in for a kiss.

Instantly Dev was kissing her in return, deep and full and filled with longing, passion and memories. They were kissing as though their lives depended on it. It was a kiss that went on and on and was even better than any of the kisses they'd shared so far. She never wanted to stop, or to leave his arms again. Even better, it seemed he felt the same.

There was still a lot between them that needed sorting out before they took this too far, but she was hopeful they'd get there.

Dev shifted, now holding her even closer to that warm, masculine body as he kept kissing her.

To hell with being sensible. It was impossible when she needed him, wanted his naked body up against hers. Now. He was the only one she'd ever known such longing and escape with. Twisting in Devlin's arms, she found a hand and began pulling him along to her bedroom. Bedroom? Who needed a bed for this? Stopping, she pressed him against the wall and returned to kissing him. Her hands tugged at his jacket, pushing and pulling it off his shoulders and downward until his arms were free.

Shucking it away, he reached for her, lifting her up against him, his mouth still covering hers, his tongue rediscovering hers.

Chloe cried against his lips. More, more, more. His

skin was hot against her palms when she managed to shove her way under his clothing. His hard, throbbing need for her was pressing into her belly. Desire pulsed at her centre, ready for Devlin to join them together. Her fingers were thick and clumsy as she tried to undo the zip on his jeans.

His mouth jerked away from hers. 'Let me.' His hand pushed hers aside, then his jeans were sliding over his hips to his thighs, and beyond. And he was back to kissing her.

Even though it had only been a few days since they'd made love it wasn't enough. She'd missed this. Missed Dev. Missed *them*. Reaching for him, she wound her fingers around his need for her, absorbed the pulsing heat, the length, the passion she knew was coming.

Somehow without letting go of him, she managed to shove her knickers down till they reached her feet and she could step out of them, all the while sliding her hand up and down Devlin's response to her.

Then he was lifting her so she could wind her legs around his waist and take him inside. Fast. Hot. Deep. Her body was imploding, her head wasn't thinking, and her heart was dancing.

'Chloe, love, wow.' Moments later, Devlin was still holding her tight against him, breathing fast, and looking astonished and happy.

Thankfully, happy. She'd fall apart if he hadn't been happy. 'Yeah, Dev, wow.' Placing a kiss on his chin, she smiled with everything she had. 'We're still so good together.'

'We sure are. I can't believe how we do that. Read each other so easily and quickly. It's how we've always been together.' Was that longing of another kind in his voice? In his eyes?

'It is.' Snuggling into him, she couldn't stop smiling. Everything about her was warm, soft, tender, and so happy. Yep, she too was happy.

Somewhere her phone was ringing. 'I'll ignore that.'

'Might be important.' Devlin leaned back to look at her in his arms. 'Seriously.'

Nothing could be as important as being right here with Devlin. Nothing. No one.

'Come on. You'd better answer it.' He was heading towards her kitchen, where she thought the sound was coming from, his arms still wound around her.

Glancing at the screen, she grinned. 'Giuseppe. Is that where you bought dinner?'

'Yes. Bet he's ringing to check up on me.'

'Why?'

'I told him to prepare your favourite meal plus something for me. I think he worries about you, though I was only bringing around dinner.' Heat suffused his cheeks. 'Which is probably getting cold as we stand here practically naked, staring at a phone you don't seem to want to answer.'

Laughing, she picked up the phone. 'Hey, Giuseppe, dinner's delicious. Nothing less than I'd expect. The company's good, too. Let's catch up when I'm not working crazy hours.' She pressed off and put the phone back on the counter. 'Okay?'

Shaking his head at her, he grinned. 'I'd better grab the food so we can eat. Can't have you lying to your friend.'

'I'll get you an old robe Jack keeps here for whenever he and Mum stay. As much as I'd prefer you remained naked, it isn't that warm in here.' She glanced across at the firebox and groaned. A few bits of well-burnt wood glowed but it wasn't exactly a roaring fire. 'I did light it when I first got home but there hasn't been much time to add more wood.'

'Genie's curled into such a tight ball I'm surprised she's breathing.'

'I'm more surprised she hasn't been nudging me to do something about warming the house up.' That would've been an interesting interruption to what had been going on in the hallway. After handing the robe to Devlin, she threw a couple of pieces of pine at the firebox, rubbed Genie's head, and went to pour two glasses of Cabernet Merlot before sitting down to eat.

'You bought in red wine in case I visited?'

'Caught.' She grinned. So much for her plans of eating toast in bed before falling asleep for the next few hours. What an entrance Devlin had made. Food. Kisses to die for. And sex that cut through all the pain and cruel words of the past like a knife through soft butter. 'What made you decide to go buy me dinner instead of going home?'

'I was hungry, and I kept seeing your face, full of exhaustion, and figured, hey, why not share a meal together? It was something I could do for you.' Devlin drew a slow breath. 'Besides, I didn't want to go home to an empty apartment. Or stay there after I'd had a much-needed hot shower.'

He was lonely? Or at that point of tiredness where everything was too much of an effort to do just for himself? Winding her fingers around his hand on the counter, she said, 'I know that feeling. I'm glad you came back.' More than anything that's what had tickled her buttons tonight. Everything felt different between them. The underlying tension that crept up on her at unexpected moments at work seemed to have disappeared completely. Everything about her was relaxed. She was probably heading towards disaster. 'I mean that. We've got on well these past couple of weeks, but there have been times I've wondered where we might be headed. Now it seems like old times where everything happened fast and was so good.'

Careful, Chloe.

There was a lot to move on from still. Or was it best to let go of everything that had happened seven years ago, including the miscarriage, and just move forward? He had apologised for his mistakes. Going over and over what had happened and upsetting them both wouldn't be of any benefit to either of them and might even drag them down into a dark hole again.

Looking thoughtful, Devlin put the containers of food on the bench. 'Want these heated up? I'm okay with them as they are. We didn't spend a lot of time being distracted.' If he hadn't been smiling that gentle, loving smile she'd missed so much she might've wondered if he thought they'd been too rushed.

There was something he was avoiding saying. She still knew him that well at least. She also remembered that pushing him wouldn't get her anywhere, so, placing a hand on the container labelled meatballs, she shook her head. 'That's still very warm. It'll do fine.' She found plates and cutlery, and spoons to dish up. 'Let's eat. I'm starving.'

The silence between them as they ate their delicious pasta meals and drank their Cabernet Merlot was comfortable. An ease she hadn't felt in years. One she'd only known with this man, and then not often. Back then they'd both been busy with their careers, studying and working lots of shifts. There'd also been lots of questions for her about her future, mostly from his mother. Did she want to be a nurse once she was married, or was she going to become a society wife going to an array of functions to raise funds for those less well off? Her choice without a doubt was to continue in her chosen career. Nursing was so important to her, made her feel needed and filled her with joy at being able to help people who were medically in dire straits. It was hands-on caring, not anonymous support to people she'd never meet.

'You were never cut out to be like the women my mother mixes with.' Devlin was watching her as he forked up a mouthful of pasta.

'How is it you've always been able to read my mind so easily?' It was unreal at times. And a little nerve-racking. No secrets. Except, of course, the one time he'd misread her with dire consequences. But here she was, ready to try again. Try? Leap in, boots and all, more like.

'It's something we've always had. It was just there, if you remember.'

There wasn't much she had forgotten. Including how they liked to cuddle up in bed after making love, their legs entwined, arms around each other, and talk nonsense. 'Eat up. I'm shattered, and the bed's waiting.'

Devlin couldn't help thinking back to the many other occasions where they'd shared sex and a meal, and more sex, not least the night they'd spent together only a few days ago. And he couldn't wait to do it all again tonight. He forked up more pasta and sauce. 'Those guys really know how to cook. This is excellent.' So was Chloe. He grinned. Who'd have thought when he knocked on her door that they'd get wild and passionate within minutes? Certainly not him. He might've wanted it, but he would never have gone out to make it happen. But then, often when he and Chloe got together things just happened. They were meant for each other.

But he couldn't prevent a knot of fear from starting to wind up in his gut. Walking away from Chloe last time had decimated him. Even though he'd been proud and determined not to be taken for a ride by her, the pain of losing the love of his life, the woman he'd believed he'd spend the rest of his days with, had left him empty and bewildered. He couldn't face any of that again if this didn't work out for a second time.

Nor could Chloe.

'You've gone serious on me.'

'Sorry. I didn't mean to.' Which was true. Enjoying this evening was what was important. He did want to try again with Chloe. He'd stop overthinking everything and try to take it slowly.

A soft hand touched his. 'We're just being us. This is how we do things.'

He couldn't help himself. He laughed. 'You're right. So, let's finish up here and head to bed.' He wanted to make love to Chloe again, and sooner rather than later. And, honestly, he could do with some sleep. He'd forgotten how tired they'd been when they knocked off work. Too many distractions going on. Distractions he loved.

'The Devlin I know.' She was grinning and yawning at the same time.

Reminding him again that they both needed sleep. But it wasn't going to get in the way of him showing her how much he cared about her. He could do showing, but not telling. Not yet. That might take a little longer.

CHAPTER NINE

CHLOE STRETCHED HER legs to the end of the bed. At least she tried, but a big lump was in the way. 'Genie, what are you doing on my bed?'

'She's been there for a couple of hours,' grunted the other, warmer bundle beside her. 'I thought it must be normal for her to sneak onto the bed once you were asleep.'

'Yes, but I usually wake enough to send her back to her doggie bed. She probably thought if you're allowed here then why can't she join us?'

'And how do you explain that to a dog?' Devlin laughed.

'Down, Genie.'

'Like she's taking the slightest bit of notice, Mum.'

Chloe smiled and snuggled closer to that divine body. It was awesome having him here after staying with her the whole night, laughing, warm and cuddly in bed. This was something she hadn't had in years. Since he'd kicked her out of his life. The few men she'd dated and ended up in bed with hadn't given her the same sense of ease, of being at home and comfortable, and she'd never stayed with them all night long. Not one of them had attracted her in the off-the-chart way Dev did. He always had, and it seemed he always would. 'Genie, down.'

At the stronger command Genie slowly rose up and jumped down to the floor to stroll out of the room as though she were really the one in charge, not Chloe.

'Typical.' Rolling away from Dev before she lost her mind all over again, she tossed the covers aside and sat up. 'Better let her outside before there's trouble.' The last thing she wanted was any lovemaking to be interrupted by a dog with crossed legs. 'Want a cuppa?'

'Since it's the best offer I've had since I woke up an hour ago, I'll say yes.' Devlin shuffled up the bed and clasped his hands behind his head on the pillow.

Cheeky thing. 'Lots of milk and three sugars, right?'

He just laughed.

But he spluttered into his mug when he got exactly that. 'You— You—'

'Yes?' she asked smugly as she settled back into bed with her perfect cup of tea. 'Problem?' The laughter dried the moment he stood up from the bed stark naked. Her dream man. Not overly muscular but built exactly how he should be. From those gorgeous wide shoulders, his lean body tapered down to his tight abdomen, and beyond, to his strong thighs. Her mouth dried.

'It certainly appears you've got one.' He laughed. 'Would it be childish to say ha-ha before I go get a drinkable cup of tea?'

She finally managed to find her voice. 'Wouldn't matter if I said it was.' This was fun. Silly conversation, if it was even that, about nothing. Relaxing, endearing. Although she'd prefer it if that sexy body weren't striding out of her bedroom… 'Devlin,' she called seductively.

He flapped a hand over his shoulder. 'Keep your

tricks to yourself. I'm getting a cuppa before I do anything else. Then I'm going to see what's in your fridge and pantry that I can cook for breakfast.'

Reality check. 'You'll need to go to the supermarket if you want more than chocolate cereal.'

He poked his head back around the door. 'You still eat that disgusting stuff?'

'I need a chocolate fix some mornings, all right?'

'Chloe, Chloe. How do you look so stunning and lithe while eating sugar-laden cereals?'

'By running around the emergency department nonstop for at least eight hours on end, five days or nights a week.' Snuggling down the bed, she drank her tea. Thank goodness for days off. She wasn't due back at work until tomorrow night and she'd make the most of her time. She and the girlfriends were getting together for a birthday lunch today, and she might see if Devlin wanted to go to dinner somewhere tonight. There was something else she had to do, if she could remember it. Apart from the usual walks with Genie and doing the loads of washing that had accumulated over the week, that was.

Devlin went past the door, a steaming mug in one hand. 'Genie's out in the yard. I'm grabbing a shower, then heading out to get some supplies.'

'Don't forget I'm going to fix your leaking tap too.'

He appeared in the doorway, all of his splendid body on display for her to ogle. 'I'll cook you the best breakfast you've had in a long time and you can deal with the tap.' He disappeared, taking her favourite morning image with him.

'Come back and make love,' she whispered to thin air as the bathroom door snapped shut. Guess that meant she'd better get up and start her day.

* * *

Devlin sat back and rubbed his stomach. 'Nothing like a full breakfast to start the day.'

'Not bad.' Chloe grinned around the forkful of bacon, egg and hash brown she was slipping into her mouth.

Cooking didn't used to be her thing, and from what he'd seen of her pantry and fridge still wasn't. There was a stack of heat-and-eat meals in the fridge, but no fresh meat and eggs. Not a lot of butter or cooking oil anywhere to be seen either, which said it all. 'So you didn't learn to cook while you were in Italy?'

A smug look filled her gorgeous face. 'I can do a mean pizza, a not too bad macaroni cheese, and even a pasta dish with packet pasta and tinned sauce.'

'But you can change tap washers. Guess we all have our specialities.' He enjoyed cooking. It relaxed him at the end of a hectic day, and gave him pleasure to eat something he'd put together.

Now he did the same for Chloe. At least, he hoped she'd be happy with his input to their morning. Speaking of which. 'You got anything planned for the day?'

'First thing is a walk with Genie. Might go past the supermarket to pick up a few bits and pieces. I'm out of soap powder, for one.'

'Nothing that needs cooking?' He ducked as a scrunched-up paper serviette came his way.

'There's heaps of food in the fridge.' Chloe shoved out of her chair and dumped her plate in the sink. 'You want some bones, Genie?'

The dog's wagging tail whacked the chair her owner had just vacated.

'Thought so.' Chloe filled her mug with more tea. 'More for you, Dev?'

'Nah.' He began rinsing plates to put in the dishwasher. 'Two's more than enough. I feel wired already.'

'So you won't join us for coffee at Bengie's? It's part of the walk routine on my days off.'

'Bring it on. Coffee is my preferred kick-start to the day.'

A small frown appeared on that beautiful brow. 'That's new.'

He had always been a tea man, but not any more. Coffee and more coffee, to the point he sometimes got a throbbing headache, but it was worth it. 'Shows I'm open to change.' Wasn't he? He thought so. He could admit to himself his feelings for this woman. That was a change in capital letters right there.

Biscuits clinked into the tin dog bowl. 'You moved from Auckland to Wellington, drink coffee when you barely used to touch it. What's next?' Her grin was mischievous. 'Let your hair grow below your shoulders?'

I'll tell you what could be next, if I can let go my fear of being hurt if this doesn't work out again.

Because even though he knew now that she hadn't done what he'd believed, he did understand how vulnerable he'd felt when they'd broken up. 'I was thinking more along the lines of getting a pet guinea pig.'

Her eyes were sparkling in the way that tightened his gut, and other places. 'Genie would have it in one hit.'

Genie stopped scooping up biscuits and looked at Chloe.

Chloe rubbed her head. 'Sorry, girl. Devlin won't be providing you with a live toy. Unless he gets a cat. Then there'd be some activity going on whenever we visited.'

She was intending to keep this relationship going? On what level? Friends or lovers? Which did he prefer? That didn't even warrant asking. He knew the answer.

After last night there was no way he could walk away from her again. He either went into this full on or not at all. If he held a part of himself back trying to protect himself, too much hurt would ensue, and neither of them deserved that. 'Chloe.' He paused, his breakfast suddenly heavy in his belly.

Her head shot up, that twinkle in her eyes instantly replaced with caution. Doubt, too. 'Yes?'

Why had he started this? What was wrong with just getting on with the day? They didn't need to go over things again, or talk endlessly about the past. They could have fun, enjoy being together and see where it led, couldn't they? Except... 'We've done it again, haven't we? Gone fast and furious. No looking back or even sideways, just caught up in the moment, and now we've slept together again. That's twice within a week.'

Her knuckles were white at her sides. 'You're regretting making love?'

'No.' It was almost a shout. 'No, not at all,' he said a little quieter.

Her fists didn't relax one bit.

'I was thinking aloud. The first time we met and got together, it all happened so fast, like we were meant to be together.'

Stop. Take that back or you can't follow up. You'll put your big flat feet right in it.

Devlin looked away, came back to face Chloe. He didn't do avoidance any more. 'We seem to be doing the same thing again. But I don't want us to rush it too much this time. We need to get to know each other again.'

'I can understand that. I feel the same way,' she said in a stronger voice than he'd expected, and with a direct look that said, *Don't mess with me.*

She was less willing to rush in and try to please

him. Some of the tension slipped away. They still hadn't touched on their feelings for the situation or each other, but she wasn't going to let him walk all over her. He gave a mental fist pump. He'd loved Chloe before, and he liked this Chloe even more. He loved her. But that wasn't for saying. Not today. Not until he felt safe.

'When I learned you worked here, too, I admit to feeling knocked sideways. Suddenly I started wondering if there was something unfinished between us, when it had never occurred to me before.' He leaned his hip against the counter and folded his arms over his chest. And watched Chloe as he let go his hold on the words that had been building up for two weeks. 'I never believed we'd be able to have an ordinary, friendly conversation without accusations creeping in. Our break up was loud, nasty and complete, yet once I saw you the day you returned to work, I knew we weren't finished.'

Her hands tightened just as they'd been relaxing. 'We were over.'

'True. So why are we getting along so well? Hell, we made love twice on Monday night and twice again last night. We're planning on going out for a walk and coffee soon. You're going to fix my tap. What is going on?'

Chloe stared at him as though he'd grown a second head.

He waited. He'd put too much of himself on the line to go on without some hint from her that she might be feeling the same as him. She didn't know he was having doubts about himself. Any minute now she'd burst out laughing and point at the front door.

Two steps brought her to him, where she placed a hand on his chest.

She was being friendly, not sending him packing. That had to be good.

'It seems we just can't stay away from each other. Forget the last seven years.' Her shoulders dropped briefly. 'No, we can't forget what brought us to this point, and we shouldn't. We've both learned lessons from it. What I mean is we seem to have a knack of leaping into each other's arms without overthinking it. There is something between us that we can't seem to control. Like we're either meant to be together or we should live poles apart.'

'Exactly.' He could see in his mind's eye the first time he'd ever seen her. Chloe had been standing in her uniform on the opposite side of the ward where he was with a specialist learning everything he could. She was gorgeous and she'd had him hot in an instant, and he hadn't even known her name. He'd gone across and asked her out, and within days they were sharing a bed, and sometimes his apartment, and were never going to be apart again.

'Dev, I don't know where we're headed any more than you do. I do know I want to find out, though.' Her faced had paled, but determination highlighted those eyes.

He pulled her into him. 'Starting with a Genie walk, coffee and a dripping tap.' Man, he loved holding that soft, hot body, breathing in the essence that was this woman, knowing she was his other half—if only he could let go of the fear. His arms dropped away. But his mouth gave him away. He couldn't stay away from Chloe. 'Let's go out to dinner tonight. Somewhere down on the wharf, overlooking the harbour.' His heart was pounding. Would she or wouldn't she?

'I'd love that.'

Phew. The breath he'd been holding spilled out. 'So

would I.' It was as close to mentioning love that he was likely to get for some time. But it was a start.

'I think we do need to slow down a bit, get to know each other more thoroughly. Not take everything at face value.'

'You think that's what we did last time?' he asked.

Chloe nodded. 'We got into a close relationship fast. We fell apart almost as quickly. Not once did we stop and consider what we were doing and what it all meant for each of us.'

His head dipped in acknowledgement. 'You are so right. Does slowing down mean I can't take you to bed and make you cry out with pleasure?'

'Do it slowly and I'll be very happy.' She grinned.

Chloe headed for the shower, a smile lingering on her mouth. Devlin was her man. How could she have thought otherwise? Or thought she'd stopped loving him? She'd been fooling herself for seven long, lonely years. He was her other half, her soul mate, her love.

He meant everything to her.

The hot water streamed over her achy body. Filling the palm of her hand with liquid soap, she massaged her arms, legs, stomach. Everywhere. All the while Devlin filled her head.

Dev, you make my heart sing.

And her head spin, and her stomach soft and gooey.

Her hand paused over her belly. Where a baby might one day grow. A baby. Perhaps it was something to look forward to in the future when they both were more settled in their new relationship. Her hand tightened briefly.

Her heart dived. She had to tell Devlin about the baby she lost. Had to tell him before they went any further.

Despite her wondering if perhaps it might be better to draw a line under the past in case it overshadowed the present, there could be no secrets between them going forward. Time had healed most of her hurt, although it would never go away completely. She'd miscarried, accepted it after a lot of pain and crying, and had eventually moved on knowing that one day she'd still have a child if she met the man she wanted to live with for ever.

But the thought of telling Devlin was making her nervous, and she didn't fully understand why. He wouldn't be upset that she'd kept it from him; he'd understand that it was a sensitive subject for her and she'd needed to pick the right time to talk about it. She could have sworn there'd been a look of love in his face when they'd been talking. These past hours had shown that they could and did get on so well, that they knew each other beneath the exterior face they showed everyone else. So what did she have to worry about? Devlin would hug her, kiss her and accept that she'd coped.

Overthinking things again, Chloe.

She snapped the water off, grabbed a towel and rubbed herself dry hard and fast. In her bedroom she pulled on jeans and a thick red jersey, tied her hair into a ponytail, ignored the make-up on the shelf, and headed out to the kitchen where Devlin was wiping down the bench.

He looked relaxed and happy.

Chloe hesitated. This could wait. They were heading out for a walk and coffee. Why bring it up now?

Because I'm Chloe Rasmussen, the woman who doesn't dodge problems.

Anyway, there wasn't going to be a problem. They just had to discuss it and then draw a line under it so they could carry on getting to know each other again.

'What's up?' He was leaning against the bench, watching her.

'There's something you need to know before we go any further.'

'Sounds serious.' Caution was darkening his eyes.

'It—' Swallow. This shouldn't be so hard. 'It's important to both of us.'

'Go on.'

She had his undivided attention, and it didn't sit well. Again she wasn't sure why. Not when her biggest issue about their break up was how he'd refused to listen to her.

'Four weeks after we broke up I had a miscarriage.' There, it was done. Now he could hug her and say he was sorry to hear that, and how had she managed?

'You what?' He stood straight, his shoulders tight, his face blank with shock. 'I didn't know you were pregnant. Why didn't you tell me?'

'I didn't know myself.'

Hug me, Dev.

'You didn't know? How far along were you?' Now he reached over to caress her cheek with the back of his hand.

Some of her tension leeched away. 'The doctor thought seven weeks.'

'And you really didn't know?' Bewilderment blinked at her.

Similar to how she'd felt when the bleeding began. 'Not a clue. But life was a bit hectic around then. It never registered with me that I'd missed my period.'

'I suppose so.' He didn't believe her?

'Probably.'

Don't let him do this to you. Don't do it to yourself.

'It was a shock when the pain struck and I started

bleeding. I had no idea what was happening at first. I mean, as a nurse I did, but it was happening to me and I didn't even know we were having a baby.'

'Why didn't you tell me?'

Don't lose it. Stay calm. 'Dev, I tried, you know I did. More than once. I phoned, left messages, came around to your apartment and left a note. I even tried visiting you at work once. You refused to talk to me. I know you thought I was looking for a reconciliation, another chance—'

'Oh, my God,' he groaned, reeling back from her.

'But there was so much more to it.' Breathe slowly. In, out. In, out. 'I wanted you to believe me when I said I hadn't cheated on you.' In, out. '*And* I wanted to tell you about the miscarriage. Until then having a baby was something for the future, but the moment I understood what I was losing I was gutted. It hurt so bad, so deep, I became very withdrawn for a while. I wanted that baby. *Our* baby. I loved you, Dev. I still do.'

He continued watching her, his eyes tortured in a white face, holding himself tight, his hands now at his sides, flat and tense.

Reaching for his hands, she found them cold and shaky as though he was in shock. 'I do love you, Dev,' she repeated softly, and waited for his response. And waited.

She'd heard it said, but never believed it until now. Silence could be deafening.

Say something. Anything. Tell me you're falling in love with me again. Or that you don't think you can and you're sorry but you're leaving. Stop this silence. It's frightening me.

Finally he whispered, 'I am so sorry, Chloe. I should

have been there for you, but I let you down so, so badly. It won't happen again.'

This crushed response was not what she'd hoped for. 'Devlin, I got through it. I'm here, happy, and stronger. You're here, and we're making inroads into fixing past mistakes. That's all that matters. I didn't tell you so you could take the blame or hate yourself. I told you because I don't want any secrets between us. It has always been something I wanted you to know if we caught up again. I just had to work up to telling you.' She paused.

She was talking to air. Devlin had gone, head bowed as though the weight of the world were on his shoulders, closing the door ever so quietly behind him. So quiet it spoke of finality. Dinner was clearly off.

She straightened her shoulders. 'I'm not giving up on you that easily, Devlin. You walked away from us once before. Don't think you're getting away with it a second time.' That would make both of them stupid and they weren't. Not even close. They belonged together through all the love and pain that life would inevitably bring them.

Chloe had been pregnant—with his baby.

Devlin strode down to his car, his neck tight with anguish as he fought the need to look back. He couldn't for fear he'd run up to her front door and beg to be allowed back in—into her life for ever. And he didn't deserve her.

He'd wrongly accused her of having an affair. Refused to listen to her telling him she had not, that she loved him and would never deliberately hurt him. He'd refused to hear she'd lost their baby which meant he hadn't been there to support her through what must've been agonising, both physically and mentally. She'd have wanted that baby. Absolutely. So would he.

He could feel her hurt now, understood it for what it had been back then, not what he'd interpreted it as. He'd thought she was just angry at losing him and her ticket to a better lifestyle. That had been his excuse to protect his already battered heart by not engaging with her at all. He'd thought she was the second woman to treat him wrong; he hadn't stopped once to think that he might've been hurting Chloe as much.

If only he'd known how much more he'd hurt her.

If he had listened to her just once, he might've been there to hold her, soothe away the agony of losing their baby, to reassure her they'd try again when they were ready. Instead she'd faced it all on her own. With her mother and Jack, most likely. But that wasn't the same as if he'd been there for her. He'd been her fiancé, he'd loved her. It had been his place and he'd relinquished it without realising. Which was not an excuse, because if he'd only paused to hear her out then none of this might have happened.

He slammed the car door and pushed the ignition button hard. He could hardly breathe. He had to get away. Put some distance between them while he absorbed what Chloe had told him and how terribly he'd let her down.

Something penetrated his agony.

She'd said she still loved him.

How could she? Couldn't she see he wasn't good enough for her? There had to be men out there who'd love her as she should be loved. Who'd never hurt her, never let her down as he had. His hand tightened on the steering wheel as he headed down the road, away from her little house as fast as possible. Away from the temptation to go back to her and promise he'd never, ever let her down again if she'd give him just one more chance. But he had to be strong and put himself second. He loved her with every fibre of his being, and then some. But she deserved a better man than him.

She loves me.

He was sorry about that. It wasn't going to do her any good. But she'd get over him and find someone else. He couldn't be trusted to have her back, to protect her heart over everything that might break it, including himself.

In the apartment block underground parking area, he braked abruptly, pushed out and slammed the door in frustration. He'd found Chloe again. Found love again. Screwed it all up spectacularly again.

What was wrong with him?

His phone rang. 'Chloe' showed on the screen. He ignored her, shoved the phone into his pocket and headed for the road and the beach beyond.

The phone rang again. 'Chloe.' The phone went back into his pocket.

Storming down the beach, dodging kids and dogs and couples strolling hand in hand, he aimed for the far end.

The next time the phone went he was tempted to hurl it into the sea, but managed to refrain. Perhaps he should answer, explain to Chloe that he wasn't good enough for her. But hadn't he avoided her last time and been wrong to do so? Yes, he had. But he had to sort his head out before he said something that might cause more repercussions for Chloe. She'd had more than her share of heartache because of him. Chloe came first. Not him ever again.

But this time it was his mother calling.

Good. Now was his opportunity to finally say his

piece, to let her know that by saying Chloe was having an affair behind his back she'd gone and broken his heart completely. His finger hovered over the icon.

I'm more guilty for believing her. It was all my fault I didn't listen to Chloe. Not Mum's. Or anyone else's. I really don't deserve another chance with her.

He put the phone on silent and dropped it back into his pocket, continued striding along the wet sand as though an infuriated bull were behind him.

'So that's the way he wants to play it,' Chloe muttered and dropped her phone back on the bench. No surprise. She'd give him some time and try again. Because she wasn't giving up. Been there, done that, and look where she'd landed. On her own and still in love with Dev.

No, this time she would push every button he had to get his attention. They *would* talk about this and if he still wanted to walk away afterwards, then so be it.

Making another mug of tea, she leaned against the bench where only a short while ago Devlin's tight butt had been resting. She sipped the hot liquid and shoved away the urge to cry. Crying achieved nothing except puffy eyes and a headache.

Damn you, Devlin Walsh. You have the power to hurt me so much. Why can't you just stop and talk to me? Listen to me? Tell me what you're thinking. How you feel. What you want.

She'd give him some space to get his head around the fact she'd been pregnant with their baby, and hope he saw the light, and realised there was no point holding onto the past. They'd both moved on. That had been pretty apparent over the past couple of weeks. And making love with him this week had shown how much they were still so in tune with each other. They belonged together. They were two halves of a whole.

No matter what, he wasn't getting away with a repeat of last time. They would talk, and make up, and get on with living the life they'd once dreamt of having together.

Her phone rang.

Her heart lifted.

That hadn't taken long.

But it was Jaz's name on the screen. Ignore her? To hell with that. 'Hey, what's up?'

'What time are you heading into town?'

Eek. She'd forgotten the birthday lunch for their pal, Mackenzie. She couldn't go. What if Devlin tried to get hold of her when she was out with her friends? He'd think she didn't care. But if she sat here waiting for him to call she'd get into a funk. 'The table's booked for one and Mackenzie wanted to go for a drink at the Harbour View first, so how about we meet there at midday?'

'Perfect. I've got the handbag, by the way, and it's gorgeous,' Jaz said.

The present they were giving their friend. 'Thanks for doing that. See you soon.' Chloe stared out of her front windows, willing Devlin to come walking through her front door.

I'm missing you already.

Thunk. Genie head-butted against her thigh.

'Walkie time, huh?' Might as well, since Genie would be alone for a while this afternoon. And who knew? They might bump into Devlin walking on the beach. Except if he was avoiding her phone calls there was no chance he'd be on the beach he knew she frequented. 'How am I going to find the strength to wait him out, Genie?'

Thunk.

'Fair enough. One walk at a time.' But how long did she give him before banging down his door and demanding he talk with her?

Once back inside his apartment two hours later, Devlin finally checked the messages on his phone. He couldn't go on hiding from everyone for ever. What if he was needed in the ED? That would take his mind off everything for a while. The walk had done nothing to calm the turmoil in his head and heart. He loved Chloe. Which was why he had to stay away. He couldn't risk hurting her any more.

'Urgent.' His mother.

'Please call me.' Chloe.

'Got an hour to catch up for a drink?' Mark. His mate from Auckland was in town with his wife to see an art show.

Who to answer? Who to ignore? Damn but it was like juggling melons and knowing there was going to be a mess when he missed the lot. His sigh was harsh. 'Urgent.' Everything was urgent with his mother, but at the moment she would be the easiest to deal with, because he would simply say no to going up to Auckland for whatever dinner or function she had in mind today.

'Mum, what's up?'

'It's your father. He's had a heart attack and is having surgery late this afternoon.' She sounded oddly fragile and his heart missed a beat.

'Surgery for what?'

'Stents. Why aren't they doing it now? He could have another attack before then.'

'No, Mum. That's unlikely. The medical team will be watching him like a hawk.' Hell, Dad, you'd better hang in there, and get through this one. 'I'll be there as soon as possible.'

'Of course you will. I'll let you go so you can arrange a flight.' Just like that, she hung up on him. She knew he'd do what was right.

What she wouldn't understand was that he'd do it because he loved his father despite the difficulties they'd faced over how he wanted to take a step back from the family commitments. He wasn't going up to be by his bedside to please either of his parents. This was about love, pure and simple.

Sorry, Chloe, we'll have to talk later.

When Devlin walked into Auckland General's ICU nearly three hours later he still hadn't called her or left her a message. It didn't sit well, but what to say? He didn't want her rushing to his side because of his father's medical event. When he next saw her it would be because he was ready to discuss their future.

The sight of his father looking so small and frail in bed shocked him. 'Hey, Dad.' A lump filled his throat and he couldn't say any more.

Carefully avoiding all the tubes attached to him, Devlin gave him a gentle hug. And shook his head. 'What are you doing trying to scare us?'

'Scared me, too,' his father gasped.

'You won't know yourself once those stents are in.' Three, according to the cardiologist he'd just spoken to. 'You'll be running round the golf course soon, and won't even need the buggy.' He was a doctor, and he hadn't noticed anything wrong with his father's health.

He got a weak smile for a reply.

'They're taking you down to Theatre in a few minutes. I'll sit with you until the orderly comes for you.'

'Th-thanks, son.'

Devlin stretched his legs in front of him and watched the shallow rise and fall of his father's chest. A strong, forceful man, dropped to his knees by his own heart. A man who never paused to listen to other people's opinions or needs lay there looking lost and a little frightened. That was natural. Devlin had seen it often with patients. Yet it was hard to get his head around the fact his dad could be the same. Not when his word had always been law, his way the only way.

That's not what you're doing to Chloe, by any chance?

No, he was protecting Chloe from himself, by not screwing with her life any more.

You sure about that?

No. Not at all.

An orderly appeared around the end of the bed. 'Right, Mr Walsh, let's get you down to Theatre.'

Devlin gripped his father's hand for a moment. 'See you in a while, Dad.' He watched him being wheeled away and then went to join his mother while she waited for the surgery to be over.

At first neither of them said much, lost in their own thoughts. Devlin kept fidgeting with his phone, wanting to call Chloe and tell her what was going on. He'd give almost anything to have her with him right now. But he couldn't do that. It would be selfish. He'd walked away from her again, so he couldn't ask anything of her. He owed her that much at least.

'Your father's strong. He'll get through this,' his mother said with her usual determination.

Was that how she'd always approached life? It was the only way he and Patrick had known her. A force to be reckoned with. Someone who'd always wanted things done her way, and that way had to fit in with their father's world. 'Why did you lie to me about Chloe having an affair, Mum?'

'To get rid of her.' No lies, no gentle cover-up. Just the blatant truth.

He'd more than suspected it, but it still hurt to have it confirmed. 'What about me? My feelings for her?'

She took her time, surprising him. Finally she told him, 'Chloe was busy dragging herself out of poverty and nothing would stop her from reaching for a better life. But she wanted to focus on her career; she wasn't really prepared to devote her whole life to you and to the family. She was all wrong for you. I didn't want you being hurt.'

'Your lies hurt me.'

'Chloe would have hurt you more. I saw her out with that man more than once. It was only a matter of time before she betrayed you. Best she went before she made a mockery out of your relationship.'

His anger was rising, but he held it in check enough to say, 'You didn't know Chloe. You only saw what you wanted, and were convinced she didn't fit into your expectations of what my wife should be like. Yet she tried. Oh, man, how she tried.' He stood up and paced to the window and back, stared down at this woman who'd raised him and watched him get his heart thoroughly broken. 'Chloe is the most unselfish woman I've ever had the good fortune to fall in love with. I didn't deserve her.'

'You don't mean that. It's been a long time since you broke up. You should be thinking about settling down now and having children to continue the family name.'

'Mum, stop it.' The words exploded from his broken heart. 'You have no idea what you're talking about.'

Back at the window, he stared out onto the busy street below, not really seeing anything but the face he'd loved for years. The endearing smile and cheeky grin, the twinkling eyes that had sometimes filled with tears or love or shock. Shocked betrayal was the last vision he'd had of Chloe as he'd left her that morning.

Was he the same as his mother? Intent on getting what he wanted from people and not really giving enough back? If that was the case, then he didn't have to stay like that. He could change. Would change. If Chloe would give him a second—no, a *third* chance.

Turning, he crossed to sit beside the woman who'd raised him to her exacting standards. 'Chloe is strong and determined to be herself, but she also gives so much of herself to others. She is not, and never was, out to tie herself to someone else's good fortune. She stands tall and proud.' And has her heart bruised and broken, and yet gets back up to fight another day.

'You're seeing her again.' There wasn't even a hint of pleasure in her voice.

'Yes.' At least, he had been. Who knew what his chances of reconciliation were? No, he really didn't deserve to be given another chance. But she had phoned and left messages to call him back. That wouldn't be so she could just vent her spleen. He would crawl over broken glass to win her back. 'I'll stay until Dad's out of Recovery and I've talked to the surgeon, then I'm going home. To Wellington,' he added, in case his mother still believed she ruled him.

'You can't do that.'

'I can and I will,' Devlin said firmly. 'It's for the best, Mum. For all of us. It's not that I don't care about the family. I do. It's that I have my own life to live.' Hopefully he wasn't too late for Chloe to be a part of that.

* * *

'He's either not home, or he's ignoring the intercom,' Chloe told Genie as they stood outside Devlin's apartment block the next morning. 'Might as well go home for breakfast.' Not that she felt in the slightest bit hungry, but she'd go through the motions.

It had been a long, sleepless night after she'd got home from the birthday celebrations that had gone on and on. She'd felt guilty for not being full of life during lunch with her friends. When she'd finally managed to sneak away and grab a taxi home, she'd been ever hopeful that Devlin would be sitting in his car outside her gate, waiting to tell her he was sorry for disappearing and that he'd never do that to her again.

Once again she'd been living in la-la land. There'd been no car, no Devlin, no apology.

'Come on, girl.' She tugged the lead, and they began walking home, stopping in at the supermarket for some crumpets in the pathetic hope she might feel like eating when she got home.

What happened to being strong? Twenty-four hours and she was coming apart at the seams. Hadn't she meant it when she said he wasn't getting the better of her this time? That she'd at least try to talk to him and make him see they could make a go of a relationship? Yeah, she had.

Woof, woof. Genie pulled at the lead.

'Hey, steady, girl.' Chloe looked around to see what had got Genie excited, and her heart slammed into her ribs. Devlin. Really? Really. The lead slipped from her lifeless fingers.

He was striding towards her, purposeful and yet visibly worried. 'Chloe.'

'Dev.'

'I tried to get here last night. But it wasn't possible.'
Then his arms were around her, finally giving her that
hug she'd hoped for during their last conversation. Followed by a kiss. Oh, and what a kiss. It reached to every
part of her, loosening the tightness that had held her in
a vice-like grip from the moment she'd watched him
walk out of her front door and down the path to his car,
touching her as only Dev's kisses could. Making her
feel whole and real and happy. Happy? She jerked away,
locked a fierce look on him. 'Where have you been?'

'Auckland.'

Her arms fell away. The family. Right. 'You couldn't
have let me know something, anything, about where
you were?'

'Chloe—'

'This reeks of last time. You.' She poked him. 'You
refused to talk to me then. What's happened to owning that? You admitted you'd made a mistake and now
you're doing the same thing again. No way.' Hadn't he
learnt a thing?

'I wanted to be certain of where I stood, what I was
going to do. I owe you that much at least.'

'So you went back home to Auckland.' Great. Nothing had changed.

'This is not an excuse, please understand. But Dad
had a heart attack yesterday. I flew up, stayed until he
came out of surgery and then headed for the airport. Unfortunately there were no seats available on any flights
until this morning so I stayed overnight at a hotel at the
airport.' He did look remorseful.

But that wasn't enough. 'I'm sorry your father is ill,
Dev. But was your phone completely flat? You couldn't
even text me to tell me where you'd gone? I've been
ringing you, been to your apartment block, even asked

if you were at work. Did you think I'd walk away again, let you go without a fight?'

Firm hands gripped her shoulders. 'Look at me, Chloe. I know exactly what I want with you. For us to be together for ever, to have that future we'd once dreamed of. Going to Auckland was out of my control, and I deliberately didn't tell you about Dad because I didn't want you turning up out of sympathy after how our last conversation ended.'

But she would've been supportive and loving—and hopeful. 'Is your father going to be all right?'

'Yes, as long as he's sensible. They put in three stents and when I left he was sitting up in bed demanding to know when he could go home.'

Dev hadn't hung around then. Because their future was more important to him? She had to know. 'You're either all in or you're all out when it comes to us. No half measures, Dev,' she said firmly.

'I am not going back to Auckland for any events or dinners, or any other damned thing my mum comes up with. I'm here, in Wellington, and I've found you again and that's all that matters to me. Nothing is ever going to come between me and you again, Chloe.' He hesitated.

'Go on,' she pushed.

'I don't deserve you but I'm all in. Right over my head.' His hold softened, pulled her a little closer. His eyes gleamed with light and happiness. 'I love you, Chloe Rasmussen. With all my heart and then some.'

Phew. They'd finally done it. Got back on track and were heading towards happiness and an exciting future. She pulled back just enough to be able to lock her eyes on his. 'I love you, Devlin Walsh, and you do deserve me. Nothing else matters.' Very happy. 'Dev, I know

there are things to talk about, but I promise you I've
never stopped loving you since the day I first met you
all those years ago. Will you marry me?'

A smile lifted that amazing mouth. 'Yes, Chloe, I
will. I love you with all my heart and don't want to
spend any more time without you at my side.' He pulled
her close again for another kiss.

Some time later Chloe leaned back once more to look
into those superb, sexy eyes. 'Let's do it soon. There's
no reason to hang around for months when we've already wasted years. I'd like to get married asap. And to
keep it simple.' She wasn't letting him out of her sight,
at least until they'd tied the knot.

'You're on. What are you doing next week?'

'Putting in for leave for our honeymoon.' It had all
come together just as she'd hoped.

Giuseppe lifted his glass of champagne and tapped the
glass. 'Let's drink a toast to Devlin and Chloe Walsh.'

'To Mr and Mrs Walsh,' Lorenzo said gruffly.

Chloe grinned. 'To us.'

Dev laughed. 'To us. And to you all, family and
friends, for celebrating this special day with us.'

Eight weeks after her proposal, Chloe was still pinching herself. She and Dev had talked a lot about what
had come between them and finally laid everything to
rest. How could they not when their love for each other
had weathered seven years in purgatory? They'd both
changed in that time and were ready to fight for what
they wanted. Not that there'd been any fighting. Just
lots of laughter and loving and happiness.

Devlin wrapped his arms around her. 'You look
beautiful, Chloe love.'

'Oh-oh. Time I brought some food out or these two will become an embarrassment.' Lorenzo laughed.

'I'll give you a hand,' Chloe's mum said.

'I'll help, too,' Ruth Walsh said loudly, always the controller. But at least she and Dev's dad had accepted the wedding was going ahead and it was here, in this small family restaurant with no onlookers, no big society fuss, only family and close friends.

'Of course you can. Giuseppe, what needs doing first?' Lorenzo said.

'Nothing. The mothers are meant to sit down in regal style and enjoy the occasion.'

'Oh, no.' Chloe's mum laughed. 'I can't sit around being useless.'

'And I intend doing something to help.'

Chloe sighed. Ruth had come around to the fact that she was in Devlin's life for ever. It wasn't always going to be easy between them, but Ruth had apologised, albeit stiffly, and they were all trying to move on, and that was good enough for her and for Dev.

Chloe leaned against Devlin, looking around at the people who were here in Giuseppe and Lorenzo's restaurant to share this perfect day with them. 'I have never been so happy.'

'I'll second that,' Devlin said quietly. He tapped his glass against hers. 'To us.'

* * * * *

FORBIDDEN FLING WITH DR RIGHT

JC HARROWAY

MILLS & BOON

To Dr. H, my own medical hero.
Your years of dedication are truly inspirational.

CHAPTER ONE

DARCY WRIGHT FIRMLY believed in good impressions, which were never more important than on the first day in a new job. So where the hell was her pen when she needed it? She absently tapped the pocket of her navy-blue surgical scrubs and then scanned the nurses' desk for a stray pen, but no luck. How could she show her new boss what a great surgeon she was when she didn't even have a pen to sign a consent form?

The man would be here any minute and she wanted to wow him, present the sick patient she'd just finished examining, who urgently needed surgery.

Her career, helping people and easing suffering, was the most important thing in her life and her new boss, Joe Austin, was the last thing standing between Darcy and her career pinnacle: being a consultant, important enough to be ultimately responsible for the patients under her care.

'Mr Clarke in room three will be going to Theatre today,' she told Isha, the staff nurse behind the desk. 'If I had something to write with, I'd consent him...' Darcy blew the hair that had escaped her ponytail from her forehead, her flustered search for a pen amplifying her concern for the most seriously unwell of Mr Austin's patients. Of *her* patients.

Isha nodded, took a pen from her uniform pocket and waved it in Darcy's direction.

'Thanks,' Darcy said with a grateful smile.

'Hold on,' said Isha. 'You're adding a patient to Mr Austin's theatre list without asking him first?' Her wide-eyed, slightly impressed smile made Darcy's surgeon senses flicker into high alert.

'Of course… I'm his registrar. That's part of my job.' She added her signature to the operation consent form with a flourish and passed the pen back to Isha.

The other woman's concerned expression fanned Darcy's nerves. Until thirty minutes ago she'd never heard of Joe Austin. She'd expected the kindly older surgeon, Mr Fletcher, who'd interviewed her for this post at London's City Hospital. Instead, she'd discovered that he'd recently retired and she'd been reassigned to Mr Austin's team.

Unease now slithered down Darcy's spine, her good impression under threat. 'Why…what's Mr Austin like?' she asked the wary nurse, her defensive hackles rising. Surely her diligence in arriving early and identifying a patient with an acute abdomen from those admitted overnight would only earn his praise. Or would this boss replacement want to vet every decision she made, as if she were incompetent?

Darcy dismissed the suggestion with a shake of her head. She worked hard for her patients, worked hard to prove she was good at her job. Proving herself was something of a habit, a hangover from parts of her childhood…

Surely her boss would see her dedication the minute they met.

'Hmm… All the patients love him,' Isha said. 'Even the married ones, if you know what I mean.' She grinned and winked and then typed a flurry of words on the keyboard. 'Haven't you heard of him?'

Isha's eyes sparkled with worrying mischief that tightened Darcy's now frankly anxious stomach.

Heard of him...? How formidable could he be? Did he tear the arms off his registrars for fun?

'No-o-o...' She stretched out the word as her mind raced. 'Until I arrived this morning, I assumed I'd be working for Mr Fletcher... Why would I have heard of him?'

'Oh, my...' said Isha with cryptic glee. 'Are *you* in for a treat. He's no Mr Fletcher looks-wise, that's for sure. Plus, he's an awesome surgeon and kind of famous.'

While Darcy stared with growing dread, Isha's eyes darted sideways to the ward's entrance. 'And here he comes,' she added under her breath.

Darcy's body entered panic mode. She kept her eyes in front, battled the temptation to turn around and gawp at this fearsome creature who, it seemed, might be easy on the eye but might not find her enthusiasm all that impressive given her current state: floundering—no pen, no inkling as to the credentials of her *famous* boss and no time to probe Isha for more than the vague clues the nurse had already offered.

But surely all that mattered was the wellbeing of their patients, first and foremost Mr Clarke.

'Don't tell him that I've never heard of him,' she hissed at Isha in a frantic whisper. Her first impression was not the time to make a professional faux pas. Isha winked and tapped the side of her nose reassuringly, as if to say she'd conceal Darcy's ignorance.

She'd known the nurse for thirty minutes, long enough to discern a dry sense of humour she couldn't help but warm to. Could she be winding Darcy up?

Please let this be a joke. The last thing Darcy needed was for her new boss to be some sort of bad-tempered ogre who'd make her job, the one thing she took pride in, miserable.

Darcy's fingers twitched to straighten her wayward ponytail, but she didn't want to be seen to preen. Instead, she snatched the precious seconds to prepare, brace herself mentally for this unexpected man she'd be working closely alongside for the next three months.

Then every tiny hair on her body prickled to attention as she caught a hint of delicious aftershave and sensed an impressively tall and compelling presence at her side.

'Morning, Mr Austin,' said Isha, smiling in welcome at the man in Darcy's peripheral vision.

'Good morning, Isha.' His deep voice resonated with authority despite his personal question. 'Is your daughter over her cold?'

As she could no longer avoid it, Darcy looked up at the formidable new arrival, his handsome profile doing little to settle her frayed nerves. Not an ogre after all. Smartly dressed in a navy three-piece suit, a dove-grey shirt and a burgundy tie, Joe Austin seemed reassuringly confident, with the sort of commanding air that made people hang on his every word. Tall, dark and chiselled, he could be a hotshot financial trader or a male model instead of a gastrointestinal surgeon. Perhaps that was why he was famous—he moonlighted for the top fashion houses…

A flicker of relief shot through Darcy. Despite Isha's scaremongering, Darcy imagined they'd soon come to respect each other, develop a mutually appreciative working relationship.

As if finally noticing her, his gaze swooped over Darcy.

Caught off-guard, Darcy smiled—a twitching grimace generated by his impressive presence. Under his observation, Darcy revised her opinion.

Not handsome—*hot*.

She needn't have bothered with the smile. Before she could open her mouth to introduce herself, he dismissed Darcy without acknowledgement and returned his attention to Isha.

Not a good sign.

All of Darcy's hidden insecurities, honed during a lifetime of feeling not quite good enough, writhed in the pit of her stomach like a bad case of gastric flu while nurse and surgeon conversed for a few moments as if she didn't exist. Darcy pulled herself upright; she was a thirty-one-year-old woman, for goodness' sake. She'd give Joe Austin the benefit of the doubt this once. After all, as Isha had hinted, he was jaw-droppingly attractive.

Waiting for her chance to interrupt, she used the time to observe the man the way a dieter examined chocolate cake.

He was nothing like the genial, rugged-faced Mr Fletcher, who was the far side of sixty and more of a granddad type, that was for sure. Joe's dark untamed hair sported just enough grey at the temples to promise future membership of the 'silver fox' club, and his decadent, almost sensual mouth looked as if the pinched scowl it wore when he'd glanced Darcy's way was borrowed for the occasion.

A groan filled Darcy's head. She had more pressing matters than finding the boss so good-looking that her ovaries bounced with unrestrained glee. She had an urgent case to present: Mr Clarke and his ruptured appendix. Seizing her moment during the briefest lull in his conversation with Isha, Darcy stuck out her hand in his direction.

'Mr Austin…' She was done being ignored.

Her boss turned his head and this time their eyes locked. His were conker-brown, sharp and intense.

Unease and fascination fought for control of Darcy's racing pulse. Seriously… No wonder every female staff member and patient within head-swivelling distance had a smile on their face.

'This is your new registrar,' Isha said, because Darcy seemed to have forgotten that she was a qualified surgeon, not a starry-eyed medical student on her first day on the wards, drooling at the *real* doctor.

Darcy's face ached with the effort of holding an expectant smile in place, the first impression stakes even higher now she knew that she'd be working for someone so renowned.

'Ahh…' he said, clearly unimpressed by what he saw, perhaps her wonky ponytail or her lack of a pen.

What…? She wasn't expecting a fanfare of welcome or fireworks, but he could at least be civil. If it weren't for her tendency to become overly defensive when uncomfortable or judged, she'd let him have a piece of her mind, famous brilliant surgeon or not.

He finally took her proffered hand. 'Good to meet you.' He made it sound anything but *good*.

Darcy's smile offered a final uncertain wobble before dying altogether. How could she have possibly upset him this early into their working relationship? Unless he'd noticed the way she'd checked him out…

Years ago, Darcy had developed a firm and decisive handshake in order to encourage people to take her seriously. She employed it now; she'd never needed it more. 'Darcy Wright. So pleased to meet you, too.'

She dragged in a preparatory breath, ready to bring him up to speed on Mr Clarke, to dazzle him with her diagnostic skills.

'Welcome to my team.' He returned the gesture with an equally firm touch, his conker-brown eyes both holding her captive and appraising as if she were a virus under a microscope. She pretended to ignore the fact that his words said *Welcome* but his tone asked, *Which rock have you crawled from under?* But she stiffened all the same, the delicious heat of his palm against hers no compensation for what felt like an unfair and hasty evaluation.

Perhaps she'd only imagined the way his eyes seemed to swoop from her head to her toes, forcing her feet to shuffle and her body to shudder as if she'd never been this close to a man before? She dragged her stare from his lush lips, which ridiculously brought to mind desperate kisses. She wasn't here to swoon. So he was hot. Big deal. It was just that it had been a long time, over a year, since she'd found a member of the opposite sex attractive…

Since splitting from her ex, Dean, she'd spent a year in a self-imposed dating hiatus in order to focus on the career she loved. The harder she worked to make a difference to her patients, the greater the personal reward.

She'd always needed to be good at something. She'd embraced her belief that she was the odd one out in her family and learned to stand out. The karate she'd only endured at twelve because her sisters had started ballet class. Or riding her first boyfriend's motorbike during a very brief rebellious teenager phase when even her teachers had written her off. They couldn't see past the make-up and the bad boy boyfriend to bright studious

Darcy beneath, who was hurting from the latest slap of rejection from her biological father.

But that had changed as soon as she'd started pushing her pain away and pushing herself instead. Luckily for Joe Austin and Mr Clarke, her drive had brought her here.

Now she had his attention it was time to focus on the patient. 'Can I present Mr Clarke, whom I've added to your urgent theatre list for today?'

Joe raised a sceptical eyebrow, waiting in a loaded silence. His dark stare lacked warmth, or even respect, but its penetrating quality, the length of his sooty lashes and the pounding adrenaline it evoked in Darcy made her so aware of her breathing and the whoosh of her heated blood around her body that she almost lost hold of her determination.

Typical of Darcy that the object of her lust was completely off-limits for a whole raft of reasons...

Her boss.

Probably married.

Seemed to dislike her on sight.

Inside, her hopes for a favourable first impression were rattled. Clearly Isha was right; she should have asked first. They weren't going to be chums, but he was too hot for sense anyway. She would *not* find him attractive. Working for such a guarded man would throw up many challenges she hadn't anticipated without her body reacting every time he looked her way. She needed to show him just how capable she was, not flush every time he addressed her.

'I've acquainted myself with all of your patients,' she said, pushing on regardless. 'Mr Clarke is a thirty-five-year-old man in room three with a perforated appendix who needs surgery. Today.' She handed him the tablet bearing the patient's file, her desire to schmooze her way into his good books dwindling fast. Now she prayed she'd get through her first day without telling him exactly what she thought of him and his hard to please attitude.

Stony-faced, he scrolled through the information. 'Tell me, where did you work before you arrived at City?' His tone implied that he fully expected her answer to be, *Nowhere, I just hung out at the job centre,* as if she wasn't good enough to be *his* registrar.

She opened her mouth to answer, gaping like a goldfish while her insecurities flared to life from the glowing embers she carried inside. Everyone had vulnerabilities, deep-seated fears. Hers stemmed from the childhood belief that she was somehow defective or fundamentally unlovable after her biological father walked out before her first birthday, only reappearing sporadically throughout her childhood, raising and then dashing her hopes that he'd always be a reliable part of her family, of her life.

Darcy was lucky. She had other, more constant family. She loved her half-sisters—Lily, a solicitor, and Stella, the youngest, a doctor too, with whom Darcy shared a flat. She'd had the benefit of equal adoration from her mother and stepfather, Grant, who was a wonderful man. He'd adopted Darcy and treated her just like his biological daughters.

But at times throughout her young life even that hadn't been enough to negate Darcy's feelings of rejection. She'd assumed it must have been something she'd done that drove her father away. If she was well behaved or worked harder at school then she could win back her father's love. Thus began the competitive drive that still pushed her today.

How did this man seem to detect all those insecurities with a single glance? His apparent and unfounded scorn made her blood simmer.

His dismissal was unfair.

In her haughtiest tone, she reeled off a truncated version of her impressive curriculum vitae, her stomach sinking at the tenacity of his blank expression. What *would* it take to impress this man?

'...and before moving to City I worked the surgical rotation at Hanes Hospital with Mr Clough.' She finished with a defiant tilt of her chin, trying to keep the tumult of emotions from her face.

'I know you've inherited rather than chosen me, but Mr Fletcher was delighted to offer me this post,' she said, trying to claw back some outward semblance of the mutually respectful professional relationship she craved, but instead subtly suggesting that the fault lay solely with him and his misplaced prejudices.

'Hmm...' Joe Austin muttered noncommittally as he read Mr Clarke's notes in painstaking detail, as if checking for the mistake that would prove she wasn't a real doctor after all.

The last thing Darcy needed this close to her career's finish line was an arrogant, demanding and ruthless tyrant bossing her around when she'd developed her own way of doing things. Her self-beliefs were constructed on shaky ground as it was without him questioning her professional autonomy. Her career, helping people, fulfilled her and gave her pride.

Clearing her throat, she pushed her agenda, the only real thing that mattered: her patient. 'Mr Austin, I believe Mr Clarke needs an emergency laparotomy.' She kept her tone calm but assertive, her desire to make a good impression buffeted by mounting waves of irritation caused by his impenetrable expression. 'As you can see from his notes, he has obvious signs of an acute abdomen—'

'Have you excluded non-surgical causes for his symptoms?' he interrupted, his gaze still on the screen.

'Of course.' Darcy all but spluttered at his insinuation. Did he think her totally incompetent? It was becoming increasingly difficult to extend him the benefit of the doubt and believe his unwarranted scepticism wasn't personal. She assumed that he must have had lazy trainees in the past. Or perhaps he'd lost a patient recently and had reacted with overbearing distrust. Clearly Joe Austin was unlike any other consultant she'd experienced.

No, he was hotter, but also rude and infuriating.

Darcy dug deep into her reserves of patience. All consultants had their own rules and routines. She'd never before taken it personally. So why now?

Because his attitude made her feel small, inconsequential, an afterthought, the sting too reminiscent of what she'd experienced with her father and, more recently, her ex.

Belatedly, she shot a glance at his left hand, wondering how his wife put up with him, and found his ring finger to be bare. Damn...that didn't help with the demarcation she was desperately trying to establish between his physical effect on her sad and lonely libido and the way he emotionally seemed to both press all of her soft spots and rile her up until she acted like someone she barely recognised.

She hardened her voice to the authoritative tone she reserved for inebriated relatives in Accident and Emergency on a Saturday night. 'When you examine Mr Clarke, you will see that he has guarding and rebound tenderness in the right iliac fossa.' She reeled off a list of typical signs and symptoms, her defences so high she'd forgotten that she'd set out to impress her superior. She wasn't used to explaining herself this much, not since she was a junior doctor.

Trust her to land the difficult boss. Was it too much to ask, knowing how hard the journey from naïve medical student to veteran consultant was, that he'd show her a modicum of respect and acceptance?

She shoved her hands into the pockets of her white coat with finality in answer to the blank assessing expression he wore as well as his suit. This was about what was best for the patient.

'He has textbook peritonitis,' she continued, her tone now as frosty as his, all expectations abandoned. 'My diagnosis is a ruptured appendix, so I've commenced intravenous antibiotics and consented him for Theatre.' She imagined the satisfying image of Joe Austin's grovelling expression when she proved that her diagnosis was correct in the operating theatre. 'I'm happy to operate if you have a full list.'

Something like momentary respect flashed in Joe's dark eyes, gone as soon as it appeared. Darcy winced at the way that second of recognition lit up her nervous system like a zap of forty thousand volts of electricity.

His lips tightened. 'Ms Wright...' He said her name with that bite of command, only instead of riling her up it made her breath catch and her heart race with the same excitement and anticipation she experienced with a scalpel in her hand.

'If and when,' he added pointedly, 'I'm happy for you to operate on my patients, I'll let you know.'

Darcy spluttered, dumbfounded. 'But I've done this procedure many times in the past.' The brush-off stung, even as she respected his dedication to ensure the care of his patients. Yes, she was new and yet to demonstrate her talents, but she hadn't printed a fake medical diploma from the internet and walked in off the street. She'd trained hard for the past ten years. Made personal sacrifices in order to achieve her goals. While most of her school friends were married, some of them with children, some of them bosses or running their own companies, she still had her training wheels on, both professionally and definitely in her drab private life.

'Let's start the ward round with Mr Clarke, shall we,' Joe said briskly to Isha without acknowledging Darcy's comments and set off down the ward.

Isha, who looked as if she'd won the hospital gossip lottery, shot Darcy a sympathetic but encouraging smile and hurried after the great man.

Insufferable man, more like.

What the hell just happened? Would she have to prove herself worthy over and over again?

Darcy scurried to catch up, feeling like an imposter. Excluded. Maligned. It had been a while since she'd allowed anyone to make her feel that way.

Only the memory of Mr Clarke's pain-induced pallor and clinical signs of peritonitis stiffened Darcy's resolve. Her diagnosis was correct. Joe Austin would soon discover that for himself when he examined the patient. Then he'd have to apologise—publicly, profusely and preferably on his knees.

CHAPTER TWO

JOE AUSTIN DREADED the first day with a new team of trainees. They came with bad or lazy habits they'd acquired working for less demanding bosses than him, habits he'd need to quickly and thoroughly quash. Not that he'd ever met a trainee as downright pushy and defensive as Darcy Wright.

'I'm not sure how they did things at St Mary's, Ms Wright,' Joe said as his long stride made short work of the ward corridor, 'but here at City my patients are *my* responsibility.'

He glanced sideways in time to catch the faint rush of colour to her cheeks. Damn, he'd need to check his delivery, ease her in gently to the fact that instead of working for the genial and relaxed Rod Fletcher, she now had a boss with high expectations that he had no intention of slackening.

Joe ran a tight ship out of necessity, predominantly for his emotional sanity. He knew from devastating experience the consequences of inattention. But perhaps he could make some conciliatory remarks so his new registrar realised his inflexible attitude wasn't personal. At least not personal to Darcy.

'Of course,' she said, her determination obvious in the way she hurried to keep up. 'But it's my job to evaluate your patients.' She wasn't going to accept his ex-planation at face value, and he couldn't help but respect her for the qualities that made her question.

'Little did I know,' she continued, 'that trying to do my job would earn me a humiliating and very public reprimand.' She ended with a defiant tilt of her chin.

His eyes met hers, an uncomfortable collision on multiple scores. She was inconveniently beautiful and, from his first impressions, sharply intelligent and highly driven. From the first moment he'd looked at her she also roused something in him he hadn't felt in a long time. Enthusiasm, interest, a gravitational pull.

His head still reeled from its effects. He'd spent so long living in a thick, dense fog of grief that any posi-tive feeling was notably astounding.

How had she done that so effortlessly?

'My apologies if I made you feel chastised,' he said, marvelling at the way challenge lit silvery sparks in her brilliant blue irises. 'I'm afraid that, as my registrar, you'll have to grow used to my peculiar little ways.' Even to his own ears he sounded far from apologetic.

But he'd already deduced that this particular regis-trar would present many tests, not least of all the way she'd rapidly slid under his skin.

She pressed her lush lips together as if she had no intention of granting forgiveness.

'I don't mean to be gruff,' he continued, outlining his expectations for their working relationship, 'but I do demand the highest standards.'

And, like most perfectionists, Joe required the most of himself.

'That's great.' Her smile glittered with resolve. 'Be-cause I'm passionate about my work. I take caring for others very seriously, I put in the hours and, in this case, I know my diagnosis is correct.'

He stopped outside room three and tugged a pair of latex gloves from the box attached to the wall. An admiring smile pulled at his mouth. 'I'm glad to hear that—there are no slackers on my team.'

True to form, she practically spluttered at his insinuation.

'Mr Austin—' she spoke through a clenched jaw '—I, of course, respect your authority, and I'm here to learn from you, but in my previous positions I've worked with a great degree of autonomy. My former consultants were only too happy to leave the routine ward work and patient pre-op prep to me so they could focus on their theatre lists and clinics.'

At least she'd cut the combative tone from her voice somewhat.

Joe nodded. She'd made a perfectly reasonable observation. That was how he too had once worked. Before his personal life fell apart and his job became his only solace. Back then he'd been self-absorbed, too focused on his work to see what was happening at home, with his family.

And he'd paid the ultimate price.

'You have the benefit of an experienced registrar before you.' Darcy ploughed on. 'There's no point keeping a dog and barking yourself, as it were…' she finished with a smile that hinted at her playful sense of humour.

It transformed her face so that Joe took a second look. She wasn't merely beautiful, she was stunning. What would she look like in her own clothes and with her hair down? She certainly rocked a pair of shapeless surgical scrubs, alluring curves in all the right places.

'I agree to a point, Ms Wright,' he said with the calm

but inflexible authority he didn't usually need to work at, but with this woman he'd have to stay on his toes. 'But when it's my scalpel, my name next to the patient, *I* need to decide who goes onto my operating list.'

He sighed internally, realising belatedly that he should ask her to call him Joe. But the thought made his skin prickle with heat, as if the formality of 'Mr Austin' somehow kept her abundant feminine appeal at bay, kept him distant.

No matter he was her senior. Responsible only for her training and education. He couldn't think of her any other way. He definitely shouldn't think about the brilliance of that warm, open, briefly glimpsed smile when she'd greeted him earlier and the way the minute he'd driven it away with his grief-induced foul mood he'd craved a second look.

'Are Mr Clarke's observations stable?' He directed his question to Isha, who'd watched this unusual battle of wills with amused delight.

'He's tachycardic and pyrexial, but his blood pressure is stable.'

'But I've seen patients like him deteriorate rapidly before,' said Darcy, fighting not to be excluded from the conversation. 'I think that once you've examined Mr Clarke you'll agree with my evaluation.'

Why did she need to be right? Why did he care so much about her ego?

'Perhaps I will,' he said, shoving her attractiveness aside as irrelevant, 'but I'm an uncompromising boss. I like things done *my* way. I'll likely double-check everything, so you'd best get used to it.'

Darcy eagerly stepped closer and reached for her own pair of gloves. 'I'm a fast learner, as you'll see when you allow me to operate on Mr Clarke.'

She just didn't give up.

'My CV outlines my extensive surgical log,' she continued, 'and if you don't feel comfortable taking my word for it, you're welcome to supervise the operation.'

'We'll see,' he said, her determination earning his grudging respect. Would they butt horns professionally the entire time? Without stopping to question why a part of him relished the possibility, he focused on the bigger part that needed the order and precision of his work to compensate for the mess he'd made of what had once been an idyllic life as he pushed open the door and strode confidently into the room to greet Mr Clarke.

Her diagnostic skills had proved highly attuned.

Joe blinked in the harsh operating theatre lights and swallowed a wave of guilt at the way he'd reacted negatively to his new registrar. He watched her prepare the surgical field, her long, glossy blonde hair concealed under the blue head covering, with the exception of a few tantalising wisps.

'Ready?' He looked up, bombarded anew by the flash of distrust in Darcy's bright blue eyes. Fringed with impossibly long eyelashes, her resolute stare was the only part of her face visible above the surgical mask. He should have gone a little easier on her. Theirs was not a career that tolerated hesitancy or insecurity. Had Darcy failed to diagnose the severity of this patient's condition, he might be sitting on the ward right now with life-threatening septicaemia.

She'd done well, and it wasn't her fault that this was a particularly difficult week for him personally.

The impending leukaemia fundraiser he and his ex-wife held twice a year in memory of their daughter Rosie sliced open his poorly healed wound the way he slashed through sutures. It meant well-intentioned friends asking how he was, as if the devastating emotions of losing your only child and then watching helplessly while your marriage imploded could be encompassed by a single socially acceptable word: *fine*.

If he smiled at acquaintances the guilt sliced him in two. If he showed any kind of emotion in front of Laura, his ex-wife, she'd get that glassy look to her eyes and then she'd sniff and fight tears. Then the grief, for which there was no shelf life or miraculous cure, would crush him from the inside until all he could do was wait for their guests to leave and pound the punch bag hanging in his garage until his knuckles bled and exhaustion took him to unconsciousness.

He'd spent many a night asleep on the concrete floor over the years, waking with swollen hands—the irreplaceable tools he needed to work—and swollen eyes.

No wonder meeting his unexpectedly beautiful and assertive registrar had thrown him off course. If only the balm of her attractiveness, both physical and intellectual—a likely consequence of his non-existent dating life since his divorce—wasn't completely irrelevant.

She nodded. 'Are you happy for me to proceed, Mr Austin?'

'Please continue, Ms Wright.' He stifled a sigh, dark thoughts of his past failures abolishing the foolish flickers of desire.

'You're sighing.' Darcy paused from preparing the patient's abdomen, frustration evident in the tone of her voice. 'Have I done something wrong? Is there another way, i.e. your way, that you'd like me to prepare the field?'

She'd swabbed the skin with iodine and demarcated the area with sterilised surgical drapes in a perfectly standard manner. And with swift precision that told him she had no intention of altering her technique to mollify his peculiar whim.

He cleared his throat. 'No. I was distracted by a... personal matter. Carry on.'

Darcy gave a momentary pause where she observed him intently. Then she continued.

Joe breathed again. He needed to get himself together. At this rate she'd think he was unhinged or easily preoccupied.

'While we're on the subject of doing things my way,' he said from behind his own surgical mask, 'I want you to ensure that the new foundation doctors run a blood test for pancreatitis on all of my patients admitted with abdominal pain. I have a standing rule.'

Thorough routines—another technique he used to restore some sense of order and control to his shattered existence. Ticking every box, giving his job his whole, somehow absolved a minuscule fraction of his guilt for the way he'd lost what mattered the most: his family. First his daughter and then his marriage. Because without his work who was he?

Not a husband and no longer a father.

'Of course.' Darcy nodded, her keen stare wary and suspicious. 'I, too, never pick up a scalpel until I've seen the pancreatic enzyme levels and excluded all non-surgical causes of abdominal pain,' she stated calmly, her tone full of reproof. 'The first consultant I ever worked for taught me *that*.'

Joe winced behind his mask. Perhaps he did sound a little patronising to someone of her experience. Although her implication reminded him he likely had little to teach her beyond how to become a paranoid workaholic, he couldn't help but applaud her calm persistence. She was at least ten years younger than his forty-three, and people rarely challenged his authority in the workplace.

To the casual outsider, he was the mighty Joe Austin after all, the once golden boy of gastrointestinal surgery, now a jaded and bereft shell of his former self.

He cleared his throat. 'I've seen acute pancreatitis missed before, confused for a surgical emergency.' Yes, this was rookie surgeon stuff that she already knew, but his high standards, his reminders and double-checks hurt no one and were, in fact, designed to do the opposite: keep his patients safe and ensure that his daughter's death made some sort of sense, even if only as a distraction technique.

'I won't put any patient of mine through an unnecessary laparotomy,' he said in further explanation, although he couldn't fathom why Darcy's opinion of him mattered in the slightest. Let her think him bad-tempered and demanding.

Except...

Her observant stare seemed to probe his inner thoughts way too clearly. She'd practically told him how to do his job on the ward earlier. Perhaps he cared what she thought of him because he hoped to conceal how much he needed his work—how it gave him purpose and allowed him to focus on others' lives rather than the train wreck of his own.

'On that we agree,' she said, her tone clipped as she adjusted the overhead lights to aid her clear view.

Joe watched her with renewed fascination. Was it just his gruffness that made her defensive, or had she arrived this morning already gunning to push her agenda? He knew all too well the demands of life as a consultant surgeon, and she already had many of the qualities required. Confidence, assertiveness and persistence. The attributes were practically a requirement of a surgeon who made life and death decisions on a daily basis.

But what was her personal story behind the mask? Did she have a husband or boyfriend or children that she hardly saw, the way he'd neglected what mattered most: spending time with his loved ones?

When she caught him staring her eyes hardened, as if she fully expected his interference or criticism.

'What?' she asked, pausing with her hand out-stretched for a scalpel. 'Why are you looking at me like that?'

Joe battled the urge to smile. She was so…feisty. Re-freshing. Rousing. Her apparent lack of respect for his authority should rankle. Instead, she made him feel… lighter, as if at any moment he might burst into laugh-ter at his own absurdities. When was the last time he'd been gripped by such a spontaneous positive emotion? And what was it about this woman that awoke him to amusement, among other emotions?

He blinked and tried to clear the insanity in his head. He could *not* find his junior colleague attractive, desir-able or fascinating. Aside from the ethical barriers, the fact he was her boss and therefore held the balance of power in their professional dynamic, he'd hadn't had a single date since he and Laura split three years ago.

Rusty would be an understatement.

Whenever he'd thought about dating in the past, he couldn't move past how undeserving he was of a sec-ond chance after his family's tragedy. He'd had his shot at happily ever after and he'd messed up.

Now, there was only work and keeping fit, both physi-cally and mentally so he could work some more, the cycle rewarding and absorbing but also addictively numbing.

He'd all but given up on those vital parts of his masculinity still functioning but Darcy Wright, with her bright eyes and her dazzling smile, could restore the sex drive of a monk.

'How am I looking at you?' he said, the foreign heat of intrigue shifting through his veins, where normally work was a place to keep busy, to lock down any thought beyond patient care and avoid feeling anything at all.

Darcy huffed. 'As if you're waiting for me to make a mistake.' The briefest flash of vulnerability lit her eyes before she looked down again, focused on their patient.

His gut tightened with renewed regret and something more. Shame. He didn't usually care what anyone thought of his high expectations. Most staff had been around long enough to know the old Joe Austin, the surgeon he'd been before his life fell apart, and cut him the according slack. But unless she'd already had time to catch up on hospital gossip, Darcy didn't know that there'd once been a more relaxed and engaging side to him. That he'd enjoyed a joke with his patients, played soft rock ballads in Theatre while he operated and showed the nurses photos of Rosie—proud dad moments, the memory of which now turned his stomach.

Perhaps if he'd been at home more, he might have noticed her rapid deterioration and Rosie would still be alive. The dull ache of self-hatred somewhere under his ribs grumbled awake like an ill-tempered bear disturbed from hibernation.

Of course, none of this was Darcy's fault and he'd need to apologise.

Shoving his feelings of inadequacy back down, he returned to their conversation. 'It's my job to observe your technique, supervise and evaluate you in preparation for your next job as a consultant.' A good reminder to stave off those wayward moments of attraction.

'I know,' she said, sounding completely unconvinced, 'but there's observation and then there's *observation*.' She handed the scalpel to the theatre nurse and asked for a forceps.

His lips twitched once more beneath his mask. 'Am I making you uncomfortable?' Interesting... Had he rattled her as much as she'd unnerved him? Would her time working for him be filled with these...sparks?

'Not in the slightest,' she said, but her evasive stare said otherwise. 'Are we still good?' Darcy asked the anaesthetist, checking that the patient's level of anaesthesia was satisfactory.

Joe deserved the dressing-down he suspected she'd held back after the way he'd grilled her on the ward. Old habits reared their heads, and his gloved hands itched to take over control of the instruments. Her confident incision on Mr Clarke's abdomen was textbook—right over McBurney's point, the anatomical landmark for the location of the appendix. He agreed with her diagnosis: peritonitis secondary to a likely ruptured appendix. He'd expect a trainee with her experience to easily recognise and treat the surgical emergency.

So why had he been so hard on her?

Because he hadn't expected Darcy herself. Her tenacity, her determination, her spirit had made him take a second look beyond his first impression. And then a third and fourth look. She'd roused him from emotional detachment, made him feel something after years of trying to feel nothing. He hadn't cared about anything beyond his work, his patients, for so long that the emotion—any positive emotion—felt...alien, as if it was her probing him with uncomfortable questions, not the other way around. With his guard erected, he'd gone overboard in questioning her diagnosis.

'You didn't say I told you so,' he said as the collection of pus making the otherwise fit and healthy Mr Clarke sick came into view through the small incision she'd made.

Her eyes clashed with his in surprise, quickly replaced by resignation. 'I want a glowing reference when I leave, not to score petty points.'

Her tone was clipped with concentration, her movements precise and practised in a way that told Joe she possessed that innate instinct which turned a skilled technician into an intuitive surgeon.

'Besides,' she added, 'I'm here to learn from you so that I can be the best surgeon I can be. Maybe even as good as you.'

Joe said nothing. He'd once shared Darcy's ambition, and he still did to a degree, only now his motives were as much about self-preservation as they were about wanting to save the world one sick patient at a time. His perfectionism had become another shield he used to ward off regret.

'I'll teach you everything I can.' Although, he'd learned life's most valuable lesson outside the hospital, the hard way—a lesson he would wish on no one.

'I look forward to it,' she said. 'Although, I didn't realise that I'd be working for someone so notable when I arrived on the ward this morning.'

He winced—he most certainly didn't deserve her awe. She obviously knew of his work in the development of the RA Clip, a now universally used surgical clip that cut the risk of post-operative bleeding in half.

Yes, he was good at one thing: his job. But he'd been a largely absent father and, at the end, an inadequate husband. He'd once had it all. But he'd ruined it all, too. Did Darcy know about Rosie's death, about his failure as a father, the only truly important role he'd ever had?

'I've designed a surgical clip, not cured cancer.' Joe's insides twisted with familiar remorse as surely as if Darcy were probing inside his abdomen, not their patient's. If only he *could* have cured cancer. He might still have his darling little girl…

Nausea swirled in his gut, resurrecting the intrusive thoughts that plagued him day and night. He'd once been so busy treating others at the hospital that he hadn't been home when his daughter's health had rapidly deteriorated four years ago, following a short illness he'd thought was common viral gastroenteritis. By the time his wife and six-year-old daughter had arrived at the hospital Rosie had been unconscious from a brain haemorrhage—a rare complication of her undiagnosed acute leukaemia—and admitted to intensive care. He'd missed his chance to speak with his beloved girl one last time. To remind her that he loved her and always would.

A wave of grief slashed through the sutures barely holding his heart together, the pain snatching his breath away. He should have noticed something was seriously wrong. He was a doctor. Observation, intuition, diligence were vital parts of his role. He'd let Rosie down. There was no going back to save her. God knew he'd prayed hard enough for that impossible second chance—one he didn't deserve.

'Well, as you can see, I'm a perfectly competent surgeon and you're going to have to trust me a tiny bit if you ever plan on sleeping again.' She deftly directed the scrub nurse's suction to where she wanted it. 'We're on call tonight—it's going to be a long shift if you insist on shadowing every move I make, double-checking things a medical student can do unaided.'

She was right. He had plenty to do.

'I'm sure that my little foibles seem...over-cautious.' Helping his patients allowed him to focus anywhere other than on his own messed-up head and tattered heart. 'But you do seem to have things under control.'

While he'd been half overseeing, half ruminating on his failures, Darcy had cleared the abscess collected around Mr Clarke's appendix and tied off the artery in preparation for removing the perforated structure.

'Thank you, I think...' Her lips twitched under her mask with what he guessed was a sardonic smile. After years of working with the face coverings he'd become adept at reading people's eyes. She adjusted the retractor to open up the wound. 'Now you can see that I'd never allow professional awe or first day nerves or even self-doubt distract me from a patient's diagnosis or care.'

Her subtext added, *Even when my senior colleague gets in the way.*

Self-doubt? She seemed extremely confident. She'd given him what-for, hadn't she?

The scrub nurse held out a clamp. On instinct, Joe reached for it at the exact same moment as Darcy. Their gloved hands collided, the brush of her fingers against his, followed swiftly by the locking of their stares.

Awareness permeated the sterile atmosphere as they stood face to face, hands frozen, his atop hers, on the handle of the surgical instrument.

It could only have lasted a split second, but it was enough time to flood Joe's body with the same restless heat he'd experienced when she'd first turned to smile at him this morning on the ward.

He'd had to suppress the feeling then, as he must now.

He relinquished the clamp and Darcy recovered first. 'I'm more than happy to finish up with Mr Clarke alone. Unless you have any last advice?' Darcy asked, hinting that it was high time he left her to operate unaided.

The feeling of her fingers under his persisted, forcing him to gather all of his best coping strategies. 'Just a mantra I find useful: mistakes cost lives.'

'They do,' she agreed, her blue eyes softening with the compassion of their profession. 'Although, inevitably, we can't save every patient. That's a reality of the job, isn't it?'

Damn, he didn't need her seeing him so intuitively. He didn't need this…distraction. And yet she brought his emotions, good and bad, to the surface with her smile and her grit and her…dogged persistence.

He offered a single brisk nod that made his neck feel like a brittle log about to crack and splinter. 'I'll leave you to it then…' Like it or not, he couldn't oversee every aspect of patient care himself. There weren't enough hours in the day, and God knew he'd tried to fill every second as an antidote to being alone with himself. With his vicious thoughts and weighty regrets.

For now, he needed Darcy as much as she needed him.

'I'll be next door dictating letters if you want me.' Joe left the theatre, disposing of his gloves, mask and gown, wishing he could dispose of his remorse as easily.

Here in the confines of the hospital where he'd lived out the worst day of his life, he'd found a modicum of not exactly peace but routine in his life, and that was all he deserved.

No, Darcy Wright was a fascination he couldn't indulge. Not now. Not ever.

CHAPTER THREE

DARCY RETURNED HER toothbrush to her bag and splashed her pale face with cold water. She was used to long sleepless nights on call, but she'd never grown accustomed to the icky dry mouth and gritty eyes of sleep deprivation. It was amazing what a three a.m. mouthful of toothpaste and an invigorating face splash could achieve in lieu of an undisturbed eight-hour sleep.

Almost as invigorating as spending the day and most of the night with the most infuriating man she'd ever met: her control freak boss.

If only she didn't respect his surgical skills and bedside manner so much. If only he was gruff with the patients. But he seemed to come alive when he was helping someone, showing tantalising glimpses of the Joe who was caring, kind and dedicated.

She exhaled, drained by the emotional gamut she'd run since she'd first laid eyes on him the day before. Never had she met someone who simultaneously left her both frustrated and in awe. Who, for every spare second of her long first day, occupied her thoughts in good ways—his skill in the operating theatre and the calm reassuring tone he reserved for his patients—and bad. His ability to push her buttons was unsurpassed and, no matter how many times she told herself it was pointless, ridiculous and, above all, forbidden, she couldn't switch off her attraction.

Fortunately, they'd been too busy with admissions and surgeries for her to dwell on Joe's magnetism and her body's persistent weakness.

Darcy brushed her hair and retied her ponytail, her stomach in knots at the thought of spending the next three months working in close proximity to such an absorbing and exasperating mentor. She could keep her head down, avoid him and ignore the fact that he made sexy look…drab. But if he kept up his hovering and taking over, she might snap and do or say something…stupid.

Darcy's cheeks warmed. If her sisters could see driven, career-minded Darcy now, all rattled and riled by a man, they'd die laughing. Then they'd probably remind her that before her ex, before she'd sworn off dating, Joe was exactly the type of man she'd once fantasised she'd end up with.

'I'm going to marry a builder, like Dad,' said Lily, aged eight.

'I'm going to marry a superhero,' said Stella, aged six.

'I'm going to be a doctor and marry a doctor and live in a castle in Scotland,' said Darcy, aged ten.

Even in childish fantasies she'd felt the need to outshine her sisters and distinguish herself somehow, because she'd grown up uncertain of what she'd done to make her father stay away for increasingly long periods. She'd acted out, imagined a 'them and her' distinction between her sisters that only existed in her head. She'd convinced herself that she must be different if she wasn't even good enough for her own father, who would appear for a wonderful but brief flash and then disappear into the endless passage of time. Darcy never knew when he'd show up again or which of his promised visits he'd keep.

Joe's far from welcoming attitude today had once more brought out those deep-rooted fears of being... inconsequential. Trying to impress such a man would only lead to the kind of heartache she'd experienced over and over as a girl, waiting for the phone to ring. Now, all she hoped was that they could work alongside each other in relative harmony.

Somewhat refreshed, Darcy emerged from the bathroom and came to an abrupt halt. Joe was sprawled on one of the comfy chairs in the theatre staffroom, his hair dishevelled from removing his surgical hat and the fatigue of their long day and night finally haunting his intelligent deep brown eyes.

Her pulse flew. 'Um... Hi, Mr Austin. I thought you'd left,' she said, a rush of compassion hijacking her surprise. His tiredness made him seem more human, more approachable, more real. Positive feelings Darcy wanted to reject and instead question why he hadn't gone home or sloped off to sleep in an on-call room like all her previous consultants.

'I think it's time we use first names, don't you, Darcy?' he said, catching her completely off-guard. 'Is it okay for me to call you Darcy?'

The sound of her name on his lips body-slammed her, robbing her of breath and any hope of coherent conversation.

Every time she succeeded in grappling her opinion of him under control, he morphed again, showing another side of himself, clouding her judgement. Because where yesterday those eyes of his carried nothing but suspicion and distrust, now they seemed haunted by a whole raft of more complex emotions, expressive and open. His tall, lean body—so sexy in his scrubs, which revealed a triangle of dark chest hair, and his powerful arms, corded with muscle—was relaxed. Even his hands were elegant and yet capable in a totally arousing way.

Everything inside Darcy clenched in anticipation. Her head contained a riot of confusing feelings—attraction, exasperation, excitement and exhaustion. But, for all his sex appeal, he was still the man who'd doubted and patronised her all day. She could find him attractive and irritating at the same time.

No—she couldn't find him anything! He was her boss.

'Um… Okay… Joe…' she said in response to his request for informality, his first name intimate on her tongue, sending irrelevant flutters through her belly. 'Do you need me?'

A hint of a roguish smile tugged at his mouth and lit his eyes.

She flushed as she realised that her question sounded…suggestive. More alarming, though, was her insane desire for him to reply 'yes' for all the wrong reasons.

To cover her body's inappropriate, sleep-deprived reaction, she pretended to check her phone for a missed call from Accident and Emergency. All doctors were highly attuned to the sound of a pager or the ringing of their phone—but she needed the valuable seconds to regroup her defences and battle that pesky buzz of attraction that showed no signs of abating, no matter how confounding she found her boss.

'No, I don't need you.' His stare lingered on Darcy as if he had something else momentous to say. It propelled Darcy's frantic pulse to a dizzying new high.

Please, no... The first name thing was shock enough.

'Okay…' she croaked, trying to rein in the physical interest she was certain her weary body couldn't have mustered five minutes ago.

They'd just emerged from a six-hour surgery—a multiple abdominal stabbing case of a man in the wrong alleyway at the wrong time, but fortunately on Joe Austin's watch. Darcy found Joe a fascinating surgeon. He worked with the same dogged precision and minute attention to detail he applied to checking up on her. No blood vessel was too fine to escape cauterisation. No corner or crevice of the abdominal cavity was too obscure to warrant checking. And, unlike Darcy, whose feet and back had ached, leading to the odd fidget and position readjustment, Joe's energy levels had seemed as unwaveringly constant as his concentration and focus.

Their chosen career carried its own unique set of challenges. But the hint of vulnerability she'd seen in his stare when he'd said *'Mistakes cost lives'* was like a shot of curiosity to Darcy's bloodstream. What forces had shaped brilliant and dedicated Joe Austin to be so hyper-vigilant to the point of obsessive? A bad experience? The shock of losing a patient?

And why did she find his intelligence and commitment, even his humanity—on first impressions she'd have declared him incapable of the chink in his armour—the regret she'd spied, so bloody seductive? It would be much easier to dislike everything about him, his overbearing attitude *and* his looks.

'Our stabbing victim is stable and on his way to Intensive Care,' he said.

Darcy sighed, all thoughts of gently enquiring why he was so over-the-top-dedicated evaporating. 'Post-op checks are my job. I just wanted to splash my face with water first.'

He shrugged in explanation and tapped the folder on the seat next to him. 'I went back for my notes.'

Why did his diligence seem to bring all her worst traits to the surface, make her feel…small, somehow not good enough? Was it just admiration for someone she now knew was a surgical legend? Or was it that he didn't seem to see or understand the importance of her career to Darcy, how helping people filled a hole in her heart?

The academic success of her teens came with the kind of praise and accolades that told her that, despite her father's waning interest in her as a daughter, she was okay, good at something. She'd become addicted, her competitive nature blossoming as she chased one success after another. Not that she could have anticipated how fulfilling she'd find a career in medicine.

'Why are you so defensive?' he asked, questioning the shell she used to protect herself when he'd spent the day reminding her of those childhood inadequacies by niggling at the career she took pride in. His expression was infuriatingly steady, as if he had no part to play in erecting her barriers. With a chill that poured through her veins, she realised how effortlessly Joe had jarred defences she'd spent her life fortifying.

But his attitude also reminded her of her ex, Dean's fault-finding, which by the end had felt pretty constant.

'You're rarely home.'

'You work too hard.'

'You put us last.'

Dean was a sculptor. He'd never really understood her drive or career choice, as if wanting to become a surgeon was merely playing at make-believe when the only truly noble endeavour was art. Realising they were headed for angst and heartache, she'd broken off her engagement and made her choice: work.

Joe watched her now, his stare tracing her flushed features as if she had some fascinating and newly discovered disease. Could he read her mind? Could he sense how she'd failed to balance her career and her one serious relationship?

Instead of answering his inflammatory question, she bit out, 'Why are you so intent on doing *my* job before I have a chance to do it first? You said overcautious, but it comes across as…paranoid, as if you trust no one.'

She pressed her lips together tightly. She shouldn't have said that. She shouldn't have argued with him at all. But the same fatigue she'd seen on his face dragged at her, and he'd been a constant burr beneath her skin since he'd walked onto the ward.

'Paranoid…?' he drawled, quietly serious, eyes disturbingly watchful and glittering with provocation. 'Perhaps it's because I hate learning something the hard way.'

Darcy vibrated with remorse. What lesson had he learned that caused such profound over-vigilance?

Joe narrowed his stare in a way that made Darcy think of a powerful predator, lightning fast and ruthless. 'But I asked first.' He raised his eyebrows, waiting.

Darcy sighed; she had some insight into her pushiness. The pain of repeated rejection from her father over the years had made her self-reliant, out to prove herself. It also made her judgement sensitive and conflict avoidant.

Except with this man, with whom clashes came readily.

'I'm a surgeon,' she said. 'It's my job to be assertive

and decisive.' She held his watchful stare pointedly. 'Perhaps *I* hate being underestimated.'

It reminded her that, no matter how hard she tried to be a good daughter, nothing she did helped her to hold onto her father.

She cleared her throat. 'Surely you can see why your tendency to question me as if I'm a novice med student might cause me to be a little…prickly.'

'Noted,' he said, dragging in a prolonged breath and whipping the wind from Darcy's sails. 'Sit down, Darcy.' His face wore a conflicted expression, as if he wanted both her company and to be alone.

She, too, could do with a reprieve from his all-consuming masculinity and the way he seemed to bring out the worst in her.

But as he'd already checked on their last patient she couldn't avoid his order/invitation. But where to sit? Too far away might seem rude, but too close and he might feel crowded, not to mention that she'd end up… distracted.

A small sigh escaped her lips. She was a grown woman for goodness' sake. She wanted nothing to do with her ridiculous…crush. Pulling herself together, Darcy took the seat next to Joe.

Big mistake.

Not only was she close enough for her strung-out senses to detect the subtle spicy tones of his aftershave and body heat, his proximity also reminded her how she'd almost burst into flames when she'd accidentally brushed hands with him in the operating theatre. Time had slowed to a standstill at the connection, a frozen split second where their eyes locked as if seeing each other for the first time all over again. His strong, glove-covered fingers had been warm against hers and, as if defibrillated, Darcy's heartbeat skittered faster than when she'd peered inside the incision in Mr Clarke's abdomen and saw that her diagnosis of a ruptured appendix had been correct, the thrill acute and blinding.

'Why don't you try to get some rest?' she said, newly annoyed by her physical reaction to the man.

Joe shook his head. 'I don't sleep well at the best of times, so there's no point even trying here.'

Something dark shifted in his stare, something she'd seen the first time their eyes had met this morning, only she'd been too caught up in impressing him to attribute the look she now identified: tortured.

Joe Austin was tortured.

By the mistake he was so keen to avoid in future, the bitter lesson he'd learned. All doctors feared losing a patient through some sort of human error.

Darcy swallowed the lump in her throat. The ghost of regret in his eyes called to the part of her that wanted to help people. She still remembered the buzz of caring for her sister, Lily, when she'd broken her leg as a child. She'd felt needed. Valued. It was the first time she'd considered the possibility of becoming a doctor.

But she knew very little about Joe, beyond what she'd gleaned on the internet during a lull in their operating list when she'd snatched a quick sandwich from the cafeteria. Not only famous in the surgical world, Joe was also well-known on the UK celebrity scene as the husband of internationally bestselling fiction author Laura Knight.

Operating on Mr Clarke had cut her fact-finding mission short at that point, his ruptured appendix taking priority over her rampant curiosity and strange and inappropriate dejection.

She forced herself to raise his marital status now.

Hopefully it would act as the final nail in the coffin of her preoccupation with him. 'Won't your wife be expecting you at home?'

The same sinking feeling she'd experienced on seeing a photo of the glamorous, beaming Mr and Mrs Joe Austin earlier today swooped in her stomach. Stupid because of course someone like him—handsome, successful, intelligent—would have a beautiful, talented wife.

'I usually spend my on-call nights here, catching up on work.' Joe's stare took on that intensity he wore when he wielded a scalpel. Directed her way, it made Darcy's breathing shallow.

'And I've been divorced for three years.' A hint of amusement tugged at his mouth as he dropped that bombshell as if he'd seen through her lame fishing attempt.

Divorced...

A worrying wave of relief washed through Darcy's veins. He no longer had a beautiful, talented wife.

Poor Joe...

This was bad news for her, too. Off-limits due to his marital status threw up an instant brick wall. But simply off-limits because he was her boss became a much flimsier barrier.

Darcy looked away—there was no way he could ever know about her secret lusting. Professional judgement she could handle, but another personal disaster at this stage in her career...?

No way.

CHAPTER FOUR

'So why did you choose medicine as a career?' Joe asked, placing an empty coffee mug on the table in front of them.

Darcy's body overheated at the pressure of making conversation with a man who didn't seem to like her in the slightest, perhaps even suspected her inappropriate crush and made her feel like both a siren and a simpleton whose professional input—the one thing in her life she took pride in—was superfluous.

She would have preferred to talk shop, ask him why he'd favoured nylon over silk sutures in the stabbing case, to distract her wayward hormones, which were determined to see him as some sort of sexy doctor pin-up from one of those medical soaps.

'My younger sister broke her leg falling from a trampoline,' she said. 'She was six and I was eight. It was summer, so I spent the school holidays entertaining Lily—fetching her glasses of lemonade, reading to her, scratching her toes and drawing cartoon cats on her plaster cast.' Darcy chuckled at the happy memories, shoving away the recollection of other feelings from that summer. She was supposed to have gone on holiday to France with her father, their first holiday together. She'd been looking forward to it with giddy glee, dancing around the house with excitement and probably annoying her parents with a constant barrage of questions. Then he'd cancelled out of the blue, two days before he was due to collect Darcy.

She could still hear her mother's end of the ensuing tense telephone conversation and how her mother's obvious annoyance with the man who'd flitted in and out of Darcy's life had somehow increased Darcy's disappointment. It had been the first time her blind adoration for her larger-than-life father wavered, her heart breaking, confused over what she'd done wrong. It had also set in motion years of Darcy trying and failing to regain the closeness she'd felt for her father as a young girl, years of seeking his attention, battling the guilt she felt for loving Grant, as if she was somehow betraying her *real* father.

'I liked nursing Lily so much, I knew I wanted to help people,' she said, aware of Joe's continued observation while her insides were so raw.

'What about you?' She tried to brush off the claws of those childhood demons. 'Did you always imagine you'd be a surgeon?'

'My mother was a nurse.' He shrugged as if that explained everything.

Darcy wanted more. Her brain bombarded her with questions to which she wanted answers: *What happened to cause your divorce? Have you moved on? Do you have any children?*

Then he changed tack. 'I took your advice and re-read your CV earlier.'

'Oh...?' Darcy smiled. So he knew her academic accomplishments and her employment pedigree. Perhaps he'd respect her professionally after all. Perhaps their disastrous first day was a blip. Hopefully, without the emotional ups and downs—nerves, the pressure to impress and him chipping away at her confidence—her silly infatuation would evaporate. Before she knew it, she'd be applying for a consultant post with Joe's glowing endorsement.

'I was particularly interested to see you were featured in that TV show—the one that followed a cohort of medical students through university and into their first job. I watched a clip after our ward round this morning.'

Chills doused Darcy, as if she'd dived into the Arctic Ocean. 'Did you?' She clenched her jaw and looked away.

Just when she thought she'd earned a few crumbs of his respect, he seemed to be taking a subtle dig at one of her bad choices. She only kept that show on her CV because the series had gone on to win several TV awards in the reality category, but she'd grown to regret her participation. In her first year at medical school she'd naively signed up, thinking it would help her to stand out from the crowd and a fun way to document the start of her career. Except some of the early episodes showed her and her fellow students letting their hair down. Darcy hadn't taken herself as seriously back then as she did now. She'd been young, uncertain of who she was because she'd recently reached out to her father again, in the hope of forging an adult relationship now that she was a daughter he could surely be proud of.

She'd called him out of the blue, taken the train to Edinburgh, where he'd settled, her heart so full of hope that he'd want to have an adult relationship with his daughter that she could barely breathe. What she'd discovered had torn that foolish heart in two. He had two more daughters. It wasn't that he hadn't wanted a child; he just hadn't wanted Darcy enough to stay in her life.

Young, newly away from the security of home and heartbroken by her father's ultimate act of betrayal, she'd acted out, developed a bit of a reputation as the party girl of the show. The director had delighted in portraying her as the flaky one, not really there to become a doctor. But she'd quickly learned that wasn't who she was. That her father wasn't who she'd hoped he'd be. That she could neither impress him nor make him love her.

Some blinkers could never be replaced once they were removed, and she'd stopped reaching out to him.

Since then, she'd worked hard and made it through med school and earned her job as registrar to the mighty and famous Joe Austin…

Who, of course, would put her in her place, focus on a time from her past that made her seem…frivolous and attention-seeking, when in reality she'd been desperate to prove she deserved to be at medical school, that she'd work harder and longer than the next student to show her father that she could do anything, be anything, even without him.

Darcy's hackles rose to new heights. Of course, Joe wouldn't compliment her research on cirrhosis patients or the fact that she'd presented her scientific paper at the Surgical Advances and Innovations Forum to a delegation of eight hundred in the field last year. He'd formed opinions about her even before they'd met, perhaps because he hadn't chosen her himself. He'd made it clear that he didn't think she was good enough, didn't want her. Why else would he give her such an undeserved hard time? He'd insinuated she was slack about her work, someone he needed to watch closely for mistakes and check up on.

If she hadn't been awake for more than seventeen hours she might have slept on her conclusions, modified her tone, even bitten her tongue.

'If you've read my CV then you know that I take my work seriously. As seriously as you do, in fact,' she said, levelling him with an unflinching stare. She must have sounded highly strung, but Joe's condescending reminder of something she wasn't totally proud of brought her repressed frustrations and the fear of not being good enough to the surface.

'I didn't know it was a touchy subject.' Joe winced, looking immediately contrite.

But it was too late for Darcy, who'd tolerated him hovering and questioning the most basic of her decisions. She wouldn't accept him putting her down after the years of hard work and the sacrifices she'd made for her chosen career.

'You know, I've tried my best to impress you and show you that I'm responsible and diligent and competent in caring for your patients.' With her reserves of resilience against his criticisms drained, Darcy muttered, 'Now I understand the divorce…'

Heat raced up her neck and flooded her face. She'd never before spoken to a senior colleague, or any colleague, like that. What was she doing? She'd sabotage this position and any reference he might give her in the future. She'd blown it within her first twenty-four hours on the job.

She clamped her hand over her mouth, ashamed of her rudeness. She blamed fatigue and stress or her tendency to be prepared for an attack. She'd had a long, emotionally fraught day. Clearly, she wasn't thinking or acting straight.

'Now who's making assumptions?' he replied before she could apologise. 'My marital failure is none of your business.' He leaned forward in his seat so his stare sparked with hers. 'Are *you* in a relationship?' His gaze fell to her left hand, where she'd once worn Dean's engagement ring.

Clearly, she'd touched a nerve, too.

She opened her mouth to tell him, to explain herself, but he ploughed on.

'Have you successfully managed to combine an intense and demanding career with a blissful personal life?' His mouth flattened into a terse line.

For one euphoric second his probing personal question, his interest in her marital status, made her wonder if he was as fascinated by her as she was by him, until she recalled her humiliation and sense of failure when she'd realised that she hadn't been able to make her personal life a success, that she and Dean were incompatible. She'd once thought she'd had it all. The career she'd always wanted. An understanding fiancé. But it hadn't lasted. Dean's support had dwindled as Darcy's hours grew longer, the exams harder, the stresses more absorbing. She'd had nothing in common with his friends and their differences had seemed to amplify in importance as time went by until she'd felt like the outsider the young Darcy had feared she was.

'No, you're right. I've been single for a year.' Darcy braced her hands on the arms of the chair and swivelled her body to face him. 'I put my career first before my fiancé and I called it off. That same career you seem to be implying that I neither deserve nor value. But, as

I see it, we have at least one thing in common—we're both married to our work.'

A glimmer of respect hovered in Joe's steely stare. 'I never said you didn't deserve your career. Of course—'

'You've doubted me at every turn,' she interrupted, her pulse flying as they faced off. 'You know, I never expected us to become friends, but I at least hoped you'd respect my work ethic and the long hard years of dedication and sacrifice I've invested to reach this stage in my career. You know what I've done to get here, because you've done it, too.'

She ignored his deep frown. Ignored the warning bells that she'd made her point and said enough.

'You may not like me, Mr Austin,' she said, returning to their earlier formality, 'but we're very similar, you and I. We put our patients first. We put in the hours. Perhaps because neither of us has anything else in our life…'

Her harsh words hung in the stiff silence. The tense seconds in the wake of her outrageously rude accusations made Darcy's breath come in incensed pants. He too was breathing hard, his dark eyes locked with her blue ones.

Had she flushed her career down the drain? She'd likely lose her job.

And yet a current of suspense hung in the air, tendrils of energy snaking between them, sparks of heat and fire.

Darcy's indignation became swamped by the absurd urge to kiss Joe's arrogant sculpted mouth. It made no sense, apart from the fatigue surely clouding her judgement, the unfairness of her current situation and a sick sense of self-sabotage.

If she was going to be sacked, she might as well go

out with a bang, end her terrible first day, perhaps even her long-coveted career, on *her* terms, not his. Payback for him making her doubt herself all over again when she was within spitting distance of her consultant job and the security of her own achievements.

She could make herself feel a tiny smidgen better and kiss the furious look from Joe's face.

No! Madness.

Except he seemed to sense her wildly inappropriate thoughts. His gaze dropped to her lips. He inhaled sharply. His eyes landed back on hers, their dark depths now glowing with intensity and maybe even the barest hint of challenge, as if he too had felt the same illicit urge.

It happened too quickly to analyse. Darcy sensed movement on Joe's part, but she'd already acted on the insane impulse and actually kissed him, her heart rate galloping so high that she grew dizzy.

For a coherent moment of doubt she gasped against his lips, her eyes searching his, but Joe's fingers were curled around her upper arms and showing no sign of letting go. He kissed her back, those strong, capable hands holding her like a vice, his blazing eyes locked to hers as if he too would make some sense of this risky, ill-judged act neither of them seemed able to resist.

He was party to the same madness that had accosted her. Contagious madness that came from being sleep-deprived.

But Darcy was too far gone to consider the fallout of kissing her boss. Her lips tingled where they were crushed against his, darts of electricity firing through every nerve. For the first time today, she felt like herself: strong, capable, determined.

For a heady moment with his mouth on hers, her

choppy breaths mingling with his rough exhalations, all the blood in her body pooling in her pelvis, she soared. Every deep-rooted doubt planted in the fertile soil of her insecurities dropped away, lighter than feathers, and she surrendered to pure sensation.

Joe's kiss was firm, commanding and inflamed, and it carried a whiff of desperation, as if he'd thought about kissing her long before this moment of joint insanity. As if he hadn't kissed a woman in a while and the desire was bottled up inside him like oxygen compressed inside a cylinder.

The thought of her hot, divorced boss's sex life made her entire body shudder against his chest. But Darcy hadn't thrown caution to the wind, perhaps even thrown away her glowing reference, in order to swoon at her master's touch.

Owning the kiss, she slid her hands from his broad shoulders, where hard muscles bunched under her palms, and tangled her fingers in his hair, directing his head and touching her tongue to his. He grunted out some unintelligible but sexy sound to which Darcy was deaf. All she could hear was the urgent whoosh of blood through her ears. All she could feel was the exhilaration of the endorphins lacing that blood, the high of kissing Joe a fantasy she realised belatedly she'd secretly harboured since she'd witnessed his first unimpressed sneer.

Joe might not respect her professionally but he seemed equally powerless to their ill-judged attraction.

The reminder that they were colleagues and at work elbowed its way to the forefront of her mind. He was her boss. A man she could grow to loathe if he continued to make her job as difficult as he'd made her first day.

She needed to stop this insanity. Now.

With worrying reluctance, she abandoned his hair and positioned her hands to push at his shoulders, even as her lips clung to his in the dying threads of their reckless and forbidden lip-lock.

In that second her pager emitted an eardrum-shattering bleep. Darcy snatched her mouth away, simultaneously shoving at Joe and jerking to her feet. His hands left her waist with almost unwilling slowness. Confused and disoriented, Darcy looked up from silencing the pager clipped to the waistband of her scrubs.

Joe had retreated behind his scowl once more.

Darcy swallowed, trying to ignore the demands of her libido and quash her disappointment, while trying to appear as unaffected as Joe. They were right back where they'd begun. She'd risked her career for nothing.

'If I still have a job,' she said huskily while she willed the colour in her face to fade, 'I'm needed in A&E.' She tightened her haphazard ponytail, avoiding looking at a gloriously dishevelled Joe—messed hair, dilated pupils, bruised mouth.

He raked his hand over his face, where his stubble darkened his strong jaw, his stare somewhere between bewildered and displeased, and gave her a single curt nod.

'Do you need me?' He stood, his voice gruff and his body rigid, as if trying to claw back a shred of their proper professional relationship. Or perhaps already preparing his dismissal speech.

Who knew what would happen in the cold light of a regular work day? Surely she'd be fired for her outspoken attack and for crossing the line and kissing City Hospital's golden boy.

Darcy touched her mouth. Her cheeks tingled from

his stubble, a reminder of the most self-destructive thing she'd ever done. 'Um… I'll let you know.'

What she needed was distance. A chance to analyse what the hell she thought she was doing first arguing with and then kissing her consultant and why she still hadn't outgrown that urge to push herself, be the best she could be, to stand out.

Now look where it had landed her.

She made her way to the emergency department with a sinking stomach as glints of brilliant orange pierced the windows, heralding the dawn of a new day. Too bad it was too late for first impressions.

CHAPTER FIVE

THE FOLLOWING WEEK Joe entered the theatre scrub room, the memory of that kiss thrumming as fresh as if they were still lip-locked. His feet skidded to a halt. He'd been expecting Darcy, of course. He'd requested her assistance in today's complex surgery.

He'd even expected the same euphoric thrill he'd experienced with his mouth on hers—the first woman he'd kissed since his divorce—before his remorse killed the high like a vile-tasting antidote to a sweet, addictive poison.

The door swung closed at his back. Darcy twirled to face him, that now familiar flash of confusion, bravado and need bright in her ocean-blue eyes. He hadn't meant to upset her that night, but he'd seen that look a lot since the kiss—every time they interacted on the ward, in clinic or in Theatre.

'Darcy,' he said in greeting, his voice a grunt strangled by his guilt. Not for the kiss, which while totally unprofessional, he couldn't bring himself to regret, but for bringing his emotional hang-ups into the workplace and making her defensive. To her credit, she hadn't reported him to management for his inappropriate behaviour. She'd merely navigated her job with the same thorough persistence he'd learned was her default position.

But it had left him with more questions than answers.

She'd chosen her career over her fiancé. Why couldn't she have both?

She had regrets. Was that the reason she pushed herself so hard, as he'd once done?

She'd been underestimated, even dismissed in the past, perhaps the reason for the self-doubts she'd confessed. But couldn't she see how exceptional she was?

'Joe,' she said, acting as if everything was normal between them, but up close her eyes were bright with those emotions she'd been trying to conceal all week. Her face was flushed, perhaps with embarrassment, and those delectable lips he recalled the taste of were pursed in defiance. The reminder smacked him in the head with the same force he'd felt when she was crushed against his chest.

But for the shocking intrusion of her pager blaring through the charged atmosphere of the theatre coffee room, she might still be there, captive to the desire she'd awoken in him.

'Thanks for coming to assist.' Joe offered Darcy a tight smile as if they were strangers. He should have apologised sooner, dispelled some of this awkwardness.

'Of course. Where else would I be?' she said, acting with forthright professionalism, when he wanted some answers now that they finally had five minutes alone.

Darcy tied her surgical hat in place. It forced her breasts up and out in his direction, and he had to consciously tear his eyes from the blood-stirring sight she made, his heart slamming against his ribs. He reached for his own surgical hat to stop himself from tucking away that stubborn strand of her blonde hair that always escaped her hat. Now he knew its softness, the faint scent of some sort of floral shampoo, the tickle of it against his face, his fingers burned to touch.

But he had no right. She was his trainee. He'd kissed her like a man starved, tasting her, consuming her throaty little whimpers, learning what made her tremble.

But why had she kissed him back?

Rampant curiosity goaded, made a mockery of his attempts to stay professional.

'Have you performed a Whipple procedure before?' he asked, trying and failing to project a normal tone. Hell, all he wanted to do was kiss her again. Perhaps then he could figure out why those few blissful seconds they'd shared had silenced even his darkest, most intrusive self-recriminatory thoughts.

'Not single-handed.' She cast him a wary look as she tied her mask in place over her beautiful but distracting mouth. 'I've assisted in a handful of cases though, so I'm glad you asked me to help.' She looked away, blinking rapidly.

She clearly wanted to forget the kiss, otherwise she'd have brought it up—Darcy wasn't shy in pushing her agenda or broaching the difficult topics. Perhaps she simply wanted to return to a professional footing. Exactly what he should want.

Except, if forced to admit his deepest darkest desires, he'd need to acknowledge that he wanted Darcy Wright the way he hadn't wanted anyone since his life imploded. A huge part of him was in no way sorry that he'd learned the soft taste of her sensual mouth or the warm feminine scent of her close up or the arousing crush of her breasts against his chest.

Three years without sex was clearly detrimental to his decision-making processes.

But they still needed to work together. It was his job to clear the air. He tied a mask over his mouth to stop any wayward and unprofessional confessions.

'Before we start the surgery, I'd like to apologise.' It was long overdue, his only excuse that he'd tried to maintain some sort of distance over the intervening days, as if to raise the subject of what happened that night would force him to admit the rush he'd experienced when that long-dormant part of him had roared alive at her touch. He'd been Frankenstein's monster reawakened—still cobbled together pieces of his former self, but surprised to find that his bruised and battered heart still functioned.

'I made your first day...difficult.' He winced. 'It's no excuse, but I was going through some...personal stuff. I want you to know that it wasn't my intention to upset you when I mentioned your CV, which, by the way, is very impressive.'

For a second she stared. He braced himself for the inevitable questions or contradictions. 'Thank you.' Then she stepped up to the stainless steel sink and switched on the taps. 'So, I've reviewed the scans and I can see why this case is so complex.' She continued their prior conversation as if he hadn't changed the subject.

What? Where was the tongue-lashing he deserved? Why wasn't she putting him in his place? Unease slithered down his spine—she did seem a little subdued today.

'Darcy,' he said, his tone serious.

She glanced his way and their eyes locked, the connection instant and exaggerated now that they knew the taste of each other. Joe almost forgot himself and where he was, almost reached out and touched her.

'We need to discuss what happened.' He needed to

dissect it and then put it to rest. Then he needed to keep his eyes, hands and lips to himself. Joe started the taps next to hers, doused his hands and arms in the warm water.

Perhaps she'd be more amenable to hearing him out while they prepared for surgery.

Joe reached for a single use scrubbing brush from the dispenser. Darcy reached for one at the same time. Their arms collided. Their hands tangled.

Darcy yanked her arm away as if she'd been scalded.

'After you,' said Joe, breathing through the jolt of heat incinerating his body.

Kissing her that night should have brought him to his senses, shocked his system back into the soul-draining numbness he'd inhabited for the past four years, the place he preferred because that was where he felt closest to Rosie. Only Darcy plagued his every non-work-related thought. Not just the kiss, which was unforgettable enough and fodder for some pretty erotic dreams, from which he woke sweating and hard, but also the flashes of vulnerability she'd shown him that day.

She snatched a packet from the dispenser and tore into it. 'I guess the fact that we're still on first name basis and you haven't fired me yet means we can't avoid this conversation any longer.'

'Why would I fire you?'

She flicked her stare his way, her eyes sincere above her mask. 'Because I shouldn't have done…what I did on call. I was obviously stressed and exhausted. So I'd like to apologise, too. For…you know…the kiss.' She attacked her forearms with the scrubber, the suds stained yellow from the iodine.

Wait… She was taking responsibility for the kiss? Had she missed the way he'd fixated on her mouth, his brain foggy and distracted by the apparent softness of those full lips? Had she forgotten the way he'd crushed her to him like a drowning man, the way that even after the violent and unwelcome intrusion of her pager he'd struggled to relinquish his hold?

For something to do other than yank her back into his arms, Joe began the second-nature ritual of scrubbing up, leaving his mind free to fill in the blanks. Had she needed the balm of his lips as much as he'd needed to taste hers? Something primal shifted inside him. He got to her. It seemed only fair—she'd been under his skin since the moment they'd met on the ward.

'I'm your boss. I crossed a line, Darcy.' Not that he'd change a thing about the kiss itself.

He looked over at her stilled form. He could tell from the look in her eyes that her mask concealed an astonished expression. 'No, *I* crossed the line.'

Joe grinned behind his mask. Typical that Darcy needed to win the pointless argument of who'd made the first move when the real issue was ensuring that it never happened again.

But now she'd given his curiosity an open door.

'And why exactly did you do that?' Joe's nervous system sparked alive. It shouldn't matter why, only he was having a hard time stopping himself from peeling down her mask and repeating the error, God help him.

Darcy's eyes went wide with a flicker of fear, gone as soon as it appeared. She scrubbed at her hands hard enough to leave red welts behind. 'I don't know...'

'Liar.' He stepped closer, his stare laser-focused on hers, water and suds dripping down his arms and onto the floor at their feet. 'Don't forget that I felt your heart thunder and your breath gust. I heard the throaty little moans you couldn't hold inside.'

Why was he pursuing this, goading her to admit something that was irrelevant? Was he a glutton for punishment? Or simply already addicted to the feeling of being alive, to the transient amnesia he suffered around Darcy?

She sluiced her arms under the water, feigning indifference. 'Perhaps I was frustrated that my first day had been a battleground. Perhaps it was payback for how you rattled my confidence with your…hovering. Or maybe it was just plain old temporary insanity.' Abandoning her composure, she whirled to face him, her eyes ablaze. 'Take your pick.' She reached for her mask and tugged it down.

'No, no, no.' His voice was a seductive growl he barely recognised. 'Temporary insanity is *my* excuse.'

Except he'd known exactly what he was doing. She'd awoken him from an emotional drought with her sass and grit, evoking a rampant desire to know if her lips would taste as good as they looked.

They had. Better, in fact. And he hadn't wanted to stop.

'Another thing we have in common then,' she said, with a tremulous quality to her normally clear voice that heated Joe's blood.

'Perhaps…' Lust punched him below the waist as she looked up at him with widened pupils. 'But I don't routinely go around kissing my registrars; in fact, I haven't kissed anyone since my divorce.'

Joe inched closer. 'I've never met a woman so…provoking.' His eyes strayed repeatedly to her mouth, the urge to kiss her again so intense he almost forgot that he'd spent the past five minutes rendering his hands and arms sterile for the impending surgery. Because with their stares locked, and her lips parted, he was struggling to care.

'So why kiss me?' Her chest moved with her rapid breaths.

'Perhaps I hoped that tasting your lips would shunt me back to normal, knock the sense back into me.'

Only it had backfired. Her lips had been soft and desperate, her soft moan barely audible but resonating so deeply with his own desperation and need he'd had to curl his fingers around a handful of her scrub top to stop himself from uttering the feral growl trapped in his throat.

For endless seconds they stood facing each other, too close for colleagues, wet arms and blazing stares the only barrier to everything Joe wanted to say and know and do. The patient wasn't in the operating theatre yet. For one unthinkable second he fantasised about reigniting the madness that had clearly infected them both that night. Every cell in his body felt the urge to pull down his own mask and take her mouth, lose himself until she looked at him the way she had in the on-call staffroom, just before that kiss.

She hadn't been able to stop herself from kissing Joe the man, and he'd been whole for a few minutes, not the damaged animal he'd been every day for the past four long years.

But Joe was that broken man and all the other complex permutations of himself to boot.

'So, what now?' she asked, her voice a whisper, her eyes searching. The newly awakened man in him wanted to see the same wild desperation he'd witnessed when she'd dragged her wet mouth from his, her lips swollen from his desire. It was there in the background, but there was also what looked like understanding, compassion.

That he didn't need.

Joe reined in his urgent and highly inappropriate thoughts, fresh regret dragging at his limbs as he turned back to the sinks. 'Now we perform this Whipple together. I need your help.'

Darcy stood frozen for a few seconds and then nodded with resignation, her long lashes fluttering as she glanced down at the floor. 'Of course.'

Joe resumed scrubbing his hands. Earlier he'd put Darcy's sudden reserve down to embarrassment or lingering resentment for the way he'd treated her that first day. But what if her change in demeanour these past few days meant something else?

With a blow that winded him somewhere in his midsection Joe connected the dots. Her shift in attitude wasn't fear for her job or awkwardness following the kiss.

It was pity.

She knew. About Rosie and how the man she'd wanted that night was a shell—cracked, shattered.

'You know, don't you? About my daughter.' With fiery shame in his veins, he scrubbed his forearms with over-enthusiastic vigour until his skin turned red. 'You've availed yourself of the hospital gossip network.' He couldn't have kept his past a secret for ever, but he'd have preferred that she hear the truth from him direct.

She had the decency to flush, but Joe couldn't bear to see the sympathy in her eyes. He wanted to forget again, to have her look at him the way she had when she'd been in his arms, her breath mingling with his, her fingers tangling and tugging his hair. She kissed like she operated, like she fought her corner. With determination and assertiveness that had somehow roused the man in him from a soulless four-year slumber.

Of course, he was gossip fodder at City Hospital. Even before they'd lost Rosie, his surgical renown and Laura's public persona had created a stir when he'd first arrived, giving him minor celebrity status he'd always dismissed. But did she also know the sordid details of his inadequacies and deepest regrets? How the mighty Joe Austin had once had it all, taken it for granted, been too busy caring for others to notice the seriousness of his own daughter's undiagnosed condition?

'I… I'm sorry.' Darcy dragged him from reliving his pain. 'I promise you I wasn't prying or gossiping.'

Joe couldn't bring himself to look at her again, his unfocused stare aimed at the suds swirling in the sink.

'Some of the surgical staff mentioned the open invitation to your garden party on Saturday and…'

Joe ignored her reasonable tone, brushed aside the fact that he'd meant to issue the invitation to her himself. 'And you discovered that it's in memory of Rosie. Is that why you've been avoiding me? Why you stopped pushing on every patient management decision we've made this week? Out of pity for the broken man who was desperate to forget his grief for a few seconds and kissed you?'

The scrubbing brush dug into the sensitive skin under his fingernails and he welcomed the pain. Perhaps it would act like acupuncture, the physical sting overwhelming the emotional.

'Don't be ridiculous.' Her fire returned. 'Empathy for your loss isn't pity, Joe.' She braced her hands on the edge of the sink as if collecting herself and then pinned him with her determined gaze. 'I'm a doctor; caring for other human beings comes naturally. And I'll always push my own agenda. That's who I am.'

Until now, that facet of her complex personality had earned his fascination and respect.

'Of course you will.' He'd never met anyone with more to prove than Darcy. 'Well, don't worry—your efforts haven't been in vain. I've noticed your dedication this past week—you're on the ward before me every day, leave after me every night, which, considering that I practically live here, is impressive bordering on sycophantic.'

Outrage returned to her glare. 'I'm not sucking up to you. It's my job, a job I love, and I want to be good at it.' She looked deflated and Joe glimpsed that vulnerability once more, his heart thumping with gratitude that he wasn't alone.

She glanced up. 'I need to be good at it.'

Joe frowned. Why? And why would she confess such a thing, to him of all people? To her he was a demanding, unreasonable boss at best and a sad grief-stricken divorcee at worst. But it was all irrelevant. He'd been carried away by that addictive mental silence when he'd kissed her, consumed by feeling normal, like a red-blooded man, indulging again, when all she felt for him was sympathy.

'Listen,' Darcy said, interrupting his reverie, 'I won't come on Saturday if it would be…inappropriate.'

Oh, no, he couldn't leave things this way. They faced a complicated procedure this afternoon, so he needed to wrap up this disastrous conversation. But he *was* a red-blooded man. He was broken, yes, but he wasn't dead. If he focused on their attraction, one he knew she reciprocated, perhaps he could distract himself from the self-loathing he felt at any mention of Rosie's name, and distract Darcy until she looked at him like she needed the connection, the life-affirming thrill as much as he did. Indulging his attraction was risky; he was her boss. But he could detach his feelings from the workplace. Darcy would soon move on and he'd never allow his attraction to influence her career.

He smiled, the expression brittle. 'You're very welcome—I'd planned to invite you anyway. The weather is forecast to be glorious, the food will be delicious and it will be a great opportunity for you to socialise with the rest of the surgical staff.' He rinsed the iodine-coloured suds from his arms and turned off the taps with his elbows, holding his wet arms up between them. 'But by all means stay away if our obvious attraction will make you uncomfortable.'

She swallowed, her inhale shuddering through her as she tried to grapple control over her body.

'As for the kiss...' He slowly traced her parted lips with his stare. 'I would apologise, too, only I just can't bring myself to regret it.'

He moved to the swing door to the operating room, casting her a final pointed look. 'But for your pager going off, I might not have stopped. Think on that next time you feel sorry for me.'

The desire that lit her eyes momentarily pierced the shock on her face, but it was little comfort. For now, she'd infected his blood and no amount of scrubbing could eradicate the truth. He wanted to be immune to the way she made him feel. Now that she saw him for who he was, knew all his sordid little secrets, he *needed* to be immune. And, like any disease, there was only one way to build up that resilience, to remove Darcy from his system so he could again feel normal: greater exposure.

CHAPTER SIX

DARCY NIBBLED AT her lip and glanced around the immaculate garden of the family home in the Surrey countryside just outside London. Joe was nowhere to be seen. A stitch settled under her ribs and the delicious mouthful of Pimm's and lemonade soured on her tongue as her gaze swept over the back of the house and the open French windows. She couldn't seem to stop her almost frantic search.

Just one glimpse of him; that was all she wanted. So she'd know he was okay, surviving this difficult day and all its memories.

She thought back to the day of the Whipple surgery, the stomach-churning mix of desire and doubt. No one liked to think they were the source of local gossip, but why was Joe so defensive about his daughter's death? The tragedy of losing his little girl, while devastating, wasn't his fault.

Unless he blamed himself somehow.

At least his personal experience explained his caution and conscientiousness.

She'd tried to stay away from today's event, to show him that the last thing she felt was pity, that the last thing she wanted to do was pry into his still raw grief, but his words had swirled through her mind, drawing her to him like a constant lure.

As for the kiss... I just can't bring myself to regret it.

Neither could she. Her stomach swooped, all nervous anticipation and fizzing excitement. Surely he'd make an appearance soon.

'Beautiful, isn't it?' said Isha, who had one eye on her energetic daughter. Together with a ragtag group of other children of varying ages, the sweet ten-year-old with her mother's eyes was trying to negotiate the rules for the croquet set up on the pristine lawn.

Darcy nodded, fussing with the frilly neckline of her prettiest sundress. She'd spent way too long preparing for this event, gone all out with subtle make-up and products designed to transform her poker-straight hair into a careless, textured style as if she'd spent the day at the beach. Perhaps Joe had been and left and wouldn't even witness her efforts to look good. For him.

'I'm not sure I should have come,' said Darcy, nerves jittering in her chest. 'I feel like an imposter.' Especially after her last real conversation with Joe unrelated to work had ended in confusion and renewed wariness. 'He doesn't even like me and I'm standing on his lawn sipping Pimm's.'

This was a mistake. But after the shock of discovering that Joe had lost his only child, she'd needed to reassure herself, to witness his resilience and to be there if he needed...

What? She snorted. If he needed to talk he wouldn't seek out Darcy. Their current communication style was formal and polite, to say the least.

'Don't be ridiculous,' Isha said. She'd been the one to encourage Darcy to attend the garden party, which, together with the infamous Christmas party fund-raiser, seemed to be the talked-about surgical department so-cial event of the year. 'He's asked about you every day this week.' Isha took a sip of her drink and waved hello across the garden at a striking, heavily pregnant bru-nette who looked vaguely familiar.

Darcy practically cricked her neck with the speed she swivelled to stare, gobsmacked, at Isha. 'He has not.' Treacherous fingers of delight danced down Darcy's spine. She hadn't been able to stop thinking about Joe; had he been similarly preoccupied?

Had he scoured the hospital for a chance glance of her? Had he awoken from hot, sweaty dreams where the unwelcome interruption of that call to A&E had never happened?

The nurse nodded slowly, a knowing grin compress-ing her lips. 'He has. But don't worry. He's careful to ask under the guise of checking that you've settled at City. But he can't fool me.' Isha tapped the side of her nose and winked. 'I've seen the way he looks at you when he thinks no one is watching.'

'Oh, stop. He's my boss.' Darcy hid her conflicted euphoria behind an exaggerated roll of her eyes. She was the one who needed reminding that Joe was strictly off-limits. She jammed her sunglasses back on her face and looked away to where Isha's husband was discuss-ing football with a few theatre staff and nurses she rec-ognised.

'Don't believe me, huh…' said Isha. 'Well, how do you explain that he never asked about your predeces-sor's well-being? Not once in six months. Whereas with you he seems to require a daily update.'

Just like she sought him out at every opportunity. Oh, she was careful to disguise her obsession—seeking his medical advice or updating him on a particular patient. But perhaps she was fooling only herself.

Despite her sternest internal lecture to discount as preposterous the information Isha had just shared, elation sang through her bloodstream, making her hot and restless and even more desperate to see Joe.

The unfinished business between them was stacked sky-high.

Darcy bit into a chunk of ice, the well-timed frigid shock the jolt she needed. What was she thinking? She was his registrar—they couldn't happen. Only they kind of already had—that kiss, their botched apologies, his startling and extremely hot confession that he was as into that kiss as she'd been.

Darcy fanned her face and stepped further into the shade of a giant oak tree in the centre of the lawn. 'That's because he's a control freak who doesn't trust me to order an X-ray without his say-so.'

She winced at her disloyalty. He was *her* control freak.

Now she knew that he'd lost his daughter she understood that he had good reason. She couldn't blame him for being thorough, overly cautious, meticulous. Doctors set higher standards for themselves when it came to the health of their loved ones, probably the reason they weren't allowed to treat family members—too close, too emotional, no perspective.

Which also accurately described her Joe-seeking behaviour today.

She scanned the party once more, eyes burning for sight of him, fingers tingling to touch him the way she almost had in the scrub room the other day. Darcy swallowed the anticipation lodged in her tight throat. Despite

Isha's insinuation, anything beyond the wary tension they currently shared seemed insurmountable.

She needed to confront him again, outside of the hospital. To work out this mess away from the expectations of their professional roles, where they could just be Joe and Darcy, a man and a woman having an honest conversation about how to navigate their undeniable attraction.

Recognising the direction of her thoughts, she swallowed hard. What was she thinking?

Darcy's priority had to be her career. She'd abandoned the small gains and big losses of dating to climb this final slope to the pinnacle, her consultant job. She couldn't risk it all for a…fling, no matter how tempting.

Fortunately, Joe was too professional to put them in that position. He hadn't dated since his divorce. Despite returning that kiss she'd smacked on him, he'd given no sign he intended to allow this to go any further. Like Darcy, he valued his job. And besides…everything she did seemed to provoke him.

This mounting evidence to support her decision should reassure, only she felt…deflated.

'It looks to me that you're equally invested in his whereabouts,' said Isha with a smidgen of sympathy in her perceptive eyes. 'You haven't stopped searching him out since we arrived.'

Darcy glanced down at the ground, pretending to examine the heel of her sandal. She needed to be more careful if her growing infatuation was that obvious.

All week she'd tried to focus on work, on their patients and the million jobs in a standard day in the life of a surgical registrar, but respect for the man she was desperately trying to ignore had become overwhelming. He spoke to the patients with a compassion and honesty she tried to emulate. He knew them as well as she did—every blood result and X-ray finding, the names of their loved ones and favourite pastimes.

'I want to know that he's okay with my being here, that's all.' And that caring part of her needed to be on hand to offer comfort. She couldn't even fathom what it must be like to lose a child.

Just then Isha's husband called her over. Darcy smiled and wandered over towards a stunning wilderness area alive with bees dancing between every type of flower.

'Darcy...that is you?' a male voice said.

Darcy looked up, her disappointment that the man addressing her wasn't the one she wanted to see locked behind a polite smile.

'Aaron—what are you doing here?' She shook his hand and he pulled her close for one of those awkward hug and cheek-kiss combinations of people who came from the same place but only really knew each other in passing.

'I heard you'd taken a job at City. I'm tutoring the newest intake of general practitioners there this term.'

Darcy, nodded, a stab of homesickness catching her by surprise. Aaron was a rural GP from Abbotsford, Darcy's home town. 'Look out for Stella. She's on the GP training programme, so she might be in one of your lectures.'

At the mention of her sister's name, his smile seemed strained, his expression shifty. 'I will...'

Darcy's curiosity flared. Stella had a bit of a crush on Aaron years ago. Could there be something going on between them...? She'd have to push her sister for details later.

'So, you're working for Joe?' said Aaron, collecting himself.

Darcy nodded, her pulse picking up at the opportunity to talk about the man never far from her thoughts. 'How do you two know each other?'

'We met at med school, flatted together for a couple of years, back in the old days.' Aaron looked across the garden with a fond smile, 'Molly and I were friends with Joe and Laura before…well…you know.'

Before Aaron's wife Molly died, leaving him a single parent to their newborn baby—the story was the local tragedy back home—and before Joe and Laura divorced.

'She looks great,' Aaron continued, his gaze focused on the gorgeous pregnant brunette. 'I'm happy for her. If only Joe could move on, too.'

Darcy followed his line of sight to Joe's ex-wife, who Darcy guessed was in her third trimester. 'That's Laura Knight?' Of course Joe's ex would be here.

Aaron nodded. 'Have you met her?'

Reeling, Darcy shook her head. Before she could acknowledge the inappropriate rush of possession she felt for Joe, her breath trapped in her lungs. Joe chose that moment to appear from the back of the house and join his ex and the tall greying man with his hand in the small of her back, who was presumably the bump's father.

Blind to the others in the group, Darcy's eyes stung at the sight of Joe dressed casually in faded jeans and navy T-shirt. Still heart-stoppingly gorgeous, he looked…different. The relaxed outfit somehow softened him, made him more complexly human, more three-dimensional and real. It was as if the ex-husband and father elements of him amplified outside of the hospital environment.

Here, in his former back garden, he seemed like just a man. A virile, steadfast, reliable and honourable man, who was nonetheless driven by demons, loss and grief.

Darcy's heart clenched violently. Why did that call to her on so many levels? Why couldn't she keep Joe Austin and all his niggling negatives at arm's length emotionally? Was it just her doctor's gene, a reflex need to help people in pain? Or was it the fact that, professionally, since the Whipple operation, she felt that he needed her, trusted her a little more?

Darcy gulped her drink to hide the glut of confusing feelings from Joe's friend.

Just then Joe glanced in their direction. His eyes locked with Darcy's and her body actually shuddered. The warm summer-scented air stilled. The hum of insects and the chatter of surrounding conversations dimmed.

Stripped bare, Darcy wondered if all of the assembled guests, Joe included, could see every one of her emotions.

They hadn't been alone since the Whipple operation. Since they'd acknowledged the kiss—Darcy with an apology and Joe with his stark admission that he hadn't wanted it to stop. And they weren't alone now, but they might as well be for the heat and awareness that connected his stare to hers as if by an invisible thread that stretched across the lawn.

All of the reasons they couldn't be that she'd cemented in her mind crumbled.

He wanted her. She wanted him—he was gorgeous, and that single half-arsed kiss had blown her mind. Darcy felt as if she might actually melt into a puddle. Her body came alive, her breasts tingled and heat pooled between her legs.

Joe pressed a kiss to his ex-wife's cheek, shook her new partner's hand and then made a beeline for her and Aaron. Every relaxed step he took across the grass jolted through Darcy's weakened body like a shockwave. When his stare swooped from her eyes to her chest, and lower, she felt it caress her skin as sure as if it were his warm, confident touch.

Darcy swallowed past her dry throat. She was in so much trouble.

While Joe and Aaron exchanged warm greetings with mutual back slaps and genuine laughter, Darcy contemplated running away. She'd done what she'd come here to do: ensure he was okay. Except it made her breath catch to see Joe's face transformed during the moment of unguarded joy as he welcomed his friend. How was it possible for him to be any hotter, and why was she so desperate to be the reason for his happy, relaxed smile?

'Darcy, thanks for coming along.' His voice carried none of the anger and accusation of their last personal conversation, only warmth and something else, something exhilarating that sounded like a secret code. He kept his hands to himself, to Darcy's relief. If he'd touched her or politely kissed her cheek in her current conflicted state, she might actually hurl herself into his arms in front of all assembled.

'You were right about the weather,' she said in a panicked search for appropriate words. 'What a beautiful day.' She chewed the inside of her cheek, disgusted that, after waiting so long for him to appear, her concern growing with every second, all she could dredge up was an observation on the weather, when she had so much to say, to ask, to understand and explore.

She searched Joe's eyes for his feelings. Should she

offer words of condolence? Would he want her sympathy when things between them were so…complicated and strained? She hated that he thought she pitied him, when the opposite was closer to the truth. In the face of his loss, she respected him even more for being the man she'd come to know: kind, dedicated, sexy as hell…

'I'll leave you two to catch up,' croaked Darcy, shuffling away from the friends when all she wanted to do was get Joe alone. But this wasn't the time or place and being alone with him was…dangerous.

At least she'd seen with her own eyes that he seemed fine.

Joe's hand landed on her arm, halting her escape. 'Can you spare me a minute?'

She froze under his touch, which was warm and electric and way too tempting to deny. Aaron muttered something about refilling his drink and sauntered casually away.

Finally alone, Darcy faced Joe, tongue-tied for the first time in her life.

'It's good to see you away from work.' His stare was banked with sincerity, searching and intense. The force of it, the way heat burned across her skin confirmed that at least to her body Joe was primarily a man, not her boss.

He stepped infinitesimally closer, the way Darcy longed to do, but her feet were stuck on the grass, her knees so wobbly she'd had to lock them to stay upright. 'We need to talk—I've been…thinking.'

Yes, her too! Only now he stood before her in the flesh, his dark hair lifted by the breeze, his haunted eyes narrowed against the sun and his familiar scent bathing her in a delicious cloud, she had the strong urge to hide from his extreme magnetism and her convoluted feelings.

'I know this must be a very difficult day for you.' *Don't touch him. Don't touch him.* 'I'm so sorry, Joe.'

His sadness-touched smile was unadorned. 'No more difficult than every other day.'

Darcy's heart cracked for him. The gift of his honesty and openness pulsed through her until she was certain she'd act on the compulsion to hold him. He flashed the guarded smile he usually wore at a group not far from them, reminding Darcy that while she might feel as if they were the only two people who existed, they were no more alone than at the hospital.

Would she need to wait for their next night on call to get him to herself? Except she wanted, no, needed, all the barriers she could find. They kept her on course, reminded her why she was single. Because sometimes, like now, when she caught Joe's eye, momentarily forgot he was her boss, she questioned her choice.

But that was just lust.

'What were you thinking?' Could those around them see her body's desire for him? Could they tell, even as she clung to her denial, that if she wasn't careful she'd have to acknowledge other feelings, alarming feelings?

No—it was just professional respect.

Joe winced, his expression torn. 'Now isn't really the time.' He glanced back at his ex-wife, who smiled. Darcy sensed their ongoing connection and shuffled her feet, unsettled. What must it be like to lose a child? How did Joe feel, seeing his ex move on? Were they still as close as they seemed, and why should it matter so much to Darcy, who neither wanted nor had any claim?

'Can we meet for a coffee, outside of work?' he said, sending her pulse galloping. 'Are you free tomorrow?'

The strength to make an excuse drained away. 'Okay…' Her voice was an anxious croak, as well it should be. Meeting away from the hospital sent a certain message. They weren't friends. Would it be a date? Would he suggest a wild sex-only fling so they could get all of this tension out of their systems? Would she run for safety or leap into his arms, lips first?

Just then a cry startled them both from their bubble of intimacy. Darcy's eyes flew to the source of the sound, her adrenaline soaring to high alert.

She heard Joe's gasp at the same moment he grabbed for her hand, as if acting on instinct. He jerked into action, taking Darcy along too.

Hand in hand, as if it was the most natural thing in the world, they raced across the lawn towards what was clearly some sort of emergency. Darcy's drink spilled over her free hand before her brain kicked in and she passed the glass to a startled guest.

Joe and Darcy skidded to a halt at the small huddle of horrified adults. The child at the centre was no more than eight years old and lay, pale and lifeless, on the grass. Flecks of bright green pond weed clung to her hair, making her pallid skin even more waxen.

Darcy dropped to her knees on the other side of the little girl. Joe leaned over the girl's head, checked for signs of breath on his cheek. Darcy fingered her tiny wrist and then her neck for a pulse.

Their eyes locked over the girl's lifeless form. Darcy nodded and Joe shook his head, silent communication loud and clear between them. She had a pulse but wasn't breathing.

'What happened?' asked Joe as he rolled the child onto her side to clear the water from her mouth.

'She was running,' said the mother with imploring

eyes. 'She tripped and fell into the pond. I think she must have hit her head because she can swim, but she didn't. Please help her.'

Joe rolled the girl onto her back and inflated her chest with a rescue breath. 'Can you still feel a pulse?' he asked Darcy.

'Yes, but it's faint,' said Darcy, focused on Joe and the girl. 'Could be a concussion.' She quickly examined the girl's head and found a scalp contusion under her hairline. 'Looks like she did bump her head, perhaps on one of the rocks.'

Joe nodded and continued resuscitation, his calm determination a wondrous sight in the highly emotive atmosphere.

Darcy took command of the surrounding situation, recruiting Aaron to herd the guests inside the house and give them space. Every face was etched with distress and they didn't need an audience.

'Does she have any health conditions?' Darcy spoke to the child's parents, gleaning her medical history, while Joe breathed for her. 'Is she on any medication?'

The frantic parents shook their heads in unison. Darcy felt again for a pulse and gave Joe a reassuring nod.

With that the girl spluttered and coughed up a mouthful of water. Joe turned her onto her side and placed her in the recovery position, elation bright in his eyes. Eyes that clung to Darcy's as if he needed her presence in order to breathe.

Darcy's heart swooped in her chest, her own relief for the little girl, her parents and for Joe a high in her blood. She recalled the way he'd gripped her hand almost instinctively, as if he'd needed her in that moment of surging adrenaline.

Darcy sagged back on her heels. Her feelings for Joe roared out of control. The event had been scary enough for all of them, but for Joe, today of all days, a near miss like that would likely trigger all sorts of sorrow.

Darcy took the blanket someone had retrieved from the house and draped it over the child's slender body.

Joe rested his hand on top of Darcy's on the girl's shoulder. 'Thank you.' He swallowed. His low words were just for her and emotion blazed from his eyes, dragging an answering surge from deep within Darcy's chest. It was as if they were the only two people in the garden again.

Or maybe it was just the adrenaline, pure and simple. It was one thing to tackle medical emergencies at the hospital, but out in the community, without equipment or drugs, another matter entirely.

'*You* revived her,' Darcy said, checking the girl's pupillary reflexes, although she knew from the pink tinge to her skin that she was out of imminent danger.

Her sobbing parents knelt and talked to their daughter, whose name was Holly, soothing her with comforts and reassurances.

'She'll need to go to A and E,' explained Darcy, because Joe had fallen into a pensive silence. 'She'll need to be checked out and she might need a scan to exclude any head injury.'

Darcy wanted to hold Joe so badly; she had to remind herself where and who they were. Just because she felt a greater connection to him, felt as if he truly valued her as a colleague, didn't mean he had any feelings for her as a woman, beyond simple physical attraction.

And she shouldn't have feelings for him either.

When the paramedics arrived Joe and Darcy handed

over Holly's care, supplying a succinct history of what
had occurred to the ambulance crew.

Once more alone, side by side on the lawn, Darcy
sensed Joe's withdrawal, chiding herself for her flight
of fancy. Of course, he had no feelings for her. He was
grieving. He was the host and, even though it seemed
the party was over, he had friends, family, responsibilities here.

Yes, he'd needed her at a time of medical crisis, but
life had taught her to never place her vulnerable heart
into the hands of another. Ten minutes ago she'd wanted
to get away from Joe and the way he made her feel the
first tender shoots of romantic possibility.

She should trust that instinct.

CHAPTER SEVEN

JOE'S ENTIRE BODY sagged with relief as his car rounded the bend in the gravel driveway of the house he'd once shared with his wife and daughter. Darcy stood outside the gates under the shade of a tree, her face downturned to her phone. How could just the sight of her in her pretty floral sundress be such a balm, today of all days, especially in light of the close call with little Holly?

Because he couldn't get her out of his mind, that was why.

How had she, this fiery, forthright woman, penetrated the fog he'd lived under for four years, like a lone but warming ray of sun? How had she somehow kickstarted a part of him relegated to irrelevant while he'd dealt with his grief over his inadequacies as a father and husband? Not that he was miraculously cured—he'd never be free of his regrets. But perhaps the universe was trying to tell him that he still had worth as a man, not just as a doctor. That he needed more than work.

But did he deserve more?

He pulled up and jumped out of the car. He hadn't realised how much he needed to see the smile in her eyes, albeit hesitant, until he basked in it now.

'I thought you'd left ages ago.' While he'd wrapped up the party and reassured the guests that he, Laura and Holly would be fine. The minute he could reasonably leave he'd snatched up his keys and made a bid for escape, that part of him that had reached for her hand seeking Darcy out among the last party stragglers.

'Isha and her family had to leave,' she said in explanation. 'But I wanted to make sure that Holly and her parents were okay.'

Joe nodded, grateful now, as always, for her compassionate and professional nature. 'Do you need a lift?' He breathed through the rapid thumping of his heart, refusing to acknowledge how much he needed her to say yes.

'I was just going to order a ride.' She waggled her phone in his direction.

Her eyes, those deep pools of blue, saw way too much of his shredded composure. While he prided himself as a guarded and private man, Darcy seemed an expert at peeling back his layers. Was that why he'd reached for her hand the minute the emergency registered in his head? Because he needed her in order to feel…better, to feel something other than the flat, colourless emotional void of his pre-Darcy existence?

'I'm going back to London. I can take you.'

She frowned and he shoved his hands into his pockets.

'I'm trying to get you alone, Darcy, for that talk we discussed earlier.' And because she filled his head morning and night and something had to be done. Should he find her another position, out of temptation's way? A surgical registrar of Darcy's calibre would be an asset to any team. She'd be snapped up. He'd come to depend on her, handing over more and more responsibility this week while he'd left work at a reasonable hour in order to assist Laura with the preparations for today's fundraiser.

More importantly, though, the thought of not seeing her every day left him hollow and restless.

Joe opened the passenger door and shot her his *I mean business* look. 'Just get in so we can get out of here—it's been a long day.'

'Okay, sure. Thanks,' she said, her smile wobbling as if with nerves. Without further argument, she slid into the passenger seat and buckled her seat belt.

Joe climbed in and set off. For a long time they sat in loaded silence, as if neither of them wanted to break the tension that filled the car. Joe wound through the country lanes, his focus on the road but his awareness of Darcy breathing next to him, her light floral scent rousing his senses, made him grip the steering wheel tighter in case his hands decided to tremble. In case he pulled the car into the nearest lane and dragged her to his kiss.

'I called the hospital and spoke to Holly's mum,' said Darcy, her tone soft and reassuring, the way he'd heard her speak to distraught relatives or seriously ill patients. 'They're keeping her in overnight for observation, but the CT scan was all clear.'

'That's good.' Joe hid the mess of his conflicted emotions behind a tight smile.

'She was lucky that it happened in your garden,' she said, respect clear in her expression.

Darcy's calm, confident presence had soothed the rage of his pulse and the roar of his adrenaline-laced blood. Not that he'd forgotten his first response training, although it had been a while since he'd managed an emergency outside of the hospital and without a team of other staff. But the seriousness and timing of the incident—a day when his thoughts naturally revolved around Rosie and how she should be there, running around the lawn in her bare feet, dark hair flying behind her—struck him with a wave of fresh grief.

'Or unlucky—I should have drained that pond years ago,' Joe said pointedly, his regrets returning tenfold.

While focused on providing mouth-to-mouth resuscitation to the child, he'd had to stop himself from imagining it was Rosie whose life he'd been attempting to save. The relief of Holly's first spluttered breath had been overwhelming and disorientating because she was another man's beloved daughter, not his.

Rosie was still gone.

'That's not true, Joe. Accidents happen every day. She tripped and hit her head. That can happen anywhere, and we both know that children can deteriorate quickly, but also recover just as speedily.'

As if realising that recovery wasn't always the case, she sucked in a gasp.

Joe glanced at Darcy. She wore the same expression she'd had when his eyes had sought hers after reviving Holly. Her gaze filled with understanding, as if she knew his innermost thoughts, understood his conflicts and wanted to comfort him.

'Are you okay?' she whispered, conveying their new and growing intimacy.

He swallowed, feeling anything but okay. He wanted so many things in that moment. He wanted Darcy with something close to a terrifying ferocity. Because the way he felt around her confused him, as if she lessened his pain and he'd forgotten how to live without his grief. His grief was his only connection to Rosie. He'd cling to it until his own final breath.

'Define okay?' He focused on navigating the roundabout, when all he wanted to do was touch her face, trace the sun-kissed freckles across her nose, slide his fingers through her hair, drag those lush lips to his until the noise in his head fell silent. He'd tried but he couldn't stop craving the release he'd experienced when they'd kissed that first night. He couldn't switch off his eagerness to know everything about her, not just as a doctor but as a woman, a friend, a sister and daughter...

She sighed, her hand twitching in her lap. He curled his fingers around the steering wheel to stop himself from reaching out to hold that hand once more, because it had felt so good there during those few brief moments.

'Today can't have been easy for you,' she said. 'I guess I'm asking in a not-so-subtle way if you want to talk about it.'

He swallowed, so tempted to lay himself bare to her. Perhaps he'd scare her away and he wouldn't need to deal with his feelings of inconvenient attraction. Normally he avoided talking about Rosie. While he thought about her constantly, discussing his little girl amplified his guilt and failure as a father.

Words couldn't bring her back.

'Not easy on you either, with the unexpected emergency,' he hedged, waiting for the lid on his emotions to snap closed, as it usually did when anyone strayed too far into his personal territory. 'Are *you* okay?'

'I'm fine.' She smiled and something shifted in his chest. 'I was shaken, of course. The adrenaline and the thought of the possible consequences.'

Joe nodded. Darcy was right about how rapidly children, in particular, could deteriorate. Rosie had gone downhill over a few short hours.

They stopped at traffic lights. 'I'm... I'm glad you were there,' he said. This time he did reach for her hand.

'I'm glad you were there, too.' She gripped his fingers the way she'd done as they'd run to help Holly.

They both stared at her lap, at their hands entwined there, neither speaking or moving a muscle as if acutely aware of the momentousness of the simple comforting gesture.

The lights changed. He released her hand reluctantly. 'It's been a while since I performed CPR out in the field.' Darcy's junior status meant she'd much more likely have encountered an acute head injury emergency more recently than him. In the few short weeks they'd known each other he'd come to rely on her clinical acumen and clear-headed decisions.

'You were great,' she said.

Their eyes met. They were skating the issue, the big conversation.

'You know I mean it, Joe... If you want to talk, I'm happy to listen. I can only imagine what you and Laura have been through.'

'You met Laura?' Why was the idea of that so strange? Laura was remarried. He respected Phil, her second husband, even liked him. Were his feelings for Darcy, his strengthening obsession, bordering on more than desire...?

No, he couldn't allow that.

She nodded, her stare wary. 'She found me afterwards and thanked me for helping to handle the emergency. She seems lovely. She's very beautiful and talented—I've read a few of her books.'

Joe nodded. 'She is all of those things.' *As are you.*

His mind veered close to disintegration as his worlds, past and present, desires and despair collided. He had to stay strong, as he'd always been. He couldn't fall apart then and he couldn't succumb to emotion now.

'Thanks for the offer, but there's nothing to talk about.' He changed lanes and put his foot down as the familiar shame made his hair stand on end. 'I was an absent father. My daughter died. My marriage couldn't survive. End of story.' His tight throat strangled his voice. He'd passed the point of wanting to impress Darcy. In fact, a part of him wanted to let go. To pour out his every ugly, loathsome feeling and see what she'd do with the mess.

'You were *not* an absent father.' The force of her vehemence startled him.

'How would you know?'

'I know because I had an absent father, literally,' she continued, pain in her eyes. 'I still do.'

So this was the issue at the core of all her vulnerabilities. Was the man she described, the one clearly responsible for her self-doubts, the reason she pushed herself so hard? Did she need to feel worthy of his love? Was that why she'd given up on her fiancé too? To protect herself from being so...vulnerable?

He fought the rampant urge to ask her for all the details. What right did he have picking over her pain when he fiercely guarded his own?

'I'm sorry that you had that experience,' he said, hating the idea of Darcy being hurt.

'It's okay.' She stared at her lap, where her hands twisted. 'I'm better off without him, although it took me a lot of years to realise that.' She looked out of the window as they covered some miles back to the city, the traffic building and the fields of gold fading.

Joe ruminated over his own regrets, comparing himself, his desire to provide well for his family after growing up in relative hardship, to the painful picture of absent fatherhood Darcy painted.

'Was he ever in the picture?' he asked.

'My parents split before my first birthday. He visited sporadically for the first few years, took me places, brought gifts. Then as I grew older the visits dwindled to once a year. He always had a believable excuse, just enough of an explanation for me to feel somehow guilty for missing him. I had romantic childhood dreams that one day he'd come back for good, settle close and be a real father, like Grant, my stepfather,' she said, her wistful tone tugging at a place in Joe's chest that had become way too invested in her well-being. 'I spent hours lying on my bed, staring at my ceiling, waiting.'

She turned back to Joe, her eyes hard. 'Then I grew up.'

She sounded matter-of-fact, but he could see that the rejected little girl still resided inside Darcy. Joe ached to hold her. No one should experience that level of deep-rooted abandonment, constantly raised and then dashed hopes. Darcy was a bright and bubbly woman— warm, caring, funny. It was a privilege to know her. Who wouldn't want to be a part of her life?

Of course, she'd hate his sympathy as much as he'd refused hers.

'I know we haven't known each other that long, but you were a great father, Joe. Trust me. I saw the photos of you and your family when I used the bathroom earlier. You and Rosie adored each other—it's there in your eyes, in your smiles, in all those experiences you shared. You showed up, you cared and she knew you loved her; that's what matters.'

Joe's throat tightened until he considered pulling over in case he grew dizzy. Yes, he'd been there, largely, for the big days. The birthdays and Christmases, the first day of every school year and the annual holidays. But he hadn't been there for all of the little things, the everyday moments. He'd been too focused on his career aspirations, in part to provide for Laura and Rosie and give them the best life he could, but also to fulfil the needs of his ego. Now he ached with how much he wished he could turn back the clock and relive every ordinary second better, cherish the little things, the quiet moments, the beautifully mundane.

'I spent too much time at work for stupid superficial reasons,' he admitted, his throat raw.

Darcy shook her head, as if confident in her belief. 'Wanting a career and excelling at it isn't stupid.'

'Maybe, but my main motivation was to take financial care of my family. After my father died my mother struggled to be the breadwinner and the single parent to my sister and me. I vowed to do better, to provide well, to ensure my family had more. And for what? It was all pointless. I lost all that was important.'

'You did your family proud—your home was beautiful and, by the looks of those photos, you gave Rosie a wonderful childhood full of laughter and rich experiences.'

Joe's heart stuttered painfully as he thought of the photos Darcy referred to. Rosie had been the happy, vibrant girl Darcy saw. She'd loved to tease Joe and always had some scheme on the go, be it to enlist his help with her latest craft project or game of hide and seek, the rooms of that family home he'd once occupied alive with chatter and giggles.

He glanced Darcy's way, marvelling at her sharp observation and intuition, wondering what kind of little girl she'd been. Just having her at his former home had made him want things—things he'd long ago sworn off. Even before the emergency he'd wanted to leave, to take Darcy with him and escape the place where he felt the biggest failure of all. His past. She grounded him somehow. Made him feel more like his old self. Oh, he'd never be whole again, but Darcy's presence, the way she looked at him, the way she asked his opinion and advice without taking any of his nonsense… it made him glimpse a part of the man he'd been for a while, as if discovering a dusty old photograph.

At his silence, Darcy continued. 'All parents worry about balance. That doesn't make you a bad person. It doesn't mean you were negligent or in any way to blame. Rosie had leukaemia.'

'I went overboard.' He clenched his teeth, spurred on now that he'd started to expose his ugly parts. 'I became lured by the long hours and the personal gratification of my job. Pushing myself for the next promotion, consumed by the responsibility and the knowledge that I was needed, making a difference.' Joe cast her a cautious look. 'I think you might understand how that feels.'

Darcy gave a small hesitant nod. 'There's nothing wrong with being good at your job.'

'No, there isn't, as long as it's for the right reasons. But let my life be a cautionary tale of ambition and what truly matters. Yes, I once had it all, but I'm also living proof of how quickly it can all vanish.'

Darcy touched his arm and his body shuddered at the glimmer of pleasure.

'It wasn't your fault, Joe.'

He looked away from her compassion-darkened stare.

She was right. Sadly, knowing that didn't help in the slightest.

CHAPTER EIGHT

DANGER SLITHERED OVER Darcy's skin like the lick of a flame as Joe parked outside her flat in the vacant space that her sister usually used. She should get out of his car, thank him for the lift and watch him drive away, because her wants and needs were overwhelming.

The house was dark, empty. Stella was working a late shift at the hospital.

'Do you want to come in?' she asked, irresistibly drawn to this open version of Joe.

His heartbreaking confession during the ride back to London had ignited not only her innate compassion but also deepened the connection she felt. She'd had to sit on her hands for the rest of the journey in order to stop herself from taking him in her arms and holding him tight. Now, she wasn't ready to say goodbye, even though she should—she wanted him close after such an intensely fraught day.

Just for a little longer.

Darcy risked a sideways glance, immediately regretting it. His hair was ruffled where he'd run his fingers through it. A dark shadow of sexy stubble covered his jaw. And his eyes... So many emotions swam in their dark brown depths, Darcy felt at risk of drowning. He looked so conflicted, as if he were two men, two sides of a coin. A man who looked at her with desire, the same man she admired and respected at the hospital, and the shadow of that man. Hurting, tortured, punishing himself.

How could she resist that call? Her woman's heart wanted him with similar desire and the doctor in her yearned to help him heal. Darcy was a giver, empathetic. She was fulfilled by reaching out, human to human.

But that was all it could be for them. Physical—yes. Practical—all good. Emotional—no way.

Joe hesitated. *Sensible man.*

Darcy saw potential risk stamped all over him, but surely if she kept her head, indulged only in her attraction and ignored the way he made her crave more, she'd be safe, especially away from work. She'd given her career her all since her split from Dean and she was almost there, at the top of the mountain. She and Joe had an expiry date. Soon she'd move on and likely never see him again.

He'd made a valid point about priorities and the importance of family and work/life balance. Darcy drove herself hard, set high standards and was goal oriented, but Joe had been wrong about one thing: she no longer wanted it all. She'd put herself out there emotionally with Dean and it hadn't worked out, although with the tumult of her feelings for Joe racing around her head she belatedly realised that she perhaps hadn't committed her all to her previous relationship.

There was a part of her that had entered into it with pretty low expectations, as if waiting for it to fail. And, like all good self-fulfilling prophesies, it had.

But a relationship was the last thing on her mind.

She craved the return of the visceral bond they'd

shared when Joe had reached for her hand, the pride that lit her up like a firework when he'd looked to her for reassurance while they'd worked side by side to save Holly. He'd shown her that he valued her medical skills.

'It's been a moving day, and I make a mean cup of tea if that will sway you.' She tried to keep things light. Perhaps he'd open up even more. Perhaps she could help him unravel his regrets. She wanted to understand why he punished himself for what was surely a great and unfair tragedy but definitely not his fault, because she sensed that he didn't believe in his own innocence.

Joe smiled, his gaze both lost and somehow searching in a way that lured Darcy, physically and emotionally, the way lungs needed oxygen. 'Tea would be great, thanks.'

He killed the engine and unclipped his seat belt, his T-shirt rising up to expose a strip of toned abdomen, the sight of which left Darcy salivating. At her front door she fumbled with her key in the lock, her heart pitter-pattering in anticipation and fear of them being alone in her empty flat.

Darcy breathed through the panic of her ill-judged invitation. Already she had a head full of erotic visions involving Joe, except now that they'd worked as a team to save Holly, now that he'd needed her in a moment of alarm...that meant something more to her than the physical attraction there since that first day they'd met.

Did he see her as an equal?

In the kitchen Darcy dropped her bag, flicked on the lights and then the kettle. She reached overhead for two mugs with jittery fingers, the hair at the nape of her neck rising with awareness of Joe in her kitchen, filling her personal space with his magnetic aura. When she turned to face him, prepared to fake a bright smile and make small talk or resurrect the personal conversation they'd begun in the car, he'd stepped closer.

Face to face, a mere pace apart.

Darcy fell into the depths of Joe's stare and all thoughts of conversation dispersed.

Heartbeats pulsed through her like lightning strikes, marking the seconds they stood in tense silence.

He raised his arm, slow and steady, to brush back that stubborn lock of her hair determined to reside on her cheek.

As if conditioned to his touch, Darcy turned her face into his palm, part of her craving more, craving it all. 'Joe…' His name passed her lips, all breathy and pleading. For what? She wanted him physically, of course, but they had complication written all over them, the space between them an emotional and professional minefield.

He was still grieving the death of his daughter and perhaps even the demise of his marriage, and before meeting him she'd sworn to focus on her career, a career she stood to jeopardise if they started something personal. Even sex would be a far from straightforward exchange between two people who shared insatiable chemistry, for good or bad. Come Monday morning she'd have to face him; he'd still be her boss. She needed his reference for her consultant position applications.

Could she risk clouding their work dynamic just for sex?

'I want you,' he said, his expression starkly open and honest.

Overwhelming need built inside Darcy, its pressure centred between her legs.

'I've tried to resist,' he said, his voice full of gravel, 'but I'm failing badly.'

Darcy wavered. Joe's eyes brimmed with repressed

emotion. He was clearly experiencing the same conflict tugging Darcy in two different directions.

If only they were strangers. If only they'd met in a nightclub and shared a passionate one-night stand...

Darcy's eyes fluttered closed, defending herself against his intense stare and the call it issued. 'Me, too.' The release of admitting her feelings rushed her bloodstream like a potent shot of morphine. 'But...this isn't a good idea.'

She clamped her hand over her mouth—she'd spoken that aloud. It waved the red flag and her body, the neediness for his kiss, his touch, hated her for the unguarded outburst. Her eyelids blinked open to find Joe resolute, his jaw set, his eyes ablaze with desire.

As if deciding to swim against the tide and face the consequences when they reached the shore, they lunged for each other in unison. Their kiss landed, lips colliding, a desperate union of people who'd fought their hunger for too long.

The catharsis after all of the denial and reasoning, confusion and conflicted feelings almost buckled Darcy's knees. Joe's strong arms scooped around her waist, as if he sensed the physical cost of her surrender. Darcy's hands clawed at his wide shoulders, dragging him those last few millimetres closer.

'Darcy,' he grunted against her sensitive lips as he tightened his grip and hauled her body up his firm chest until she was balanced on tiptoes. Darcy parted her lips to the invasion of his tongue, the sensual glide making all the difference to her inflamed libido, which sparked and fizzed like a lit fuse.

Unlike the kiss in the on-call staffroom, which had been angry and full of frustration, this kiss exploded with pure, uncontrolled passion, blast after blast in a chain reaction that left Darcy a slave only to her body's needs. She weakened against Joe's strength and hardness. Through the lust fog in her head, she grew aware of movement and felt the edge of the kitchen table against the back of her thighs.

Fantastic idea.

She jumped up and spread her legs so that Joe's hips could slot into place. They fitted so perfectly she wanted to weep. How could something that felt this right be a bad idea? It was just sex, chemistry, a release. This tension had been brewing between them from day one.

A sense of blissful inevitable release washed over Darcy. Her fingers curled in his silky hair, his stubble rough against her palm as she kept him where her lips wanted him.

The shock of his warm palm on her thigh, where her dress had ridden up, added fire to her veins. She shunted her hips to the edge of the table, needing more friction, needing him closer, needing to feel him on every part of her body at once. His other hand skimmed her waist and travelled up her ribs to her breast and she tore her mouth away from his and opened her eyes, lost in his pleasure-darkened stare.

This was happening. They were doing this, crossing the line that kept them safely out of reach. Joe's handsome face was cloaked in arousal that made Darcy applaud her instincts. Their panting breaths mingled, their lips only a whisper apart.

'I wanted you from the start.' Joe cupped her breast, his thumb tracing the sensitive peak through her dress.

Darcy gasped at the sublime and foreign contact. It was as if she'd never been with a man before. His touch combined with his bold stare and stark declaration felt so good she knew this must be the worst idea she'd ever had. As Joe's erection pressed between her legs, she dredged her conscience, searching for the inner strength to pause and reflect.

Yes, it was just sex, and they were adults, capable of keeping things professional at work, no matter what happened here between them tonight.

But…

This day carried momentous significance for Joe. It wouldn't be just sex, not today, and Darcy couldn't afford for it to be anything more.

She pressed her mouth back to his in denial, trying to shut out the anguish she'd seen in his eyes when he'd talked about his daughter, when he'd looked at Darcy with both relief and despair after successfully resuscitating Holly. He'd been so haunted it hurt Darcy's soul.

Hating herself, she pulled back and searched his heated gaze for what she knew she'd find there—the one thing that would stop this where her willpower and common sense had failed miserably.

Grief shone through the desire. A warning light, glaring, blinding.

She couldn't do it. Selfishness was not a part of her nature. She cared about Joe too much to take advantage of his vulnerable state, and she couldn't have him resent her down the track.

She needed him. At work, for his expertise and training and as a person she admired, liked, respected.

She placed her hands on his chest and gently pushed. 'Stop. We need to stop.'

Her body rebelled, flames leaping over her skin. She slid from the edge of the table, her breasts grazing his chest and his delicious scent a cloud of temptation from which there was no escape.

To Darcy's shame, there was also an aftertaste of relief as she withdrew from the emotional temptation of Joe's pain. Taking care of herself didn't come naturally, but she'd vowed, after Dean, that her career must take priority. It was her chance to lay all of her own demons to rest. To finally make it and know that she was good enough, despite the trials that had shaped her.

Face taut with confusion and resignation, Joe backed up. His warm touch left her so rapidly she shivered.

He speared his fingers through his chaotic hair. 'Hell…yes. You're right.'

No…convince me I'm wrong…convince me that it's just sex.

'I don't want to be right,' she choked out, guilt that she'd not only allowed things to go so far, but she'd also rejected him when she knew the size and shape of that emotion so well gripping her vocal cords. 'I don't want this to be a bad idea, but sense tells me it is.'

Grief was such a complex process. She couldn't bear to bring up the subject of Rosie when his mouth was still bruised from their kisses, his arousal still pushing at the fly of his jeans.

'What about Monday, at work?' she said, trying to reason her way back to some semblance of normal when she felt anything but. No matter how much her libido hated her right now, this was the right decision.

Joe's grief and pain must be amplified after today's party.

Darcy pushed down her dress, self-conscious and suddenly cold. 'It feels like I'd be…taking advantage.' She hesitated. Joe would hate to think she was motivated by pity. 'Today was rough, for many reasons… I just—'

'No, you're right,' he interrupted. 'It was rough.' He tugged at his hair. 'I am all over the place.' He set about composing himself, tugging the hem of his T-shirt and scrubbing a hand over his face.

Darcy looked away to give him some privacy. Her heart broke for him. He clearly blamed and punished himself for his daughter's death, but he deserved the happiness and healing his ex had found. She ached for herself too—she struggled with trust, and one of the reasons she was so drawn to Joe, beyond the fact that he was so sexy, was his integrity. She had to stop herself from grabbing him again, kissing him again and forcing the insight and compassion from her mind, acting purely on sensation, taking everything she wanted right here, right now on her kitchen table. To hell with the consequences.

But she couldn't risk the emotional outpouring she suspected would follow. She couldn't sleep with him *and* care. It was too risky.

'I should go.' He headed for the door.

'Wait.' She had no idea what she wanted to say; she just needed him to understand. 'Joe, I want to be there for you.'

Joe winced as if she'd insulted him. 'Just not for casual sex... I get it.'

'No... Yes...' Horrified, she sought the right words. 'Casual sex is all we can have. I've tried to have more than that in the past, and right now... I need to focus on myself, my career. I just don't think we should make such a momentous decision to cross the line when you might be lonely or reeling from a tough day.'

Who was she trying to kid? There was no one lonelier than her.

Apart from her sisters, with whom she'd once, as a little girl, felt like the odd one out, she had few friends. She'd always told herself she was too busy with work.

But, in truth, she either held herself distant or pushed people away before she could be hurt, the way her father had hurt her. Again and again. She'd even withdrawn from Dean the minute he'd proposed. At the time she'd convinced herself it just didn't feel right, that their differences were insurmountable, but now she suspected she'd been predominantly motivated by the fear of possible future rejection.

Joe's expression had turned granite-hard.

Darcy flushed. 'Sorry… I didn't mean the lonely comment… I just… I think this needs more thought than either of us has given it. Don't you agree?' This must be a big deal for him if he hadn't dated since his divorce. It was a big deal for *her*. She could allow herself a casual fling, but she couldn't become distracted at the final career hurdle. She'd worked too hard. And the way she'd become ensnared by caring for Joe and wanting to help him, the risks of emotional entanglement were amplified.

Joe held her eye contact so she felt naked, exposed. 'I've thought about it plenty,' he said with soul-searing honesty. 'But you're right about the timing; this was… ill-judged.'

He pressed his gorgeous lips together, and Darcy's stomach plummeted. She wanted them back on hers, wanted to rewind and keep her mouth shut, keep every one of his kisses and lose herself in pleasure.

'I'm sorry, Joe.' Her throat ached. 'I want you, but I don't want to hurt you.' Or herself. 'You're punishing yourself enough as it is.'

His grim smile cut like a knife. 'I understand. This is why I didn't initially tell you about Rosie, why I shouldn't have opened up to you in the car, because now I'm no longer a man you're attracted to; I'm just a man who can't get over the fact that his daughter died.'

He hardened his jaw, and Darcy almost caved and begged him to forget the last few minutes.

'I wanted to be that first guy for a while, that's all...' He shrugged.

And then he left, taking with him a tiny piece of Darcy's heart.

CHAPTER NINE

A WEEK LATER Joe forced his eyes to linger on the city lights of Amsterdam beyond the window of the swanky Italian restaurant while the conversation around the table droned on. He curled his fingers into a loose fist where his hand rested on his thigh. Only a few inches separated his thigh from Darcy's. A few promise-filled inches that might as well be an entire universe.

His regret returned full force like a blow to the chest, winding him.

She'd been right to call a halt that night a week ago. Right to declare them complicated. Right to worry about any fallout from a reckless affair that might affect her career.

And he *was* punishing himself, or he had been before she'd pulled him up on that, forcing him to examine the contents of his head and acknowledge that he was stuck, suspended in his grief, because to acknowledge any positive feelings like those he'd experienced since Darcy had blasted into his life, to move on as Laura had done, shot panic through him like white-hot laser beams.

What if he allowed himself joy? Would that diminish or invalidate his love for Rosie somehow?

Wasn't a part of him relieved when Darcy had applied the brakes? Because a distraction that good, letting go of his pain and embracing his out-of-control attraction to Darcy, might change him, or make him forget.

Not that sex could heal, of course, but he'd started to care about Darcy. It wouldn't, couldn't, be just sex. Was he strong enough to keep those emotions off the table?

He'd certainly clung to his pain for so long—it was his only connection to Rosie.

Except all of this self-reflection hadn't lessened his desire for the woman he craved day and night, the woman sitting next to him now. Her delicate scent and the rich timbre of her voice dragged him from his thoughts. Spending time with her equated to a kind of torture.

Restlessness coiled in his stomach as he tuned back in to the largely medical chat happening around the table. He and Darcy were attending a conference— the European Surgical Innovation Summit. Ever since they'd left London he'd wanted Darcy to himself. He wanted to show her that he was more than a damaged man in need of her compassion. That she'd been the one responsible for waking that dormant side of his masculinity. That she was wrong; he could separate sex from his emotional life because, no matter how much he cared about Darcy, the woman he'd come to know and respect, sex was all that he could offer. The rest of him was all tied up.

'You're drifting off again,' she side whispered in his direction, a playful smile tugging at her gorgeous mouth, reminding him of frantic kisses and the way his arousal had sought the heat between her thighs.

Joe grinned, casting her a wink for good measure; he actually winked. All day they'd achieved a lighter, flirty vibe. Being away from the hospital changed their dynamic enough that they could be more open and honest, more real without professional restriction.

It was a revelation. Joe hadn't felt so…joyful for years.

'I've heard all these chats before,' he whispered, inhaling her warm Darcy aroma. And he'd had to share the one person he wanted to talk to—her.

He checked his watch, desperate to get her alone. They'd never had that coffee date.

'Was that your excuse for inattention during the lectures today?' she said, calling Joe out with a knowing look. Away from work she was relaxed and flirtatious. It gave him hope that they could work this out in a mutually beneficial way.

He shrugged. 'You noticed that, huh?' He'd barely heard a word of the varied and informative presentations today, ones he'd anticipated with interest before meeting Darcy, because she'd been at his side. All day. A constant distraction, a reminder of that seriously heated session in her kitchen and all of the almost moments in between then and now.

He hadn't felt that wild loss of inhibition for decades, since he was a teenager. For a moment when she'd pulled back he'd been utterly dazed, so lost was he in the blissful oblivion of the physical pressure valve release.

He looked away from the temptation of her teasing stare. Darcy deserved more than his uncontrolled lust, more than he had to give.

But she didn't want more. She wanted just sex. That she wanted him at all in all his ugly, broken glory was miracle enough. And once the emotional turmoil in him had settled the next day he'd almost driven back to her place, hammered down the door and presented himself as the ideal casual sex candidate.

Only the honest part of him knew his feelings were already engaged. He cared that she'd been hurt by her father in the past. Now he simply hoped he could hide those feelings and take what was on offer.

Joe watched her lips caress the tines of the fork as she ate. The urge to touch her, kiss her, explore every inch of her body overwhelmed him once more, an itch along his spine that he couldn't quite reach.

'How did you find the symposium?' he asked, dragging himself back to a professional footing.

'Are you asking as my boss?' she said. 'Because then my answer would be: it was extremely useful and professionally enlightening.' She raised her eyebrows in that taunting way of hers that never failed to make Joe's heart race.

He lowered his voice. 'What if I'm asking as the guy you made tea for on Saturday evening?' He shouldn't raise this subject, especially not here, in front of colleagues, but the flecks of silver in her irises which sparkled in the candlelight spurred him on. He was done pretending. To her, to himself. Time to lay his cards on the table.

'Ah…' She smiled, a hint of colour in her cheeks. 'Well, to him, I'd have to confess I was somewhat… distracted, too. By the guy sitting next to me.'

Joe latched onto her stare, his blood rushing around his body. 'Perhaps you're tired,' he said, playing along. 'We've had a busy week at City.'

'Maybe a little. My boss is this extreme perfectionist, demanding an even greater standard than I put on myself, which is up there.' She raised her hand overhead, indicating what he already knew. Now he wanted her to know that, no matter what had happened in her past, she needn't try so hard, that she was enough exactly as she was—perfect.

'Guy sounds like a jerk with nothing else in his life but work.' Joe smiled when he really wanted to take her hand. 'Don't be like that guy.'

'Oh, he can be…challenging.' Her mouth twitched with mirth and Joe sucked on his bottom lip, remembering how her kisses tasted and the breathless quality of her soft moans. 'But he's a very dedicated and instinctive surgeon…' her eyes softened and his throat went dry '…so I can't help but respect him.'

Her words buzzed through his head. Joe sat frozen, mesmerised by what he saw in her stare, the understanding, the heat, the promise. The rest of the restaurant's patrons, including the handful of colleagues at their table, faded away, leaving just him and Darcy and…possibility.

Just then a surgeon Joe had known for years, Professor Jensen, who sat to Darcy's right, engaged her in conversation.

Joe pushed some pasta around his plate, trying not to eavesdrop but failing.

'Yes, I've read your paper on hepatic complications of bariatric surgery,' Jensen said. Joe's possessive side flickered to life. Of course, Jensen had made a beeline for the seat next to Darcy the minute the small group had entered the restaurant. The guy had a wife Darcy's age and a dreadful reputation for philandering. Joe's blood still simmered after he'd already monopolised her time over dinner.

'I found your review interesting,' Jensen continued, his pompous voice grating on Joe's nerves, 'if a little…

sketchy in places,' he finished with a superior air, shovelling a forkful of pasta into his mouth.

Joe had attended many of these symposia over the years and had never found the man worthy of particular note in the past. Now he had the ludicrous urge to defend Darcy. The conference was over for the day. This was supposed to be a social event.

Joe sensed her stiffen slightly beside him. 'Yes, the nature of review articles, I fear, Professor Jensen, but thank you for your invaluable feedback.'

Joe concealed his ready grin against the rim of his water glass. Of course, Darcy knew how to put the old buffoon in his place without breaking a sweat. The man wouldn't win Darcy's sycophancy or flirtation. One of the things he admired most about her was her ability to straight talk, even with people who deemed themselves superior from time served in the profession.

He should keep his nose out of it but some irritation, perhaps that itch up his spine, the urge to get her alone, forced him to intercede.

'I found Ms Wright's review excellent, actually.' Joe caught the tiny shocked intake of Darcy's breath. 'She's certainly a great asset to my team. In fact, I hope to persuade her to co-author a paper I'm planning for *The Lancet* before she leaves for her consultant post.' He cast a glance sideways in time to see Jensen lose interest and address another colleague across the table.

He looked at Darcy. She hid her surprised expression behind one of mild censure. 'Thanks for sticking up for me,' she said in a hushed tone, 'but I had it in hand.'

'I know you did, but I couldn't stay silent.' She didn't need him to defend her against an egotistical professor looking to rattle a young, beautiful colleague so he could flex his intellectual muscle.

Except Joe couldn't help himself.

Her pressed together lips twitched, her mock stern-ness dissolving into a playful look full of delicious se-crecy. 'Shh. He'll hear you.' Then she smiled her lovely relaxed smile and Joe breathed freely for the first time since they'd boarded the plane to Amsterdam.

They'd come a long way since their first tense and prickly meeting when he'd been the one to ruffle her feathers. She trusted and respected him professionally and he valued her more than he could articulate.

Perhaps too much.

'Did you mean that?' she asked, glancing his way with hopeful curiosity. 'About the paper?' Darcy pushed away her half-full plate, her appetite clearly as non-ex-istent as Joe's.

When could they politely get out of here?

'Of course. I've been meaning to raise the subject when I had a chance. Perhaps we can discuss it on the plane back to London tomorrow.'

She nodded, her eyes big expressive pools reflecting a whole raft of emotions he wanted to dissect. Did she still see him as an irritating boss? Or just a grieving father? Alone with Darcy, he felt as if he could be so much more. For the first time in years what he wanted had become crystal-clear.

Her.

'You didn't have to walk me back to the hotel,' she said, shivering slightly at Joe's proximity and pulling her car-digan closed over her chest.

'I wasn't going to let you walk the streets of Am-sterdam alone,' he said, stepping closer so their arms almost touched. 'And I want to talk to you as much as

I want to ensure that you're safe, for my own peace of mind. Would you like my jacket?'

She shook her head. Darcy's body trembles were down to full-blown anticipation. Especially when he looked at her the way he'd been doing all day, as if she were a dessert he wanted to devour.

Heaven help her...

'I've wanted to get you alone,' he said, placing his hand in the small of her back as the crowd of passers-by clogged the pavement. Not that she minded. Ever since she'd watched him drive away from her street she'd craved a return to this closeness. No matter how many times she'd reasoned that it was better if they never happened, she couldn't be convinced.

Darcy forced herself to breathe in something approximating a normal rhythm at his sure and resolute touch. 'Have you?'

Me, too, a voice yelled inside her head as she recalled the torture of being at his side most of the day but also surrounded by people. Because spending the day with Joe, away from their professional roles and with no emotional triggers to cloud the issue, she'd been consumed with him so she hardly knew the contents of her own sensible mind.

He glanced her way, his eye contact bold and steady, as if he knew exactly how paper-thin were her defences and arguments. 'Yes, I want to thank you for sensing my extreme vulnerability and kicking me out that night.'

Darcy's heart clenched at his honesty. The longer she knew Joe, the more she learned that what you saw was who he was. No games, no tactics, no hidden agenda. He'd sat next to her in the lecture theatre rather than sitting with consultant colleagues. He'd asked for her opinions on the topics presented and introduced her to the internationally renowned surgeons that he knew.

He'd even stood up for her to the self-important Professor Jensen. She couldn't recall the last time anyone had done that. Self-reliant Darcy could take care of herself, but it was nice to know that he cared.

'You're welcome.' She smiled and her cheeks ached; she'd smiled so much today. 'Although, at the time I regretted it immediately.'

Her breath stuttered in her chest at admitting how much she still wanted him. But she refused to enter this fling based on just common or garden lust. She cared about him as a person too much.

And you've never felt lust this powerful before.

Because things had changed. Finally, she felt like his professional equal, as if Joe understood her, respected her, valued her. Her whole life she'd craved the acceptance that she was okay, that she wasn't defective because of her father's repeated and confusing abandonment. To feel it from Joe, a man she respected in return, both personally for what he'd been through and professionally, brought a rush so powerful her head spun with yearning.

There was no longer any point denying her feelings for Joe. They must be written on her face. But if they were to cross the line that they'd only narrowly avoided last time, they'd need to do it together.

They paused at a zebra crossing and Joe placed his hand on her elbow as he scanned the traffic. She hid her smile. Joe was old-school, a gentleman, and she surprised herself with how much she liked the small signs that he cared for her well-being. It called to the part of her that craved his touch as if it were the oxygen she needed to breathe.

She could become seriously addicted to him.

A niggle of lingering doubt forced its way into her conscious thoughts. 'How have you been this week? I haven't liked to ask at the hospital, but I've been thinking about you.'

Darcy held her breath, wary of prying into his grief. Except his emotions, his feelings of loss, were normal and nothing to be ashamed of. It was human, understandable, expected. Could a parent ever get over the death of a child? She suspected not.

'I've been good. Thanks for asking.' He glanced her way, looking at her as if he wanted to say a whole lot more. As if he wanted to kiss her here under the Amsterdam streetlights.

Then he dragged in a breath, as if making a decision. 'You'll think I'm mad, but I've taken to talking to Rosie sometimes.'

Darcy's heart clenched, desperate to hold him. Instead, she reached for his hand and squeezed his fingers. 'I think that's lovely and completely normal.' Emotion clogged her throat but she swallowed it down, moved to show him that she understood.

'When I was a little girl I used to talk to my real father in my head at night. I'd pretend that he'd ask about my day at school, just like my stepfather did, or praise me for my artwork or spelling test results.'

Joe raised her hand to his mouth and pressed a kiss on the back of her hand. 'I'm sorry that he wasn't there for you. He doesn't deserve a daughter as wonderful as you.'

'You're right there.' The heat of tears threatened behind her eyes, not only for her own loss but for Joe's, too, because if ever there was a deserving father it was him. 'Sadly, I only discovered that years later, after repeated rejections. It took being let down again and again for the fantasy bubble I'd invented to burst.' Darcy shrugged, forgiving herself anew for her naive hopes.

This time Joe pulled her against him and pressed his lips to her forehead. 'You are perfect, a daughter anyone would be proud of. I bet your parents are.'

She laughed, snuggling into his chest and inhaling the clean and erotic scent of him and his shirt. 'My sisters and I are very high achievers.'

'Healthy sibling rivalry?' he asked.

She sobered as he struck an exposed nerve. 'Something like that, although for a while I convinced myself that I was the odd one out, because they had the same father where he'd only adopted me. It's silly, I know, and totally down to my messed-up way of thinking and nothing my family did.'

'That doesn't mean he loved you less,' said Joe with understanding in his eyes.

'No. He's a great dad; I'm lucky to have him. Sometimes I feel guilty, even bitter, that I might have held back from loving Grant completely out of a misguided sense of loyalty to my father.' That same part of her that held back had also felt not quite good enough, despite her wonderful upbringing.

They'd veered close to an emotional hotspot for both of them, Darcy suspected. For a short distance they walked hand in hand in pensive silence.

'About last weekend…' he said as the hotel came into view. 'I wouldn't want you to ever feel…used or convenient. That was never remotely my intention. I *was* in an emotional place that day, but I need you to know that I'm also a man—a man who wants you more than I have any right to.'

Darcy's pulse raced, speech almost deserting her.

'Joe... I see you that way, and I want you, too... I just needed us to make a clear-headed decision.' She didn't want to think about her complex situation with Dean when her head was filled with Joe, but she needed the reminder of their turbulent times, their fights and resentments, the way Darcy had often felt misunderstood or unappreciated, in order to guard her emotions and keep this explosive connection brewing between her and Joe light and temporary.

Except tonight she wondered if it was a warning she needed more than Joe.

'I understand—it's just sex.' Heat flared in his stare and deepened the tone of his voice. 'Neither of us is looking for more.'

She nodded, her stomach strangely hollow when she should feel nothing but relief and excitement. 'I need to focus on my upcoming consultant job interviews and I'll be moving on in a couple of months...'

Joe nodded. 'We're both mature and dedicated enough to safeguard our work above all else. We're on the same page.'

Joe was saying all the right things. She wanted to sleep with him. Yes, it was risky, it could potentially alter their professional relationship, but her libido didn't care one jot. Even her intellect was struggling to mount coherent objections now they'd established the rules and found themselves back where they'd always been: undeniably attracted to each other.

As for her other feelings for Joe, it was natural to care about someone she liked and admired so much, but surely she could set that aside for one stolen night...

They crossed the threshold of the hotel and Darcy dropped his hand to press the button for the lift. It was now or never, sink or swim. She risked a look in his direction and all but spontaneously combusted from the look of sheer need in Joe's eyes.

'So you're saying you'd accept if I invited you to my room?' She tried to exhibit the same cool pragmatism while her insides had turned molten. But she needed to approach this fling with the same calm rationale she gave to her career moves and clinical decisions. She'd chosen that career over a relationship in the past.

Unlike her ex, this man understood the sacrifices required to succeed at this job. He wouldn't make her choose, and he couldn't let her down because she had no expectations beyond tonight.

He stepped closer, his own feelings on the matter clear in the intensity of his stare and the increase in his breathing rate. 'Look at me,' he said. 'You'll see my answer.'

He swallowed, and Darcy saw the cost of his vulnerability, his ceding control. He wanted her and she'd exhausted all of her excuses.

Tonight, he wasn't her boss. He wasn't a man wrapped up in grief. He was Joe.

In silent agreement they stepped inside the lift.

To her dismay, they weren't alone for the journey to the fourth floor. Had they been, Darcy might have succumbed to the urgent need to leap at Joe and kiss him the way he'd kissed her last Saturday. From the look of polite impatience on his face, Joe might have pressed her up against the wall the way he'd pressed her back into her kitchen table, his hard body commanding, his control barely leashed, his need for her decimating all else.

The furnace built inside Darcy until she was certain her face glowed. Their lift companion smiled as Darcy and Joe exited on Darcy's floor, telling her that sexual tension cloaked them like a fog. Every step Darcy took trembled with urgency.

Inside her hotel room, Darcy dropped Joe's hand and placed her bag on the desk. She needed a moment to slow the crazy swirls of desire making her dizzy.

She sensed his body heat at her back and her knees weakened. She spun slowly to face him, needing to spell out her terms and conditions. For her sanity or for his benefit?

'Just tonight,' she said, although it came out as a whisper. 'We can't let this affect working together.'

He hadn't touched her again since letting go of her hand in the lift, but her skin was aflame, her blood supercharged as it raced around her trembling body.

'I agree.' His stare devoured her. 'But if you've changed your mind...'

'No.' She'd die if he left her now. 'I haven't changed my mind.' She stepped closer, reached for his hand and squeezed, to comfort herself more than him, to stop his escape, although his eyes told her everything she needed to know about Joe's wants and intentions.

'I want this,' she whispered in confirmation. He understood her. He accepted her just the way she was, and she recognised the limits to what he could offer. They weren't embarking on a relationship. It was just one night. They'd quench this insane attraction and move on as if tonight had never happened.

Darcy forced herself to ignore the trickle of cold in her veins at that idea. Before she could reach for him, Joe cupped her face, his thumbs tracing her cheekbones with aching slowness. Darcy stared into his eyes until her vision swam and her heart pounded almost out of her chest. Perhaps *Wham-bam, thank you, ma'am* would have been better than this slow, seductive burn they generated. She wanted to tear his clothes off, but she also wanted to honour that they'd have only one night. That they'd needed time to process their feelings after their last encounter when she'd slammed on the brakes. That she needed time to slow the frantic race of her pulse and ensure she kept her emotions off the table, focus only on the way he made her feel physically.

Already she felt close to disintegration and they'd barely touched.

She circled her hands around his wrists, clinging to him for balance. 'Kiss me, Joe. Kiss me the way you wanted to the other night. I won't stop you this time.'

As if waiting for her permission, he unleashed himself with the same steady and meticulous attention to detail that he applied at the hospital. His fingers speared her hair and dug into the back of her scalp. His strong thigh stepped between her legs and his lips settled over hers, slow and sensual, consuming her every sense, commanding her body in a kiss that felt way more than a kiss.

A melding of two imperfect people who understood the limitations of the other. It was so freeing that Darcy practically levitated.

Joe slanted his mouth over hers and she yielded on a gasp, lips parting to the welcome invasion of his tongue. He backed her up against the desk, scooping one arm around her waist to hoist her from the floor and deposit her on the surface. They momentarily broke apart while Darcy spread her legs and impatiently tugged the belt loops on his jeans to bring him closer.

'I can't stop wanting you,' he said, his voice cracking as he trailed kisses over her jaw and down her neck until her eyes rolled back at the delicious sensations, which were amplified by his heartfelt admission.

'Me neither... I've tried.' Oh, how she'd tried. Since day one she'd done her best to hate him, ignore him, dismiss him and resist him. Look where all that fight had ended.

Right here in his arms, sharing his kisses, wanting more, so much more.

He nodded. Clearly, they'd been trapped in limbo together, each battling this, battling themselves, battling their pasts. But now that they'd laid down the rules and showed mutual trust and respect, surrender felt harmless.

It was perfect.

Passion without consequences.

No longer willing to wait another minute for her reward after the denial she'd suffered these past weeks, Darcy hurriedly unbuttoned Joe's casual shirt. The fabric smelled of detergent and of Joe, but when her palms skated over the smooth warm skin, the ridges and dips of his abdomen and the soft hair of his chest, she closed her eyes against the heady rush of overwhelming sensation.

With a bone-dry swallow, Darcy leaned back to look her fill, tracing every defined muscle with her unapologetic stare. He was beautiful, so sexy she wanted to photograph him for posterity. Her keen doctor's eye mapped the anatomical landmarks of his male perfection, and she spotted a scar across one of his ribs. She traced the slight bump with her fingertip, fascinated because it was Joe she was touching and everything about him was new and compelling.

If only his emotional wounds could heal so easily. If only he'd stop blaming himself, stop clinging to his pain... Perhaps then he'd be ready to allow himself the happiness he deserved.

He removed her hand and lifted it to his mouth, kissing her fingertips and then the inside of her wrist where her pulse fluttered.

'It's from a chest drain,' he explained. 'I broke a rib playing rugby at school—ended up with a pneumothorax.' He rolled his eyes and grinned, his lips still pressed to her sensitive skin so that electricity skittered along her nerves.

Darcy shuddered the way she had when he'd cupped her breast on Saturday, her whole body reacting to his smile, which occasionally, like now, reached his eyes with blinding effect.

How could he do this to her? Undo her so effortlessly with a single self-deprecating smile?

Because this proud, capable, life-saving man had made himself vulnerable to her, shared his deepest regrets and made her feel that she wasn't alone with her own demons.

She cupped his face, his stubble scraping her palm. She wanted to kiss him from head to toe. To taste his skin, find his ticklish spots, soothe away the lines from around his eyes, unless they accompanied that devastating smile.

Reminding herself that this was about sex only, Darcy slid from the table and lifted her dress over her head, tossing it away. She flicked her sandals from her feet and unclasped her bra, her body warming and her belly fluttering at Joe's appreciative stare.

His expression grew more serious with every passing second. His nostrils flared, his eyes raked her near nakedness, telling Darcy what it cost him to keep his hands to himself. Instead of touching her, he removed his jeans and shoes and socks, matching Darcy item for item until their clothing lay in a heap.

'You're so beautiful,' he whispered huskily and then stepped close once more. His feverish skin made contact with hers, inch by inch, flames licking at the points of contact.

'So are you,' she croaked, recalling the sight of his thick muscular thighs and the rigid length of him behind tight black boxers. 'I have a condom,' she said, reaching behind her for her bag, ever the practical, safety-conscious doctor.

'So do I.' Joe raised his eyebrows and smiled his dazzling smile. 'What a team we make.'

They laughed together and then he grew serious, tugged her close and took her mouth in another heated kiss that left Darcy weak-kneed.

What a team we make. If only he knew what those words meant to her.

CHAPTER TEN

JOE PRAYED DARCY couldn't feel the trembles racking his body as he laid her back against the cool white sheets of the hotel bed. Every muscle in his body screamed at him to speed this up, to surrender to his base desires, which had been tightly coiled like a rusty spring and ignored these past four years, and lose control of his powerful desire for this woman. But another part, the part of his brain still functioning, knew instinctively to cherish every second of tonight, as that was all they'd have. Tomorrow, they'd go back to London, pretend this had never happened, their chaste workplace dynamic restored. He her boss and she his junior.

Because, no matter how good she felt in his arms, no matter that he'd never felt more alive, more optimistic, more like himself, he had nothing more than this to give. Relationships took time and commitment and posed a massive potential risk for crushing heartache. All of Joe's energy was consumed by work and remembering, honouring and grieving Rosie.

A flicker of hesitation made it to the functioning part of his brain. He didn't want to hurt Darcy, or mislead her. But he'd been as upfront as he could, and she knew what she wanted—one night. He'd never met anyone more certain of her path.

'How did I get so lucky?' he asked, covering her sublime body with his, marvelling at the softness of her skin, the hunger in her passion-glazed stare and the sexy splay of her silky hair across the pillow. He wanted to bury his face in the golden strands and inhale her unique Darcy scent, commit it to memory, because he'd want to remember tonight, this amazing woman who somehow brought a flicker of life back to his battle-weary heart.

Instead, he kissed her once more, consoling himself by tangling his fingers through her hair while he trailed his lips down her neck.

'Joe,' she moaned, her breathtaking face soft with desire. Desire for him. This smart, funny, dedicated woman saw something worthwhile in him, despite his broken pieces.

She understood his crazier moments—he'd never told another soul how he still talked to his dead daughter as if she were still with him, not even Laura. She laughed at him when he took himself too seriously. And for all she'd been through growing up—feeling rejected by the one man who was supposed to love her unconditionally—she wasn't afraid to be vulnerable with him. Now he understood her constant need to prove herself and how it helped her to reach her career goals. But some part of him wondered if it wasn't holding her back from being happy, fulfilled.

Darcy's hips rocked under him, reminding him that Darcy's happiness wasn't his business, at least not beyond tonight. Her fingernails bit into his upper arms, dragging his mind back to the physical sensations he could indulge. A great wave of desire rose up inside him at the sight of her parted lips, her slumberous eyes, her passion. She needed him in this second, this strong, independent woman, but somehow she also held him together with her fearless forthright tenacity.

Joe bent to suck her nipple, loving the whimpers he drew from her throat and the way she gripped his hips with her thighs. Hunger roared through him, splintering him apart. How had he done without a connection like this for so long? Darcy had given him back this vital side of his maleness. He'd never forget that gift. The least he could do was rock her world and give her a night to remember when she moved on.

Done being patient, Joe knelt back on his haunches and slid her underwear down her legs. 'We might need to take this slowly,' he said. 'I'm a bit rusty.'

He wasn't certain how long he'd last after four years of abstinence, but he'd been none too shabby at this in his heyday. He likely still had the moves.

She chuckled, cupping his face. 'Me, too—let's take all night.'

His heart surged with renewed vigour. Could she be any more perfect? He kissed her again, his hand sliding between her thighs to the slickness there. She gripped his wrist and held him in place, her hips rocking in rhythm, telling him she liked his moves just fine.

Joe's wicked side roared to life and he dipped his head, murmuring, 'We are so unprofessional. What would our patients think?' He took her nipple back into his mouth and watched desire flicker across her features, colour blooming under her skin.

'Yes...'

He wasn't sure if she was agreeing with his statement, encouraging him or both, but he kept up his attentions, a man on a mission. When she shattered, he kissed up her cries and rode out every second of her pleasure at her side, privilege soaring in his chest until he felt like a king.

Finally spent, Darcy threw her arms up over her head, looked into his eyes and grinned. Then she laughed, a throaty, sexy laugh filled with delight. 'Oh... wow...' She giggled some more and Joe had to hide his own smile.

'That was funny?' Amusement spread, twitching at his lips, his spirit so light he struggled to recall if he'd ever felt so...euphoric.

'Amazing,' she said, tugging his mouth back to hers and peppering his face with kisses. 'You. Are. Amazing.' She stretched like a contented cat.

'Plenty more where that came from.' He winked, fresh urgency clawing at the layers of levity she wrapped around his heart. Of all the fantasies he'd had about this moment, he'd never once expected to laugh, to feel frivolity, but wonderful, beautiful Darcy brought that to the surface.

Darcy took him by surprise anew, shoving him flat on his back and straddling his hips. 'Don't make promises you can't keep,' she said, her voice sexy and husky. 'You said you were rusty before.'

Joe grinned, reached for the condom. 'Haven't you learned by now that I'm sometimes full of nonsense?'

Darcy laughed, nodded vigorously and then trailed distracting kisses over his chest.

Joe covered himself with the condom, his hands shaking with the effort of taking his time. She was driving him crazy, that sensual mouth of hers finding all his erogenous zones. Done being passive, he cupped her hips, positioning her over him, where he wanted her.

'But I never break a promise.' He stared up at her to see mischief light her eyes.

'Don't worry,' she whispered, temptation itself, as she jutted out her breasts. 'You said it yourself—we're a team. Why should you do all the work?' She took him inside her with frustrating slowness that tested his limits to the max.

Heat boiled in his veins. She felt so good. 'Darcy...' he warned, fearful for his out-of-practice stamina. She bit down on her bottom lip and watched him with pleasure-drunk eyes. She was gorgeously dishevelled, flushed, her hair a wild tumble. He momentarily closed his eyes against the perfect vision, his chest crushed with too many feelings that he should have expected.

From day one this woman had challenged him, surprised him and somehow saw deep inside him. Of course, she'd be an almost overwhelming, hard to resist combination.

Biting the inside of his cheek to stave off the rush of pleasure as she began to rock her hips in a sensual glide, he closed his eyes once more. He wanted to see everything, feel everything, savour everything. But he also needed to keep a measure of mental distance from this incredible sexual experience. To remind himself that he couldn't get used to this degree of rapture. That a part of him, the part he couldn't forgive, didn't deserve such a life-enhancing experience as having Darcy in his arms, riding him, consuming every sense he possessed.

He'd always imagined himself a man of strength but, weak to Darcy's lure, he slammed his eyes back open in order to watch.

'Joe... You feel so good.' She braced her palms flat on his chest, her hair falling forward in two golden curtains framing her stunning face.

Joe forced his hands to stay curled into fists at her hips, fought the battle to take every scrap of pleasure she'd give him, to touch every inch of her and lose himself completely. This was too good, too intense, too much.

What if he'd never be the same after all this feeling? What if she changed him and he couldn't find his way back to the comfort of his pain, his grief, which for the past four years had preoccupied and sustained him?

As if sensing his struggle, Darcy bent over him and rubbed her lips over his, half kissing, half talking. 'It's okay, Joe. It's just for tonight.'

Could she sense his struggle? Did she understand his deepest fears? Of course, sex, even sex as wonderful as this, wouldn't change him, couldn't miraculously heal his scars, not that he wanted to be fixed.

What the hell was he doing? He should just enjoy his amazing good fortune and keep his promise to give Darcy way more than she'd given him.

For a few seconds more he allowed her to rock above him, lose herself and take him higher and higher.

Then, set free, he abandoned the fight to only half enjoy this as some form of penance for past crimes and jumped back into the driving seat. He gripped Darcy's hips, guiding her rocking motion, and gritted his teeth against the renewed rush. He flipped them, changing positions as need chewed him up and spat him out. He ran with it, greedy now in his intention to keep his word and keep this about pleasure, with all the feelings she awoke in him locked away.

'Yes, Joe...' she panted as he powered his hips into the cradle of hers '... I'm here with you.' Her fingers bit into his skin as her second climax struck and fuelled his own in a cataclysmic release. When spent he collapsed his weight on top of her, buried his face in her hair and indulged in a prolonged, restorative inhalation of her scent that he never wanted to end.

Then he too burst into laughter and agreed with Darcy's earlier assessment. 'Yep...amazing.'

Darcy breathed but the air quality seemed off; she couldn't get enough oxygen into her lungs. Joe lay spooned behind her, his sweaty chest stuck to her back, his arms tight around her waist as if he'd never let her go and his breath caressing her shoulder, raising fresh goose bumps. He shifted, quickly disposing of the condom, and then returned to the exact same position, his lips brushing her ear.

'I'm sorry... I'll let you sleep now, I promise.' He pressed a kiss to her neck and Darcy sighed as her libido cracked open one eye, fatigued but still keen.

They hadn't stopped. One round of incredible sex had turned into another and another until, with horrifying inevitability that stung the backs of Darcy's eyes, the first rays of dawn light peeked through the crack in the curtains.

Darcy lay still, scared to move and break the spell. Scared to begin the end of their physical relationship because, despite the deadline, the one night being at her insistence and what she wanted, she couldn't shake the feeling that she'd made some terrible mistake.

Intertwining her fingers with his, she sighed with contentment. She couldn't help it. Joe the lover was a revelation, a game changer. Attentive, tender and commanding, funny and relaxed. A different man, one she could become seriously addicted to if she hadn't made her choice, sworn off relationships, set her priorities.

Joe didn't seem to be in any hurry to release her or sleep himself, so she sank deeper into his embrace for a few more indulgent minutes, lying to herself that they had all the time in the world rather than the hour maximum of reality.

Not even Joe could be ready again so soon, so Darcy took the opportunity to ask the questions she couldn't voice at work.

She stroked her fingertips along his forearm. She wanted to ask about Rosie, how she'd died and why he blamed himself. Instead, she chose what she hoped was the least emotive of her burning questions. 'Why did you and Laura divorce?'

Right about now, after countless orgasms and the most tremendous sexual experience of her life, Darcy rated Joe as a pretty perfect man—smart, dedicated, hard-working and attentive and considerate in bed. She couldn't imagine that he'd cheat. He even put the toilet seat down.

His fingers, which were laced with hers, tensed for a split second. His sigh gusted over the back of her head.

'We tried to stay together after Rosie died.' His voice started off husky like the lover she'd come to learn intimately overnight, but then he cleared his throat as if clearing his mind and shifted at her back. 'At first we grieved together but then, somewhere along the line, something changed. Laura joined a support group and began to share her grief outside of our joint experience.'

Darcy held her breath, aching to hold him, to offer comfort.

'I was glad,' he continued. 'It helped her. She saw that, sadly, we weren't alone in losing a child. She felt consoled to know that we weren't the only ones living the nightmare. That we were one of many families torn apart.'

'And you?' Darcy already anticipated his answer.

Because where Laura had seemed to move on, to find love again and embrace the hope of creating a new life, Joe was stuck, punishing himself and living some sort of work-focused half-life.

Not that she could talk… They were similar, she and Joe. Would she too one day regret devoting so much time and energy, so much of herself, to her work instead of finding and treasuring personal happiness?

She felt his body stiffen a fraction, his heart pound a little faster at her back. 'I already knew that we were one of many couples living with loss from my work. The knowledge didn't help me at all. I didn't want to be part of a group with such a hideously unfair shared tragedy. I wanted the impossible.'

'To have Rosie back?' Darcy's voice was barely a whisper now as she crept closer to his deepest pain, feeling as if she had no right. They were just colleagues, temporary lovers. She didn't want more than that, and yet she couldn't ignore his torment or her own desire to know him just a little bit more.

She felt the brisk shake of his head. 'To go back in time.'

Darcy understood. She often regretted the amount of time she'd wasted missing, waiting for and fanta-sising about her biological father. As if wishing could change things, but it never had. He'd continuously dis-appointed her and let her down—forgotten birthdays, broken promises, hollow words.

'We started to grieve separately,' Joe said. 'Laura needed my support and I needed nothing, because in my experience nothing made the slightest bit of differ-ence to the pain. The only time I could forget for a few seconds and feel something resembling normal was at the hospital.'

Darcy nodded. She, too, had often patched at the holes in her life with her love of her work—especially after that final rejection from her father and later when she'd broken things off with Dean.

'It was no solace. Feeling normal made me feel guilty, as if I'd forget Rosie without the constant ache of her loss. But I started working later and later anyway, determined to distract myself from the agony gnawing at my insides, even if it was simply from fatigue. At least I felt needed at the hospital. Laura continued searching for her support outside of the marriage and I couldn't blame her. I'd have done the same if I thought anything would stop the pain. We moved in different directions.'

Darcy gripped his fingers tighter, his grief slicing into her like a razor-sharp scalpel. 'I can't imagine what you're feeling, Joe, but I hope that, for your sake, you find something that eases your grief. Perhaps the passage of more time…'

He had so much to offer, the thought of him still alone five years from now made her stomach pinch. But the idea of him with another woman… That made her nauseated, so she forced herself to voice the unthinkable. 'Or when you start dating again, the way Laura has.'

His withdrawal happened swiftly. He rolled away, stood and scrubbed his hands through his hair. 'I know the stages of grief, Darcy.'

'Whoa… I'm sorry.' Darcy sat up and tugged the covers over her instantly chilly upper body. 'I didn't mean to upset you. I was just trying to help.'

This was why she'd fought her attraction so hard. It was virtually impossible not to feel more, after all they'd been through together.

'I appreciate your sentiments,' he added, his mouth a tight line.

He sounded as if he felt the exact opposite, as if she'd pried too far or knew nothing about his feelings. Yes, she had no personal experience of his level of profound grief, but she was a doctor. She knew that Joe's coping mechanism of choice—to work until numb and punish himself—was in no way a healthy long-term strategy.

Not if he ever wanted to move on.

She knew because spending last night with him had made her realise how empty her own life was. She missed the physical and emotional connection and wanted that in her future. What if she strived and achieved and proved she could make it as a consultant surgeon, only to mourn the things she'd sacrificed, like finding love? Because she'd never truly given her past relationship a proper chance, she saw that now.

Had she ever opened up to Dean the way she had with Joe?

'I didn't mean to overstep the line,' she said, pushing as she always did. 'I just see that you could have so much more, if only you felt you deserved it.' Surely after the night they'd spent together, after the physical intimacies they'd shared, he'd see that her comments came from a place of caring and a genuine desire to help.

He shook his head and reached for his boxers, tugging them on with abrupt efficiency that told Darcy their lost night of passion was over.

'I know we are putting last night behind us—' if she could '—but that doesn't mean I don't care about you, Joe. Don't you want to find meaning again, to have a second chance at being happy?'

Just like she hoped one day to be. It had to be possible. For both of them.

'Don't doctor me, Darcy.' He jerked on his T-shirt. 'That isn't what this was about. We agreed—just sex.'

Darcy sighed, strangely bereft. He was right. She'd laid down the rules. So why did his emotional withdrawal sting so much? Caring wasn't something you could easily switch off. This was who she was, who she'd fought long and hard to become, despite her own obstacles, her shaky self-belief.

She saw Joe's point of view. 'I don't mean to doctor you, as you put it, but this is how I felt before we slept together and I'm not going to keep my insights to myself if I think it might help you to one day move on.'

Joe shook his head as if in disbelief. 'Maybe this is as good as I'll ever get. I told you I had nothing to offer. Maybe this is as far as I'll move, as much healing as I deserve.'

Darcy's horrified gasp seemed to shock them both. 'You deserve as much as the next person, Joe, as much as Laura.'

And so did she, if she could just stop that fear from holding her back.

'Do I? I put my career before spending time with my family, before my little girl. The day she died I went to work, my head full of other people's illnesses, and I never got to speak to her again.' His eyes hardened and Darcy shivered at how quickly things had turned sour. 'We've both made sacrifices for this job, Darcy, the difference being that I know the high price of those decisions, and it's not a choice I'd make again.'

Darcy swallowed, fighting the irrational fear that he'd just criticised the choice she'd made when she'd picked her career over her relationship. He was in pain. He didn't mean it that way.

Or perhaps, despite the past twenty-four hours, their

shared confessions and intimacies, he didn't really understand her after all.

Darcy watched his retreat to the shower, the sense that finally she'd met someone who not only saw her for who she was but valued her, too, deserting her with sickening realisation.

Until he understood himself they'd never see eye to eye, and Darcy was running out of time.

CHAPTER ELEVEN

'MRS O'CONNOR, I understand you're upset but I assure you that we are doing everything we can.' Darcy kept her tone low and reassuring, feeling every scrap of the woman's frustration. 'Your husband's post-op pneumonia is a recognised complication of surgery, especially in someone with his co-morbidities, but we're doing our utmost to help him turn the corner.'

Darcy's temples throbbed. She needed to go home, to leave the sterile hospital environment for a while and recharge her batteries and her reserves. She hated conversations like the one she'd been trapped in for fifteen minutes with this anxious relative, because she was already doing everything she could—for the patient and his family, who'd naturally assumed that he would quickly recover from his routine hernia operation. But sometimes fate had other ideas.

These situations brought up the inevitable conclusion that Darcy's utmost wasn't enough. Sometimes it couldn't be. With the best will in the world, you couldn't save or cure or even help everyone.

She'd tried to help Joe in Amsterdam after their intimate night, and she'd been knocked back.

'You never explained he might end up here...in Intensive Care.' The woman's pale face haunted Darcy, her pain reminiscent of what she'd witnessed from Joe. This was the worst part of her job and the irrational, vulnerable part of her feared that Joe would side with this relative and blame Darcy too.

They'd left with such a cloud over their relationship as they'd travelled back to London, back to their once more distant and untrusting reality. Darcy knew only one thing for sure: she had no idea what their new dynamic would be and no idea how to untangle her convoluted feelings about the mess they'd made of what should have been a simple one-night stand.

'No one could have predicted the complication,' she said. 'He was moved here so we can monitor him more closely and supplement his breathing with the ventilator. And while it seems alarming, Mr O'Connor is in the best place and receiving the best care.'

Darcy knew that for a fact. She herself had spent the better part of the night checking on her patient and speaking with the ICU team who had taken over management of his care. But she could see nothing she said would make Mrs O'Connor feel reassured.

Darcy couldn't blame the poor woman. She was angry, upset and Darcy had been lashed out at before, more times than she cared to remember. It was part of the job and she always tried not to take it personally. People reacted to stress and grief in different ways. And there was no situation more stressful than a threat to your loved ones.

Look at Joe. Hadn't he too lashed out at Darcy in Amsterdam, snapping closed the lid on his emotions when she'd tried to explore the deepening connection she'd felt after their night together? Understandable after his tragedy. He was protecting himself, the way she tried to avoid her own pain with her pushy, sometimes prickly attitude. She always expected the worst; her father's constant let-downs had conditioned her that way. But a part of her had hoped that she and Joe had moved past shielding and distrust.

Obviously not.

Darcy swallowed down her own hurt.

He'd been inside her, as close as it was physically possible for two people to be, caught her when she'd fallen apart in his arms, their eyes locked. She'd felt so close to him in that second, but it had been an illusion, one she should have known better than to believe.

He didn't want her caring. He didn't want her, and she should be okay with that; after all, she'd been the one to establish the rules.

Through the fog of bitter realisation that she cared too much for Joe, Darcy sensed someone approach. She turned to see the man himself arrive at her side.

An overwhelming sense of relief washed through her. Not relief that he'd wade in and smooth things over with Mrs O'Connor, but a sign of the sustenance she felt in his presence, as if she needed him beyond the physical desire, which if anything had only amplified in the two weeks since Amsterdam.

This. Was. Bad.

She couldn't allow feelings to rule her head, and her head told her to stick to their one-night rule. They certainly seemed to have effortlessly slipped back into their former strained relationship since their return.

'Ms Wright.' Joe cast her a brief look—long enough for Darcy's silly heart to pound and for her to see that he, too, appeared to share her fatigue if the fine lines and dark shadows around his beautiful eyes were any indication. Perhaps he was having trouble sleeping since the conference, just like her.

No, he probably slept like a baby knowing his emotions were safely locked down, out of harm's way. Knowing she'd soon be gone and he could resume, unscathed, his solitary, self-inflicted prison sentence.

'Mrs O'Connor, I'm Joe Austin, your husband's consultant.' He shook the woman's hand and reached for the observation chart, which would tell him that their patient was seriously unwell but, for now, stable.

'Good to finally meet you,' Mrs O'Connor said, her tone brisk with recrimination.

Darcy held her breath, waiting for what came next. She'd experienced this before. Patients often felt they weren't receiving top notch care unless the consultant themselves undertook every aspect of their treatment. But Joe was only one man—he couldn't possibly be in all places at once, operating and in clinic and there on the wards to administer every dose of antibiotics and perform every blood test.

He probably wished he could be. Then he could keep busy enough to distract himself and keep running from life. Did he fear that the memory of Rosie might slip out of his grasp if he allowed himself to be happy?

Couldn't he see that he carried her with him inside, safe and secure and permanent?

He'd made it clear that Darcy had no place in pointing out any of this.

'Yes, Ms Wright and I are incredibly disappointed that your husband's routine operation has resulted in a post-operative chest infection. Understandably, you are very worried.' Joe's quiet tone rang with calm authority. Unlike when they'd first met, when this had rubbed her up the wrong way, Darcy hoped Mrs O'Connor felt its soothing power, just as she did.

At least he still referred to them as a team, even if he no longer felt that they were one.

'Well…' Mrs O'Connor's anger deflated a little now that Joe, the big boss, was here simply repeating all the assurances Darcy had already made. 'I'm sure you'll do everything you can to get him well again.'

Darcy bit her tongue, pretending she didn't exist. If a relative felt comfort from hearing things from the horse's mouth, she couldn't complain. If only it didn't make her feel written out of the equation.

But perhaps her confusion over Joe and where they stood was more to blame. In Amsterdam she'd felt valued and accepted, but that was before he'd rejected her compassion and care. Now she was back to guessing his opinions.

Joe subtly stepped closer to Darcy, bringing her back into Mrs O'Connor's line of sight. 'Ms Wright and the intensive care staff have acted quickly in transferring Mr O'Connor here. He's in the right place, with an amazing team of doctors and nurses to care for him. Be assured we will continue to do everything we can to treat his pneumonia. From a surgical standpoint, Ms Wright informed me that his operation ran smoothly and that his scar is healing beautifully.'

Darcy unfurled under his praise like a flower in the sun. At least outwardly he supported her and her management of Mr O'Connor.

Joe's acknowledgement shouldn't matter, but it reminded her what she already knew: she *was* good enough to work for him. She was his equal. But did his professional consideration on top of their growing intimacy prove that somewhere, beneath his grief and pain and guilt, he cared about her, just as she'd begun to care about him?

Joe's magic touch worked on Mrs O'Connor, too. While Darcy tried to still the rampaging of her foolish heart that seemed to want impossible things, the other woman cast a small relieved smile in Darcy's direction before turning her attention on Joe once more. 'Yes... So will you be coming back to check on him later?'

'I'll check in tomorrow, but in the meantime I have the utmost faith in the medical team on ICU and in Ms Wright, who takes excellent care of all of my patients.'

Darcy swallowed convulsively, her reaction telling her how invested she'd become in Joe and how close to the surface her feelings lurked. Close enough that she could be seriously hurt.

She couldn't be falling for him. She refused to allow it.

Mrs O'Connor cast Darcy one last speculative look and hurried back to her husband's bedside.

Awkwardness descended, cloaking Darcy in its icy tentacles. She didn't want to look at Joe in case it confirmed all of her worst fears—that, despite her best intentions, she was in too deep.

'Shall we continue the rest of the round back on the surgical ward?' Joe looked down at her with an expectant expression, no hint that he in any way struggled with the post-sex boundaries they'd imposed in Amsterdam, when all Darcy wanted to do was either rip off his clothes or force him to let her in, emotionally. Preferably both.

No, no, no...

Darcy nodded woodenly, her head a mess. Every step back towards the surgical wing of the hospital along the sunlit corridor might as well have been on broken glass, so stilted and uncomfortable was the atmosphere. Eventually, Darcy couldn't stand the silence.

'Thanks for smoothing that over,' she said.

'I hope she wasn't too rude to you,' said Joe. 'It's hard to stay objective and calm when your loved one's fate is uncertain.'

'Of course.' Darcy glanced over at his stoic profile, knowing he must be thinking about Rosie. Unable to read him, she wished she could simply pull his X-ray and blood work and know exactly what he felt inside.

But maybe she didn't want to know. Maybe it would only confirm she was alone in wanting more than that one night. She sighed; she couldn't face another slap of rejection.

'Don't take it to heart,' he said. 'Sometimes patients and relatives need to know where the buck stops. It will stop with you soon enough, when you move on from City.' He paused outside the surgical ward and faced her. 'By the way, I forwarded the reference you asked for to Manchester Hospital. When is your interview?'

He gave so little away. Where had all that openness, the easy non-verbal communication between them gone?

'Next week.' Darcy's stomach cramped. His reminder that she'd soon take up a post in another hospital, which could be anywhere in the country, amplified the panic fluttering in her chest. She'd likely never see Joe again. Well, perhaps at a surgical conference in the future. Would they both still be single? Would they hook up for old times' sake? Would that be enough?

Five weeks ago that scenario might have sat comfortably with her, but now she found the idea of casual sex, even if it was with Joe, depressing. She wanted more; she wanted it all—her career and a meaningful private life—and for a moment in his arms that had seemed possible.

She imagined bumping into him down the track, seeing him happy, a shiny new wedding ring on his finger. Inexplicable emotion gripped Darcy's throat so her words emerged strangled. 'Thanks...for the reference.'

She thought back to her first day, when a letter of endorsement had been all she'd wanted from Joe. Now her wants were so much more...complex. Impractical and terrifying.

'All part of my job,' he said, pushing open the door to the ward and stepping aside for Darcy to pass.

Yes, that was all she was to him—work, a colleague. He'd warned her there was no room inside him for anything else and she'd believed, hoped, that one night would be enough.

Only now...

Joe paused just inside the ward and levelled his stare on Darcy, the intense, soul-searching one she'd grown to expect during their long sleepless night in an Amsterdam hotel. Despite their location, her own warnings and plain old common sense, which demanded she not over-interpret that look, her pulse flew, buzzing in her ears, the danger deafening.

Careful...

'We should talk,' he said, 'before the ward round.'

There was a utility room at the entrance to the ward. Before she could argue or agree, Joe glanced toward the empty nurses' station and then gripped Darcy's arm and ushered her inside.

Darcy backed up into the small room, lost for words. Her heart hammered against her ribs, which was silly because he wasn't likely to pounce on her and rip off her clothes in a room regularly entered by ward staff. So why did she suddenly wish the door had a lock?

He paced close, his stare intent. The appearance of

an urbane professional man slipped away, replaced by the look of a hungry predator. Darcy shivered. Her reaction to this unexpected diversion confirmed what she already knew. Despite the danger, she craved more than the night they'd shared, more than to be a part of his work, a colleague. More of them together.

Could he want the same?

'What are you doing?' she asked, her voice wobbling with anticipation.

Please let him be about to kiss her.

'This.' In two swift strides Joe closed the distance. He scooped one strong arm around her waist and, with a triumphant grunt, slammed his mouth over hers in a frantic kiss that answered every one of Darcy's unspoken prayers.

Feeling as if she were levitating, she parted her lips, her tongue meeting his, duelling, thrusting, devouring. This was what she'd missed since Amsterdam. It was reckless and perilous and alarming, but she could no more resist than she could switch off her feelings.

They broke for air, Joe's lips continuing a trail of kisses over her jaw towards her earlobe.

'What are we doing?' panted Darcy, curling her fingers into his hair and tugging at the lapel of his suit jacket, bringing him closer and dragging his lips back for another kiss.

'Taking a big risk, but I don't care.' He crowded her back against the counter, his big body trapping her exactly where she wanted to be.

'I can't stop thinking about you,' he said, his words muffled against her skin. 'Every time we've seen each other I've had to stop myself from touching you, reaching for your hand, kissing you. I almost broke on ICU and dragged you into my arms.'

Joe's thigh pushed between her legs. 'I brought you in here to apologise for the way I reacted in Amsterdam. But I can't seem to keep my hands off you.' He gripped her waist, hoisting her backside up onto the table. Darcy closed her eyes, lost to physical sensation as Joe snaked his hand around her waist and trailed his voracious lips down the side of her neck.

She should curtail this. Anyone could come in at any second. She was certain that fornicating in a storage cupboard was a sackable offence, but she just couldn't bring herself to care enough, already lost under the hypnotic spell of the way Joe made her feel.

As if, with the right man, she could have it all. She could feel whole for the first time in her life. But Joe couldn't be the right man. He wasn't ready to forgive himself. His determination to be alone put Darcy in a highly risky position. She'd been the one to make all of the concessions, all of the sacrifices in the past. She'd done it with her father growing up—holding out hope that they'd resume the closeness they'd shared in those first few years, forgiving him when his broken promises broke her heart, over and over, keeping a distance from Grant in case it provoked her father's disappointment—and also with Dean out of ingrained habit.

But with Joe she was in deeper water.

'We said we wouldn't do this again,' she said, hooking her fingers through the belt loops of his trousers so he couldn't escape. 'You said you kept your promises.'

Was that her desperately breathy voice goading him to ignore the rules they'd agreed on and be exactly what she needed?

Please let him break this promise...

'I never promised to stop wanting you, to stop craving you,' he said, the words pressed against her skin as he kissed a delirious path from the vee of chest her top exposed to the angle of her jaw.

'Don't stop,' she said as his tongue flicked at the lobe of her ear. They couldn't have sex in the utility room at the hospital, but perhaps there was little harm in continuing this relationship until she left City. It was only a handful of weeks, a nice tidy deadline she had time to get used to.

But could she ever get used to the way he made her feel?

He pulled away enough to pin her with his sexy stare. 'Are you free tonight?' Joe cupped her breast and rubbed her nipple through her layers of clothing.

She bucked against him, her body incinerating at his touch and all the erotic memories it evoked. Not fair.

'Um…' She wanted to ask, *Free for what?* To cover an extra shift, a date, more sex? Despite the warning exhilaration rendering her virtually speechless, she was definitely ready and willing for the latter two.

'I'm sorry…for the way things ended in Amsterdam.' His gruff voice, his warm breath on her neck, did things to her willpower. 'I hoped you might allow me to make it up to you…' his other hand slipped under the hem of her top until he brushed bare flesh; her body sprang alive, like the jolt from a defibrillator '…with dinner.'

No, say no.

'Um…' Were there no words left in her vocabulary? Had she become a gibbering wreck of hormones and emotions, too addicted to Joe to make any sense?

He cupped her cheek, swiped the pad of his thumb over her bottom lip, sincerity and that hint of vulnerability in his beautiful eyes. 'We could go out to a restaurant if you want, or I could cook. I only live two Tube stops away from here.' He pressed his hips forward between her legs and her body melted, all fight draining away until she was left with only need and feelings.

Feelings that erred perilously close to the edge of the fall.

No, she couldn't. She mustn't.

'Okay...' Darcy sighed, helpless to resist as his tempting kisses resumed.

Uninhibited by the way he made her feel complete, she slipped one hand under his suit jacket and around his waist, her fingertips tracing the muscles of his back through his shirt. Her other hand found the hard length of him behind the zip of his trousers and they groaned together.

Darcy closed her eyes against the spiralling sensations he effortlessly created. Could she wait until tonight? She dropped her head back, exposed her neck to his mouth in utter surrender.

With a thud, the back of her head hit the shelving that lined the wall behind. A cacophony of packages— syringes, gauze, catheter tubes—rained down on them like medical confetti.

It broke the tension. Darcy laughed, clapped her hand over her mouth. Joe rested his forehead against hers and chuckled, the fraught arousal draining from his features.

'Perfect timing,' he said, pressing one last kiss to her lips. He helped Darcy slide from the counter and speared his hand through his hair, trying to make himself presentable once more.

Her heart clenched. He looked so sexy she was certain she wouldn't have stopped without the interruption. Was she so far gone that she'd forget where they were, forget that they'd both sworn off relationships and this had no long-term future?

They righted their clothing and picked up the fallen

equipment, shoved it into the correct cubby on the wall, their matching knowing smiles infectious.

'So...' Joe said, 'meet me at six, my office?' The excitement lingering in his eyes called to the part of Darcy that was now full-blown addicted to Joe Austin. For her self-preservation, to protect that last part of her heart, she needed to know how he saw this panning out.

'So, will it be like a date?' she croaked, chiding herself for the hope that bloomed inside.

He shrugged, a moment's hesitation confirming that he too was in uncharted territory. 'If you like. After all, you'll soon be moving on. I need to get my fill of your company before you leave.'

That he wanted more, just like her, terrified and elated her. That he'd, too, identified a natural and convenient deadline should reassure her. But she no longer wanted just sex; she craved their emotional connection, the depth of which she'd never before experienced. Could she take more incredible sex without needing him to open up emotionally? Could she protect herself if he once again shut her out?

She trembled, her nerves frayed. One thing was evident; she couldn't risk falling all the way in love with a man incapable of giving her what she needed. She couldn't be second best or an afterthought or good enough. Next time she committed to a man she wanted to be everything to him, his world.

'Okay, a date it is.' Darcy nodded, her heart fluttering wildly. While good, her diagnostic skills struggled to determine the cause of her palpitations. The euphoria she craved or trepidation for the rejection she expected?

Only time would tell the outcome for her and Joe.

CHAPTER TWELVE

JOE PLACED A bowl of steaming pasta in front of Darcy and refilled her wine glass before taking his seat opposite. Lightness rose in his chest. It was good to have her all to himself, in his home. No demons, no pressure, no expectation.

Just the constant and undeniable need to be with her, talk to her, touch her.

His growing obsession was understandable after being alone for so long. And he'd convinced himself that there was little risk; she'd soon be moving on.

But...

He couldn't seem to shake the hollow dread that settled in the pit of his stomach when he imagined the end of this.

Darcy leaned over the dish and inhaled the fragrant steam and then offered him an impressed smile that warmed the coldest recesses of his soul. 'This smells delicious. Thank you.'

'It's just pasta...' He wished he had more to offer her than a simple home-cooked meal. She deserved champagne and caviar, satin sheets and a whirlwind romance.

She shrugged. 'No one's ever really cooked for me before.' She took a sip of wine and picked up her fork, her eyes alight with reflections from the candles.

'Really?' Joe hid his surprise. 'Not even your ex?' He frowned. What sort of a man would propose to Darcy and then allow her to escape?

Darcy swallowed the mouthful, her eyes darting away from Joe's. 'No...' She bit her lip as if choosing her words carefully. 'Dean was...an artist. The practicalities of everyday life—cooking, shopping, paying the bills—often passed him by while he worked.'

Joe's irritation flickered to life on Darcy's behalf. Laura and Joe had shared the household responsibilities. Working from home was still working. The idea of Darcy returning home after a long gruelling day at the hospital with no support or understanding left him itching with exasperation.

'Did you live together?' he asked, trying to picture the driven, ambitious woman he knew in a serious relationship. 'I can't imagine you happily working a sixty-hour week *and* doing all of the household chores.' Nor should she have to. This wasn't the Dark Ages. Her career was just as important as Joe's.

Darcy looked uncomfortable but then, with a small sigh, dropped her guard. He hadn't realised how much he'd held out for the return of their confidences, how he craved her trust as strongly as he craved her lips.

'We did live together,' she said. 'Divvying up the everyday tasks became a bone of contention. Among others.'

Joe raised his eyebrow in enquiry. Relaxed by the wine and the soft music he'd selected, Darcy seemed to be in a confessional mood that lessened Joe's guilt for pushing her away after they'd slept together. Their night had shocked him, not only the violence of his insatiable physical desire for Darcy, but also because he wanted more, wanted to know every fine internal intricacy of her mind.

Like why she was still unattached. It seemed preposterous that she hadn't been snapped up when she was most guys' dream woman.

'He never really understood my career. Our career.' Darcy twirled her wine glass by the stem, watching the deep red liquid catch the light as she talked about her ex. 'He thought such a utilitarian job should keep regular hours.' She rested her elbows on the table and sought Joe's eyes. 'We had ups and downs like any couple. He'd complain if I was late to one of his gallery exhibitions or if I couldn't socialise with his friends because of my on-call commitments. I guess he never really understood me either, or my drive.'

A surge of protective feelings welled up in Joe. 'It's a common point of friction between doctors and their non-medical spouses.' He and Laura had had their fair share of trials and tribulations. Darcy deserved a partner who appreciated her qualities.

'So you called it off?' he asked, although she'd already admitted this. But he wanted to know why. He wanted to know if Darcy's heart had been broken by this man who'd made her doubt herself, made her choose.

'I did,' she said, meeting Joe's gaze. 'I'm not saying I was perfect. At times, I might have acted as if my job was more important than his... I've always been ambitious. I guess I needed to prove to myself that I could be and do anything after growing up with so much... rejection. He asked me to marry him, and initially I said yes, but the minute the word left my mouth it felt like the wrong decision.'

Joe tried not to give rein to the envy that she'd almost married this guy. 'Why was it the wrong decision?

Don't you want to get married one day?' Now why the hell had he asked that? What business was it of his? Except he cared about her and wanted her to be happy. She deserved to have it all one day, as he had.

She swallowed, her eyes brimming with vulnerability. 'I felt like he'd never fully accept me for who I am—my motivations and values. I'd already sacrificed so much of myself trying to be the kind of daughter that my father would want, not that I knew then what would make him want to stay around. For a long time I made myself feel like an outsider in my own family. I never knew when he'd reappear, so it was as if I felt the need to keep a part of myself constantly ready for him to show up and whisk me away for a one-on-one. I was a child. I guess I thought I couldn't have both. Now I see that I was emotionally withdrawing from the people who loved me the most, Grant, my sisters to a degree, even my mother. Because I tried to hide some of my disappointment when he let me down for the times my father would return. I didn't want her to be angry with him on my behalf. It took most of my late teens and early twenties to untangle those childhood beliefs and embrace my family one hundred per cent.'

Joe nodded, new respect for her strength and determination making his breathing tight.

'With Dean,' she continued, 'it felt as if one day I'd have to choose again, sacrifice our relationship or my job.' She shrugged. 'I knew there was no contest, so I called it off before either of us could get hurt.'

Joe sensed there was more to the story, more to her motivation. Most people successfully combined a career and a personal life. Darcy's polarised view smacked of self-preservation, fear. No one understood that better than Joe. 'So you pulled the plug pre-emptively, before giving commitment a try?'

Her eyes flashed to his, a flare of defensiveness, then resignation. 'Yes... I suppose I did. I wanted to save myself the emotional fallout when our relationship broke down, as it eventually would. I guess I didn't love him enough to take that chance.'

Unease prickled along Joe's spine. It shouldn't matter to him that she, too, had relationship reservations. Why was he pushing this? He wanted to be with her, to take as much of her as she'd give him in the time they had left, not dissect her past choices to determine where he would fit into her life. He wasn't offering her long-term, so why did it bother him that she'd shied away from committing to another man?

'It might have lasted,' said Joe, playing devil's advocate even as his blood pumped harder, knowing that Darcy hadn't loved this man from her past enough. 'None of us can predict the future,' he said. 'No one knows what awaits us around the bend. If we did, maybe we'd never do anything. Never grow or thrive or experience wondrous joy.'

Her eyes softened. She was thinking about him and Rosie, he could tell. Yes, Joe had first-hand experience of life's highs and lows and fickleness.

'I guess I was scared,' she said, her voice breaking.

Joe held his breath, desperate to hold her but needing to complete the Darcy puzzle, too. She was opening all the way up to him and his greedy, selfish side craved everything she was willing to give. Perhaps talking about her past would help her, the way telling her small things about Rosie had helped him. When she left City he'd sleep better at night knowing that he'd done everything in his power to support her onward journey, as a clinician and as a person.

'I did hold back from Dean, from full commitment.' Her candour, her bravery mesmerised him. 'I thought our differences, which at times seemed insurmountable, would push us apart eventually.' She shrugged, her small smile shifting something inside Joe.

'So you pushed first, to protect yourself.' His voice was low, coaxing, pleading for her to share this part of herself that she normally guarded. He was in no way judging. Humans were at their most unpredictable and complex when frightened or in pain. 'It's understandable after what you went through growing up.'

Her father's abandonment, his repeated rejection, would have affected bright, emotionally intelligent Darcy. The feeling of being somehow unworthy of his love might have eased the more she pushed herself academically and later in her work as a doctor, but the belief would ultimately hold her back from deep connections with others, from true contentment.

He knew. He'd deliberately withdrawn and avoided developing bonds since he'd lost Rosie, but he wanted more than that for Darcy.

She shrugged, her colour high. She was intuitive enough to read between the lines. He'd hit the nail on the head.

The thought depressed him more than it should. It wasn't his place to fix her, not when he'd promised her nothing beyond a few more nights of incredible sex. Except he couldn't stop himself, just as he'd been powerless to deny his urges in the utility room earlier.

'What about you?' she asked, turning the tables. 'Do you think you'll ever want another shot at happiness?'

Doubt flashed in her eyes, brief and unfamiliar. Did she imagine more between them?

Joe's stomach pinched with unease. 'Ah... I've already experienced love *and* its flipside. At first it feels great, you feel invincible, but then...' He swallowed his own fears gripping his throat. 'I never want to feel that degree of pain again.' He looked away from her searching stare, his resolve hardening. 'It's not for everyone, but I'm happy with my lonely, risk-free existence.'

He couldn't bear to see the emotions in Darcy's eyes. Sorrow for him, perhaps disappointment that he wasn't just like her, pushing for the best outcome, to be the best version of himself.

How he wished he could be different, open to exploring this connection with Darcy beyond a few passionate nights. A part of him would love to be the kind of man she deserved, the kind who would love her unconditionally and chase away all of her doubts about her worth. But he'd been there before, and nothing he'd done could stop it all slipping through his fingers.

Already he felt his insatiable need for Darcy had begun to dictate his emotional happiness. When she smiled it elevated his mood. If she challenged him he felt enlivened, cheerful, animated. And when she returned his kisses, her passion burning as brightly as his own, he became convinced that *anything* was possible.

But that was a lie. He couldn't rely on another person to that degree.

'I guess we're similar in avoiding risky emotional fallout,' she said, and Joe's skin crawled with unfamiliar dejection. Maybe they were too similar—Darcy and the old Joe. The man he'd been before he was forced to realise that without your loved ones there was no one to strive for. What would stop Darcy pushing away the next man who got too close?

She settled those defiant and determined eyes on his. 'Dean wasn't the one for me. I'm glad that I chose to focus on myself instead of investing valuable time and energy on the wrong priority.' She lifted her chin and Joe saw the flicker of fear behind her bravado.

Wasn't that how he felt about his job and all the missed chances to spend time with the most valuable people in the world: family?

Joe reached out and took her hand, needing her touch to remind himself that their physical connection had to be enough. 'Good for you.'

He didn't want more than this, but to hear her fear, how she ran from commitment, reminded him that waking up from the past grief-dulled four years, embracing something life-enhancing and passionate with this woman, was one thing. But chancing more than that when there were no guarantees in life and Darcy, for all her amazing qualities, had been a flight risk in the past... That seemed unthinkable.

Darcy accepted another glass of wine and made room for Joe on the sofa, her emotions conflicted. She'd been warmed by his attentiveness, touched by his cooking and even welcomed his gentle enquiries. They finally had a chance to be alone and explore each other on a deeper level and it felt good to open up to him. She trusted him.

But a niggle of unease permeated her relaxed, hopeful mood.

Joe understood her past fear of commitment because it was something they had in common, for different reasons. Only, for the first time in her life, Darcy glimpsed a way forward, the possibility of having it all. With Joe. If only he could meet her halfway along the same path.

But no matter how hard she tried to imagine a future where she could have everything—a relationship with a man who understood and supported her and a career she found fulfilling—she always circled back to the same roadblock: Joe's grief.

She saw shadows of it whenever she looked into his deep brown eyes. He was trapped by it, scared to let go in case he lost the memories, lost more of his little girl than he had already.

And she couldn't blame him for clinging to the one thing he felt connected him to Rosie. She'd do the same.

Except she wanted more for him than half a life, which was tinged with so much sadness. She wanted him to be the wonderful man he was and to find self-forgiveness.

She took his hand, curled her fingers into his palm. They looked down at their entwined hands. Darcy's pulse throbbed to the tips of her fingers at the thrill and decadence of Joe's touch.

'Tell me about Rosie,' Darcy whispered. 'I'd love to have met her.' Her enquiry was long overdue, but there was never the right time for such an emotive conversation at the hospital, and until recently she'd been too unsure of Joe's emotional shield to ask. Even now, when they'd spent an evening learning new things about the other, warning signs flashed in her mind. He'd withdrawn in Amsterdam. Would tonight end with a repeat? Him defensive and her pushing him further away?

Joe's breath shuddered out on a slow exhale. He stared at the flickering candle flame on the coffee table, lost in his thoughts. 'She was the sweetest little girl. So precious, as all children are. I adored her.' Their stares connected and Darcy was crushed by the outpouring of stark emotions she saw.

She smiled, steering him away from Rosie's final minutes, the mechanics of which only appeased her doctor's curiosity. She cared much more about Joe's recovery. 'What was your favourite thing to do together?'

Darcy's heart banged against her ribs. The urge to hold Joe in her arms and never let him go, to always be there for him in whatever capacity he'd allow, was almost overwhelming. She realised way too late that where Joe was concerned she seemed to have forgotten her suit of armour.

He smiled, remembering, and her spirit soared. 'We would cook breakfast together on the weekend. Her favourite—pancakes with banana and maple syrup.' He talked with his hands, so Darcy could vividly picture the scene. 'We'd trash the kitchen and then eat the results, but we always needed a story before tackling the washing-up. My girl was a bookworm.' Pride warmed his expression. 'She loved it when I read to her.'

Darcy struggled to speak past her choked throat. 'What a beautiful memory, Joe.' She cupped his face and stroked her thumb over his stubble-rough jaw. 'Your relationship sounds so close. You were both so lucky to have each other.'

Joe stared, nodded, his eyes full of love for his daughter and sympathy for Darcy. 'Yes, we were. She was a gift. I miss her so much.'

Joe's love for his daughter, the simple but special moments he described, amplified Darcy's own sense of loss for something she'd never had—that one person to share everything with. To build a life, a family, love. She wrapped her arms around Joe's shoulders and held him close, more for her own comfort than his.

'It would have been her tenth birthday next week,' he said, gripping Darcy with equal compulsion, the thump of his heart against hers sure and steadfast. 'I try to imagine how she would look, how she'd have changed as she grew, who she'd resemble most, me or Laura.'

Darcy glanced around the room, spying only one or two framed photos of them together on the mantelpiece. No wonder he was lonely here, with his sparse reminders. He clearly thought about Rosie all the time, but where the family home she'd visited in Surrey, the home he'd left to Laura after their split, was alive with the presence of their daughter, Joe's house, but for those two framed photos, resembled more of a bachelor pad.

She pulled back to look into his face. She cherished his trust. 'Will you celebrate the day?'

He frowned as if she'd suggested something he'd never considered. 'Last year Laura and I visited Rosie's grave and took toys and flowers, but this year...' he swallowed, clearly struggling '... I suspect she'll want to go alone, with Phil.'

Darcy's soul ached anew. She wanted to volunteer to go with him, to be whatever he needed in his time of grief and remembrance. But he'd never accept that from her. She wasn't his partner. She wasn't even his girlfriend.

To keep her mouth shut and her offer to herself, she leaned forward and kissed his temple. She couldn't stop herself from touching him, comforting him, connecting.

'Why don't you have a party—make a stack of Rosie's favourite pancakes and decorate them with ten candles?'

He frowned and Darcy worried that he'd see her suggestion as interference.

'I'm sorry, Joe. I don't mean to upset you. I can only

imagine how you must feel. But it's okay to learn to live with your wonderful memories of Rosie in a different way. It's natural for a parent-child relationship to change with time. It won't mean that you love her any less because you smile.'

Joe scrunched his eyes closed and dropped his forehead to hers. He was silent for so long Darcy squirmed that she'd overstepped the line and ruined their evening.

Then he drew back, a small frown between his brows. 'When did you last reconnect with your biological father?'

Darcy stiffened, withdrawing from the pain still potent enough to sting. A part of her wanted to protect her deepest shame, that for her father she hadn't been good enough, but Joe had shared so much with her. She wanted him to know that he wasn't alone with his regrets. She had them too.

'I looked him up when I started medical school,' she said, the humiliating memories flooding back. 'I hadn't seen him for years. Part of me hoped that he'd want a relationship with the adult me. I wanted to show him that I was someone he could be proud of. I was going to be a doctor and, thanks to that show I participated in, I was going to be on TV.'

She shook her head at her naiveté, struggling to finish the story because it brought out all of her most painful insecurities—the last thing she wanted with Joe, the man she was falling for. 'He invited me to his home—he'd moved to Scotland. I almost threw up on the train journey; I was so nervous and excited and hopeful.'

Joe cupped her cheek and pressed his lips to her forehead, anticipating the *but*. She fell a little harder in that moment, grateful that he understood her so intuitively. Grateful for his strength.

'I arrived to find that he'd remarried. He had two new daughters, one six and one a year old, the age I was when he first took off. It was hard to see how much he adored his girls.'

She blinked away the sting of tears. 'I felt betrayed—it wasn't that he didn't want children; he just didn't want *me*. The visit was a disaster. I couldn't hide my anger, my...disappointment. I lashed out at him with some home truths and haven't seen him since.'

Air rushed from her lungs on a cathartic exhale. The only other people she'd told the details of that story to were Stella and Lily.

'I'm so sorry.' Joe held her close, his heart thudding against hers in solidarity. It felt like all she'd ever need to tackle life's future obstacles. But the bitter taste in the back of her throat reminded her that she couldn't rely on Joe. As wonderful as he was, Joe wasn't ready to be the man for her.

'It's okay.' She sniffed, put on her brave face. 'It was good for me in a way. I started taking myself more seriously, stared knuckling down even more with my studies and planning my future. It gave me renewed purpose, the work ethic I still have today. Perhaps I wouldn't have even become a doctor if he'd accepted me with open arms.'

Joe pulled back to look at her, his thumb caressing her cheek where he still cupped her face. 'Of course you would. You're an innate healer. You were always going to be the gifted surgeon you are now. You were always destined to be your amazing self. Don't give him credit he doesn't deserve when your success, your inspiring qualities, are down to you and you alone.'

He brushed his lips over Darcy's in a whisper of a kiss. 'Sometimes it's easier for people to move on and try to forget their past mistakes. Staying with them and working for redemption is harder, takes more self-reflection and honesty. Humans are essentially lazy cowards who avoid pain at all costs.'

Darcy understood that he referred to her father, but instinctively knew that Joe's condemnation also included himself. She gripped both of his hands, demanding his attention.

'Joe, you didn't do anything wrong. You are an incredible man.' She pressed her hand to her breastbone. 'I know in here, deep down in my soul, that Rosie would be so proud of her dad. I know because the little girl I was, the one so desperate for her real father to care, would have done anything for a father like you.'

His tight swallow told her anything he might want to say was trapped in his throat. She hated the remaining distance between them so she leaned in and pressed her lips to his, seeking and giving refuge. He took her kiss as if reaching for a lifeline, his arms clutching her so tight she felt melded to his chest as if they were one.

His mouth grew demanding, overpowering and yielding in perfect harmony so that Darcy forgot her own pain, forgot that Joe might not want her consolation, forgot every doubt as she lost herself in their kiss.

Comfort quickly turned to passion. Darcy tugged at Joe's shirt and he unclasped her bra with one hand. Tearing his mouth from hers, he stood and lifted her into his arms.

'I want you. I've been in hell since Amsterdam.' He strode towards what she assumed was his bedroom and kicked open the door.

She'd missed her chance to slam on the brakes, reconstruct some semblance of a barrier against her feelings for Joe. They'd spilled free the minute he'd begun to confide in her, talking about his daughter, and it was too late to scoop them all up now.

She was in too deep.

'Joe, hurry,' Darcy cried as they stripped, tossed clothes away with furious impatience. As they finally found each other completely naked, skin to warm skin, their groans resounded in unison around the darkened bedroom.

Darcy knew she was making a mistake because nothing had ever felt this good, or this important. It had to be bad. It had to mean that rejection wasn't far away. She shouldn't trust it.

Except she wanted to be wrong. She wanted Joe to declare himself ready to open his emotional vault. She wanted to trust him with her heart, the way she'd never trusted before. She wanted them to face this scary new future together, as much a team as a couple, as they were at work.

When he covered himself in protection and pushed inside her she had to dig her teeth into his shoulder to stop her tears. It was too good. They were too in sync, the enormity of her feelings for this man bursting forth as she shattered around him and clung on for dear life.

Joe crushed her, spent, and then rolled to the side, taking her with him, clinging, holding, stroking as if he'd never let her go. Darcy lay in the circle of his strong arms, her cheek pressed against his slowing heart, too scared to breathe, because if she'd thought she was terrified that he'd somehow let her down, how on earth would she ever survive falling in love?

CHAPTER THIRTEEN

DARCY FLUNG OPEN her front door to find a sight for sore eyes standing on her doorstep: Joe. His dazzling smile knocked the wind from her lungs. The familiar hint of sadness around his eyes made her feel needed. That he'd come to her on this day, Rosie's birthday, a sure sign of his personal feelings.

He must care.

Her heart leapt into her throat and she threw her arms around him, pressing a kiss to his neck. 'What are you doing here? I literally just arrived home from Manchester.' She hadn't even had time to change out of her interview suit after spending the day touting her skills as a candidate for the newest general surgeon consultant post on offer.

'I wanted to see you.' He kissed her long and deep, and Darcy forgot how to breathe. How could she have missed him so profoundly? She'd only been away one night. How would she survive working three hundred miles away when her body felt starved of him after only twenty-four hours?

When they broke apart she invited him in and closed the door.

'How was the interview?' he asked, placing the shopping bag he carried at his feet to shrug out of his jacket.

For the first time since she'd opened the door to find him expectantly seeking her out, the nauseating taste of failure returned. 'It seemed to go well.' She looked at her feet, which were bare and still protesting the heels she'd worn for her interview. 'The panel were friendly and interested in my past research, but...'

She glanced up at Joe, knowing he'd understand what today's failure meant to Darcy.

'But you didn't get the job?' He looked disappointed, gutted on her behalf, tired.

The mean little doubts that had plagued her on the train journey home—that perhaps his reference hadn't been the glowing endorsement she'd needed to secure the job—now seemed trivial and disloyal. Perhaps her thoughts had been a desperate diversion from ruminating on her feelings, because Darcy was more certain than ever that she was falling deeply in love.

Stupid, foolish woman.

'No. They chose the guy from Scotland, the one with a PhD and a large portfolio of research.' Darcy hung Joe's coat on the rack in the hallway and led him into the living room, where Stella lounged on the sofa after her shift at the hospital.

'Joe, this is my sister, Stella. Stella, this is Joe Austin, my consultant.' Darcy winced inside. She wanted to be able to introduce him in another more personal way but, regardless of her feelings, the fantasies she'd allowed herself to concoct—that he'd realise he couldn't live without her, beg her to stay in London and ask her to move in with him—that was all he was to her in reality.

Stella flushed as she uncurled herself from the sofa and shook Joe's hand. 'I know who he is.' She rolled her eyes at Darcy and then to Joe said, 'Nice to meet you. I…uh… I was just about to go for a run so I'll… um…leave you two to it.'

With all the subtlety of a baby rhinoceros, Stella jogged upstairs to change.

Darcy bit her lip and searched Joe's face for signs that he was upset by her sister's obvious assumption. 'Sorry. She's figured out we're sleeping together. You can't hide anything from sisters!' And, of course, Darcy had in turn questioned Stella about Aaron's cryptic reaction to her name. 'But she's the soul of discretion, I promise.' She didn't want him to feel uncomfortable if he ran into Stella at the hospital after Darcy left.

'I'm not worried.' His apparent ease rankled. Perhaps he wouldn't even miss her. Perhaps he'd move on, too, seek physical comfort from his next registrar.

'Have you eaten?' He held his shopping bag aloft.

Darcy chided herself for her irrational hope and her pointless jealousy. 'No—are you cooking?' How could she resist any part of him? She'd take whatever he was willing to give her until she left, and somehow try to get over him from afar.

Hopefully she'd be too busy working to give him a second thought.

Joe nodded, tugging her back in for another kiss that felt loaded with all the unspoken confidences and confessions Darcy wanted to hear.

I'm falling for you.

I don't want you to move so far away.

I'm ready to give us a try.

'Today's the day,' he said, sliding his hand under Darcy's jacket to stroke her back.

She nodded, pressing kisses to his face in order to chase away the shadows haunting his expression and

her own desire to blurt out her feelings. 'I know. Joe…
I'm so touched that you called around.'

Surely the fact that he'd come to her, of all people,
meant that he cared more than he'd expressed. That a
part of him already considered them more than a casual, sex-only fling.

'I brought steaks and salad.' His open smile faltered.
'And pancake mix… I thought we could…celebrate. I
don't want to make too big a deal out of it, but I wanted
you to be there, as it was your clever idea.'

Hot tears prickled Darcy's eyes. 'Of course. I'd love
that.' How she longed for him to say that he needed her.
That he couldn't get through today without her by his
side. She kissed him, her empathy ever-present. But
also to stop herself from pushing for the impossible.

Now wasn't the time.

'Thank you…for asking me to share this with you
and Rosie.' She stepped back from the warm, safe circle of his arms. 'I'll just get changed—help yourself to
wine in the kitchen.'

Darcy raced upstairs and stripped off her interview
clothes, choosing a comfy pair of jeans and her favourite snugly jumper. Ignoring why she needed its soft,
fluffy comfort, she pressed her hand over her fluttering heart to steady her whirlwind thoughts. He'd come
to her to share a massive emotional milestone. Could
it mean that he'd opened his heart to the idea of more?

As she headed back down the stairs in her bare feet,
the clatter of pots and pans making her stomach rum-
ble, she tried to shove all doubts aside and just be there
for Joe.

'Smells good,' she said, coming up beside him and
taking a grateful sip from the glass of red wine he

handed her with one hand while jiggling the pan containing the sizzling steaks with the other.

Abandoning the cooking, he turned, scooped his arm around her waist, kissed her. She wanted to forget the demands of her unfed stomach and drag him upstairs now that they had the house to themselves. But tonight wasn't about her and her constant need for Joe. It was about him and Rosie, remembrance and celebration for a life cut too short.

Joe served the steaks onto two plates already laden with delicious salad and they carried plates and wine glasses to the table, where he'd even lit a bunch of candles Stella liked to burn.

So thoughtful. So romantic. So Joe...

'What reasons did they give for not offering you the job?' asked Joe, slicing into his perfectly medium steak.

Darcy shrugged, desperate to avoid voicing her biggest fears about him, but needing to know all the same. She wanted to trust him one hundred per cent. To give all of herself. More than that, she needed to know that he was on the same page as her when it came to them.

'Oh, the usual...' she said, her stomach now too unsettled to eat. 'Personality fit and experience.' She loaded her fork with salad anyway, ready to fill her mouth so she couldn't say anything to ruin tonight, but the words escaped anyway. 'A part of me was worried that perhaps you'd based my reference on our disastrous first meeting...'

Joe frowned, even though she'd punctuated her outrageous and unfounded accusation with a nervous giggle to soften its impact.

Darcy looked down at her plate and ploughed on, all her fears now rising to the surface as if she'd cut herself open. 'Or they could somehow tell from what you'd written that we're sleeping together... I know—silly.' She shook her head but the fear lingered, that rejection-sensitive part of her convinced that Joe's professional respect was a figment of her imagination. Waiting for his true colours to emerge, for him to condemn her surgical skills or, worse, to push her away.

She swallowed hard, her throat raw. She had to keep her feelings a secret. She couldn't tell him how much she cared about him, how she was falling in love with him. Not until she was sure that he was ready to accept her feelings.

Darcy pushed the food around her plate. She was already way more emotionally invested in Joe than he was in her. Part of her had hoped that he'd be overjoyed when she didn't get the job. That he'd admit they had something worth exploring beyond the handful of weeks she had left at City Hospital.

He shook his head and wiped his mouth with a napkin. 'Not that silly. I did struggle to stay professional when I wrote about you.'

Her heart surged, only to flop in the next heartbeat.

'Well, it's Manchester's loss. Let's hope that Thames Hospital—', which was not far from City Hospital '—or Newcastle see what an asset you'd be.'

Oh, how easily and with a sense of inevitability he compartmentalised what they'd shared.

Darcy nodded and swallowed her mouthful of salad, which tasted suspiciously like broken glass.

Darcy pushed the final birthday candle into the stack of pancakes and Joe lit it, his heart heavy as he tried to recall Rosie's incandescent smile. The only thing stopping him from breaking down completely was Darcy's encouraging, beautiful and genuine smile. Over the flickering candles, her eyes glowed with understanding and compassion so he almost lost himself in their depths.

With a heavy sigh, Joe finally admitted to himself why he'd come here tonight: he'd missed her, he needed her. She made him feel better, lighter, more like himself, his real self. His relief that she wouldn't be moving to Manchester was selfish and twisted, soured with the guilt that sliced between his ribs, because he had little to offer her in compensation.

She wasn't his therapy. He was responsible for his own emotional happiness, so he wanted—no, needed—to stop the panic that he could once again lose the only precious thing he had in his life. Before Darcy that emotional happiness hadn't mattered to him in the slightest. He'd been quite content to dwell with only his pain and his guilt.

But now…?

He couldn't shake the intrusive feelings that he could have more. Darcy was right. Joe's grief wouldn't bring Rosie back or keep her close. It wasn't his only connection to his little girl. There were so many other ways to honour and remember her, and she'd always live in his heart and soul.

'Will you sing with me?' His voice choked. Darcy squeezed his hand, her caring so humbling that all the things he wanted to say to her fled his mind.

'Yes, of course.'

They started singing 'Happy Birthday'. To his surprise Joe felt his smile come readily, naturally, his gaze flitting from the magical beauty of the ten tiny flames to the woman who'd given his life new purpose. Meaning. Hope.

He watched her watch him, emotions shifting inside him until he felt a wave of motion sickness. How would he get through the Christmas leukaemia fund-raiser without her? Christmas Day, a day he dreaded, the anniversary of Rosie's death and her eleventh birthday…? Darcy was leaving, and he had no right to ask her to stay.

Being what she needed, a man who'd love her with everything he had, terrified Joe.

She had an exciting and fulfilled life ahead of her, but while she'd helped him realise that his future could be brighter, he had so far to go in order to be the man she deserved. He wouldn't hold her back on a false promise and he wouldn't let her down as her father had so many times.

The song ended. Joe blew out the candles and closed his eyes for a private second. 'Happy birthday, my darling,' he whispered, clinging to Darcy's hand tighter than ever, even while his mind rebelled at the idea he was growing too reliant on this woman.

He raised Darcy's hand to his mouth and pressed a kiss over her knuckles. 'Thanks for being there for me and for Rosie.'

'You're welcome, Joe,' she said, her eyes brimming with feelings it was hard for him to witness, because while he couldn't stay away, spending time with Darcy drew him closer and closer.

What if he unintentionally made her promises he wasn't sure he could keep?

'I need to go, actually,' he said, genuine regret tugging at his gut. 'I have to visit a private patient who's having a Hartmann's procedure the day after tomorrow.'

At her flash of disappointment, he tugged her into his arms and pressed his mouth to hers. 'Would you like to assist? I'd really appreciate the help.'

'Of course.' Darcy nodded, opened her mouth as if she wanted to say something and then closed it again.

He saw the yearning in her eyes. He wasn't stupid—he knew they'd diced with danger since Amsterdam. If Darcy felt even half of the emotional connection to him that he felt for her, she must wonder what their future might hold. He couldn't give her much in return for all the amazing gifts she'd given him, but he could at least be honest.

'You know,' he said, brushing his thumb across her soft bottom lip, 'I wish we'd met in another life, one where we were both open to finding love.' His stomach turned, but he pushed on. 'You are the whole package, Darcy. One day someone is going to love you and cherish you as you deserve. Maybe that someone is waiting in Newcastle.'

Joe swallowed the envy he had no right to feel.

'Maybe,' she said, her voice hollow. 'Come on.' She rose to her feet and reached for his hand to pull him up. 'You don't want to be late.'

No… And there were so many more things he wished he could make right as easily as showing up on time.

CHAPTER FOURTEEN

You have to tell him.

Stella's words ran through Darcy's mind from their late-night chat after Joe had left. Stella was a master at interrogation, and Darcy had blurted out her confession in a purgative rush. She was deeply in love with Joe. She'd never realistically be able to hide that from her sister for long. Stella knew Darcy wasn't the type to fall constantly in and out of love, so it was obvious to anyone with eyes.

Anyone except Joe.

Joe had been open and honest—the man to love and cherish Darcy, as he claimed she deserved, wasn't him. Why else would he suggest that she look for this mythical man in Newcastle? She hadn't even had her interview up north, but already he had her packed and delivered!

No wonder her emotions had got the better of her after he'd left.

They were equally fragile today, but there was a glimmer of hope. Perhaps Stella was right. Perhaps Joe was determined not to stand in the way of her career. Perhaps his feelings matched hers, but he was too wrapped up in his fear to give them a voice. Perhaps if he knew how she felt about him, he might not relinquish her to a non-existent Geordie lover quite so readily.

Darcy breathed deeply against the nerves churning in her stomach. She dumped her scrubs in the linen bin near the door of the staff changing rooms and headed out to the foyer of the private hospital where she'd assisted Joe in the Hartmann's procedure. They'd spent the day operating together, both work-focused and avoiding any personal interaction. But the things she had to say bubbled up inside her, desperate to escape. They'd reached an impasse. She was moving on—the prestigious job at Thames Hospital, while her preferred position, wasn't guaranteed—and she didn't want to leave London, if she secured the Newcastle post, without him knowing her feelings.

She spotted Joe, a tall handsome figure near the exit, his head bent over his phone. Her pulse accelerated as it always did when he was close. Would she ruin their last few weeks together with her confession? Or would she earn what she wanted, working for it the way she'd always achieved?

Resolute, she crossed the foyer. Her feelings weren't the only thing they needed to discuss. This morning she'd calculated that her period was five days late. Intellectually, she knew it couldn't possibly mean she was pregnant—they'd used protection—but the niggle of doubt lodged in her brain all the same, and for a few minutes she allowed herself to wonder what if...

What if they could forge a future together, be a team in their private lives as well as at work? What if Darcy could finally put all of her fears aside and commit everything she had into making this relationship with Joe real and enduring? What if he could love her in return?

She saw the fantasy in her head and for the first time

ever it seemed tangible and barely out of reach. Thrills of excitement danced along her nerve-endings as, side by side, they headed out to the car park.

When they were seated in Joe's car, driving back to City Hospital, Darcy could wait no longer. Perhaps their discussion around contraception would be the catalyst to a discussion of their future. Then she could tell him how she felt and perhaps that would be enough for him to realise he felt the same way.

Darcy dragged in a deep breath, actually tempted to cross her fingers for the first time since she was a kid. 'I um… I have something to tell you,' she said, choosing the easier of the two confessions to begin.

Joe raised his eyebrows in invitation, his focus on the traffic.

'It probably means nothing—' she brushed a speck of fluff from her trousers '—but I'm a few days late this month.' Darcy cleared her throat, which was gripped by nerves. 'I might just do a pregnancy test to stop myself worrying and waiting.'

Joe said nothing, sat frozen, staring straight ahead at the car in front.

Prickles of unease crept down Darcy's spine. The nerves flared and she prattled on, filling the loaded silence. 'I…thought you should know, but I'm sure it's no big deal…'

Of course, he'd be shocked initially, especially if he assumed she *was* pregnant, as she'd done for a split second that morning. But, of course, she wasn't. Any minute now they'd laugh about the absurdity of that likelihood, she'd pluck up the courage to tell him that she loved him and they'd move on to play the *what if?* game for their future.

Wordlessly, Joe pulled off the road and parked up in a side street lined by trees frosted with autumn colour.

The wait for him to speak seemed endless. How had this taken such a serious turn so quickly? It wasn't going at all to plan.

Joe killed the engine and turned to face her. 'How late?' His tone was clipped, his mouth pinched in a small scowl. It reminded Darcy of the day they'd met, of his…disapproval and unfair judgement.

'Five or six days.' Her stomach griped, uneasy. He looked as if she'd punched him in the gut. 'But it's irrelevant. I can't be pregnant.'

His frown persisted as Darcy's indignation cracked open a sleepy eye.

'Are you normally regular?' he asked in his surgeon's voice, as if taking a medical history from a poorly compliant patient. Darcy felt like a naughty little girl.

'Yes… But I figured it was the stress of job hunting.' She had the Thames interview tomorrow. 'Perhaps we should have had a discussion around the consequences before we started sleeping together.' She pointed out the obvious now that she knew his opinion, which was etched on his face.

His expression, the frustration in his eyes, bordered on horrified. Darcy shivered, chilled to the bone by his cold reaction. Did he not want children full stop, or just not now? Perhaps he didn't want them with *her*.

She just about stopped her hand from covering her mouth.

'We used condoms,' he said, matter of fact. 'I know they're not foolproof, but you can't be pregnant.' It sounded as if he was forbidding it rather than rationalising the probability.

Darcy closed her eyes as nausea threatened. He'd offered no reassurance, no consideration of how she might be concerned, no promise that whatever happened—positive or negative—they'd work out the consequences together, as a team.

Because he didn't see them as a team outside of the hospital. He didn't have feelings for her.

'I agree. It's highly unlikely.' Darcy swallowed the irrational tears clogging her throat. Deep down she knew the possibility that she might be pregnant could be a trigger for Joe, but a part of her had hoped their discussion would turn to their future or the growing seriousness of what had started as a fling between colleagues but was now more.

Except in Joe's eyes it wasn't. That seriousness was one-sided, representative of *her* feelings, not his.

How could she have been so stupid and so blind?

Joe's emotions were still locked away, safe and secure and unchanged from the first day they'd met, despite all they'd shared. He couldn't have any feelings for her, otherwise they'd be able to talk about this, laugh together, figure out a plan, as she'd fantasised.

But fantasies were pointless. Hadn't she learned that by now?

The slap of rejection landed like a blow. Darcy snatched her gaze away from the sickening view of Joe's conflicted expression and stared blindly out of the car window. What had she done? She'd fallen for a man who was aeons behind, emotionally. She was about to confess that she loved him, that she'd embraced the belief that she could finally have it all, the career she loved and a happy personal life. That she could at last be enough, be everything to someone.

How had she fallen for the wrong man again? This time one who could never love her back because somehow he believed that opening his heart to her meant betraying the memory of his daughter.

Joe gunned the engine. 'We'll get a test right now,' he said, all businesslike and assertive, the way he behaved in Theatre. 'There's a chemist down the road.'

He'd slipped so effortlessly into control mode, the perfectionism he used as a shield, that she almost agreed to his irrelevant and invasive suggestion. But she wasn't a patient, or something to be managed, fixed and filed. An inconvenience.

'Stop. I'm not a problem you can fix with your usual thorough approach.' The low volume of her request impressed Darcy. Outwardly she must appear calm, but inside she boiled and bubbled like molten lava.

'This isn't about an unplanned pregnancy,' she said, humiliated that he couldn't see the problem here for himself. Devastated that she'd misjudged him so spectacularly.

Joe stared, a confused furrow between his brows. 'Of course it is...'

Fingers of dread gripped Darcy's throat. She had two choices. One, take Joe's urgent pregnancy test, fake jovial relief when it was negative and forget about confessing her feelings—they were clearly horribly unrequited anyway. Or two, put Joe on the spot instead and demand that they have the second conversation about his feelings for her.

'What else is it about?' Joe rubbed a hand over his face, clearly confused and perhaps a little impatient.

She understood that he'd be keen to have this matter nicely rectified so he could shuffle back into his emotional hermit hideaway.

Looking into his eyes, which showed only fear, a piece of Darcy shattered like the handle snapping off a fine bone china teacup. For self-preservation she should back down, pretend that all she wanted from him was a cordial end to their fling, along with his glowing professional reference, and move on, forgetting that she'd opened herself up to a world of pain by falling in love with her unreachable boss.

Except Stella was right—if you didn't try you couldn't be rejected, but nor could you be accepted. Joe had shown her that she was good enough, despite her past. He believed in her and if she could reach the pinnacle of a stressful and demanding career she could do anything, including being brave and honest, even if he might not be ready to hear it. She needed to lay everything on the line, for herself, to prove that she'd been all in, before he…freaked out.

Now was the time for the biggest push of her life.

'It's about us, Joe,' she said, her vision blurring with the effort of staring at his handsome face and panicked eyes. 'About the chasm between us emotionally.'

Joe's frown deepened as if he genuinely had no clue that her feelings might be involved. He looked so aghast that a wave of empathy might have swiped her feet from under her if she hadn't already been seated.

Darcy hardened her resolve, prepared to hammer the last nail in the coffin of their relationship. If he couldn't see a future with her and a life they might create together, he'd definitely be unprepared to hear what she was about to say next.

'I love you.' The words flew free at last, but minus the expected wave of euphoria she'd imagined. 'I've been desperately trying to hold that inside because I knew you might not be ready to hear it.'

She couldn't switch off her empathy for him. That he could offer her nothing in the way of commitment was due to him clinging to the fear that he'd somehow love Rosie less if he allowed himself to be happy.

'I thought when you shared Rosie's birthday with me,' she continued, 'that you might be moving in the right direction, that you might trust me and want more from me, but you don't. Your face tells me exactly what you're feeling—terrified and about to retreat.'

He winced, looking down at his lap. 'Darcy, I—'

'It's okay.' She couldn't hear his excuses and platitudes—they'd destroy what was left of her composure. He'd never promised her love and for ever. He'd promised her nothing. 'I should have known better than to trust my instincts. They've always landed me here—hurt and alone.'

She needed to escape. To get away from his sympathetic stare.

'You're not alone,' he said. 'You're pushing this too far... I—'

'Oh, don't worry, Joe,' Darcy interrupted. 'I know you're an honourable man who would support me and our non-existent child, but I don't need that from you.' Darcy sucked in a breath laced with her last shred of courage. 'I needed a sign that we were on the same path, that this relationship was going somewhere. And now I have my sign. You're not ready to feel anything for me and the worst part is that... I understand.' A film of tears blurred her vision. 'I'm not even angry. I'm just empty.'

Yet again she'd chosen a man who didn't see the real Darcy, didn't *want* the real Darcy. The reality of any future they might share was one of Darcy making all of the sacrifices, never quite sure if she was good enough, and Joe lagging behind emotionally, scared to commit in case it changed the status quo he'd built around his wounded heart.

Darcy reached for her bag from the passenger side footwell and pulled at the lock on the car door.

'Wait—you can't just leave. We need to talk about this.' Joe shook his head as if trying to clear the fog from his brain. He seemed dazed, as if the idea of feeling something for her was so alien to him he couldn't quite grasp the concept. 'I'm not saying the right things…' But where he might be uncertain, Darcy now saw everything clearly.

Her heart clenched in one final spasm as she traced his features with her blurry stare. She swallowed, hardened her faltering heart, ignoring the pain that had nothing to do with the anatomical muscular pump in her chest and everything to do with her foolishness.

Of course he'd rejected her. Hadn't a part of her always expected it?

'Words are overrated, Joe. Promises are broken every day. I'll get over this, don't worry.' She'd got over her father's trail of dismissal and indifference and she'd got over failing Dean's expectations. 'I'm just embarrassed that I was stupid enough to believe my own hype when I know differently.'

Before she could bare her soul further, she fled, jogging towards the main road and jumping aboard the first bus that stopped. She had no idea where it was going, just as she had no plan for how she'd face him tomorrow. All she knew was that her tomorrows wouldn't include Joe.

CHAPTER FIFTEEN

JOE STARED AT the computer screen, hollow-eyed and hollow-chested from reading the contents of his latest email from Darcy. She'd secured the consultant position at Thames Hospital and handed in her notice. Taking her fortnight of unused annual leave into account meant she'd only be with him at City for another three weeks.

Then she'd be out of his life for ever, just the way she must believe he wanted.

Joe scrubbed a hand over his face, frustration a tight knot in his stomach. She'd told him that she loved him and he'd said nothing. He must have acted as if falling in love again was the worst thing that could happen to him; the fear of exactly that had certainly ground all his mental faculties to a halt. He'd been in shock, yes, and she hadn't given him the chance to explain his thoughts and feelings after her double whammy bombshell she'd delivered in his car. She'd pushed him away and pushed onwards regardless, the way she'd always done. To prove that she was okay without him?

That should bring him relief. He had no doubt that she would be fine. But he couldn't claim the same.

Joe felt as if he'd been hit by a truck and he only had himself to blame.

He and Darcy had come full circle. She warily

avoided him in the hospital and he'd focused on his busy week in order to ignore the fact that he was floundering around for a way to make it right.

All he could think about was his future and how it compared to the images that had flashed briefly and brilliantly before him when Darcy had told him that she loved him.

Sick to his stomach, he pulled out his phone and opened her last text message, which had been sent the night everything around them had collapsed.

Pregnancy test negative.

Three little words. Three enormous words, because they forced him to truly search his heart in a way he hadn't done for years. They forced his past and his future to collide, forced him to acknowledge what was becoming increasingly unthinkable.

Life without Darcy.

His throat closed in panic; he couldn't allow her to leave this way.

A knock at the door prevented further futile self-reflection. Laura entered, carrying a small bag.

'Is it that time already?' Joe asked, rising from his desk to meet her halfway across the room. He pressed a kiss to her cheek in greeting and glanced down at her baby bump. 'How was your appointment? Is he growing and healthy? The right number of digits?' She'd been at City Hospital this morning for an obstetric appointment and ultrasound scan.

'Yes, all perfectly normal.' Laura smiled, kneading the small of her back with her free hand. 'I brought the things you asked for.' She held the bag aloft, her eyes clouded with understanding.

Joe stared at the bag as if it contained the secrets of the universe—wonderful but terrifying. Then he breathed through his gut reaction and took the offering, peeking inside.

'Thanks for this; I appreciate it.' Joe placed the bag carefully on his desk as if it held fragile birds' eggs. 'Do you want a seat? A glass of water?'

Laura settled into the sofa with the protracted sigh of a heavily pregnant woman. 'Yes, please.'

Joe collected a glass of water, eyeing the bag of Rosie's things with longing. He'd examine the contents later. At home. Alone. So that he could fully immerse himself in the memories the items would surely evoke. Happy memories. Treasured memories.

At Darcy's suggestion he'd asked Laura to select some keepsakes from Rosie's room at the house that he could hold onto. It was time he stopped punishing himself and started honouring Rosie in a way that would make her proud.

If only he could fix what he'd allowed to happen with Darcy so easily, not that he was a fully recovered grief addict, but he wanted to find balance. To be a better version of himself. To be worthy of the wonderful woman who'd shown him another way forward. Darcy.

He and Laura chatted for a few minutes about due dates and baby names, the nostalgia heavy in the air. But neither was it as overwhelming as it had once been. That was down to Darcy. She'd showed him a path through the trees that he couldn't see alone. She'd led him to that first clearing in the woods when she'd awoken him to emotions, negative and positive and so human he was ashamed to acknowledge he hadn't found the way unaided. But they'd been a team. He was man enough to accept he wasn't an island, that he needed people.

Really, he just needed Darcy.

'That's the third sigh in as many minutes,' said Laura. 'Why don't you ask me for advice so I can waddle off home and put up my swollen feet?'

Joe sighed again, this one deep enough to operate all of the hospital's ventilators. He looked at his ex-wife, marvelled not for the first time at the contentment glowing in her features, at the hope shining in her eyes.

'How did you do it?' he asked. 'How did you move on without feeling as if you were losing more of her?'

Laura stared at her lap, the flash of pain moving across her face telling Joe that their daughter was never far from her mind either, in spite of appearances. It buoyed his spirits. Laura had found a way to live with her grief and allow herself to be happy.

'I love Rosie as much as the day she was born.' She put her hand on her belly, over her second child. 'Perhaps even more.'

'Me, too,' agreed Joe, sorry that he'd brought sadness into the room, but needing to be a man who could face his demons and be what Darcy deserved.

If only he could grasp that elusive thread, that lifeline Laura seemed to have caught hold of. Was it just as Darcy said—choosing to live with the memories in a different way?

'I didn't want to be alone for ever,' she said. 'I wanted to smile again, laugh again, find other joys. The small things, you know?'

Joe nodded, a secret smile tugging at his mouth as he recalled flickering candles atop a stack of pancakes and the way they'd reflected in Darcy's beautiful eyes.

'Remember her infectious giggle?' Laura smiled at him through the sheen of tears. 'One of us would crack up, and then she'd start, and then we'd laugh harder because her laughter was such a delightful sound we never wanted her to stop.'

Joe nodded, his chest in a vice as he held onto the image, the memories.

'Somehow,' continued Laura, 'I just knew that Rosie, our wonderful girl, would want me to be happy. That she's watching me and when I laugh she laughs. She can't help herself.' Laura blinked rapidly, clearing the moisture from her eyes. 'I want her to laugh, Joe, every day. Wherever she is, I need to know that she's giggling.'

Joe nodded, his grin wide and spontaneous at the image Laura created. 'That's perfect. I want that, too.'

She nodded and rose to her feet. 'Good, that's the easy part. The hard part is finding out what makes you happy and doing that every day.' She cast him a speculative look, feminine wisdom etched into her insightful smile.

'I think I might know what that is.' Joe's heart hammered. He needed to talk to Darcy.

'Good.' Laura squeezed his arm as she skirted him on her way to the door. 'And another piece of advice, which I kind of shouldn't need to tell you, but will hopefully steer you in the right direction in the future.' She turned in the doorway and pointed at his chest. 'Never make a pregnant woman cry.'

Joe grinned. 'Thanks. I'll remember that.'

Hiding away in the office beside the on-call room, Darcy pulled up the erect chest X-ray of the seventy-year-old woman she'd just admitted, noting the two crescents of black under the diaphragm denoting escaped air. She made a note in the patient file and ordered a host of blood tests on the computer. Then she texted the foundation doctor with instructions to start working up the patient for Theatre. Mrs Hancock would need a laparotomy. Perhaps she'd invite the foundation doctor to scrub in and assist. She had no idea where Joe was, despite them being on call tonight.

Perhaps he was avoiding her, the way she'd been keeping too busy to bump into him...

Darcy pressed her hand to her breastbone, breathed through the tightness which had settled there the minute she'd walked away from Joe's car and jumped on that number ten bus. Yes, her professional confidence was at an all-time high. Under Joe's tutelage these past months she'd flourished, become even more autonomous. A good thing, as she was about to become a consultant, in charge of her own team of junior doctors and ultimately responsible for the patients under her care.

But personally... There she seemed to be travelling backwards. Still making errors of judgement, still choosing the wrong man. Still scared to fully commit and push for what she truly wanted. What she deserved: love.

The door swung open and in strode Joe. His eyes lit up with relief, and Darcy had to look away to stop herself flying into his arms, divesting him of his scrubs and forcing him to love her in return. Because, no matter how deeply she'd retreated into her protective shell at the first hint of his rejection, if anything she felt worse, not better.

So fight for him. Push.

Only it was easier to focus on the here and now rather than dissect the mess that was them. Did she have it in her to commit to the added responsibilities of a new job and to struggle over her feelings for Joe?

They were so emotionally distant she might as well be going to Newcastle.

Walking away, no matter how much it hurt, would save her heartache in the long run. Wouldn't it?

'I've just admitted a seventy-year-old woman with abdominal pain and pneumoperitoneum,' she said, her tone businesslike, reminding her of that first day when she'd shoved her diagnostic skills under his nose for Mr Clarke and his appendix. 'Her blood work is underway. She has no pre-existing medical conditions apart from well-controlled hypertension. I'd like to add her to to-night's op list for an exploratory laparotomy.'

Surely she must have imagined the flicker of amused indulgence in Joe's eyes as he stared back. 'Since when did you need my permission?'

Darcy shot him what she hoped was a look that re-flected her incredulity. 'Since we started going back-wards—you disapproving of my every move and double-checking my work was how we began, after all.'

Darcy turned back to the computer and logged off. It hurt to look at him, knowing that he'd never be hers. She sensed Joe move closer and her hand faltered on the mouse.

'We're not moving backwards, Darcy—only for-wards. Together.'

Darcy snorted, shoved down the flare of hope that warmed her blood and rose to her feet. 'I don't think so.' She turned to face him, forced herself to meet his deep brown eyes. 'I'm moving to Thames and I truly wish you well, Joe.' Her voice almost cracked because she'd never meant anything more. She loved him and she wanted his pain to lessen, to end, even if she wouldn't be around to witness his ongoing journey of healing.

Sometimes people were too broken to be there for

others, and Darcy deserved a man who loved her with everything he had.

She looked down, away from his searching stare, which left her raw and exposed. 'Excuse me.' She stepped sideways to bypass his solid presence blocking her escape.

'Oh, no.' He reached for her arm, his touch everything she wanted. 'No more running and no more pushing me away.'

Darcy levelled her least tolerant glare on him while her heart raced way too fast for safety. 'I'm too tired for this, Joe.'

Heartsick more like.

Because he was right; she had pushed him that day she'd told him that she loved him. As much as she'd expected his rejection, known deep down that Joe was still working on some major personal stuff, she couldn't bear to hear her worst fears vocalised. That he could never love her back. That she wasn't enough. That he didn't want her.

Joe tilted her chin up until their eyes met once more. Her heart leapt, pulsing to her extremities. Being this close to him, a step away from everything she wanted, was torture.

How would she survive the next few hours, let alone the next three weeks?

'Too tired to love me?' he asked, pushing that stubborn lock of hair back from her cheek. 'Or too tired to hear how I love you, too?'

Darcy's heart stopped for a beat, a second, a third, stuttering back to life with her short gasp. He'd never be so cruel as to toy with her emotions, and yet he couldn't mean it…

Joe ignored her shocked expression and ploughed on.

'I never got to have my say that day when you thought you might be pregnant.'

Hadn't he received her text, telling him of the negative test? Was he simply saying all of this out of some sense of twisted loyalty?

She couldn't process his words. She couldn't organise her own thoughts.

'Well, I'm not pregnant—' she stepped aside, away from the wall of his body '—so this conversation doesn't need to happen.'

He stepped in front of her once more, gripped her upper arms, forced her eyes back to his. 'If you'd given me a chance to organise my thoughts that day and disentangle them from my emotions, you might have learned that I felt a thousand things during that conversation and only one of them was fear.'

Darcy nodded, only hearing him admit to being too scared to give them a chance.

'I *was* scared,' he confirmed. 'I still am. I never thought I'd have another chance at love, at happiness. For a long time, I felt unworthy of a second shot. But I realised that my fear was a symptom that I'd already fallen in love. With you.'

'Joe…' She couldn't bear to hear any more; her battered heart was too fragile.

He swallowed and she saw his turmoil swirling in his eyes. 'I'm not going to sugar-coat it, Darcy. The idea of being a father again terrifies me.'

'I understand.' Her heart cracked a little more. She'd always imagined that one day she'd have children, but right now she loved Joe enough to promise never to put him through that fear.

'But you ran,' he said. 'You did what you've done since the day I met you: push. You pushed me away.

I understand why, and I ache here—' he pressed his hand over his sternum '—for the rejection you've been through. But just like I need to work on my grief, learn to express it in healthier ways, you need to work on your knee-jerk reaction to anything you perceive as rejection.'

She nodded, her eyes stinging, because they were no further forward. He was right, his conclusion one she'd come to herself in the past few days when she'd thought they were over and she'd been forced to self-reflect. She *had* pushed him away at the first hint of negative reaction. She'd pushed before she could be pushed.

It didn't lessen the pain though.

'Thanks for the analysis. I'll be sure to take your comments on board next time I get involved with the wrong man.' No, she didn't mean that. 'I'm sorry, you're right. I have pushed people away first.'

But with Joe she'd been finally ready to let go fully and risk it all.

'There won't be a next time, Darcy.' He stepped closer, his hand sliding down her arm to grip her hand. 'I regret my slow reaction when you told me you loved me. But we're stuck with each other.' His smile all but broke her in two. 'We love each other and we're going to work this and any other snag out during our relationship.'

'You want a relationship...?' Blood whooshed through her ears.

'Of course.' He smiled and her eyes drank in the beautiful sight. 'Did you miss the part where I told you I love you?'

She nodded, her eyes filling with moisture.

He raised her hand to his mouth and kissed her knuckles slowly, one swipe, two, tender and reverent.

'Joe, I want a relationship, too. I promise we can take it as slow as you need.'

He shook his head, his self-assured grin telling her everything would be fine as long as they were together. 'I don't want slow. I want you as you are.' He brushed his lips over hers. 'Humans aren't perfect,' he said, his eyes brimming with a million emotions. 'We make mistakes. We say the wrong things. We feel too much sometimes, and it makes us a little bit crazy. But I've been married before, so I'm the one with the experience here. You're going to have to trust me on this one. A marriage, lifelong commitment, takes work and just wait until our family comes along. That will test us in ways we never even considered. You'll probably constantly push your agenda and I'll likely consider every possible consequence in minute detail, but we'll always get there in the end.'

Was he saying he wanted for ever with her? Marriage? Children?

Could she do this? Take the leap, put in the work and last the distance, despite the bumps in the road that might make her nervous? Yes! She was Darcy Wright. She could do anything she set her mind to, including loving Joe without reservation, wholly and fully vulnerable.

He cupped her face, holding her eye contact. 'I know you're scared,' he said, breathing against her lips. 'I am, too. But I'm more terrified of the pain of losing you than I am of risking my heart again. So I need you to trust me. To put your hand in mine and come with me on this journey. I need you, your strength and your determination and instincts. I need you on my team.'

Darcy nodded, too choked to speak.

'You make me happy, Darcy, and I want to be happy every day for the rest of my life. I'm ready.'

Just like the first time they'd kissed, which was full of frustration and pent-up emotion, Darcy flew at Joe, slamming her mouth over his to shut him up. His *I love you, too*, rang in her ears. In her yearning and disbelief she'd missed at least half of his spiel, but she understood the gist.

She could have everything she wanted and she was ready too, to hold on tight and never let go.

Joe banded his arms around her back and hoisted her feet from the floor, stumbling the few paces into the on-call room. He slammed the door closed and pressed her back up against it, jamming his leg between hers and tangling his hands in her hair so he could kiss her back. Darcy never wanted this moment to end, except reality beckoned…

'Joe…' she said, a million explosions detonating in her nervous system, which struggled to process so much happiness. 'I need to go and fix Mrs Hancock…'

He nodded and took her hand, his confident smile filling her with hope and certainty that working together, being together, loving each other, they could achieve anything.

'First we fix Mrs Hancock, then we focus on us.' He raised her hand to his mouth and kissed it, his eyes promising everything she'd ever wanted.

'Deal,' Darcy agreed.

EPILOGUE

Three months later

A MILLION TWINKLING lights sparkled overhead, cloaking the ceiling in festive magic. Darcy blinked, glancing over at Joe. She already had enough stars in her eyes just looking at her man.

Joe filled a tuxedo like no other man on earth, almost as good as he looked in his scrubs. Her mouth dried as she performed a quick calculation of the time remaining before she could drag him home and worship every inch of him. There weren't enough hours in the day...

Joe finished his brief conversations with the chair of the Leukaemia Foundation and slipped his arm around her waist, directing her to the terrace, where a million more lights twinkled overhead.

'It's freezing. Where are we going?' she said, surprised that she was getting Joe to herself earlier than expected.

Joe shrugged off his jacket and draped it over Darcy's shoulders, the warmth seeping into her skin and his scent filling her head. 'I want to get you alone. We haven't had two minutes to ourselves tonight.'

'Well, you're the host,' she reminded him. 'This fundraiser wouldn't have happened without you. You're a man in demand.' Since he'd joined the board of the Leukaemia Foundation charity he'd found renewed purpose. He still operated four days a week at City, but that he'd begun something for himself, a job that refilled the tanks, told Darcy just how far he'd come.

Joe pulled her into his arms and settled his mouth over hers in a long, slow and thorough kiss that left Darcy weak-kneed.

'What was that for?' she said, gripping his biceps.

His eyes shone with his feelings, so open and vulnerable she was humbled by his courage. 'I love you.'

'I love you, too,' she whispered, her head spinning at how lucky she was to have found Joe.

'I missed waking up with you this morning.' He nuzzled her neck, his lips soft and his stubble tickling a path of delight to all of her erogenous zones.

Darcy closed her eyes and dropped her head back, giving him access. 'I had to go into Thames early. I had a new registrar to welcome.' Only now work was the last thing on her mind.

'Did you go easy on them?' To Darcy's dismay, he stopped the path of kisses, wrapped his arms around her and began to shuffle his feet, swirling her around in a slow dance under the lights and the stars.

Darcy smiled up at Joe. 'I took your advice and told him that I liked things done a certain way and he'd just have to get used to it.'

Joe grinned with approval. 'Is he any good? Because a competent registrar is worth their weight in gold, in my experience.'

Darcy rolled her eyes, her mind anywhere but at the hospital now that his hands were caressing her bare back underneath his jacket. 'I don't know yet... It's early days.'

Joe held her close and lowered his mouth to her ear so she shuddered. 'But the best registrars show you what they are made of from day one.'

She laughed again and Joe took the opportunity to plunder her neck, laying down a trail of kisses in her most sensitive spots.

'Well, train him up quickly,' he said as he reached her exposed collarbone.

'I will…' Darcy's mind grew foggy as arousal dragged her away from the topic of conversation. 'Why do you care? Can't we stop all this chit-chat and just go home?'

Joe pressed his hand into the small of her back and crushed her to his chest. 'He'll need to be proficient enough to hold the fort while you're away.'

Away…? Perhaps she was too aroused to keep track of the thread of the conversation. Had she missed something?

'Where am I going?'

Joe smiled, reaching into his pocket. 'On our honeymoon.'

He stepped back, dropped to one knee and opened the ring box. 'Darcy, you've given me so much, and all I have to give you in return is me. Will you be on my team for ever? Will you marry me?'

Darcy gasped, blind to the beauty of the diamond, seeing only the dazzling love shining in Joe's eyes.

'Yes,' she said, her voice wobbly with tears. 'Will you be on my team, too?' she asked, dragging him to his feet.

'Always.' And then he kissed her.

* * * * *

MILLS & BOON®

Coming next month

SHOCK BABY FOR THE DOCTOR
Charlotte Hawkes

'First, however, we're going for a scan.'

Fear rose in Sienna's chest.

'We most certainly are not. I told you, I don't want the entire hospital gossiping about me, which will be inevitable if they know I'm pregnant. Let alone if you're the one accompanying me. I've had a scan. Everything was fine. I am definitely not going for another with you.'

He cast her a cool look.

'Are you quite finished with your rant?'

'I'm not being that conversion nurse who got pregnant with Bas Jensen's baby.'

'You will have that scan, Sienna. And I will be with you.' He folded his arms again, and this time she was struck by quite how authoritative the man was. How had she failed to appreciate quite what power looked like on a man? He didn't just bear the Jensen name, rather he epitomised everything it represented.

She glowered at him, but it seemed to bounce off his solid chest without making a dent.

'So you're...what? Taking charge now?' The idea of it should baulk more. So why didn't it? 'I told you, I don't need your help, I'm perfectly used to taking care of myself.'

'And I'm beginning to think you tell me a few too

many things whilst you aren't as keen to listen. But I suspect that part of the reason for telling me now is because this is beginning to overwhelm you.'

'You're deluded.'

'No, I'm not, but I think you are,' his voice dropped to a sudden, quiet hum. 'I suspect that whether you want to admit it or not, deep down, you don't want to be the one taking care of everything. You want someone to take the reins for once.'

And it was odd but it was still there, that lethal air, swirling beneath the surface like a rip-tide, just waiting to drag her under. But he was controlling it with a fierceness that struck an unexpected cord in her.

As though by controlling that, he could control some dark secret of his own. As if a man like him had dark secrets at all.

Continue reading
SHOCK BABY FOR THE DOCTOR
Charlotte Hawkes

Available next month
www.millsandboon.co.uk